HEIR OF GODS

HEIR OF GODS

Copyright © 2022 by Elizabeth Menozzi

All Rights Reserved.

Except as permitted under the U.S. Copyright Act of 1976, no part of this publication may be reproduced, distributed, or transmitted in any form or by any means, or stored in a database or retrieval system, without the prior written permission of the publisher.

Cover design by Elizabeth Mackey

Editing by Shannon Page

The following is a work of fiction. Names, characters, places, and incidents are fictitious or used fictitiously. Any resemblance to real persons, living or dead, to factual events or to businesses is coincidental and unintention-al.

ISBN-13: 979-8-9856303-3-6

First Edition: December 2022

HEIR OF GODS

MAGE LORE BOOK 1

E. MENOZZI

For Mom and Kaitlin, who believed in this story even when I didn't.

1

THE dust cloud on the horizon, rising and billowing over the fields, signaled the arrival of the Ruhl. Each hoofbeat brought him closer to our compound. I lifted my hand so the swirling debris haloed my fingers. Squinting, I twisted my wrist, letting sunlight and shadow play across my palm, imagining for a moment that I could cast magic to send him and his party away. But if the clans ever had access to magic, that power was long gone. Traded away to the Inahi in exchange for the gods' protection.

But that protection was weakening—the raiders had returned. Somewhere deep in the forest, the veil was fading, and the Inahi were hiding. I'd left a bit of travel cake on a flat rock next to the creek, but the messengers of the gods continued to refuse my offerings. It was beginning to look like my father was right to insist I leave communicating with the Inahi to the Ruhl, as much as I hated to admit it. Perhaps the Ruhl would succeed where I had failed.

I shifted to a more comfortable position on the boulder at

the edge of the creek, stretching my bare feet into the water. The cool, clear liquid caressed my ankles, providing some relief from the late afternoon heat. I wiggled my toes as I returned my attention to the edge of the forest, even though I knew I'd stayed as long as I could. It was time to go home.

With a sigh, I lifted my dripping feet from the creek and pressed them against the warm boulder to dry them. Then I stood, brushing the loose dirt off my leggings. Taking my time. Delaying the confirmation of my disappointment. Finally, after slipping my feet back into my boots, I walked over to get a closer look at my offering.

I inspected the travel cake first. *Not even a nibble.* Then I spotted a tiny blue flower with no stem resting on the dirt next to the rock, as though it had blown there on the wind. Two more identical flowers lay nearby. Each had five sky blue petals surrounding a bright golden center. They appeared to have fallen around the rock, marking the points of an invisible triangle centered on my untouched offering.

Those had definitely not been there earlier. I released a small squeak of excitement, careful not to be too loud or move too fast and risk scaring the Inahi if they lingered nearby. My hands clenched and flexed as I scanned the ground between my offering and the brush that bordered the forest.

There was no obvious sign that they'd been here. Not that I knew exactly what I was looking for. The clan folklore offered little in the way of descriptions.

The rhyme the mage taught us as children was: *Gods above and gods below with Inahi to go between. Always watching, always listening, even if they walk unseen.* If the Inahi had emerged from wherever they hid, then they hadn't left even a footprint in the soft soil to give their presence away. Only the stemless flowers near my offering hinted at anything unusual.

I picked up one flower to study it, careful not to damage the delicate petals. Their familiar scent, like honey drizzled over ripe marsh berries, triggered a memory of fishing with Rys along this same stream at the bend where the water pooled deeper in the woods. He'd picked one of these flowers and tucked it into my hair. My heart raced as I remembered what had come next: our first kiss. My lips tingled, but I pushed away the memory and focused on the soft petals tickling my palm.

These flowers were a sign. They had to be. Moonbursts only grew under the shade of the tall trees, deep in the forest, not out here on the plains. So, it wasn't likely the wind had carried them this far. My mind raced through the stories I'd memorized, trying to remember if any of them mentioned these particular flowers. If I hurried, there might be just enough time to search Father's books before I needed to join my parents in the great hall for the Gathering.

Adrenaline pumped through my veins, and I cupped my hand around the flower, careful not to crush it in my palm. I left my offering behind and began running through the fields, back toward the gates of the compound. Tassels of tall grasses brushed against my leggings, and dry stems crunched under my feet. The tents inside the tall wooden fence surrounding the compound grew larger on the horizon as I approached. Figures scurried between them, setting up for the Gathering festival that celebrated the start of the winter season, when our clan retreated to the safety of our walled compound to weather the storms.

I smiled and waved to the guards at the gate as I raced past them. They stood at attention, waiting to relax until after I passed. When I reached the market, I slowed to pick my way through the maze of brightly painted hides stretched taut over tent posts. I swerved around people carrying baskets of harvest tithes for the blessing and armfuls of purple lantern stars to hang in the courtyard for the festival.

Slipping between two of the tents, I emerged with a clear view of the only permanent structure within the compound—our clan's winter lodge. Shaped like a rectangle with an open, interior courtyard, the stone building held a large, empty room for clan meetings that doubled as a dining hall, plus adjacent wings that housed my family, the clan elders, and any visitors from the neighboring two clans who shared our sacred peninsula.

I headed for an archway on one side of the building that led to the courtyard at the center and joined a family carrying benches for the feast, following them through. Inside, I spotted my sister Cala's auburn hair. Lorjad's Luck, she had her back to me, shouting instructions and standing watch over the festival preparations. So I ducked behind another group and slipped into the lodge near the great hall.

With the clan preparing for both the arrival of the Ruhl and the start of the festival, there were people everywhere. Pushing through the crowds already clustering in the great hall, I hurried to the far side, then slipped through the archway that led to the family wing.

The first door I passed led to my father's private meeting chamber. I would need to cross through that to get to the small study where he and Mage-nah kept the books of lineage and folklore.

I took a breath, hoping Lorjad's Luck would hold, and the room would be empty. Then I pushed aside the tapestry hanging across the entryway and immediately crashed into another body going the opposite direction, too thin to be my father, but tall like him. I glanced up and breathed a sigh of relief when I realized it was my older brother, Dern. At least it was him and not Goff.

"What are you doing?" I asked before taking a quick peek at the flower cupped in my hand to make sure I hadn't damaged it.

"I could ask you the same." Dern towered over me, blocking my path. "You're going the wrong way, Ayla. Cala sent me to find you. She wants our help in the courtyard."

I cringed and tried to squeeze around him. "I can't right now. I need to look something up in the study."

"Hiding in the study is a terrible idea." He grinned and moved to block me again. "Everyone knows it's the first place to look for you. If you want to avoid work, come with me. I'm going for a ride."

"Tempting." I tried again to push past him. "But there's something I need to do first, so move."

He refused to budge. "You're not actually planning on wasting your day memorizing the Ruhl's lineage, are you?"

My eyes narrowed as they met his. "I'll memorize the lineage of his stone-loving Shal clan when they can recite the five blessings."

He laughed and stepped out of my way. "That sounds more like my favorite sister."

"Give Arge a carrot for me," I called over my shoulder.

"Cover for me at the meeting," he called back.

Once Dern was gone, I hurried to the opposite side of the meeting room and pushed back another tapestry, this one marking the entrance to Father's study. Inside, I inhaled the smell of leather and dust, instantly relaxing as I exhaled.

A large table sat at the center of the room, piled with books. I recognized the leather-bound volumes my brother Goff had left out for me. This was where I should have been all morning, studying the lessons he'd assigned. I twisted the stack so I could read the titles. As I suspected, they were all related to clan politics or the lineage of the leadership families.

Mother had been the one to supplement the basic clan education of my three older siblings. She had taught Goff, Cala, and Dern everything they needed to know to serve as Father's heirs. They were the ones meant to play all the important leadership roles. Including educating their younger siblings. That's how Kilm and I ended up with Goff assigned as our tutor.

Even though he was younger than me, Kilm didn't need extra lessons, but I did. At least according to Goff. He wasn't wrong, exactly. Kilm was better at this sort of thing than me. And my inability to retain any lesson unrelated to magecraft or folklore was especially infuriating for Goff now that the newly confirmed Ruhl was visiting.

But I didn't need Goff's books this time. I knew all I needed to know about the former heir to the Shal clan leadership that had been chosen as Ruhl. His grandmother had been the last person in any of the clans to have direct contact with the Inahi. According to our treaties, the title and ability to speak with the Inahi passed to her eldest child. But that child died just a few years after coming of age, and the clans were left without a Ruhl until the eldest of the next generation reached their maturity. For eighteen years, the clans had been unable to communicate with the Inahi.

Until now. I uncurled my fingers to check the flower in my hand.

The only problem was no one was going to believe me. I had no connection to the Ruhlini. According to the elders, I shouldn't have been able to receive a message from the Inahi.

Though, there was nothing written in the folklore about the Ruhlini. Based on what I'd read, I believed that anyone could petition the Inahi and potentially receive a response.

After receiving what seemed like a message, I needed to figure out what it meant. Then I could prove that I was right, and the elders were wrong. Then they might believe that we didn't need the Ruhl to save our clan from the raiders.

Cradling the flower in my palm, I hurried over to the shelves that lined one wall of the study and searched our small collection for our book of folklore. I let my fingers crawl along the spines until they touched the familiar worn leather cover, imagining what it would be like when I finally got to attend the Magery in the spring. They had shelves and shelves of books that contained all the knowledge an apprentice needed to eventually become clan mage. Once I used this discovery to prove what a good mage I would be, there was no way Father would refuse my request to go after I came of age. And then, like my elder siblings, I would be able to finally have a place of importance in our clan.

With the book in one hand and the flower in the other, I returned to the table and collapsed into one of the hard wooden chairs. I pushed Goff's selections off to one side with my elbow to make room and gently set the book down. Before I opened the cover, I released the flower from my cupped hand and set it next to the book.

Flipping to the first story, I skimmed through the familiar tale of how the Inahi led our people to this land. This was one of the few legends that spoke of the Inahi revealing themselves to a human. My eyes scanned the page as I read the story of the last true mages.

I thought I'd memorized every word, but there, near the bottom of the first page, was a sentence I'd nearly forgotten.

A single, stemless purple flower rested in its place.

I kept reading until the rustle of the tapestry in the entry caught my attention. Then I lifted my head toward the sound and prepared my excuses.

My shoulders relaxed as Rys stepped into the room, still dressed in the black tunic with orange sunburst embroidered on the shoulder, marking him as a guard of the Nahl clan. Over his tunic, he wore a long vest woven with armor threads. His sword and a hunting knife hung from the belt wrapped around his narrow waist. My whole body warmed at the sight of him.

I leaned back in my chair and smiled. "You found me."

"I thought you might be here." He took a few tentative steps into the study. "I'm off duty until the clan meeting, but Dern said that I might find you here. He also said I should tell you that Goff's looking for you, too, now."

I sighed. "Is that supposed to be a warning? Or am I being summoned?"

Rys shrugged. "I'm just the messenger." He lifted the corner of his mouth in a half-grin.

I pushed my chair back from the table and stood. "Can I pretend I didn't get the message?"

Rys took a few more steps toward me. "And allow Dern to think that I ignored orders from a Nahlo?"

I closed the distance between us and reached for his hand to pull him closer. "Do you think he knows about us?"

Rys frowned. "He might suspect." He looked down at me and reached to rub a smudge of dirt off my face before letting his palm rest against my cheek.

I leaned into his hand. "I don't care, you know."

I searched his face, watching for a reaction. The Gathering festival marked the start of our courting season, and I would come of age at the Midwinter festival in a few moons. It wasn't too soon to hope he might declare for me.

Rys leaned toward me and rested his forehead against mine. I shifted my weight onto my toes and pressed up until my lips were touching his. Then I wrapped my arms around his waist.

His lips brushed against mine with a teasing kiss. I pulled him closer, and he slid his palm from my cheek down along the side of my neck before kissing me again. I melted against him as his fingers slipped under my braid and caressed the back of my neck.

My lips parted under his, and for a few moments, there was nothing else. Just me, and him, and every place where our bodies touched. Then Rys pulled his lips from mine and sighed. He kept his arms wrapped around me and his forehead pressed to mine.

I opened my eyes. "Why did you stop?"

"We shouldn't. Not here."

"Where someone might see us?" I narrowed my eyes. "You think we should keep hiding?"

His thumb brushed against the side of my neck, just behind my right ear. Directly over my clan tattoo. The horizontal black bar had been inked into my skin during my thirteenth-year naming ceremony. The same tattoo marked my siblings and my father. It claimed me as part of the direct lineage of the leader of the Nahl clan, even if I was just an insignificant spare.

"This isn't the way I want them to find out," he said.

Hope flared in my chest, but before I could respond, Rys let his hand drop to his side. His eyes drifted to the table behind me. He nodded at the book and the flower lying on the table. "What's all this?"

"I think the Inahi left me a sign." I stepped away from him and lifted the flower off the table. "I went to the edge of the forest to leave an offering, and I waited."

"Did you see them?" he asked, eyes sparking with excitement.

"No. But..." I held the flower out to him. "This time, when I checked, I found these scattered around the rock."

Rys pulled my fingertips closer so he could get a better look at the flower. "Moonbursts? Don't they grow deep in the forest?"

Of course he recognized the flowers from our childhood afternoons spent hunting for signs of the Inahi and the fierce stormcats the folklore said they rode. All that changed the summer before my Naming, but the fact that he remembered stoked the little flame of hope that had sparked at his earlier response. I banked the embers and focused on my discovery.

"That's what I thought too. But there were three of them spaced around the rock." I drew a triangle in the air between us to illustrate. "They weren't growing there. There were no stems, just the flowers."

"What do you think it means?" He cocked his head to one side and lifted the flower to inspect it.

"I think it's a sign. I've been re-reading the legend about the origin of the three clans. The one where Ruhala leads our ancestors to safety in the lost lands beyond the mountains. You remember that story?" I gestured at the book I'd been reading when he arrived.

"Of course," he said. "Doesn't she speak with the Inahi in her dreams?" He glanced down at the text. "I don't think she ever sees them, does she?"

"No. She doesn't. But listen to this." I plucked the flower from his hand and set it down on the table before pulling the book toward me so I could read the passage I'd found aloud.

"When they rested each morning at dawn, Ruhala would prepare food, leaving a portion of their meal for the Inahi. She stayed awake long after her children had fallen asleep, hoping the Inahi might come to her and offer their guidance. They never appeared before her eyes closed and she fell into dreams. In her sleep, she saw villages burned, destroyed by the invaders. She saw the last two mages drained of their magic. Thick grey clouds shielded her people from the eyes of Estrel, god of miracles and guidance. But Estrel's son, Lorjad the Lucky, beckoned to Ruhala from the mountain peaks. Ruhula woke to find her offering had disappeared. A single, stemless purple flower rested in its place."

"This has to be a sign from the Inahi. I'm so close. I know it." I searched his face for a hint that he felt the same excitement bubbling inside that I did, but the only change I noted was a crease in his brow.

Rys bent over the book, but his eyes weren't on the text. He studied the inside margin, then skimmed the pad of his forefinger down the crease between the pages. "It looks like there's a page missing here."

I nudged him over so I could look. Hidden deep within the crease were the jagged edges of a torn page. I flipped ahead a few pages, checking each seam. Then I flipped backward, checking again. "You're right."

Rys scowled. "I'm surprised no one noticed."

I pointed at the text. "You can't tell unless you look closely, and it seems like a reasonable end to the story. The next one starts on the next page. I wonder what could be missing. Maybe Mage-nah knows."

"Maybe." His hand rested lightly on the hilt of the knife in his belt. "But listen, if you go back out to the edge of the forest, promise me you'll be careful. Please?"

I squinted at him, wondering what he wasn't telling me. "Why? The last attacks happened a full day's ride from here."

"Still. Did you bring your hunting knife with you?" His hands gripped my waist and guided me closer to him.

I nodded. "Of course. And the ones you gave me." I tilted my head so he could see the knives disguised as hairpins that he'd given me on my naming day. "Why are you so worried?"

"It might be nothing." He grimaced. "When I was on patrol last night, someone spotted a flash and movement in the forest. A few of us rode out to investigate. We didn't see anything, but I thought I heard something." He released me, then ran a hand through his hair. "It sounded almost like screaming, but it could have been the wind."

"You think it might be Merluks." I thought of the attack on his own family's camp years ago. The summer after his naming and before mine. Before the Scattering that year, we swore that we'd both declare as apprentice mages during the Midwinter festival. By the Gathering, everything had changed.

His family had taken their herd close to the coast to graze that summer. The elders blamed the attack on Agrion raiders that had somehow crossed the seas and made it past the veil. But Rys told me what he saw. He believed it was one of the creatures that the folklore warned lived in the deep forest. Since the veil was supposed to keep them out of our lands, no one we knew had seen one. Many in the clan believed they weren't real. Just stories meant to scare clan children away from the dangers of wandering beyond the protection of the veil.

The attack on Rys's family came in the dark of night. He stayed protected inside the tent. His father, who went out to defend them, died. His mother, who ventured out at the sound of her partner's screams, barely survived her injuries. When they returned to the compound for the Gathering, Rys announced his intention to apprentice with the clan guard, instead. Nothing I'd said would change his mind.

He caught my hands in his. "The captain still thinks it's raiders, but I'm not sure. Just be careful, all right?"

"I will." I wasn't sure which would be worse, Merluks or Agrion raiders. Both should be impossible with the magic that protected our borders.

"I should go," he said, tugging me closer.

"I suppose I should, too. I need to get ready for the Gathering. Father will confine me to the lodge for a week if I show up looking like this." I gestured at my dust-covered tunic and leggings.

He bent his head for one more lingering kiss. "I'll see you there. We can talk more about your sign from the Inahi after," he said, before leaving.

But when I returned to the table, the flower was gone.

2

I SPENT too long looking for the flower before realizing that, if it was a sign, of course it was likely to disappear. Regular flowers, ones that aren't signs from the gods or their messengers, don't just disappear.

I wanted to run straight to Mage-nah's tent to tell him everything, but then I remembered he was probably already where I was supposed to be. I hurried to my room to wash and change, knowing from the quiet that had fallen over the compound that I was going to be late.

Mage-nah was halfway through the Gathering blessing by the time I arrived. I ducked in past the guard standing at the side entrance and crept along the back wall, hoping that no one would notice. A few heads turned. I nodded politely in response, keeping my eyes on the raised platform at the front where my father and mother stood with my two oldest siblings beside them.

A quick scan of the room revealed that Dern was not there, and Kilm had found a spot on the opposite side. His eyes found mine, and he shook his head. I shrugged, then pressed my back up against a wall near a window, thankful for the cool breeze blowing in from the mountains.

Once the blessing was complete, Kilm hurried forward with a chair and helped Mage-nah sit. Then Father raised his hands. His deep voice carried easily across the gathered clan to reach me at the back.

"Welcome home. By all accounts, our harvest this season has been bountiful, despite the attacks that continue to plague us. But we are safe here, and I vow to find a way to protect our clan before our next Scattering. So tonight, let us celebrate! We will share our Gathering with the Ruhl..."

I couldn't concentrate on what my father was saying. My mind was still on my discovery and how quickly I could reach Mage-nah after the Gathering. I pretended to listen as I plotted the fastest course through the crowd. Focused on my desire to avoid anyone who might stop me, wanting to catch up after months away, I almost missed Father's next mention of "the Ruhl."

"—arrived safely. Tomorrow I will speak with him about protection for our clan." He paused. "As Ruhl, he has a responsibility to speak with the Inahi and petition them to restore the magic that protects us. To strengthen the veil that secures our borders."

When my father finished his speech, one elder stepped forward to address him. "My Nahl, what if the offerings aren't enough?"

I dug my nails into my palm and tried to force my face to remain blank, relaxing my jaw muscles, which had already tensed from biting back my response. No wonder the magic was weakening, if even our elders had lost their faith. I braced as I anticipated my father's reply.

"The gods have only turned their gaze elsewhere. Once the Ruhl alerts the Inahi, Estrel will return and repair the veil. There will be no more thieves and raiders to come in the night and attack our settlements and our livestock. The Ruhl will see to that." Father's words reassured the elder as much as they'd infuriated me when he'd said nearly the same to me, almost two years ago, just before the High Mage had announced the new Ruhl. I'd gone to him to convince him I could help, that I could find the Inahi. But he had insisted we wait and trust the Ruhl, instead.

I longed to step forward and tell everyone that they were wrong. We didn't need the Ruhl to protect us. We just needed to keep our faith and honor the traditions. I could prove it.

But not yet. I needed to wait just a bit longer. I had already received my sign that I was on the right path. All that remained was deciphering the message I'd received. Then, with Mage-nah's support, I could win the trust of my father and my clan.

My gaze drifted past where Mage-nah sat, to the archway that led to the courtyard. Two of the clan guards, clad in identical black tunics and dark green leggings, bracketed the entrance, standing watch over the proceedings. They both had the brown hair and deeply tanned complexions common among our clan, and from this distance, they appeared almost identical. But I would know Rys anywhere and from any distance. I watched him from across the room—my childhood playmate, my best friend, my secret love, and the only person in our clan who actually believed I could find the Inahi. I willed him to look at me, even though I knew he took his duty far too seriously to ever break formation.

My thoughts drifted to my costume for the festival, and the declaration that I hoped would come. Warmth burned my cheeks as another mention of "the Ruhl" broke through my daydreams.

"Will you agree to a union between the Ruhl and the eldest Nahla, my Nahl?" someone asked.

My face turned to stare at the speaker. A hot mix of fear and anger flooded my chest. I searched past the elder's creased face, past my father in his chair, to my sister, who stood in poised perfection at my mother's side.

Cala's cheeks darkened, and she tilted her head down demurely.

My father's face showed no hint of emotion when he responded. "A union between the Nahl clan and the Ruhl would be advantageous for our people. Do you not agree, Sim?"

"I do, my Nahl," he said, nodding. "But do we know where his allegiance stands? He is still young, and his mother is the Shal."

"The treaty of the united clans forbids the Ruhl from inheriting leadership in his former clan," Goff said from his position of honor at my father's side.

I held back a groan. Trust Goff to know, and to make sure everyone else knew that he knew, every bit of political trivia.

Father lifted his hand, signaling Goff to be silent without breaking eye contact with the elder. "You are correct, son. But I think Sim was suggesting that the Ruhl's sympathies may still lie with his mother, and that his potential wife's clan affiliation would not sway him." Now it was Goff's cheeks that darkened. I almost felt sorry for him.

"Yes, exactly, my Nahl," the elder agreed. "So what say you?"

"I say, if he should pursue a union, and my daughter were to accept, we would see this as agreeable and give the happy couple our blessings." He sat back in his chair, tapping his fingers on the carved wooden arm. "Yet, even if the Ruhl agrees to our terms, our needs and those of our allies in the Jahl clan come first. There will be no such union unless we get the protection we need."

I frowned. Father planned to allow the Ruhl to marry my sister, but only if the gods restored the veil. It was a gamble. I wondered if Cala knew about this plan.

If she did, she had said nothing to me. Cala had come of age last winter. She was old enough to marry, and she'd had a crush on the eldest Jahlo for as long as I could remember. He didn't visit often, and when he did, he spent most of his time with our brothers. But all of my siblings teased her about it because anyone who'd seen them together could tell they had strong feelings for each other. I couldn't imagine that Father didn't know this as well.

Would Cala really agree to be a pawn in Father's political games when she'd already given her heart away to someone else? I shivered. Knowing my people-pleasing older sister, it was possible. I couldn't let that happen.

I fumed quietly while trying to appear calm and attentive until Father released everyone to their festival preparations. Then I sprang forward, prepared to make my way to Mage-nah. But everyone was moving already, and a small group had already gathered around Mage-nah.

Rather than join them, I slipped out through the closest archway, planning to take a shortcut that would lead me around to the far side where I expected Mage-nah would exit. I would catch him there and tell him of my discovery as I walked him back to his tent.

Halfway down the hall that led to the family wing, a familiar voice echoed toward me. Just in case he was heading in this direction, I slid into an alcove to wait for Goff to pass.

"Perhaps I could take Uncle Feln's place and return with the Ruhl and represent our clan on the council," Goff said.

"Absolutely not," Father's voice cut him off.

"But Father, if he agrees to a betrothal..." Goff's voice trailed off. The footsteps stopped.

I pressed myself farther into the corner and prayed they wouldn't see me.

"Enough. It's bad enough that I have to send one of my children to that clan. You are my heir. You will stay here. Your place is by my side. Despite what you think, you have much to learn before you will be ready to inherit the title of Nahl." One pair of footsteps continued down the hall. Most likely, it was Father walking away from Goff, but I didn't dare peek out from my hiding place to check.

"Tavo-jah told me about Sera-nah," Goff called out to the retreating footsteps. "I know that's why you won't let me go."

The footsteps stopped. "There is no one of that name in this clan. That name means nothing to me, and it means nothing to you. Do you understand?"

"Yes, Father. But it was Feln-nah's vote that confirmed the Magery's decision to grant Ezri-sha the title of Ruhl when it should have been Vorn-jah."

I frowned. *Vorn-jah as Ruhl? But why? How?* I would never admit it, but perhaps Goff was right. If I'd studied those books he'd left out for me, I would understand Vorn-jah's connection to the last Ruhlini.

Ezri-sha's father was the Ruhlini's son. Perhaps Vorn-jah's mother was also one of the Ruhlini's children. It was possible she had a third child. I couldn't remember. But it didn't matter. The title would have gone to the eldest of the Ruhlini's grandchildren. If the High Mage named Ezri-sha as Ruhl, then he must be older than Vorn-jah.

My head ached from trying to make sense of it, reminding me why I hated dealing with clan politics.

"I've dealt with my brother. He should not have voted against our allies, but I understand his reasons. He will continue as our representative, and that's final." The footsteps started again, then stopped. "What other gossip did Tavo-jah tell you?"

"Nothing, Father."

Father huffed. "You'll come directly to me if you hear anything else."

"Of course, Father." They were both silent for a moment. I imagined Father's piercing gaze studying Goff, waiting for him to so much as twitch a muscle.

"All right. Carry on, then," Father said. His heavy footsteps faded, and Goff sighed before turning and walking off in the opposite direction.

Unlike Father and Goff, the council gossip didn't interest me as much as that name. *Sera.* I didn't know anyone in our clan with that name, but Goff had said "Sera-nah." His use of the Nahl clan honorific couldn't have been a mistake. Goff didn't make mistakes like that. And honorifics were only used to distinguish members of the leadership family and to identify the clan's mage. Besides, Father clearly recognized the name, even though he denied it. Perhaps Mage-nah would know.

I was so deep in thought that I almost missed Rys walking by. I waited for him to pass, then slipped out of the alcove, crept up behind him, and stood on tiptoes to slip my palms over his eyes.

Rys grabbed my wrists and spun me to face him. Once he knew it was me, he immediately looked over my head and past me down the hall in both directions before turning and meeting my eyes. "What are you doing?"

"I was going to see Mage-nah. Then I saw you." I yanked my wrists free and tried to hide my disappointment. This was not the reaction I'd been hoping for.

Rys slipped his arm around me and led me back into the alcove. "You need to be more careful. I just saw Goff walking down the hall. He could have seen us." He brushed a strand of hair off my forehead, then cupped my cheek with his hand.

I grimaced at his scolding. "I told you it doesn't matter to me."

Rys opened his mouth to respond, but I placed a finger over his lips.

"You heard them in there, didn't you?" I asked. "I know you listen. You can't possibly just stand there without listening. Father talked about marrying Cala to the Ruhl. Did you know that already?"

He kissed my finger, then slid his hand from my face. Wrapping his fingers around mine, he guided my hand down until it rested against his chest. He covered my hand with his. "That's not the first time. There's been some talk."

"Why didn't you tell me? Why didn't she tell me?"

"I thought you knew." He shook his head. "Alliance through marriage would go far to build trust with the new Ruhl."

"How can you talk like that? Like we're just objects to be moved around on a game board?" I pushed away from him. "If you don't love me enough to Declare, then just say so, because I'd rather know than foolishly hope."

Rys caught my hand and held me close. Then he leaned in and crushed his lips against mine, kissing me like he'd never get another chance. Breathless, he pulled back just far enough to whisper, "I never said I didn't love you, Ayla."

I stared at him. "Then why are you so scared to let anyone

know?"

"You don't understand." He ran a hand through his hair. "The clan needs an alliance with the Shal clan to gain the protection we need. Our guard isn't prepared for attacks like the ones we've seen. It's impossible to protect everyone when they're so spread out during the scattering season."

"But Cala and Vorn..." The frustration coursing through me mixed with cold dread. "What if it were me instead of Cala? Would you really let my father use me as a pawn to cement an alliance or improve our standing in the council?"

Rys winced. He glanced away, unable to meet my eyes. "It's Cala's duty as a Nahla to do what's best for the clan. And if she does, maybe you won't have to."

I couldn't believe he was really saying that politics were more important than love. As Nahla, I could choose my partner from among the other clans' ruling families, but if I wanted to marry someone outside those families, that person had to choose me first. They had to declare for me at one of the festivals. It was our way.

"If you truly loved me, you wouldn't talk about duty. You wouldn't stand aside while my father married me off to another for the good of the clan." I placed my hands on my hips and waited for him to agree.

When he didn't respond, I shook my head. "You would let him, wouldn't you?"

My heart clenched. Tears welled in my eyes. I turned away from him so he wouldn't see.

"Ayla," he said, reaching for me with a look of pain on his face. But it was my world that was falling apart. I shook off his hand and slipped into the hallway. He didn't follow.

As I rounded the corner, blindly running toward my room, tears clouding my vision, I crashed into a firm chest covered in a black tunic decorated with delicate red embroidery. I took a step back, raising my eyes from the tunic to the tanned neck and familiar face of someone who had no business being in this wing of the lodge.

"Tavo-jah," I said. I blinked back my tears as I bent my head briefly in greeting. "Welcome."

The Jahlo dipped his head forward to return my greeting. "Ayla-nah." A single, thin braid fell forward against his cheek before the dark waves of his long hair slid over his shoulder to engulf it. I'd lost count of the number of times I'd had to listen to Cala swoon over his older brother's nearly identical hair.

Tavo grinned as though he knew what I was thinking. Then he said, "You appear to be headed in the wrong direction. Shouldn't you be helping your family prepare for this evening?"

I scowled. "I could say the same for you. What brings you to the family wing? Shouldn't you be with the other guests?" I stressed the last word, hoping he'd get the hint.

Tavo smiled and brushed off his tunic, running his hands over the woven fabric to smooth invisible wrinkles. Then, as if that weren't enough preening, he slowly and deliberately adjusted the sash wrapped around his narrow waist before responding. "I was looking for Dern. Have you seen him?"

I averted my eyes so he wouldn't catch me staring. "He went riding."

Tavo's gaze traveled over me from head to toe as he arched one eyebrow. "You know, it's only a matter of time. If Cala-nah marries the Ruhl, I suppose you'll make a good match for my brother—once you grow up a bit. Are you still spending all your time mucking about in the fields, chasing legends?"

I narrowed my eyes to glare at him. "Not all of us care so deeply about our appearances that we can't handle a little dirt."

He laughed. "That feisty spirit will serve you well in the mountains, Nahla."

I bowed my head, ready to be done with him. "Tavo-jah, if you will excuse me, I must be going now."

"See you at the feast, Ayla-jah," he teased, laughing at my back as I retreated down the hall.

I cringed at his use of the Jahl clan honorific with my name. I would prove them all wrong. I would not marry for an alliance. Once the Inahi carried my message to the gods, they would restore the veil. Then Cala could marry Vorn, and there would be nothing to stop Rys from Declaring for me. And I could do what I was meant to do—complete my apprenticeship at the Magery and become the next clan mage.

Passing by my room, I continued down the hallway and out the door on the far side. I needed to find Mage-nah. Fast. Before someone else decided my future for me,

3

I PUSHED back the flap leading into Mage-nah's tent and stepped inside. Our clan's mage sat hunched over a book at a table that ran along the back wall of the tent. Next to him, a dark liquid bubbled in a clay pot suspended over the small wood stove. Steam rose from the concoction, most likely a batch of pain-relieving medicine prepared by the younger apprentices earlier in the day. It was always the most requested potion after a festival.

I waited for Mage-nah to notice me, but when he didn't look up, I scuffed my foot against the dirt floor and coughed softly to get his attention.

"Just a moment," he said, eyes still focused on the book in his hands. After a moment, he set down his pen and stood. "What brings you to my tent at this hour?" he asked, walking over to greet me. "Shouldn't you be preparing for the feast? You're not sick, are you?"

"Greetings, Mage-nah," I said, dipping my head in respect. "I apologize for interrupting you. I'm not sick. It's just... I found something today, near the forest, and I want to ask you about it."

"And it couldn't wait until tomorrow? It must be important. Out with it, then." He waved a hand to usher me further inside.

"Mage-nah, have you ever found flowers next to an offering you left for the Inahi?" I took a few steps, then paused, unsure if he wanted me to sit or continue on to the work area at the back.

His brow wrinkled, and he gestured me toward a chair near the wood stove. "What sort of flowers?"

"Moonbursts." My heartbeat pounded in my ears as my pulse raced in anticipation of his response.

"The flowers that grow deep in the forest? The ones that only bloom under a new moon?"

I nodded. His questions reminded me that the moon tonight would be full, as it always was at the Gathering festival. Another reason those flowers had to be a sign from the Inahi.

He scowled and shook his head. "I can't say that I have ever seen flowers near an offering. Why do you ask?"

I gripped the back of the chair, too excited to sit. "I found some. Today. Moonbursts lying near an offering I left at the edge of the forest. It says in the legend of Ruhala that the Inahi left a flower for her in place of her offering." I paused, waiting for him to say something. When he didn't comment, I continued. "I brought one flower back to the lodge with me, but then something even more strange happened. The flower just..." I gestured with my hands to illustrate my point. "Disappeared."

"I see. That is curious." He tugged on his beard, his bushy eyebrows rising.

"And that's not all. When I searched the book of folklore to figure out what it means, Ry—I noticed there's a page miss-ing." If Rys didn't want anyone to know about us, it was prob-ably better to leave him out of the story.

"Which page?" he asked.

"That's the problem. I'm not sure what's supposed to be there. I always thought that was just the end of the story, but there is clearly a page missing right after the part where Ruhala speaks with the Inahi and they agree to use the magic from the clans to create the veil." I sank into the chair, unsure what else to do.

"I'll need to have a look..." His voice trailed off. He stared at the fire for a moment. "I remember there being something else, but it's been so long, I've forgotten what. And that's the only copy of that legend we have. You'd have to go to the Magery to find another."

I leaned forward. "Do you think it means something? Do you think the Inahi are trying to communicate with me?"

"Perhaps. The only one who would know for sure is the last Ruhlini, may her soul rest among the stars. But maybe her grandson knows. Have you asked the Ruhl?"

I cringed. "I haven't seen him yet."

"He is a very nice young man. Find him at the festival and ask. But before you go, I have something for you." He turned and walked toward the back of the tent.

I followed him over to a shelf above his worktable, where he picked up a thin leather notebook. When he handed it to me, I ran my fingers over the frayed edges of the binding be-fore carefully folding open the cover.

"Kilm-nah found it when he was cleaning out the store-room to make room for our winter supplies." He reached for the notebook and flipped ahead a few pages. Ancient rune symbols, believed to be the language of the Inahi, ran down the page in a column. Precise writing labeled each symbol with a translation. "If you still intend to complete your training at the Magery, it's time you learned the runes. This should give you a good start."

My fingers hovered over the drawings. I fought the urge to curl up in a corner and devour this new treasure. "Who wrote this?"

"It is the work of an old apprentice," he said. "I didn't realize she left it behind when she departed to attend the Magery."

"Where is she now?" I closed the cover and hugged the soft leather to my chest.

He waved a hand. "Still there, I imagine."

I opened my mouth to ask why she never returned but didn't get the chance. Voices, muffled by the tent skins but accompanied by grunting and scuffling, drew our attention to the door flap just in time to see it fly open.

A pair of guards shouldered their way into the tent, carrying a limp form dressed in a familiar tunic. "It's the Nahlo! Hurry! He's hurt," one of them said.

I set the book down and ran to help. "What happened?"

"I don't know," the other guard said. "We found him like this, slumped in the saddle and unconscious. At first, I didn't think the horse had a rider. Then Gav spotted the body, and— it's a wonder he made it all the way back to the gate and didn't fall off!"

As Mir explained what she knew, I did what I could to help the pair of them carry Dern. We followed Mage-nah through a flap at the back of the tent and into the adjacent infirmary. Once we got Dern settled on a cot, I took a step back in horror. He was covered in blood.

Mage-nah's usually gentle voice had turned hard and stern

as he issued orders. "Ayla-nah, get warm water and clean cloth from the storeroom."

I hurried out as he asked Gav and Mir if they had sent a patrol out to search for the raider and if anyone had informed Father or taken care of Dern's horse. I didn't hear their replies in my rush to gather supplies.

Somewhere in the back of my head, a voice reminded me I could have been with him. Perhaps I should have been with him. If he hadn't been alone... I shuddered. My hands shook as I poured warm water from the pot Mage-nah always kept on the stove into a bowl. I refilled the pot and set it back on the stove before carrying supplies back to the little infirmary tent.

When I returned, the guards were gone. I set everything down on the table Mage-nah had pulled beside the cot where Dern lay.

"What should I do?" I asked.

"Help me strip off his tunic so we can figure out where this blood is coming from." Mage-nah took a knife to the soiled tunic, cutting it open to make it easier to remove.

As I eased the fabric off Dern's arm, I noticed he was clutching something in his hand. I pried his fingers open to retrieve a charm of some sort that had been strung onto a thin leather lace. The loose ends were still knotted together, but the strap was broken. It could have been something he'd pulled off an attacker. I didn't recognize the design.

"What's that?" Mage-nah asked, glancing up from his inspection of the deep gash across Dern's chest from his collarbone to his lower ribs.

"I don't know. I've never seen it before." I held up the charm so Mage-nah could get a look.

"Hmm." He continued his inspection of Dern's upper body,

neck, and head. "These wounds need tending, but they're not bad enough for him to lose consciousness. Ayla-nah, will you bring me the wound salve and a thimbleful of the pain potion?"

I tucked the charm into the pocket of my tunic and retreated to Mage-nah's worktable to fetch the medicines. When I reached up to grab the pot of wound salve off the shelf, my eyes fell on the little book Mage-nah had given me, and I wondered if the odd symbols on the charm I'd found were runes. I snatched up the book and stuffed it into the sash belted around my waist, then searched for the measuring thimbles.

As I scanned across the table, I spotted my name scrawled on the page Mage-nah had been writing on in his journal. I knew I shouldn't look, but I couldn't resist. I crept closer and quickly scanned the words surrounding my name.

He'd been recording a reading he'd done. For my father. I nearly dropped the salve pot. Behind me, someone rushed into the tent, and I spun around, hoping they hadn't caught me spying.

"Where is he?" Tavo asked, his voice edged with barely contained rage.

I pointed out the entrance to the infirmary tent. "Mage-nah is seeing to his injuries."

Tavo took a breath and tugged at his tunic to straighten it. "Your father sent me to sit with him until he can slip away from the festival."

"I'm here. I can stay with him." After my argument with Rys, I'd lost most of my excitement for the festival. If I stayed, I could ask Mage-nah about his former apprentice, and I could attempt to decipher the symbols on Dern's charm. It wasn't as though anyone attending would miss me.

Tavo shook his head. "He wants you there."

I sighed. "Here. Take this then." I stretched out my arms to hand the salve pot to Tavo. "I need to measure a bit of pain potion. I'll bring it in before I go."

Tavo took the pot and ducked into the infirmary. I waited a moment, measured out the pain potion, then snuck another glance at Mage-nah's book.

Jusala's Heart. Forsla's Charge. Solnat's Binding. Those were the primary runes in the reading. I scanned back to see if Mage-nah had noted the question and found my answer. *Betrothals of both Nahlas. Cala-nah to Vorn-juh. Ayla-nah to Ezri-ruh. Cards are favorable to this plan. Poor Ayla. She will be so disappointed that this is the closest she'll get to the Magery.*

I wasn't sure what hurt more. That Mage-nah knew what my father had planned and hadn't said a word to me, or that my father had never intended to marry Cala to the Ruhl. He had no intention of letting me study at the Magery. He was going to use me as a pawn in his political games.

But Mage-nah had still given me that notebook. He'd also suggested I ask the Ruhl about the flowers I'd found. He couldn't tell me about Father's reading, but perhaps he was trying to help me.

If there was a chance to salvage my future, I had to act quickly. I was so close. It was time to get to the festival and confront the Ruhl before Father ruined everything.

4

I STOOD in front of my reflection and stared down at the mask in my hands. I'd been planning my costume for weeks, excited to surprise Rys at the festival. The soft grey silk that I selected from the dressmaker's collection had been spun from delicate silver and black threads. The hint of texture as the fabric skimmed across my skin gave the impression of sleek grey-black fur whenever I moved. But I was most proud of the mask I'd made, featuring the dark-rimmed eyes and tufted ears of a stormcat. At least according to the folklore. I'd never seen a real stormcat.

According to the stories, stormcats were wild creatures, tamed by the Inahi. Based on their descriptions, I'd always imagined they were like the cats who lived in our stables, only bigger and fiercer. When Rys and I were children, we used to pretend that we'd tamed a pair of stormcats and they followed us on all our adventures. As I stared at the empty, black-rimmed eye-holes in my mask, tears pooled behind my lashes. Since I'd given up hope he might declare for me tonight, the costume felt like a waste.

I swallowed and clenched my jaw to stop the tears. I wouldn't cry. There wasn't time for that now that I knew what Father had planned for me. I needed to find the Ruhl and confront him. If he didn't have the knowledge of his ancestor to help me decipher the message I'd received, then I could reveal him as an imposter and put an end to this nonsense about needing his help to restore the veil. I would use what I learned as leverage to get him to agree to a new plan. *My* plan. One that wouldn't lead to our union.

Meeting my own eyes in the reflecting glass, I held the mask in front of my face and tied the ribbons behind my head. After adjusting a few strands of hair so they framed the outer edges, I smiled at my reflection and left to join the others, already gathered in the courtyard.

Lively music and laughter echoed down the empty corridors leading to the great hall, now decorated with painted star lanterns hanging from the ceiling. Tables of refreshments lined the outer edges of the room. And every face was half-hidden, like mine, behind a mask.

Since I'd never met the Ruhl and did not know what he looked like, it didn't matter that he, too, would be wearing a mask. In fact, I'd expected it might help me identify him. Especially if he'd chosen an animal more common to his clan's territory on the coast.

A few of the guests turned to watch me pass, but I kept my eyes on my family and our guests, crowded onto the raised platform on the opposite side of the room, the same one Father and Mother had been sitting on during the clan Gathering. My parents and sister were easy to spot, even with their masks in place. Cala had chosen an impex mask, complete with gently sweeping horns. Of course she had dressed as the graceful and agile grazing animals native to the open plains our clan called home. The slender horns made it a bold choice. The thought of Cala poking out the eyes of anyone who dared to dance with her brought a smile to my face.

It was harder to guess which of the masked figures mingling around my parents and sister were my brothers and which might be the Ruhl, or others from his party. My heart ached knowing that Dern was missing this, but Mage-nah would see that he healed quickly. And he had Tavo for company. The Jahlo wasn't who I would have chosen, but he would be a friendly face when Dern woke. And if I hoped to convince the gods to restore the veil, I needed to be here.

As I wound my way through the crowd to the platform, a hand closed around mine. I twisted toward the man who'd reached for me, and he motioned toward the people dancing in the courtyard. The fine fabric of his tunic was orange and grey with specks of gold sewn throughout, and I guessed that the pointy ears and sharp nose of his mask represented the coastal fox. I'd only ever seen a drawing of one in a book, but I couldn't think of any other animals with that coloring or those ears.

All I knew for sure was that he wasn't Rys. I guessed he was probably one of the guards from the Shal clan, traveling with the Ruhl. If I favored him with a dance, perhaps he might help me arrange a quiet meeting with the Ruhl, away from the rest of my family.

I bowed my head to accept his offer and allowed him to lead me outside. As we stepped out among the dancers, he slipped his arm around my waist and shifted his grasp on my hand until we were facing each other. I'd barely found my footing when we were off, gliding and turning over the packed dirt and smooth stone.

The festive tempo and his command of the steps soon had my pulse racing. I spun and twirled in his arms until the end of the piece. But instead of letting me go as the music drifted off, he kept his hands on my waist.

"Stormcat," he said, and grinned.

I couldn't tell if it was a question because the musicians began to play again, this time a slower tempo piece, and he pulled me close and started dancing again. I turned my head to get a better look at him, trying to decide if I'd been wrong to think he was one of the Shal clan visitors.

In the dim glow from the star lanterns, it was hard to tell, but his wavy hair seemed lighter, more sun-bleached, than the thick, dark hair common among our clan. Only city-dwellers who grew up on the sunbaked coast had hair like that. But he knew our dances and performed them at least as well as any in our clan.

At the next break in the music, I leaned toward my partner to ask about the Ruhl. But, before the words escaped my lips, he'd turned, keeping hold of my hand to lead me to the edge of the dance floor and through the gate that led out of the courtyard and into the garden just outside of the lodge.

Thinking that might be my opportunity to ask for a meeting with the Ruhl, I followed him, letting the cool night air chill my warm, damp skin. Just beyond the garden gate, he paused and glanced back over his shoulder. I turned to follow his gaze and noticed the other people gathered nearby had clustered together and were whispering. They slipped back through the gate, casting glances over their shoulders at us, as they returned to the courtyard and the dancing. I hesitated, worried for a moment that I'd done something wrong and they were gossiping about me.

If I had, it was too late. I would not waste this opportunity.

Turning my back on the festival, I faced my dancing partner. "Well, Masked Fox, I believe you are a visitor here. Welcome. Do you travel with the Ruhl?"

His lips curled upward, and he stepped closer. Then he reached behind my head to release the ties that held my mask in place, lifting it away from my face.

"Hey!" I grasped for my mask as he held it out of reach.

"Ah! Just as I suspected." His smile widened. "The stormcat is a Nahla."

"Indeed." As though he couldn't have determined as much by the bar tattooed on my neck. I narrowed my eyes at him and reached again for my mask. "And you are?"

He handed me back my mask and offered me his arm. "Come," he said. "Let's walk."

I had no intention of playing these games. "No, thank you. If you know who I am, then you know I'm overdue to greet our most honored guest."

He laughed. "I don't think that will be a problem. I'm happy to introduce you, if you come with me."

I cocked my head, then glanced back over my shoulder toward the gate that led back into the courtyard. The guests who had been watching us quickly swiveled their heads away to appear as if they hadn't been staring. I turned back to my mystery dancing partner with wide eyes, realization dawning.

"You. You're him, aren't you?"

He tucked my hand into the crook of his arm and led me further into the garden. "Depends. Who do you think I am?"

I fell into step alongside him. "You're the Ruhl, aren't you?"

"I'd prefer it if you called me Ezri, but, yes, I'm afraid so. Are you disappointed?" He glanced down at me and laughed lightly when he caught me frowning.

"I just thought... I thought you would be with my parents, and Cala." This conversation was not going as planned. Somehow, he had gained the upper hand, and I needed to get it back.

"Mmm. Good. Sounds like our carefully placed rumors achieved their purpose if they set that expectation." After we passed under the vine-covered archway that marked the start of the winding, hedge-lined gravel path that led to the reflection well, he slowed his pace.

"Then you haven't come to marry Cala?" I asked.

"I've come to discuss some business." He stopped next to the deep well of calm water and turned toward me. His hands curled around my bare arms, just above my elbows, holding me close.

"With me?" I ignored the flutter of giddy pleasure at being sought out by this man. This was business. Not personal. But it made what I had planned quite a bit easier. Possibly too easy. I needed to be careful I didn't walk right into a trap.

"Why not?" He grinned.

"Isn't that the type of thing you should discuss with my father? He's the clan leader. I'm just his fourth heir." When I said it like that, it did seem odd that he had singled out me to speak with. "Do you even know my name?"

"Ah, but I do!" He released my arms so he could remove his mask. Then he dropped to one knee in front of me. He let his mask fall to the ground as he clasped both of my hands in his and looked up at me.

Unveiled, his eyes were even more captivating than they'd been peering at me through the holes in his mask. They were framed by perfectly arched eyebrows and that wavy, sun-streaked hair that I just knew would be silky to touch.

I tugged at his hands, trying to pull him to his feet. "What are you doing? Get up."

"Ayla, my Nahla, I know we've only just met, but I would like nothing more than for you to return home with me, Ezri, Ruhl of the United Clans, as my betrothed."

"You're not seriously asking me to marry you?" I paused, wondering if perhaps he'd already arranged this with my father.

He raised an eyebrow. "That is exactly what I'm doing, my Nahla."

I slid my hands out of his grip. "I can't."

"You are already committed to someone." He frowned.

A tiny part of me cheered that I'd finally cracked his supreme confidence, but it wasn't true, and he'd find that out soon enough. "That's not what I said."

"So, you're not committed, then?" The grin returned.

If he'd arranged this with my father, he would know that. This must have been his idea. "No. I can't marry you because I'm needed here. My clan needs me."

He stood and took a moment to brush the gravel dust off his knee. "I believe that. But I also know that I need you more, Stormcat."

"What? Why?" This was definitely not the reaction I'd expected. "What could you possibly need from me?"

He sighed. "Tell me, what does Cala know of stormcats? Or of the legends and folklore?"

Cala knew everything there was to know about running the clan, but she'd stopped reading folklore shortly after her naming.

"I thought so," he said, when I didn't respond right away.

A rustling in the hedge caught my attention. The Ruhl heard it at the same time and stepped in front of me, putting the well behind us and turning toward the source of the sound. My hands flew to the pins in my hair. I slipped the two thin, sharp knives out of their decorative hairpin sheaths. Then I crouched in a defensive stance behind him and waited.

A group of guards emerged from the hedge and spilled out onto the path before us. The Ruhl immediately relaxed when he recognized the man leading the group. "Zan, I thought I told you to stay behind. As you can see, I'm fine, though a bit of privacy would be nice."

"I thought you agreed to stay where I could see you," the one he'd called Zan replied. He glanced at the knife the Ruhl was already returning to its sheath. "At least you had the sense to defend yourself when you heard our approach."

"But of course." The Ruhl cocked his head to one side. "This annoying captain of the Shal clan guard is always reminding me to maintain constant vigilance, as though he is convinced I don't listen."

"Yes. Well, that is because you don't listen. You run off into hedges with dangerous women."

"Dangerous?" If the Ruhl was trying to win me over, he wouldn't do it by sounding so surprised.

"Yes." Zan's eyes skimmed past the Ruhl and narrowed as they met mine. "I will remind you that the first rule of being vigilant is to be observant. You do remember me teaching you that, don't you?"

"I seem to remember something about that, yes." The Ruhl repositioned himself so his body was between me and the guards as Zan stalked closer.

"So, I suppose then—" Zan shouldered past the Ruhl and stepped between us. "That you noticed—" He grabbed my wrists and forced my hands open in one quick motion, removing the thin blades. "This?" He showed the blades to the Ruhl, before leaning closer so he could slide the blades back into their hairpin sheaths, still buried in my hair.

The Ruhl's mouth dropped open and his eyes went wide. Then he started laughing. "Apparently, the Nahla also has a keen sense of self-preservation."

"Or an equally cautious captain of her clan's guard," added Zan, eyes narrowing again as he studied me and watched for my reaction.

"Both," I said, attempting to keep my face blank and unreadable. I reached up to check that the knives were secured.

The recent raids had everyone in our clan on edge. Living out in the open, with our lands so close to the forest, the Nahl clan was the most vulnerable of the three clans. Everyone learned how to fight so we could protect ourselves. So, of course I knew how to defend myself, if needed.

"All right, Zan." The Ruhl broke the tense silence. "If you're done here, then perhaps you can take them," he motioned to the handful of guards who held their position near the hedge, "and return to the courtyard so that I can finish here?"

"You shouldn't be out here alone," Zan said.

"I'm not alone, I'm with Ayla-nah," he replied.

The pair stared silently at each other for a tense moment. When it was clear that the Ruhl had no intention of backing down, Zan inclined his head in a slight bow of apology. He signaled the guards, and they filed out through the break in the hedge.

Before he left, Zan slid a small vial filled with amber liquid out of his pocket and held it out to the Ruhl. "You forgot this."

The Ruhl snatched the vial from Zan's hand and shoved it into a pocket in his tunic. "I didn't forget it. I don't need it."

Zan shook his head but didn't argue. "There's something else you should know. Your cousin, Vorn-jah, has arrived unexpectedly."

Cousin? I remembered the conversation I'd overheard between Goff and Father. My speculation about Vorn's mother being one of the Ruhlini's children must have been correct. If I'd at least glanced at the books Goff had left out for me, I wouldn't have had to guess at the connection. Though, I still might not have remembered. I really only cared about who had supposedly inherited the ability to speak with the Inahi.

At the mention of Vorn, I thought I caught a brief furrow appear in the Ruhl's brow, along with a slight narrowing of his eyes. But it may just have been a shadow because then he started laughing. "Did he, then? He must have heard about my rumored interest in Cala-nah."

"Indeed." Zan remained stoic. "The Nahl is greeting him as we speak."

"All right." The Ruhl sobered a bit and waved a hand to dismiss Zan. "I just need another moment alone with the Nahla, and we'll be right behind you."

Zan bowed and retreated.

I waited for the crunch of gravel underfoot to diminish before turning to the Ruhl. "You think it will take just 'another moment' to convince me?"

"Stormcat," he said, bending to lift our masks off the gravel where they'd fallen. "I know this is likely not the future you imagined, but I need you to return with me." He gestured toward the guards and the festival. "You said your clan needs you. But if you agree to marry me, you can help more than just your clan."

"How?" I wanted to hear more before I told him about my discovery and tested what he knew.

He stepped closer, his voice dropping to a whisper, all hints of amusement gone from his face. "I'll tell you, but everything I say must remain between the two of us. Agreed?"

I nodded, eager for his secrets. "Agreed."

The Ruhl looked down and studied the masks he held, running his thumb over the soft fur I'd attached to the tufted ears on mine. "I can't communicate with the Inahi unless I can find them." His eyes flicked up to meet mine. "And before you think that perhaps the Magery chose incorrectly, I am almost certain that Vorn-jah hasn't stumbled across any Inahi, either."

"How can you be so sure?" I asked.

"About Vorn-jah?" He grinned. "I have my ways. Best not ask more questions about that. At least not now."

Spies. He had spies in the Jahl clan. If that was true, perhaps he was only pretending to be surprised by Vorn's arrival. "Why do you think I can help?"

"You've been looking for them, haven't you?" He raised an eyebrow and the corner of his mouth twitched like he was laughing at me.

"How do you know about that?" I took a step backwards. Did he have spies watching our clan, too?

He held up his hand. "Let's just say I've made a point to learn about all the Nahl's children. Your father told me of each of your talents. He speaks highly of your knowledge."

I didn't believe him. If that were true, then Father wouldn't be trying to marry me off. He'd be sending me to study at the Magery. "All right. I might have some information that could help you, but that doesn't mean I have to marry you."

The Ruhl stepped closer, eyes narrowed. "Do you realize how fragile the alliance between the three clans has become?"

"No." I shrugged. "That has nothing to do with convincing the gods to restore the veil."

"It has everything to do with it." His hand wrapped around my shoulder. "The Council of Clans put their faith in me. If they knew I couldn't find the Inahi, or if they thought I didn't have the power to speak with them, the alliance would break. And then we'd be too occupied fighting each other to fight any invaders who might cross into our lands. The Shal guard may be the best of the three clans, but the Agrion army is better. I need to find the Inahi and petition the gods to help us before it's more than just raiders finding their way past the veil."

I considered what he said. I knew nothing about our neighbors beyond the mountains and across the sea, let alone their armies, but what he told me aligned with what Rys had said about how important it was for our clan to make an alliance with the Shal clan.

Even if it turned out that the Ruhl didn't know what the message I'd received meant, he would have access to his clan's version of the legends. And, if that failed, there were always the resources at the Magery, which was located within the walls of Shal City.

I wanted to go with him, but there needed to be another way to make it happen. "I won't marry you."

"All I ask for is a betrothal. It's the best way to keep you close to me and keep your assistance a secret." He slid his hand down my arm so he could wrap his fingers around mine. "I'll arrange it with your father. Then we can return to the city and find the Inahi together."

"No. I have a better idea." I didn't want him negotiating with my father until after he made some promises to me. "Declare for me at the festival tonight."

"Declare for you?"

"It is our way. If you have someone you'd like to partner with, you declare for them at one of the festivals. Gathering, Midwinter, or Scattering. Then you can marry at the next festival. I don't come of age until Midwinter, so this is my first festival where I can receive declarations." I dropped my gaze to the masks that the Ruhl still held in his hand and tried not to think about whose declaration I had been hoping for this evening. "As the clan leader's daughter, I can't make one unless it is for another in a clan leader's line. So, I could declare for you, but I think it will go better if you're the one declaring, especially since everyone thinks you'll be declaring for Cala and not me."

"And everyone saw me escorting you into the gardens, so…" His voice drifted off as he glanced back toward the music.

"They'll think you've swept me off my feet." I swallowed my thoughts of Rys.

"All right. Let's go." The Ruhl tugged on my hand and started toward the hedges.

"Wait." I planted my feet. "Before I agree to this, I need you to promise me something."

"Anything." The Ruhl stepped closer. "What?"

I raised my chin, meeting those captivating eyes of his with mine. "After we find the Inahi and restore the veil, promise me that you will release me from the betrothal, and help me gain admittance to study at the Magery."

He nodded. "If that's what you want, Stormcat, it will be so. I promise."

"Swear it. On your grandmother's ashes." Whatever agreement he came to with my father, I needed to be sure I would have my freedom when this was done.

He released his grip on my hand so he could place his palm over his heart. "I swear it on the last Ruhlini."

"Thank you." I prayed it would work. If it didn't, and he was right, our clans would be at war, our lands would be invaded, and I'd be married to the Shal's only son. "Let's get back before we miss the declarations."

5

THE Ruhl and I ignored the stares of the people we passed as we made our way back to the lodge. He kept me close at his side, his hand covering mine where it wrapped around his elbow. From time to time he'd grin at me, his eyes sparkling under his mask. I tried to mimic his excitement, but everything felt hollow and wrong.

I should have been dancing with Rys. Dern should have been dancing as well, not recovering from mysterious injuries in Mage-nah's tent. The Ruhl should have been flirting with Cala, not focusing his attention on me. And Vorn should have been in the mountains, celebrating the harvest with his own clan.

In a moment, I would have to face my family and my decision. The sight of them as we entered the great room, greeting Vorn-jah, turned my stomach into a knot. My steps slowed as though my feet were covered with mud from the plains during storm season.

The Ruhl squeezed my hand then slid his arm from my

grip so he could press his palm against the small of my back. He guided me forward, and I let him, mustering my courage, even though I wanted to flee. Soon, he would confirm what everyone was thinking.

I shuddered as my father turned his head and spotted us. This would look like what he'd planned, but would he be pleased?

"Ezri-ruh, there you are." Father greeted the Ruhl with a slap on his shoulder. "I see you've found my younger daughter."

"Yes." The Ruhl removed his hand from my back and clasped hands with Vorn. "Vorn-jah, an unexpected surprise. Estrel's blessings to you and your clan."

"And to you, cousin." Vorn returned the Ruhl's greeting before turning to me and dipping his head. "Ayla-nah."

"Good to see you, Vorn-jah." I glanced past him to Cala, trying to judge her reaction to the unexpected appearance of the man she loved and to me, appearing on the Ruhl's arm. She had always been better than me at hiding her feelings from her face.

"Now that we're all here." Father stepped forward and clapped his hands together to draw the attention of the clan to the raised platform where we stood. He waited for a hush to fall over the festival. More people pushed inside from where they'd been dancing in the courtyard.

"We celebrate tonight the blessings Estrel has bestowed upon our clan, and we welcome our Shal and Jahl visitors who have traveled to be here with us on this festive occasion." He stretched his hands wide. "Long ago, our gods led us to this land and accepted our sacrifice so that we would forever gain their protection. Though tonight we give thanks to Estrel for our safe return, we have all five gods to thank for our abundance and prosperity. To the Five! No matter where they roam, may they always look kindly upon us!"

"To the Five!" the clan cheered.

"Now, Estrel also grants us hope. Do any of you have hopes for Solnat's blessings that you would like to declare?"

Vorn stepped forward without hesitation. "I do." He glanced back at Cala. "With Solnat's blessing, I wish to declare for Cala-nah."

Father nodded, then turned to the clan. "Do any here object or wish to counter?"

It was as though the room took a breath and held it. Many eyes glanced toward the Ruhl from behind their masks. Even Father cast him a questioning look. When he didn't speak to counter, Father gestured to Cala.

She hesitated only a moment, flicking her eyes between Father and the Ruhl before stepping alongside Vorn and taking his hand. "I accept Vorn-jah's declaration."

A cheer erupted from the clan when they kissed, followed by a flurry of new declarations. My heart sped in anticipation as I searched for Rys among the masked faces. My eyes locked with his as a voice next to me spoke.

"I also wish to make a declaration."

A few whispers flitted across the room when the Ruhl paused. Father held up a hand to silence the clan, before turning to the Ruhl and waiting for him to continue.

"Honored Nahl, I have been swept off my feet by a storm-cat." The Ruhl wrapped his hand around mine. "Though I am unfamiliar with your clan's customs, I wish to declare for Ayla-nah, with Solnat's blessing."

He squeezed my hand, and I tore my gaze from Rys to spare a look at him, knowing the part I must play to make this plan work. But I couldn't resist turning back to Rys when

Father asked if anyone objected or wished to counter.

My soul reached for Rys, aching for him to say something, but his lips, the ones I'd kissed so often I knew their every contour, remained closed. My heart broke in that moment. Tears welled in my throat, so many I couldn't hope to hold them back. I knew what I needed to do next, but I didn't trust myself to speak.

I nodded once.

The Ruhl squeezed my hand, and I looked away from Rys to meet the gaze of the Ruhl at my side. He was smiling, but I caught a hint of doubt where the corners of his mouth wavered.

"I accept." I forced the words out. Then I turned and fled.

The crowd parted before me as I hurried out, through the courtyard, out the gate to the garden, and around the stables and pasture that lay beyond. I kept going until the shouts and cheers faded into the distance behind me. Only then did I slow down.

I knew better than to venture out past the fence alone at night, but after what I'd done, I needed to be alone. I walked in a daze, not really noticing where my feet were taking me until I was there, climbing the gently sloping hill that led to a bluff overlooking the grasslands. The place I always came to when I couldn't sleep.

The fence curved around the lower tier of the bluff so as not to block the view. Even though I'd been to this lookout spot more times than I could count, all thoughts fled the moment the grasslands and the wide horizon came into focus, shining silver against the black shadows in the moonlight.

I sighed. This was my home. This was where I belonged. In order to save it, I needed to go with the Ruhl. I was always planning on leaving for a time. I just thought it would be to attend the Magery, not so I could be married off to another clan.

I lay back on a nearby boulder to look up at the sky. When I found Estrel's star, I said a quick prayer, asking for guidance. The stars glistened as I let the tears flow from my eyes and trickle down my temples and into my hair. A moment later, the dark wings of a night hawk slid across the sky, momentarily blocking the light from Estrel's star.

Forsla. I took that as a sign that Estrel was sending me strength. The strength of her daughter-god, Forsla.

Behind me, the crunch of rocks under boot heels cut through the silence. Someone was coming up the hillside on the trail. Unsure how visible I was in the darkness, I pressed my body into the boulder and turned my head to look as I reached for my hairpin knives for the second time in one night.

I squinted into the darkness, preparing to fight or flee. But, as the silhouette crested the hill, I knew instantly who it was. I would recognize that body anywhere. I couldn't see his features, but I knew the shape of him. From the way he was turning his head, he was searching for something or someone.

I sat up, and the unexpected movement startled him until he recognized me. "How did you know I would be here?" I asked.

He shrugged. "I know you, Ayla. When will you realize that?"

"Rys..." I started, but he cut me off.

"It's all right. You don't need to explain." His arms wrapped around me in a possessive hug. I buried my face into his shoulder and the tears started again.

"Why didn't you say something?" I asked, the question

muffled and spoken more into him than at him.

"He's the Ruhl, and you're a Nahla. What would you have me do?"

I pulled back from him enough to look at his face. This wasn't like him. There had to be something he wasn't telling me. The Rys I'd fallen in love with wouldn't just let me go so easily. But despite the look of pain on his face, he offered no explanation.

I struggled out of his embrace and stalked to the edge of the bluff, refusing to look at him. I pulled my cape tighter around me and shivered, thinking back over my conversation with the Ruhl and cursing the fact I'd promised to keep what he told me a secret. Would it matter to Rys if he knew I'd arranged a way out?

Rys set a hand on my shoulder, and I turned to face him. I wanted to ask him to wait for me, but I couldn't. Not without revealing the secret I now shared with the Ruhl.

"This isn't what I wanted," I said.

"It isn't what I wanted, either, but we each have our duties, and we need to accept that."

I studied Rys's face in the moonlight. I wanted to scream at how easily he was accepting this, but I just stared instead, willing him to read my mind and take the step that he would not take. If he would have spoken in that moment, I might have told him everything I'd promised to keep secret. I wished for once Rys would choose love over honor and duty, but he remained silent. Twin tears slipped down my cheeks.

"Come here," he said. "You're going to freeze."

I pulled away, dropping my gaze to the trail and starting back toward the lodge. "I'll be fine. I'm going back to my room."

He reached out and grabbed my hand as I passed. "Ayla—"

He looked into my eyes as if he was going to say more, but no more words crossed those lips I longed to kiss.

I waited for as long as I could stand it. Then, with a heavy heart, I simply said, "Goodbye, Rys," and walked away down the hill.

#

LATER that morning, I awoke to bright sunlight streaming in through the window in my room and the realization that I wasn't alone. My mother's assistant, Wyn, was bustling about, preparing trunks for my clothes and belongings. The sight of them reminded me of the agreement I'd made.

I groaned and rolled over, not quite ready to face the Ruhl and my family after running out on them. Not that Wyn was going to let me sleep while she did all my packing. I flopped onto my back and was just about to sit up when my sister's voice echoed down the hall.

"Ayla! Ayla!" Her calls were getting louder as she got closer to my room.

"Ayla." Cala paused in the doorway, nearly breathless. She must have run all the way to my rooms when I didn't appear for breakfast. "What are you doing still in bed? Get up, lazybones!"

I cringed. "Tell me how much trouble I'm in first."

"Trouble? Why would you be in trouble?" Cala came over to the bed and shook me. "Come on. Get up. I have news and we have so much to do. Wake up!"

I tossed my pillow aside and propped myself up on my elbows. "What happened? Is it Dern? Is he awake?"

"Not yet." She plopped down on the bed next to me. "Father stayed with him all night. Mother's going to relieve him soon, which is why we have to hurry."

I pushed myself up to sitting. "I don't get it. Why are we hurrying?"

"I'm getting married!" Cala squealed.

"That's not news. I was there when Vorn-jah declared for you last night." I frowned at the memory, not because I wasn't happy for her, but because it reminded me of Rys. "Is that why he was there? Did he come all the way from the mountains just to declare?"

"You'll never believe it." She bounced on the mattress beside me, grinning. Her cheeks were flushed from running down the halls, or maybe from excitement. "Vorn said that Tavo-jah sent a messenger ahead to the mountain holding to tell them of the rumors that Father intended to betroth me to the Ruhl. Vorn said he rode as fast as he could to get here before the Ruhl had a chance to steal me away. Isn't that romantic?" She sighed.

It was what Rys should have done. My foolish heart still ached over the fact he hadn't chosen to intervene. Tears pooled in my eyes, but I blinked them away and swallowed the hurt.

"Was Father really intending to betroth you to the Ruhl?" I asked, curious if she'd been told about Father's plan for us.

"I was worried that he might, even though he knew my feelings for Vorn, especially after what happened to Dern." Cala frowned. "Goff said you were there when they brought him in. Is that true? Everyone is whispering about what happened. Was it really that bad?"

"Well, I don't know what everyone is saying, but it was pretty terrifying." I twisted my hands in my lap. "His tunic was drenched in blood, and he has a gash from here to here."

Cala winced. "I should go see him. We both can. After we get our gowns fitted for my wedding tonight."

"Tonight? Your wedding is tonight? You aren't waiting until Midwinter?" Everything was happening so fast. If Cala married and moved to the mountain holding, and I left for the coast, who knew when I would ever see her again. The thought of losing Cala brought to mind an image of Rys standing on the bluff in the starlight, as if to remind me of everything I was losing. My sister, my love, my homeland. All of it gone in less time than it took to prepare for the festival last night.

"You're unhappy." Cala brought her hand to my chin to raise it so she could look more fully into my face. "Why are you unhappy?" She stared at me, waiting for me to respond.

"I... It's just..." I searched for words but could only find tears.

Cala took my hand. "Oh." She dropped her voice to a whisper. "Rys. Is that why you ran out last night?" She was the only one I'd trusted with the secret of who had claimed my heart.

I nodded, and another sob escaped my chest.

"Have you talked to him?" She glanced over at Wyn out of the corner of her eye to make sure the clanswoman wasn't listening.

I choked back my tears and wiped at my eyes. "Yes."

"And?" She leaned forward to brush a tear from my cheek.

I shrugged and sniffled. "He said he's a guard and Ezri's the Ruhl."

Cala pursed her lips. After a pause she said, "He's right, you know."

"I thought he loved me." I buried my face in my hands.

Cala gently pulled my hands away and wrapped hers around mine. "Maybe that's why he didn't counter."

I glared at Cala. "That doesn't make any sense."

"Look," she said. "Don't be mad, all right?"

I narrowed my eyes at her. I had a feeling that whatever she said next was definitely going to make that impossible.

She frowned. "I think maybe Dern might have talked with him."

"What?" I threw the covers off me. "He better wake up so I can strangle him." I scrambled to push past Cala so I could stand.

Wyn peered over her shoulder at us. I froze.

Cala pulled me back down. "No. You won't," she whispered. She put her arm around my shoulders. "If you'd pull your head out of your folklore for once, you'd realize that relations between the clans are seriously strained. You must have noticed that Father pulled Uncle Feln off the council. He's been home for how many moons now?"

I kept my voice low, but bit off the words and nearly growled them at her. "That doesn't give Dern any right to interfere and tell Rys he isn't good enough for me." I tried to stand up again, but she squeezed me against her.

"He was only trying to help. He didn't want to see you get hurt."

"But I am hurt!" I twisted away, pulling her with me, further from Wyn's ears. A part of me knew she was right. The Ruhl and Rys had both said almost the same thing about relations between the clans being strained. But I couldn't help how I felt. "I love Rys. I don't want to marry the Ruhl."

"Really, Ayla! It's not that awful. He's gorgeous and charming, and based on his declaration, he clearly adores you." She leaned over and poked me in the arm.

I swatted her hand away. "He's not interested in me that way."

"Oh really? That's not what I heard. Abi and Pim told me

they saw you two sneaking off to be alone in the gardens."

I'd expected that would be what everyone was saying. Everyone in the clan had been speculating about the Ruhl since his visit was announced, and now that I'd agreed to marry him, they'd be talking about me as well. I couldn't tell Cala what really happened. I would have to let the gossips talk.

"Fine Cala. Fine. You win. I'm happy." I reached for my clothes. "You should go. I need to pack."

"Ayla, stop. Be happy for real. Be happy for me! For both of us! Do you not see how lucky we are?" She reached out and pulled me into a hug.

Cala had always dreamed of the day she would marry. She wanted more than anything to become a clan leader. It pained her that both Goff and Dern were older than her, and Goff stood to inherit our clan leadership from Father. If she'd been the eldest, it would have gone to her, but instead she'd been cursed with two older brothers.

The fact that all three of them stood to inherit before me didn't bother me in the slightest. I had no desire to become a clan leader. For as long as I could remember, I'd only wanted to become a mage, marry Rys, and someday, when I was much older, take Mage-nah's place as head mage of our clan. I reminded myself that I could still have that. I just needed to help the Ruhl find the Inahi and convince the gods to restore the veil first.

Cala was right about one thing, though. I could be happy for her. I hugged her back and tried to smile.

"You are so impossible sometimes," she said as she released me. "Now, come on and leave the packing to Wyn. We have so much to do before my wedding tonight."

"You never explained why you were getting married tonight instead of waiting until Midwinter."

She frowned. "I know, it's sudden, but Vorn wants to return as soon as possible. The winter storms are coming, and they'll make travel through the passes too treacherous. If we wait until Midwinter, we'd have to marry in the caverns. Mother and Father wouldn't be able to attend. And who knows if the snow will be melted by the Scattering in spring."

"But tonight? Couldn't you wait a few days?"

"The Ruhl plans to leave tomorrow, and he's taking you with him. I don't want to marry without you by my side."

"Tomorrow. We're leaving tomorrow?" It made sense. The sooner we left, the sooner I'd be able to check the Shal clan folklore books. Better to get moving than delay, and it wasn't as though waiting was going to make leaving any easier.

"That's what the Ruhl told Father last night." She stood and straightened her tunic. "Come on. I told Mother we'd meet her in her rooms. I'll grab you some bread from the kitchens and catch up with you there."

"Sure," I said. "Go on ahead." I picked up my brush and stared at it. If Cala was getting married right away, and the Ruhl wanted to leave tomorrow, would Father also insist on me marrying before I left? I wouldn't officially come of age until Midwinter, but that might not be enough to stop him from insisting on it. If he did, it would ruin everything.

Cala watched me for a moment, waiting until I lifted the brush to my head and pulled it through my hair a few times before she finally took a few steps toward the door. "Don't dawdle. We have a lot to do."

As soon as she was gone, I put the brush down, tied my hair back, and pulled on my boots. Then I strapped my knife to my belt, grabbed my cape, and headed off down the hallway in the opposite direction. There was only one person who would be able to convince Father to let my betrothal be enough until after Midwinter. I needed to talk with Mother before Cala returned.

6

I HURRIED down the corridor, heading for the open door to my parents' room. A quick look inside confirmed that my mother was alone. Rather than rushing in, I paused outside to catch my breath and prepare the words I'd planned to say.

"Ayla, dear, is that you?" My mother was kneeling with her back to me, sorting fabric and boxes from one of the large trunks resting under the windows.

"Yes, Mother." I took a few tentative steps into the room.

"Where's your sister?" she asked without looking up.

"Cala said she'd meet me here. Is Father around?"

"Your father should be back soon, but only to wash and change. Ezri-ruh is expecting him. They need to discuss the details of your betrothal and the plans for your departure." She stood and smoothed the wrinkles from her long skirts. "I don't suppose I need to tell you it was very rude of you to run off like that last night."

"I... I wasn't feeling well." I twisted the cloak I held in my hands, as though wringing out the fabric might also release some of my nerves as well.

Mother crossed the room to me, cupped my chin in her hands, and turned my face to look up into hers. "How are you this morning? You look flushed."

"I'm all right now." My palms sweat under her scrutiny.

"Perhaps it was too much excitement for one night, hmm?" She smiled at me, then released my chin and paced to the window. She pushed the curtains to one side and gazed out across the courtyard. "This is an excellent opportunity for you. And for the clan."

"Yes." This was my opening. "But Mother, I'm not yet eighteen."

"Ayla, dear." She turned toward me. "I know you're still young, but you mustn't be scared. You may not see it now, but it is a good match. For both you and Cala."

"But, Mother—" I prepared to lay out my plea for her to insist the marriage be delayed until the Scattering.

She shook her head and cut me off. "I don't want you to leave, either. I will miss my girls, and I wish you could stay. But your marriage, like Cala's, will bring strength to our clan. I only hope that your brothers will make equally advantageous matches."

She looked at me for a long time. I felt as though she could see right through to my heart. As though she could read the name written there. I wondered if she would ever have approved. She had been from a clan family, not leadership like my father. She'd declared for my father because they were in love. I used that to help make my case.

"It's just... I'd hoped that I might marry someone I loved. I don't even know the Ruhl. I'm not ready to marry, yet."

"Then we'll give you some time to get to know each other." She walked toward me again, taking my shoulders in her hands and squeezing them. "I don't think your father will insist on you marrying before you leave, but I'll talk to him before they meet and make sure he asks for a long betrothal."

"Thank you, Mamma." I breathed a sigh of relief as I wrapped my arms around her waist.

She hugged me to her. "I can't promise that you'll be able to wait until the Scattering to marry, but I will ask Teron to at least give you until Midwinter. How's that?"

Someone knocked on the door before I could respond.

"Oh, good! You're already here." Cala held out the breakfast roll she'd brought for me.

Mother released me so I could take the roll. Then she returned to the trunk under the window.

"Here are the dresses." She lifted out a stack of fine silk. The fabrics shimmered in the sunlight. "Take them to the dressmaker so she can tailor them to fit you."

Cala brushed the crumbs off her hands, then removed her cloak. She stretched out the fabric so Mother could set the bundle on top. Then Cala wrapped the edges carefully around the slippery fabric to keep it protected.

"Good." Mother squeezed Cala's shoulder. "Now, both of you, hurry to the dressmaker, then stop at the jeweler while you're at the market. She should have a package for me."

"Thank you." Cala kissed Mother on the cheek and then hurried for the door.

"Go on." Mother flicked her hand at me. "I have much to do here before you both leave me."

When Cala realized I hadn't followed, she tucked the bundle of fabric against her hip with one hand and returned. Linking her free arm through mine, she half dragged me out and down the hall, through the family wing, past the great room, and out of the lodge toward the busy market tents.

I allowed myself to be pulled along and let her happy chatter wash over me as we walked between the colorful tents. The relief of knowing I wouldn't be married right away brought a smile to my lips and helped convince my sister that I was paying attention, even though my thoughts had already moved on to how I would find the Inahi before Midwinter. If only I could do something about Rys. I couldn't exactly tell him to wait for me.

Cala glanced at me out of the corner of her eyes and tipped her head closer to mine before speaking. "I went to see Mage-nah yesterday so he could cast a reading. He said the strangest things."

We squeezed together to pass between two large groups heading in the opposite direction.

"Like what? What did he tell you?" I thought of Mage-nah's notes on Father's reading and the notebook full of runes he'd given me. I'd have to make sure it got packed somewhere safe.

Cala shrugged. "Most of it made little sense. Solnat's Tears. Jusala's Crown. A death that would bring my husband to power." She paused. "At first I thought he was referring to the Ruhl's father, but I suppose the cards were referring to the Jahl? Perhaps I should tell Vorn about that..."

"I don't think you need to worry. Everyone knows that when Vehlm-jah dies, Vorn will take his place as Jahl," I said, hoping to reassure her.

"You're probably right. Let's see... What else? Oh! Forsla's Flame was at the center. Something about a conflict, but I can't think what that was about. You know me. I hate to fight. But the best part was Solnat's Seeds. He said I'd be blessed with plenty of children!"

"That's great!" I tried to echo her excitement and hoped my grin would be convincing. Children were the farthest thing from my mind. It amazed me how different we were, growing up in the same place with the same parents.

"I know." She was practically glowing as she pulled on my sleeve. The dressmaker's tent loomed before us. "Come on! We need to hurry."

Cala lifted back the tent flap and held it open for me. We slipped inside and were surrounded by colors and fabrics with barely room to walk. Ribbons of all sizes and shades hung from the tent roof supports. Cala called out to the dressmaker, standing on tiptoes to see beyond the stacks of fabrics and dress forms.

"Hello!" a clear, high voice called from the back of the tent.

Papers rustled, boxes scraped across the dirt floor, a few stacks of fabric wobbled, and then a petite woman emerged from behind two dress forms. One form had been clothed in a simple yellow tunic and skirt, and the other modeled a travel suit, complete with cape.

"Ah! Welcome, Nahlas! Solnat's blessings to you both." The small woman bowed her head to us.

"And to you." Cala unwrapped the fabric and handed it to Tia. "Mother said you could alter these for my wedding tonight."

"Yes, yes." Tia examined the fabric, then handed me the pale green silk gown and returned the blue and gold silk one to Cala. "Come try them on, and we'll get them pinned."

Cala and I followed Tia to the back of the tent and through another flap to a smaller, less cluttered area. The space contained only a few chairs and a tall looking glass. I draped the gown I'd been given over the back of one chair before removing my tattered riding cape and stripping down to my under-wraps.

I finished dressing first, and Tia spun me to face her. She studied me closely while tucking a few stray hairs into the braided bun that kept her long black hair efficiently out of her face. Then she began bustling about me, pinching and fastening fabric, inserting pins, and adjusting the hem. Finally, she stepped back to admire her work.

"Oh!" Cala reached out to touch my dress, but paused, fingers hovering above the fabric. "It's just perfect."

Tia tilted her head, nudged Cala aside, and re-pinned a fold of the skirt to adjust the hem slightly. "There you go. Take it off carefully and put this on while I pin up your sister's dress."

She set a bundle of clothes on the nearby chair while I shimmied out of the dress, careful not to disturb the pins.

"What's that for?" I asked.

"When you travel with the Ruhl tomorrow." She turned her attention to Cala.

I scowled as I pulled on the snug, smoky grey riding leggings, and the loose, light grey, long-sleeved tunic of the travel suit. While Tia bustled around Cala, I wrapped a wide, woven belt around my middle. The belt started just under my breasts and ended at the top of my hips. It kept the tunic from getting caught up in my riding gear and provided some protection to my midsection should we be attacked on the road.

Most of the fabric in the belt matched the dark grey color of the leggings. Woven through the dark grey were bright silver threads. They would shine in the sunlight, making me look very regal, but the real purpose was defense. Those lightweight armor threads would make it difficult for a blade to pass through this belt.

Most of the clan used untreated black threads, spun from the same material, for this purpose. In order to make the black thread shine like silver, they needed to be submerged in a special chemical distilled by the mage, then polished to a shine. Only once in my work as an assistant had I helped one of his apprentices make this potion. The extra expense of the process was purely for decoration and therefore shunned within our clan. Even our mother didn't have a belt made with the silver threads.

I fastened the belt in the front and picked up the cape, which was a deep twilight blue. The same silver strands had been woven into the cape, and it fastened at my neck with a solid silver bar—metal mined from the mountains by the Jahl clan and traded to us for stores to get them through the winter. The bar was shaped to look like the bar tattooed on my neck.

The riding suit fit like a glove and I instantly felt more comfortable than I had in the silk dress. Tia knew how to make riding pants and tunics that fit me just right because that was nearly the only thing I ever wore. But this suit was different. This was a suit for a Nahla—a Nahla who was betrothed to the Ruhl.

I was so lost in thought that I barely heard Tia when she turned away from Cala to check the fit of my travel suit.

"Yes. That will do nicely." She removed the cape and belt. Then she made a few minor adjustments to the tunic and pants to achieve a more flattering fit. "Before you go, I need to take down your measurements to send ahead to the dressmakers in Shal City."

"Why do they need my measurements?" I asked as I slipped out of the tunic and pants.

"By the time you arrive, they'll have a trunk prepared for you to the Nahlini's specifications." She motioned for me to lift my arms, then wrapped a tape around my chest, made a note, and moved the tape to a different part of my body, repeating the process. She worked quickly, stepping back to review her notes when she finished.

"That's it," she said. "I'll have the gowns for the wedding sent to the lodge in a few hours."

Cala showered praise on Tia and her work as she followed her into the front of the shop. Alone, I dressed quickly in my old, tattered riding leggings and tunic. Then I fastened my simple belt and cape, again noticing they both showed their wear. On the plains, we had little need for new, fancy clothes. I suspected things would be different in the city, and I was grateful my mother had thought to provide me with a new wardrobe.

I was about to leave when a voice outside the tent caught my attention.

"Are you sure his horse is in the stable?" The voice spoke in a mountain drawl that made me think it could be Tavo or Vorn.

"He's meeting with Father in the lodge, so I don't know why it wouldn't be." The reply came from Goff. I was sure of it. And the only person I knew who was supposed to be meeting with Father was the Ruhl. The fact that Goff was sneaking around with at least one of the Jahlos and interested in something to do with the Ruhl's horse seemed highly suspicious and not a bit like the brother I knew.

I hurried out, hoping to catch sight of them, only to find Cala waiting for me outside the tent. She looked more excited than I'd seen her since last Midwinter festival, when she came of age. "Will you come with me to the jeweler?"

I hesitated, trying to come up with an excuse. "If you don't mind, I'd like to go see Mage-nah," I lied.

"Oh, you should." She responded as I'd expected she would,

assuming I intended to go for a reading. "I can't wait to hear what he has to say. Just don't forget, we need to be dressed and ready by sunset."

"Don't worry, I'll remember." I gave her a quick hug and turned to head toward Mage-nah's tent.

Once I was around the corner and sure she could no longer see me, I changed direction and headed for the stables. Even though it wasn't what I wanted, I'd made an alliance with the Ruhl. Whatever happened to him now affected me as well. So if my brother and his Jahlo friends were up to something, I intended to find out.

1

HE crisp, cool air smelled like freshly harvested grain, and the market swarmed with people. Heads turned my way as I cut a path through the crowd. Whispers and stares followed in my wake. I ducked my head and tugged my cape tighter around my shoulders, trying and failing to disappear, as I headed for the stables.

Everyone here knew me, just as I knew them. Before last night, I'd been able to hide in the shadows of my older sister and two older brothers, but today I had nowhere to hide. Now that I'd agreed to marry the Ruhl, I'd been pushed out into the open, the new center of attention, even on my sister's wedding day.

I stepped inside the dim, musty-smelling stables, and started down the long row that led toward Arge's stall at the far end of the building. A muffled voice said something I couldn't make out. Then someone laughed.

I crept closer, keeping to the shadows and darting between stall doors, keeping as close as possible to an opening where

I could hide, if anyone emerged.

"It won't come to that," one voice said.

"How can you be so sure?" another asked. I recognized that voice as Goff's.

"There's nothing here," said a third voice. The speaker had a similar accent to the first voice. If Goff was still with the Jahlos, it was probably either Vorn or Tavo.

"Let's go, before we get caught," Goff replied.

"Stop worrying. No one is going to catch us." I wasn't sure which of the Jahlos was speaking, but guessed that was probably Tavo.

Movement in the stall across from me caught my eye. I stared, willing my eyes to focus in the dim light, and was rewarded with a flash of pale hair. Someone else was here spying.

"We'll have to check his rooms. Are they guarded?" asked the first voice, probably Vorn.

I stepped back slowly, reaching for the closure on the stall door behind me and hoping that whoever was hiding in the empty stall across from me hadn't spotted me yet.

"He brought four guards with him, not including the captain. Two accompanied him to his meeting with Father. If the others are guarding his room, then I suppose we know there must be something worth guarding inside," Goff responded.

But what were they searching for? I unhooked the closure and edged the stall door open a crack, preparing to slip inside. The horse inside swung its head around to investigate.

"I'm surprised that the captain isn't with him. I haven't seen our cousin without his devoted bodyguard since we arrived," an unknown voice said, and laughed. This one sounded younger than the others, but had the same clipped mountain accent.

"Interesting, isn't it, that he thinks he needs so many guards just to come negotiate a treaty with your father," the first voice said.

"I told you. He's weak." The door to the stall they'd been inside swung open.

I backed inside with the strange horse, who immediately plodded over to sniff my pockets, then pressed the door closed and waited until I could no longer hear their voices or their footsteps before peeking out of my hiding place. A quick look down the row assured me they were gone. But when I reached over the door to let myself out, a hand closed over my wrist. I froze.

"Looking for something, Nahla?" The captain of the Shal clan guard stood opposite me. He pinned my wrist down with one hand and held the stall door closed with the other.

My heart hammered as I realized he must have been the person I'd seen in the stall across from me. He'd been listening just like me. But maybe he didn't know I'd seen him.

"I was just going for a ride." I forced myself to breathe and tried to calm my racing pulse.

He glanced at the horse nuzzling my shoulder. "Is this your horse, then?"

"No. I just... I thought I heard something, and I thought I should check..." I gave my wrist a twist and he released me.

"Don't let me keep you." He unhooked the closure and swung the door open so I could exit.

"Thanks." I tucked my wrist against my chest as I slid out of the stall.

He pointed down the row toward the opposite end of the stables. "If you want to catch up with the others, they went that way."

I glanced in that direction. "I wasn't... That's not why—"

He cut me off. "Don't bother. I don't want to hear your excuses, Nahla. Just know that your brother got one thing right. I will *always* be there, guarding the Ruhl. If you want to get to him, you'll have to get through me first."

I had no idea what my brother and the Jahlos were up to, and I could see that Zan would not believe me. I tried to reassure him, anyway. "I don't have any intention of attacking the Ruhl."

"It doesn't matter what you're planning." He glared at me. "I don't trust you, your family, or the Jahl and his offspring."

I sighed, already dreading the days ahead. "If you'll excuse me, I don't think I have time for a ride, after all. It's getting late, and I have to be ready for my sister's wedding before sundown."

He dipped his head as he stepped aside to let me pass.

I retraced my steps, heading in the opposite direction from where Zan had said my brother went. Despite what I'd said, it was still too early to return to the lodge, so I turned toward Mage-nah's tent. If Dern was awake, I could ask him about the charm he'd been carrying. And if he wasn't, I might talk with Mage-nah a bit more about his former apprentice.

When I arrived, I lifted the tent flap and stepped inside. "Hello?"

There was no sign of Mage-nah, and no fire burning in the wood stove. His absence alarmed me. He wouldn't have left Dern alone.

"Hello?" I called, again. "Mage-nah?"

A scuffle came from the back of the tent, followed by a figure emerging from the infirmary. "Ayla?"

"Kilm?" I could just make out my little brother's face in the dim light. "What are you doing here?"

He shrugged and made his way toward me. "I got sick of

tagging along with the Jahlos. It's no fun without Dern, especially now that both Goff and Vorn are all worked up about something. They've been at it all morning, and I'm sick of it. So I volunteered to sit with Dern."

"They were arguing?" I reconsidered what I'd overheard in the stables.

"Not arguing, exactly. But they spent most of the morning debating the finer points of hereditary law. Not my idea of a good time." Kilm sighed and shook his head.

"I can see why you left." I would have to get back into Father's study if I wanted to see for myself what all the fuss was about with the Ruhl and Vorn's lineage, but with Father and the Ruhl occupying Father's private meeting room, that was going to have to wait.

"What I want to know is, what are *you* doing here? I thought you'd be with Cala or packing. I heard that you're leaving tomorrow." Kilm poked at my shoulder.

"Yeah, that's what I hear too." I twisted away and massaged my arm where I was sure his finger left an indent in my skin. "I was with Cala, but I wanted to check in on Dern. How is he?"

"Sleeping. He woke, screaming, before I arrived. Mother was here. She calmed him enough for Mage-nah to give him another dose of the pain potion."

I grimaced. "Where's Mage-nah now?"

"After Mother left, someone I didn't recognize arrived with a message for him. He said something about needing to ride out to the forest and left." Kilm squinted at me. "Are you trying to get him to read the runes for you?"

"No." Though if the runes could give me some clarity on my message from the Inahi, I'd take it. "I wanted to talk to Mage-nah about that notebook you found. Did he tell you anything about whose it was?"

Kilm frowned. "Not really. He just seemed really sad when I showed it to him. Why?"

"He told me it belonged to a former apprentice who left to attend the Magery. He said she's probably still there." I paced to the back of the tent.

Kilm followed me. "Huh. That's strange. I didn't think anyone from our clan had gone to study at the Magery. Not since Mage-nah, at least."

"That's what I thought, too." I lifted the flap to look in on Dern. "So if there was someone else, someone more recent, why didn't we know about it?"

Kilm shook his head. "I don't know. You'd think someone would have mentioned it, especially after you started talking about wanting to go when you came of age."

I let the tent flap fall closed and started toward Mage-nah's worktable. His journal was gone. He must have taken it with him. "Do you think Father knew? That I wanted to go?"

Kilm rolled his eyes. "Of course. Everyone in the clan knew. You barely talk about anything else."

I'd almost let myself believe that maybe I just hadn't been clear enough, but Kilm was right. Father knew, and he planned to marry me off anyway. "I should get back to the lodge."

"Go on. Cala will murder you if you mess up her wedding."

"I know. Are you staying?"

Kilm nodded. "Definitely. I would much rather be here than stand around watching our sister get married. Just don't ever tell her I said that."

I laughed. "I won't."

"Good. I'll see you after, at the wedding feast. Mage-nah said he'd sit with Dern after the ceremony so I wouldn't have to miss out on all the food. That would have been taking things a bit too far."

"I see where your priorities are. Good thing you don't want to be a mage." I rolled my eyes at him.

Even though Kilm had also chosen to be a mage apprentice after his naming, he wanted to become a healer and wasn't as interested in what he considered to be the more mystical aspects of the role.

He crossed his eyes and stuck his tongue out at me.

I ruffled his hair, and he gave me a friendly shove out of the tent. As I started back toward the lodge, I realized how far the sun had dropped toward the horizon and picked up my pace. The market had emptied, so there weren't as many people to stare at me and whisper when I passed.

Back in my room, the pale green dress from the dressmaker was already hanging in my empty wardrobe. It was the only hint that remained of my presence. The two trunks on the floor near the window could have belonged to any traveler.

I ran my hand over the bare wood on the dressing table and stared at the empty shelves near my bed. Then I crossed the room to check the smaller of the two trunks. The notebook with the rune translations was there, under a small box that contained my favorite pens and pencils, and on top of my hygiene case that contained my combs and other personal items.

I breathed a sigh of relief when I found it. My fingers curled around the leather cover, preparing to lift it out, when a knock at my door startled me. I tucked the notebook back inside and closed the lid before turning around to find Wyn had returned.

"Your mother asked me to help you dress," she said.

The last time my mother had sent someone to help me dress, I'd been thirteen, preparing for my naming ceremony. I was nearly an adult—a betrothed adult, I reminded myself—I didn't need someone to help me put on a gown.

"What about Cala?" I asked.

"Your mother is helping her."

It wasn't long before I realized why my mother had sent Wyn. Apparently, putting on a dress wasn't enough. Wyn insisted I wash. She wouldn't let me near the pale green silk until I'd soaped and scrubbed from my hair to my toes. While she waited, Wyn polished my boots.

Once I was dry, I slipped into the cool, clinging fabric. Then Wyn styled my hair. When she finished braiding it and sweeping it up off my shoulders, she stepped back to admire her work, and smiled at what she had accomplished.

Wyn gave me only a moment to gaze at my reflection in the mirror before ushering me out and down the hall to my sister's rooms. The hanging over the door to Cala's room was already pinned back. Inside, my sister waited.

She looked stunning, wearing the traditional gown of a Nahl clan bride. The long, pale blue material shimmered like liquid in the candlelight. Intricate braids circled the crown of her head and wove together before disappearing into a cascade of loose curls that hung over her shoulders and down her back. The pale blue faded into a deep green and gold at the hem of her dress where it skimmed the floor, symbolizing the wide-open sky of the plains meeting the horizon of the earth that was our home.

My mother rested a hand on my sister's shoulder. "Cala, dear, you're breathtaking. Are you ready?"

Cala clasped hands with Mother and they exchanged excited smiles.

I turned away and noticed my father sitting in the corner near the window. He had been watching me, not Cala or Mother. I locked eyes with him and attempted to smile. He nodded at me and opened his mouth as if to say something. Then he glanced at Mother and Cala and closed his mouth into a forced smile.

I wanted to confront him about what I knew, and I wanted to ask about his meeting with the Ruhl. But now was not the time. I'd have to wait a little longer. At least until we weren't where Cala could hear. So I followed his lead and returned my attention to my sister.

While I'd been distracted, Mother had opened a small box with a hinged lid. Inside, a gold hair comb sat on a plush fabric cushion. She held it with both hands, waiting while Wyn twisted Cala's cascade of curls into a cluster near the nape of her neck, just below her left earlobe. She left the ends to fall and skim Cala's bare shoulder.

Once Wyn finished arranging Cala's hair, Mother stepped forward with the gold hair comb. She set the comb into Cala's hair so that it sat just above the clan tattoo at her hairline, behind her right ear. The base of the comb, which was left exposed when the tines were inserted into Cala's hair, was shaped like a half moon. The ends of the moon pointed toward Cala's neck and created a partial frame around her tattoo.

I'd seen my mother wearing a comb like this for formal ceremonies, but this one looked new. Like she'd had it made especially for Cala. Even though, soon, Cala would become part of the Jahl clan. She'd have no occasion to wear this a second time.

Each clan's leadership had their own design for their ceremonial headpieces. The Nahl clan used gold to symbolize the harvest grains cultivated on the plains. The moon shape that so perfectly framed the clan tattoo symbolized the open night sky of the plains. Father had a circlet he wore that matched Mother's comb.

After some more fussing over Cala and a few more adjustments to her dress and hair, she was ready to walk to the courtyard to meet the rest of the wedding party and guests. Mother circled Cala one last time, checking to make sure that nothing was missing. Satisfied that Cala was the picture of perfection, she motioned for Father to approach. Flanked by our loving parents, Cala glided down the hall to the courtyard.

I fell into step behind them. My thoughts were on what I planned to say to my father when someone emerged from the shadows and clamped a hand over my mouth.

8

I LET out a muffled yell, but Cala and my parents were already too far ahead to hear. My heart raced as my attacker pulled me back into the shadows. Unable to twist around, I closed my mouth on my attacker's hand, biting some of the flesh. It wasn't enough to draw blood, but it resulted in a wince of pain and my release.

I spun around, prepared to deliver a more damaging blow and found myself staring at the Ruhl. "What are you doing?"

"We need to talk." He shook out his injured hand and smiled that lopsided, mischievous grin of his.

"Right now? It couldn't wait until after my sister's wedding?" Cocking my head to one side, I tried to give him a disapproving look, even though I wasn't sure he could see my face very well.

"It was either this or kiss you in front of your entire clan without talking with you first. Which would you have preferred?" I could almost see his eyes sparkling in the dim light.

I scowled. "Are those my only two options?"

"After the story I had to tell your father to get him to agree to let you come with me when I leave? Yes. Is the thought of kissing me that terrible?" His grin widened.

"What did you tell my father?" I didn't want to kiss him. Especially not in front of Rys.

"He was insisting on a lengthy betrothal, since you don't come of age until Midwinter. That part I readily agreed to. However, he used the same excuse about your age to try to keep you here, with your clan, at least until after the Midwinter festival."

"Why would he have said that?" My heart raced as worried thoughts flooded my mind. A betrothal spent apart from the Ruhl, without his help, and without the Shal clan's books, or the library at the Magery, would be pointless. I'd never find the Inahi, and I'd end up forced to marry the Ruhl anyway. "Mother sent someone to pack my things this morning. She wouldn't have done that if Father didn't intend to send me with you."

"How interesting." The Ruhl smirked. "Negotiation tactic, most likely. Good thing I didn't fall for it."

"Ezri-ruh." Zan's gruff voice interrupted us. "Everyone is waiting."

The Ruhl sighed. "There isn't time to explain all of it. Your father agreed to let you go because I told him we were in love. So we need to make it convincing."

"In love? After a handful of dances and a short walk in the garden?" I scoffed.

The Ruhl raised his eyebrows. "Are you implying that it isn't possible?"

I squinted at him, unsure if he was teasing me. The only man I'd loved had been the boy I'd grown up with. I couldn't imagine falling so quickly and for someone I'd never met. I'd also never been openly in love with anyone before. I'd always had to hide my true feelings. I had no idea how to pretend to be in love with the Ruhl.

"What...did you have in mind?" I asked.

He wrapped his hand around mine and smiled his boyish grin. "A strategically late entrance will do, for a start."

Zan stepped aside to let the Ruhl and me go ahead of him down the hall. As we entered the courtyard, hand-in-hand, I realized what this entrance would look like to the rest of my already assembled and waiting clan and family. All eyes turned to watch us, and the hiss of whispers drifted through the crowd.

I shrunk from the attention and attempted to pull my hand out of the Ruhl's grip, but he only held it more firmly and slowed his pace to match mine. My cheeks warmed as members of my clan stepped aside to let us pass, lending further evidence to whatever they all assumed I'd been doing with the Ruhl that may have caused our late arrival.

Zan stopped at the inside edge of the gathering, taking his place among the handful of Shal and Nahl guards who had been posted around the perimeter of the assembly. All wore black tunics, marking them as Forsla's devotees. The uniforms were indistinguishable except for the embroidery on their sleeves.

A cluster of roses in Shal clan pink marked the sleeves of guards who had arrived with the Ruhl, while the sleeves of our clan's guards featured a sunburst in Nahl clan orange. I resisted the impulse to look for Rys. Even if my entrance meant something to him, even if he felt a twinge of regret, he would never let it show. He was much better than me at hiding his feelings.

It didn't take long to reach the center of the courtyard

where Cala and our parents stood talking with Vorn and Tavo. Mage-nah hunched over a small table, making final preparations for the ceremony. He straightened as we approached and arranged his palms, one on top of the other, at the center of his chest.

Mage-nah's silent signal that he was ready to begin caused my family and the Jahlos to turn and look at me and the Ruhl. A flash of anger darkened Cala's face, but when I blinked, her face had brightened into a smile. Perhaps I'd only imagined the anger, but knowing Cala, she was probably just annoyed that we were making everyone wait.

With one last squeeze, the Ruhl let go of my hand so that he might properly greet the others. Following the clan etiquette, he first clasped hands with Father, bowing his head only slightly, while Father bowed his head more deeply. Then he turned to Mother, who held her hands up at chest height, slightly in front of her with her palms facing the Ruhl. He set his palms against hers and bent his fingers around her hands. Mother bent her fingers around his and bowed her head. The Ruhl dipped his head in acknowledgment, then repeated this greeting with Cala.

When the Ruhl greeted Vorn, the Jahlo only bowed his head slightly lower than the Ruhl. I stared at the open display of disrespect, remembering what I'd overheard and what Kilm had told me. Vorn should have at least bowed as low as Father. After all, he was just the heir to the Jahl clan leadership. Both the Ruhl and Father outranked him.

Distracted by my thoughts, I almost didn't notice Mage-nah step forward and lift his hands to the sky, signaling that he intended to begin the ceremony. Cala and Vorn took their places in front of Mage-nah. I stepped in to stand on the other side of Cala as Tavo mirrored me, moving to the far side of

Vorn. Behind us, the Ruhl stood alongside my parents, which puzzled me. I assumed he would retreat once the ceremony started and go stand with Goff at the front of the gathered clan.

There wasn't time to give it more than a thought before Mage-nah shifted his gaze from the sky to the pair before him and dropped his arms until they were parallel to the ground.

"Solnat, god of abundance and marriage, we call you forth through your messengers, the Inahi, so we may humbly ask you to bestow your blessing on the union of this couple that stands before me on this night." Mage-nah selected a small, flat dish from the table and held it with both hands before him. "We call you forth with these offerings, made in your name."

Cala and Vorn took a half step apart to make room for Father and Mother to step forward with their offerings. Father went first. He placed a plain cake made from the wheat that grew on the plains onto the dish held out by the mage. My mouth watered at the sight of it. This was traveling food, like the offering I'd made to the Inahi. It was food I had taken with me many times when I spent the day out riding or exploring in the hills. The cake was dense and smelled like the fresh wheat it was made from.

Mother placed a selection of tiny, tart red berries beside the cake. This was the fruit of the plains, also eaten by travelers, but gathered to be mixed into foods and medicines. Cala once got sick after eating handfuls of them when we went out riding as children. Since then, she always scrunched her nose up at the sight of them.

But the offerings were not meant to be foods that Cala liked. They were intended for the gods, by way of their messengers, the Inahi. We made small offerings whenever we wished to call upon them, but marriage pairings were one of the five blessings requested by the mage on behalf of the tribe: scattering, gathering, naming, maturity, and marriage. For those, the offerings were more elaborate.

The offering for the marriage blessing was meant as a sacrifice of the key elements of life on the plains—the nutrients needed to feed a body, and the critical elements that kept it healthy, vibrant, and, of course, fertile. If we were in Shal City, or in the mountains where Vorn's clan lived, the offering would be slightly different, but would still represent those indisputable elements of life.

After presenting the offering, Father and Mother stepped back and Cala and Vorn closed the gap between them. Mage-nah handed them the plate with the offering, and together they placed it on the hearth at the center of the courtyard. My attention was now divided between paying attention to the ceremony and monitoring the offering plate to see if it brought forth any Inahi.

In Mage-nah's ceremonies, the offering always disappeared, but I was fairly certain it was because of some secret clan mage sleight of hand because my offerings never disappeared. An offering consumed meant that the god you'd petitioned had received your request and intended to give you what you'd asked for.

It was possible that my offerings went untouched because I was asking for too much and offering too little. That's why I wanted to figure out what the moonbursts meant. Perhaps the Inahi were trying to tell me what the gods wanted in exchange for repairing the magic that protected our borders. I kept a close watch on the offering plate to test my theory.

"Vorn-jah, eldest Jahlo, wishes to join with Cala-nah, eldest Nahla. Who stands in witness of this union?" Mage-nah asked.

I stepped forward. "Ayla-nah, lesser Nahla, vouches for Cala-nah and stands in witness to this union." With relief, I stepped back, grateful that my part in the ceremony was over quickly.

Tavo's turn came after mine. He stepped forward, but I kept my attention on the offering. "Tavo-jah, lesser Jahlo of the Jahl clan, vouches for Vorn-jah and stands in witness to this union."

Mage-nah's next question pulled my attention away from the offering plate. "To which clan will this couple belong?"

"We will belong to the Jahl clan, Mage-nah," Vorn responded.

Mage-nah turned to Cala. "Cala-nah, do you give up your position in the Nahl clan and confirm your intention to join the Jahl clan?"

"Yes, Mage-nah," Cala responded. I swallowed the lump in my throat. I'd forgotten about this part of the ceremony. No matter what happened with the Ruhl, after tonight, my sister and I would no longer belong to the same clan. I bit my cheek to keep my tears from spilling out.

"Who will accept Cala into the Jahl clan?" Mage-nah asked.

The Ruhl stepped forward and said, "Ezri, Ruhl of the United Clans, accepts Cala into the Jahl clan on behalf of the Jahl, and blesses this union."

That explained why the Ruhl had not retreated to stand with Goff. Though it seemed odd that the Ruhl, who had inherited a title meant to belong to the person who could speak with the Inahi, had the power to accept my sister into a clan that was not his own. I was sure that Goff could explain why, if I asked. Curious as I was, I didn't think the answer would be worth the lecture, so I resolved to look it up myself later.

"And do you, Vorn-jah and Cala-jah, agree to this union freely and with your whole hearts, promising to be partners caring for each other until death parts you?" Mage-nah asked.

"We do," the couple said in unison.

"Then kneel before me and bow your heads." Mage-nah selected a wooden bowl from his table that contained a dark fluid. He dipped the shaft of a stalk of wheat into the bowl, soaking up some of this substance, and leaned over Cala's head. With the fluid on the stalk, he drew an upside down "V" intersecting the horizontal bar tattooed on her neck.

Then, dipping the stalk again into the bowl to soak up more fluid, he bent over Vorn's neck and drew the horizontal bar of the Nahl clan intersecting the upside down "V" of the Jahl clan. These marks were symbolic. When Cala arrived in the mountains, their clan's mage would make her mark permanent, but for now the ink was meant only to last the night, meant to serve as a visible reminder of the union between the two clans.

"Rise," Mage-nah said, once he completed the marking. He set the bowl back on the table and again lifted his hands to the sky.

"With the blessing of Solnat, via his messengers, the Inahi, this couple is now joined and will move through life together as a partnered pair." Mage-nah lowered his arms and turned toward the dish that now sat empty on the hearthstone.

I'd missed it. Again.

Mage-nah rested one palm on top of the other at the center of his chest. "The Inahi have spoken. You may go forth together, blessed in your union."

When Vorn and Cala kissed, the courtyard erupted in happy cheers. I smiled and clapped along with everyone else, but inside I chided myself for getting distracted by the ceremony and missing the moment that the offering disappeared. It kept my mind from dwelling on the shiver that ran up my spine as the Ruhl slid his hand across the thin layer of silk that covered my lower back, or the way my heart thumped when his fingers curled around my waist.

#

THEY held the celebration feast in the great room. As guest of honor, they had invited the Ruhl to sit at the head table with Cala, Vorn, Mother, and Father. I sat at one of the lower tables nearby, with my brothers and the Jahlos. From time to time the Ruhl would catch my eye and smile, and I did my best to remember to smile back to keep up our charade.

Goff and I sat at opposite ends of our table. The empty seat to my right would have been Dern's, but he hadn't recovered enough to attend. Kilm sat on my left. One of Vorn's younger brothers, Katz, sat between Kilm and Goff, and the other, Tavo, sat on Goff's other side.

Goff and Tavo were engaged in an animated conversation while Katz leaned in, eagerly absorbing their every word. Meanwhile, Kilm hunched beside me, picking at his food.

I opened my mouth to ask Kilm what was wrong, then closed it when I thought I heard Tavo mention my name.

"Ayla?" Goff frowned. "Are you serious?"

Loud as they were, I still couldn't make out much of what they were saying. I tried not to stare at them as I shifted forward in my chair in case it might help me hear better.

"You should talk with her before she leaves," Tavo said. "Maybe she can convince him to agree to our requirements. After all, your father hasn't been able to make him budge."

"She seems to have his attention," Katz added, causing Tavo to snicker.

I could feel my face flush and bowed my head, pretending to brush crumbs off my dress.

Glancing up, I caught Goff pinning the younger Jahlo with a glare. "I'm not sure Father would approve. Ayla knows nothing about clan relations or our negotiations in the Council. I think he'd rather keep it that way."

Goff's words stung. I'd weathered his lectures about the importance of understanding clan politics, even though I believed that the clans' fraying connection to our gods was a much larger problem. One that he, like our elders, frequently dismissed. But I'd never stopped to consider that my father wouldn't approve of my involvement, if I ever changed my mind. It hurt to think that they all thought I was a disappointment, or somehow inferior. Would I never have any value in their eyes as a mage? Would I only be worthy of my title if I proved I could play their political games?

Kilm elbowed me, pulling me from my thoughts. Once he had my attention, he jerked his chin toward the main table. "Why aren't you sitting up there?"

I'd wanted to hear the rest of what Goff and Tavo were saying about me, but one look at Kilm's face made me realize he was probably equally annoyed at being left out of Goff's conversation. At least they weren't talking about him. "I'd rather be down here, with you."

"You don't really expect me to believe that?" Kilm tilted his head and gave me a significant look. "I hear you two made quite an entrance at the wedding."

"We...were just talking." I could feel myself blushing.

"Really? Is that how it is?" He leaned in, set his elbows on the table, and propped his chin on one of his fists.

Before I could respond, a movement caught his attention. He turned to watch Katz get up from the table. Kilm followed him with his eyes until Katz disappeared into the courtyard.

"What's that all about?" I asked when Kilm returned his attention to me.

"What?" Kilm asked, reaching for a meat skewer I had left uneaten on my plate, even though he'd barely touched his own food.

"What's going on with you and them?" I asked.

"Nothing." He chewed and swallowed. His eyes darted to Katz, who had just stepped back inside the great room and was fetching another cup of wedding punch.

Katz and I were born in the same year, which made us both two years older than Kilm. This was the first time since Katz's naming ceremony that he had been allowed to travel with his older brothers down to the plains. Since Tavo had come from Shal City and arrived with the Ruhl, I assumed Katz must have accompanied Vorn on his journey down from the mountains to secure Cala's hand before the Ruhl could. I was getting the impression that my baby brother had developed a bit of a crush on the younger Jahlo.

"Is there anything else going on that I should know about?" I raised my eyebrows and waited for him to say more.

"No." Kilm took a long sip from my cup and set it back on the table.

"So, if I called Katz over here..." I teased.

"No." Kilm grabbed my arm and squeezed. "Please don't."

"So you do like him!" I grinned.

"Shh!" Kilm hissed at me, scrunching up his face. Then, in a whisper, he added, "Maybe."

"Does he know? Did something happen?"

Kilm let go of my arm and buried his head in his hands. "No. Nothing. It's fine."

I squeezed his shoulder. "You know I'll kick his ribs in if

he hurts you."

He raised his head. "That's the last thing I need."

"Hmph. We'll see." I crossed my arms. "I'm not promising anything."

"You will." His eyes gleamed. "Stay out of it. Promise."

I scowled. "Well, what can I do to take your mind off it, then?"

Kilm sighed. He ran a hand through his hair, then said, "You can take me with you."

I laughed. "Right. I'm sure Father will be thrilled with that idea."

Kilm's eyes drifted up just as I felt someone standing behind me. I looked up to see our father standing over us, glaring down his long nose.

"Thrilled with what idea?" he asked.

"Nothing," we said, nearly in unison.

His eyes narrowed. "Ayla, come with me. I'd like a word with you."

When he turned and walked away from our table, I glanced at Kilm and raised my eyebrows. Kilm twisted his lips into a grimace, and he rolled his eyes back into his head. I shook my head, then hurried after Father.

I caught up to him at the edge of the tables and fell into step with him as he walked through the open doors and continued through the courtyard, toward the hearth at the center. "Your mother tells me you came to see her this morning. She suggested we delay the marriage. So imagine my surprise to find out from Ezri-ruh that you two are madly in love. Is this true?"

I didn't like the idea of lying, especially when I was certain my father could see straight through to the truth, anyway. "Everything happened so quickly. I just want a little time to get to know him before we marry."

"I see." He lifted one hand to his chin and stroked his neatly trimmed beard, that had recently turned white around the corners of his mouth and just below his lower lip. "So you want to return with him?"

"Yes."

"But you don't want to marry him?" He walked to the edge of the hearth and stopped next to its warmth.

"Not until after I come of age."

Father stared into the flames. The firelight flickered across his face as he thought. Finally, after several moments of tense silence, he sighed and turned to face me. "I've agreed to let you return with him, against my better judgment. I still think you are too young, but I will not deny you the chance to get to know him better."

"Thank you."

"The city is dangerous, and his family has caused enough trouble for us already. It is time he understands the strength of the Nahl clan. Since I must allow him to take my daughter, I have refused his request for Feln-nah to return to the Council. That responsibility will fall to you, at least until you marry and leave our clan."

"Me?" I gaped at him. Perhaps Goff was wrong, and Father did trust me.

"Do not be concerned. Your task will be easy." He smiled at me as though I were still a child. "You will report back on what happens in the Council, but you won't agree to any treaties unless you have my consent. Understood?"

"Yes, Father." I ground the words out, along with any hope of him seeing me as anything more than a pawn.

"Good girl. Now, go and enjoy the party. I will inform your uncle of this change in plans and be there to see you off in the morning." He grasped both of my hands in his and squeezed them.

I forced a smile before turning and walking back the way we'd come. My stomach sank knowing that he had given this extra responsibility to me because he still thought I didn't see what he was doing. He didn't think I understood enough to recognize that putting me in this position would drive a wedge between me and my betrothed.

It could only mean that he didn't want me to marry the Ruhl any more than I did. He was just buying time. But for what?

I'd asked Kilm, and he didn't know. Goff wouldn't tell me anything without Father's permission. And Tavo thought I was just a silly girl, chasing legends.

I needed answers, and the one person who might have been willing to give them to me was lying unconscious in the infirmary. With Father's eyes on my back, I had no choice but to return to the great hall and resume my role as the besotted Nahla who had fallen for the charms of the Ruhl. I would play along, at least until I was on my way to the city, but I had no intention of being anyone's pawn. Not my father's, and not the Ruhl's.

9

ON the morning, I took my time getting dressed in my new traveling clothes. I was fastening the silver bar of my cloak when Wyn, who was carrying one of my smaller trunks to the wagons, pushed back the curtain covering the entrance to my room. I caught a glimpse in the mirror of the figure standing guard outside my doorway.

I waited until she was gone, then rushed to the door. I wasn't imagining it. Rys really was there. I held the curtain back and waved him inside.

He looked up and down the hallway and, after judging that no one would notice, stepped into my room.

"What are you doing here?" I pulled the curtain closed behind him.

"I can't stay. I just wanted a chance to say goodbye." He looked like he hadn't slept all night. "You look lovely."

"Rys." I wanted to cry. I couldn't cry now. I could feel the lump building in my throat and threw my arms around his neck. He held me tight against him, and I could feel our bodies fall into each other, fitting together like puzzle pieces. "I don't think I can do this."

He set his chin over my head and said, "Yes, you can. You're a Nahla. You were meant to accomplish great things."

"I was meant to be with you." I buried my face further into the fabric of his uniform tunic. I half-hoped he wouldn't actually be able to understand my sappy words.

He said nothing and just stroked my hair for a few breaths. Then he stepped back and held me at arm's length, placing his fingers under my chin and lifting it until I was looking at him. "It will be all right."

I nodded. "Let me just have a minute."

He kissed my forehead before leaving.

I turned back to my mirror, wiping away the tears that hadn't quite escaped from my eyes. I tidied my hair and straightened my cloak. Then I took one last look around, trying to memorize everything about my home, not knowing when I would see it again. When I turned, prepared as I ever would be to leave my room for the last time, I ran straight into Father.

"Ayla." His eyes fixed on the silver bar at my neck, and he nodded with approval. "Are you ready?"

"Yes, Father." I straightened my spine with renewed determination, ready to finally prove how much more capable I was than he had given me credit for.

"Good girl." He turned his face toward the window. "I didn't think you would be leaving us so soon."

His words surprised me since I knew what he'd planned for me. I'd seen it in Mage-nah's book. Perhaps he didn't mean for me to be leaving so soon, but he'd planned this betrothal.

"Me either." I had always intended to leave, but only for a little while, and not until after Midwinter.

"I'm going to miss you, Ayla. I..." His voice trailed off and his lips twisted into a grimace. "Life will be different in the city. I know you can take care of yourself, but be safe."

"Yes, Father. Though, with the stone walls surrounding it, and the Shal guard defending it, I can't imagine I'll be in much danger." If whatever this game he was playing was going to put me in danger, that was an incredibly vague warning.

"Yes." He opened his mouth to say more but pressed his lips together instead. "Well, let's not keep everyone waiting."

I fell into step with him, annoyed that he refused to tell me anything useful. We walked in silence down the hall and out, through the courtyard, and straight into the chaos of people moving about in the crisp autumn air, loading and unloading items into the waiting wagons. There were more than I'd expected wearing black tunics embroidered with pink roses on the sleeve.

Father led us through the chaos to a small group gathered near the stables. Vorn and Cala were there, talking with Tavo. Nearby, Dern leaned on Goff as Mother pulled his cloak tighter around his shoulders. My heart leapt at the sight of him standing.

"Dern!" I rushed forward to greet him, stopping short only when Goff helped him turn, and I caught the look of pain etched on his face. Rather than throw my arms around him as I'd planned, I reached out and squeezed his hand. "I was worried about you."

He managed a grin. "I seem to have missed everything else. I wasn't about to miss seeing you off."

Tears stung the corners of my eyes. "Do you remember what happened? Did you see who attacked you?"

"I heard you were there when they brought me in." He tugged me closer so he could drop a kiss on my forehead.

"Thank you."

The Ruhl emerged from the stables, laughing with Kilm and Katz. The sound drew everyone's attention away for a moment.

Dern leaned close to me. "Be careful."

I locked eyes with him. "Why? What's going on?"

He shook his head. "Ask Tavo. I told him to look out for you."

"Is he returning with us?" I asked, glaring at Tavo's back. Trusting him seemed like a terrible idea. I'd guessed that there was something going on between him and Dern, given how agitated he'd been when he'd heard about the attack. But just because my brother was besotted enough to trust that slimy Jahlo didn't mean I had to.

I'd ask Tavo to tell me what he knew, if I could talk with him away from the others. But, after overhearing his conversation with Goff, I doubted he'd be inclined to tell me anything.

Vorn and Cala joined us before Dern could respond. Tavo slid in beside Dern, wrapping an arm around my brother's waist, as my sister hugged me fiercely. By the time she released me, Dern and Tavo had moved further away to join Kilm and Katz, who were still talking with the Ruhl.

Cala was still fussing over me when our mother approached. She wrapped her arms around both of us, and the tears I'd been holding back all morning welled up in my eyes. I dried them on my mother's scarf and composed my face as she broke from the embrace. Then I let Cala and Mother fix my hair and adjust my cloak before turning to the others to say my goodbyes.

Vorn kissed me on both cheeks, formal and kind. Goff, serious as always, gave me a book and a kiss on each cheek.

Katz dipped his head but kept his distance. One look at Kilm, and I knew the tears would start again.

I hugged my little brother hard to keep from crying, and I promised him I'd send for him as soon as I could. When I released him, he dropped a pouch of dried herbs in my hand. Without opening it, I knew it would be childbane for the tea used to prevent pregnancy.

I leaned closer to him, keeping my voice low. "Thanks, but I don't think I'm going to need that anytime soon."

"Just in case." He closed my fingers over the pouch. "It's not much. You'll need to ask for more at the Magery. And you better, because I'm not ready to be an uncle."

A burst of laughter escaped my lips in place of the sob that had threatened. "Better not tell Cala that."

He made a disgusted face, and I took a moment to compose myself before returning to Mother and Father to say one last goodbye.

Mother handed me the box that Cala had retrieved from the jeweler. Inside was the gold comb Cala wore in her hair at her wedding. The one she wouldn't need now that she was no longer part of our clan. Mother kissed my forehead and whispered, "Wear it proudly."

Father gave me a gold ring with a small carved stone embedded in the band. The black stone was almost as wide as my finger. Embossed in the center was the horizontal bar symbol of the Nahl clan. This was another, but far less subtle, symbol of our clan. He'd given me an official seal. The ring declared to all that I served as an official emissary of the Nahl clan.

Unlike my mother, Father offered no words of encouragement with his gift. He just nodded at me and smiled.

When our parents were done, Cala linked her arm with mine, and we walked together toward the waiting horses.

"I'm scared," I admitted.

"Don't be, silly." She tugged me closer against her side. "It will be fine."

I knew she was putting on a brave face for me, so I pushed my fears down and gave her a nudge with my shoulder. "Did you get any sleep last night?"

She gave me a shove in return. "Maybe."

I stopped next to Arge and turned to face her. "Will you write to me? Will you visit?"

She looked away, toward the mountains, her cheerful smile replaced with a wide-eyed stare as she considered my question, tears welling in her eyes. "I don't know. I don't know what life will be like in the mountains."

I hugged her tight with all my strength and whispered to her, "You've always wanted this. And Mage-nah read your happiness in the cards. Be strong, Cala. I'll miss you."

She pulled back and swiped away her tears. "I'll miss you, too."

She wrapped her hand around the back of my neck and pulled me toward her until our foreheads were touching. I wrapped my hand around the back of her neck and pressed my forehead into hers. We giggled and hugged one last time. Then she boosted me into the saddle.

The Ruhl had already mounted his horse. Some wagons had already started rolling down the path, away from our clan's compound and toward the long and dusty road to the city. I took one last, long look across the plains. The grasses swayed in the light breeze and the mountains—Vorn's, and now Cala's mountains—loomed against the sky in the distance.

The Ruhl rode up alongside me. It was time. I took a deep breath and turned toward my family. Father and Mother leaned into one another, arms wrapped around each other's waists. Goff stood with Dern, and Kilm leaned on the fence post nearby. Vorn walked up behind Cala and rested a hand on her shoulder. I tried to memorize every detail of my home and my family because I didn't know when I would see them again.

I waved, and they all waved back. All except Kilm, who shooed me with his hand. I could almost hear him in my head. *Get on with it already. Go so I can come to the city, too.* I smiled.

The Ruhl reached over and brushed his fingers against the back of my hand. They froze when they reached the ring I'd been given.

I turned to face him, ready to explain. But when he looked up, there was no trace of a reaction. He only curled his fingers around my hand and squeezed.

"Ready?" he asked, releasing me.

I nodded and signaled for Arge to walk. The Ruhl's stallion fell into step beside us. Then, with one last look over my shoulder, I turned my back on my clan and faced whatever fate lay ahead of me in Shal City.

The Ruhl rode beside me through the gates. When we emerged on the other side, I realized we were at the back of a long caravan. A trio of supply wagons, each pulled by a pair of mules, rolled along ahead of us. Guards on horseback flanked them on both sides, where the road was wide and flat as it cut through the plains.

The crisp fall air chilled my cheeks with its promise of winter soon to come. At the same time, the sun warmed my hair and the dark wool of my cape, providing the perfect contrast. I adjusted the material so it sat snugly around my shoulders, conscious that every step of Arge's hooves carried me further and further from home.

As we crested a hill at a bend in the road, I caught a last glimpse of the walls of our compound and the bright colors of the tents surrounding our winter lodge. I watched until the encampment grew so small that I could block it out completely by holding up a hand. Then I turned to the Ruhl, realizing he hadn't said a word since we departed.

He stared ahead, mouth set and jaw clenched as though in a deep but unsettling thought.

"I didn't know my father was going to do that," I said.

His eyes skimmed my face but never quite met my gaze, and his mouth remained set in a grim line. "It will complicate things."

As I tried to think of something to say, he turned to me and said, "Excuse me, Nahla, I must check on some things." Before I could say a word, he had spurred his horse to a trot. I watched his back through a light cloud of dust as he pulled ahead, passing the carriages in front of us. Most of the guards surrounding us followed him.

My eyes stung from the dust, and I blinked rapidly to keep the tears from falling. I'd left everyone I loved behind to help him. We should be discussing our plans, not fussing over political manipulations. He must see that I was being treated as a pawn and had no interest in festering clan rivalries.

But I appeared to be on my own. Now that we were away from my clan, there was no reason for the Ruhl to pretend he cared for me. I might as well get used to it. I wound a hand in Arge's mane for comfort and looked down at my tanned flesh peeking out between clumps of dark horse hair. A glint of gold caught my eye, and I adjusted my fingers to have another look at the troublesome signet ring my father had given me.

My braid brushed against the tattoo on my neck, and I sat

up straighter in the saddle. No matter what happened, I was a Nahla, representing my clan, and I would find the Inahi with or without the Ruhl's help.

Zan fell in beside me. He spared one glance at me, then resumed his constant scan of the horizon.

"You don't have to keep me company," I said, giving Arge one last pat before returning both hands to the reins.

"I'm not here to keep you company." He never took his eyes off the horizon.

I watched him for a while, squinting my eyes and following his gaze. Then I gave up trying to figure out what he was searching for and began taking note of my traveling companions. Unlike the cluster of guards who had accompanied the Ruhl inside our compound, almost half of these guards were women. They all wore the same Shal clan guard uniform: black tunics with rose embroidery under woven armor vests, paired with grey-black trousers. Weapons belts cinched their waists. Traveling capes the color of treetops at dusk hung from their shoulders. The dusky rose embroidery on the back of each cape made a pattern of overlapping "O" shapes, like an echo of the Shal clan tattoo.

Beside me, Zan tensed. He whistled a few notes, and the pair of guards just ahead of us guided their horses to the edge of the road. As we passed, they turned them to face behind us. That's when I registered a new pattern of hoofbeats. This one came from behind us and was getting louder.

Zan turned to look, and I followed his gaze in time to see a man with long, dark hair approaching at speed. He swerved around the guards who had positioned themselves to intercept him, cutting through the tall grasses to overtake the caravan.

I caught a good look at his profile as he rode past. "Tavo-jah."

The guards behind us trotted up. They slowed their horses to a walk once they were ahead of us again. Then Zan whistled again, this time a slightly different melody. One of the women ahead of us turned her mount at the sound and circled back to intersect our path.

"Mia," he said. "I need to ride ahead. Take my place beside the Nahla."

"Yes, sir."

Zan spurred his horse ahead, and Mia slid her horse in beside mine. Without a word, she picked up where Zan had left off, scanning the horizon.

I studied her in brief glances, fascinated by the place where her tanned cheek puckered around an old scar. Unlike many other guards, she wore no large weapons, only a pair of long knives that hung one on each side of her belt. It was hard to say how old she might be. She appeared to be at least a few years older than me, but much younger than my parents. I guessed she was the same age as Goff.

"Mia?" I asked, hoping she might be more talkative than my previous two companions.

"Do you need something, Nahla?" she replied without looking at me. Her voice had the hint of an accent, but it didn't sound like the clipped tongue of the Jahl or the lazy drawl of the Shal, and she clearly was not of my clan.

"No." My eyes dropped, and I glimpsed the strange ring she wore on the middle finger of her left hand. It was carved from an opaque green stone and stretched almost the full width between her knuckle and the lower joint of her finger.

Before I could work up the nerve to ask her anything, the Ruhl circled back to join us. He brought his horse up alongside mine and said, "We need to talk."

10

THE Ruhl didn't say another word until Mia dropped back to give us some privacy. "If there's anything else you haven't told me, now would be a good time."

Two things came to mind. The first was about the Inahi, and the second was what I'd overheard in the stables. Since I guessed it was the second that he'd been informed of, probably by Zan, I started there. "I overheard my brother Goff talking with Vorn-jah, and it sounded like they were talking about you. I followed them because I was worried and wanted to know what they were up to. The Shal guard captain caught me sneaking around. I think he assumed I was with my brother and the Jahlos, but I wasn't. I swear. And I didn't hear enough to figure out what they were doing there."

The Ruhl stared at me for a moment. "That...wasn't what I was expecting."

"I assumed you already knew."

"Oh, I did." The Ruhl ran his hand through his hair. "Zan told me about how the Jahlos seem to think I took something

Tavo-jah gave to one of your brothers. And he said he'd seen you there, as well."

"He doesn't trust me."

He shrugged. "Zan doesn't trust anyone. Probably not even me. But that doesn't matter. I want to know about this message you received."

I gaped at him for a breath before responding. "How do you know about that?"

The corner of his mouth twitched upward. "I told you. Best not to ask how I know things. But in this case, as it happens, there is another in our party who you'll meet tomorrow. I thought she'd meet us once we were clear of your clan's compound, but she sent a message ahead, along with all but one of the guards I sent with her, to say she would catch up with us when we stop to camp tonight."

"And this is who told you about the message?" I asked, wondering how a stranger could know about something I'd only told Rys and Mage-nah.

"She said your mage asked her about a missing page in one of your folklore books?" The Ruhl sounded as though he wasn't sure if he should believe what he'd been told.

So it had been Mage-nah who shared what I'd told him with this mystery woman who traveled with the Ruhl. Kilm had said something about Mage-nah riding out to meet someone. Maybe it was her. It would make sense that he knew other mages. He had studied at the Magery once, even if it had been a very long time ago. But if she wanted to talk with Mage-nah, why hadn't she come to the compound with the Ruhl? Why had she stayed outside?

Before I could get answers to my questions, I needed to tell the Ruhl about the message I'd received. It was no more than I'd originally planned to do, before dancing with the Ruhl and allowing him to lead me into the gardens. I still wanted to know if he had some knowledge passed down from his grandmother that would tell me what the message meant.

"The morning you arrived, I went to the edge of the forest to leave an offering for the Inahi and ask the gods to repair the veil. I'd done it before. Many times. And they never touched my offering." I continued on with my explanation before he could interrupt and tell me how silly I was for attempting to speak with the Inahi when I wasn't the Ruhl. "Except that morning, when I stood to leave, I noticed three flowers positioned around the untouched offering. Moonbursts. Do you know what those are?"

The Ruhl shook his head. "Flowers of some sort?"

"Flowers that grow in the forest, under the shelter of the trees, and only blossom under a new moon."

"So they didn't grow there."

"No. Both moons were full, and there weren't any stems on the flowers. The flower tops were positioned like this." I gestured in the air between us to sketch the three points of a triangle with my finger. "Around the offering."

"What was this offering?" he asked.

I shrugged. "The usual sort of thing one offers when asking a favor from the gods."

He cocked his head to one side. "That's something you do?"

I squinted at him. "You don't?"

He frowned. "Never."

I'd heard that the Shal had lost their faith in the gods after the Ruhlini and her eldest child died, one right after the other, but the Ruhl had said he wanted to find the Inahi. I assumed that meant he believed, even if his clan did not. "Doesn't your clan have a mage?"

He shook his head. "My mother did away with that custom

when she became Shal. She banished Mage-sha to the Magery and said the poor old woman would be executed if they caught her leading blessings outside of the Magery."

I sucked in a breath, shocked at the casual way the Ruhl spoke of the Shal's actions, as though it was just common sense to make such a policy. "But what about your clan? They supported this?"

He grimaced. "There were some who were upset, at first. Mother still holds the Midwinter festival to celebrate namings and maturities. Those who want to celebrate the other blessings travel to the Magery, just outside the city."

My body tensed as I wondered what exactly I might find in Shal City, and how much the Ruhl even knew about our folklore and traditions after growing up with a mother so fiercely determined not to believe. "Do you celebrate the blessings?"

"My mother won't allow it. We don't do clan tattoos for the namings, either. So, I don't have one." He lifted the wavy hair that skimmed his shoulders to show me the bare spot on his neck, just below his ear, that should have been marked with the elongated O of the Shal clan on his thirteenth Midwinter.

"But now that I've had a chance to celebrate the Gathering, I'm excited to see what else I've been missing." He grinned as his eyes met mine. "Of course, I think the Gathering will probably always be my favorite. At least after this year."

My heartbeat sped as I realized what he seemed to be implying. "Do you even know what we were celebrating?"

His smile grew as he noticed the blush that had colored my cheeks. "The Gathering asks for Estrel's blessing and always happens in the autumn, when both moons are full at the same time. That only happens twice a year. When it happens again, in the spring, it's time for the Scattering. That's when the clans ask for Lorjad's blessing." The Ruhl leaned closer and whispered, "He's my favorite."

I rolled my eyes, trying to ignore the warm feeling in my chest. "Of course he is."

"Then there's marriage. That's Solnat's domain. I have yet to attend a Shal clan wedding, but I don't think we explicitly ask for his blessing in our ceremonies the way you do in yours. Your sister's wedding was the first time I'd seen a mage make an offering to the gods. Do they always disappear like that? I wish I'd known that was going to happen. I would have watched more closely to see how he did it." The Ruhl rubbed his chin.

I stared at him, surprised at his knowledge and unsure what to make of the gaps in what he'd learned. "How do you know so much about the gods and the blessings if the Shal banished your mage?"

He turned his gaze to the horizon before responding. "I found a mage to teach me. Or, I suppose it's more accurate to say that she found me. Either way, it's a secret. My mother probably knows. She makes it a point to know things, just as I do. I learned that from her. But she's been satisfied enough that it's just harmless curiosity, and she's humored me by looking the other way. At least she did. Until the Magery named me Ruhl. Now her son is no longer her heir. Everyone thinks I'm some sort of mouthpiece for the gods, and she's furious. It's only a matter of time before..."

His eyes slid past mine and stared off into the distance past my shoulder as his voice trailed off. He scowled, his lips pinching shut over whatever he'd been about to say.

"My Ruhl?" I prompted.

When his eyes met mine again, there was a new intensity there. "Ezri. Please? That title...it's... Just call me Ezri."

I nodded, for the first time considering what it might be

like to be put in the position he was in. He wasn't that much different from me. Caught in a web he didn't weave. One he longed to be free of. And the only way out, for both of us, was to find the Inahi and restore the veil.

"My...I mean...Ezri." His name felt strange on my tongue. Too familiar. Too sweet. I swallowed the taste. "Do you know what the flowers mean?"

He leaned closer to me. "I am yours, you know. At least as far as anyone here is concerned. And especially now that Tavo-jah has rejoined our party."

The reminder that we were acting, that we needed to pretend we were in love, made the lingering residue of his name on my tongue turn to ash. His flirting was for those who might be watching. Not for me. "Were you not expecting him to return?"

Ezri sat back in his saddle. "I thought he might return to the caverns until after Midwinter. There won't be any need for the Council to meet before then. Which is why I'm not too bothered by your father's attempt at controlling me through you."

I breathed a sigh of relief that he understood. "If we can find the Inahi before the Council meets again, perhaps it won't matter. I can hide the ring, if that helps."

"It will be better if my mother doesn't see it, unless I can think how to use it to our advantage..." He stared off into the distance, letting the hoofbeats and jangling bits of tack fill his silence. "Perhaps we should try again with the offering. Both of us, together."

"That might help." I glanced toward the trees in the distance. We'd been traveling away from the forest all morning. "Does the road pass closer to the forest anywhere along our route?"

"How far have you traveled from your clan's compound?" he asked.

"Up to the mountains once, but it was before my naming." I had a few vivid memories of our visit to the caverns the Scattering after Vorn's naming. Father had insisted we make the trip to pay our respects to the newly named Jahl heir because Vehlm-jah had done the same after Goff's naming. "I've never traveled in this direction, though."

He nodded. "I'll find you a map so you can see where we're going, but the road does curve back toward the Barrier Forest near the river crossing." He gestured toward the trees in the distance.

"I've been thinking that perhaps a bit of travel cake isn't a big enough offering, though. Not given what we're asking for," I said.

"You've been asking the gods to repair the veil?"

I nodded.

He stared ahead at the caravan stretched out in front of us along the dirt road. "What if we asked for a meeting instead?"

His idea seemed obvious, and I wondered why I'd never considered that option. Probably because my father and the elders, even Mage-nah, had believed so strongly that only the Ruhl could speak with the Inahi. The best I'd ever hoped for was a sign that the gods would answer my plea. But now I had the Ruhl helping me. "That might work."

"Good." He nodded. "Now, about that missing page?"

I blinked. "Right. I'd never noticed it before. I just thought that was where the legend ended. But if you look closely, you can see that someone removed a page. It's right at the end of the Legend of Ruhala."

"Ruhala? Is that the one where Lorjad borrows Forsla's Flame without asking?"

"Um. No." Just when I'd begun to think he knew more about the gods and the folklore than I'd given him credit for, he went and said something that proved the gaps in his knowledge were truly concerning. "You're thinking of the goddess Jusala. Ruhala was one of the last true mages. She's the one who led the refugees over the mountains to our lands."

"Never heard of her." Ezri's lips twisted and his brow creased as he tried to remember. "In fact, now that I think about it, I think the only stories I know all feature Jusala. Or Lorjad. Or both."

I gaped at him. "Have you never read a book of folklore?"

"My mother banished our clan mage. Do you really think she wanted her only child and heir spending any time reading legends about the gods?" Ezri raised his eyebrows like the reasons should have been obvious.

"I suppose if no one ever told you about Ruhala, then it makes sense why you wouldn't know about offerings." I shook my head. "I really want to have words with this mage of yours, though."

"Lucky you! You'll get your chance tomorrow." Ezri laughed. "Oh, I cannot wait. This is going to be so good."

Ahead of us, someone whistled twice. The first note was brief, as though it was meant to get the attention of the caravan. They held the second tone longer, raising the pitch at the very end.

"Sounds like the scouts found us a place to camp for the night." Ezri sat up in his saddle and scanned the riders and wagons ahead of us. "We'll be stopping soon, but we're so spread out that we probably have time for you to tell me that story before we arrive."

"All right." I did my best to tell him the tale the way it had been told to us in our clan's crèche, raising and lowering my voice the way Mage-nah did when he recited the legends.

I told him about how Ruhala and her three children escaped from the invaders who wanted to steal the magic from the mages, and how each night she left a portion of their meal for the Inahi and asked for their guidance until eventually she dreamed of Lorjad beckoning to her from the mountain peaks. In the morning she found the single, stemless flower in the place where she'd left her offering.

So she led her family into the mountains and up, higher and higher. When they finally reached the peak, her eldest son, Jahlo, told his mother that he would stay in the mountains and light fires so other refugees would know to climb to safety.

After saying goodbye, she led her two younger children down into the great flat plain that lay beyond the mountains. They traveled the plains, searching for a place to settle, until Ruhala's next oldest child, Nahla, found a bluff overlooking the joining of two rivers. They made a home there and planted the seeds they'd carried with them.

Then, one day, Lorjad again visited Ruhala in her dreams, this time beckoning her to the coast, as Solnat kept his arms around Nahla in their home on the plains. Ruhala woke knowing that she needed to continue their journey with her youngest child, and leave Nahla behind.

Ruhala and Shalo followed the river to the sea, where they slept in a cove at the base of the cliffs. She made a home on the coast with her youngest son as the surviving mages and their kin from the war beyond the mountain made their way to these new lands.

One day, while she was out riding in the forest, she stopped to rest under an ancient tree. The Inahi came to her while she napped in the shade and warned her that the invaders who were destroying their homeland were pushing closer to the mountains. The Inahi offered to create a veil of magic that would protect their new lands from the invaders, but they could only build it with the magic of the mages.

Ruhala's children, now leaders of their clans, met to discuss the threat and agreed that what the Inahi offered seemed like a fair trade. So Ruhala returned to the forest to find the Inahi and accept their offer. That was where the story ended in our clan's book of folklore.

"That's how the clans found a new home and lost their magic. Though, the mages continued to pass on their knowledge of healing and faith to any students who choose to study at the Magery." I glanced over at Ezri and noticed that Mia, the guard who had been riding behind us, seemed to have closed some of the distance between us as I'd told Ruhala's tale.

"So, Ruhala was the first Ruhlini?" Ezri asked.

I considered his question before responding. "I'd never thought of it like that, but I suppose so."

"I think we're here." Ezri gestured to the wagons, veering off the road ahead. "Let's get settled. Then we can talk more about what this means."

We were nearly the last to arrive at the campsite. The wagons had been directed into the middle of a clearing, and a ring of tents was being erected around them.

Zan rode up to meet us, nodding to Mia, who stopped alongside us. "Mia, take the Nahla and show her to her tent. I have things to discuss with the Ruhl."

"Yes, Captain." Mia dismounted, taking the reins of her horse and bringing it up alongside mine.

Ezri reached over and touched my hand. "I'll find you later."

"All right." I waited until he removed his hand and started after Zan before sliding out of the saddle.

Mia led the way to the corral where the horses would rest for the evening. I had been looking forward to the comforting routine of tending to Arge after a long ride, but one of the younger guards who didn't look much older than Kilm took our horses from us when we arrived.

As he walked away, I realized how stiff I was from riding all day, and I took a moment to stretch.

Mia watched me for a moment, then said, "The guards usually stretch and spar before dinner. You could join us, if you like."

I smiled at the invitation even as I tried not to get my hopes up that, even if Zan didn't like me, I might find a new friend among his guards. "I would love that. Thank you."

She motioned for me to follow, then led me to a tent that held four cots. "This is where we'll sleep. Your travel kit is already on your cot. If you need anything from it, you can fetch it now, or I'll bring you back here after dinner."

I spotted the smaller of my two travel trunks waiting for me on a cot at the far end of the tent but shook my head. "I have what I need."

Mia nodded. "Let's join the others, then."

We joined the flow of black-clad guards making their way to a spot just outside the ring of tents. I recognized the faces of the men who had been with the Ruhl at our compound, but there were at least ten more unfamiliar faces. I wondered if they'd all been with Ezri's mysterious mage, or if some had just camped outside our compound walls while the Ruhl completed his business with our clan.

Mia instructed me to stand near the back so I could follow along. I took off my cloak and folded it before setting it in the grass at my feet. When I looked up, Mia was no longer at my side.

She had moved to the front of the group and stood motionless, facing away from the group with her feet planted hip width apart and her hands at her sides. She waited until silence fell among the guards assembled behind her, then began a warm-up routine of fluid poses. Many were similar to ones I'd practiced for years alongside my brothers and Cala. After a few rounds, the flow between the poses became natural, and my muscles loosened and warmed.

Just as I found my rhythm, the group broke into pairs to begin hand-to-hand sparring practice. I glanced about, looking for someone without a partner. For a moment, I thought I might be stuck practicing alone. Then Mia joined me at the back of the group.

"Ready?" she asked.

I nodded. We squared off and bowed to each other. We circled once and then engaged. Mia was quick and precise. As usual, I ducked and tumbled and scrapped with little respect for form or discipline. When fighting my brothers, I'd always used my smaller size and greater flexibility to my advantage. With Mia, my strengths gave me no advantage, and it didn't take her long to pin me.

"You lack discipline, Nahla," a voice called from behind me as Mia helped me to my feet. "That jumping and scrambling will never take down a trained fighter."

I turned to see Zan standing with his arms crossed at the edge of our group.

Ezri stepped up alongside him and set a hand on his shoulder. "Go easy on her, Zan. She's not one of your guards.

Zan frowned. "She needs to be able to defend herself, and you, if needed."

"Then come on out here and show her how it's done," Mia taunted.

I joined Ezri on the sidelines to watch Mia and Zan circle and strike. Sweat gleamed on Zan's upper lip, so it didn't seem like he was going easy on her. I studied his movements to see if he was missing any opportunities to strike.

Mia was good. She danced around him, light on her feet, conserving her energy in smooth, precise strikes. The more I watched, the more I realized how much I could learn from her. From both of them. Mia shifted her weight, then attempted to lock Zan in a hold, but he slipped away. Her recovery took just long enough to give him the opening he needed. He pinned and disarmed her.

Mia laughed. "Got me that time."

Zan released her and lent her a hand getting up. "It's not funny. You need to practice striking from that side. You rely too much on your dominant approach. Run the drills again before dinner."

"Yes, Captain, sir." Mia straightened and wiped the smile from her face to echo her captain's seriousness.

"And run the Nahla through the drills. If she's going to carry weapons around, she should learn how to fight properly." Zan turned, hands on his hips, and looked at the Ruhl. "You, too. Come on."

"It's time for dinner." Ezri motioned toward the other guards, who were collecting their things and making their way back to the center of the ring of tents.

Ezri and Zan stared at each other for a tense moment. Long enough for me to wonder who was really in charge. Then Ezri shook his head. "All right. One round. Then food."

Zan waved me forward. "Nahla, come here and let's begin breaking you of your bad habits."

Mia led us through the drills while Zan stood by correcting my form, reminding me to hold in my core, or keep my hands up, or widen my stance. I'd never concentrated much on form before, and my body tired quickly. We drilled until we could no longer ignore the smell of dinner cooking over the fire. My mouth watered and my stomach grumbled in anticipation.

The sun slipped down to touch the horizon. Finally, Zan let us stop.

"All right. Enough," he said.

I collapsed onto the ground.

Ezri stood over me and held out his hand. "Come on. Get up, or you'll miss dinner."

I grasped his hand and let him pull me up until we were standing toe to toe, staring into each other's eyes. My hand, wrapped in his, brushed against his tunic with every breath he took. His eyes flicked down to my mouth, and for a moment, I wondered if he'd kiss me.

As much as I hoped I'd be able to return to Rys without ever kissing Ezri, that probably wasn't going to happen. Not if we wanted everyone to believe we were madly in love. He'd already warned me he was going to have to kiss me, eventually. It was only a matter of time.

My heart raced. I was sure it was just nerves.

Zan's voice broke the spell. "Mia, you're assigned to guard the Nahla. And I want you both back out here tomorrow morning. Sunrise. We'll drill before we break camp."

I groaned. My body ached, and Zan's insistence on me improving my fighting skills was worrying me.

Ezri squeezed my hand. "Come on. You'll feel better after dinner."

He kept hold of my hand as we followed Zan. He'd somehow already made it nearly to the outer edge of the ring of tents. Ezri didn't seem to be in a hurry to catch up to him, so I matched his pace, and Mia fell into step behind us.

Ahead of us, Zan paused at the sound of hoofbeats approaching. I searched the growing darkness for the source of the sound but couldn't make out much until the rider brought their horse to a stop next to Zan. They exchanged a few words we were too far away to hear, and then he waved the rider on toward the other end of the camp before setting out after us.

I glimpsed a long braid bouncing against a dark cloak as the rider set off toward the corral. "Who's that?" I asked.

"Mage-ruh has returned," Ezri said, his eyes following the rider.

11

ALMOST all the guards were done eating by the time we arrived. The cook had saved us steaming plates piled with roasted meat and vegetables served on top of boiled grains. None of it was recognizable in the lantern light, but that didn't bother me. I was much too hungry and tired to care about what I was eating.

Even though I only had eyes for my plate, Ezri kept glancing around like he was looking for someone. Just as we sat down and started eating, he jumped up again. After reassuring us he'd be right back, he ran off after a trio of guards who were about to leave. He was back before Mia and I finished our servings, which was good, because if he hadn't returned, I might have started in on his plate next.

He waved a rolled-up piece of parchment at me as he sat down. "I found you a map."

I took the paper from him, finished my last few bites of food, then set the empty plate aside so I could use both hands to unroll the map. Unfortunately, once I did, it was too dark to make out the markings. I tilted the paper toward the nearest lantern to get a better view.

Ezri jumped up again and returned with a lantern. He set it down between us and pointed to a spot on the map, not far from the mark labeled Nahl Compound. "We're here."

After all that riding, I'd thought we would have been closer to the city. We had been traveling east rather than south, parallel to the main branch of the river that ran down from the mountains, though it was still too far from the road to see. The river sliced through the middle of our lands before splitting in half almost directly south of where we'd stopped to camp. The road we traveled continued east before turning south, where it crossed both halves of the river and skirted the eastern forest before reaching Shal City at the southeastern-most point of our peninsula.

"Once we cross the Little River, we'll be close to Heartgrove Forest." Ezri pointed to the triangle of land between the crossings marked almost entirely with trees. "Then, after we cross the Lower Stone, we'll travel along the southern edge of the forest the rest of the way home."

Home. My eyes drifted back to the spot marked Nahl Compound. Shal City wasn't my home, but the Heartgrove Forest did look bigger than the Wandering Woods north of our compound. It would be a good place to test Ezri's idea about asking the Inahi for a meeting.

"How far will we go tomorrow?" I asked.

"Across the Stone, at least," Mia said.

Ezri grunted in agreement. He swallowed his mouthful of food before adding, "Zan doesn't like camping near the forest."

"Your captain didn't seem like the type to be scared off by tales of gods and monsters." My finger traced the edge of the eastern forest.

According to the legends, the three forests were packed with danger and considered off-limits. Each was said to be the home of one of Estrel and Solnat's children. Heartgrove belonged to Jusala. Wandering Woods was Lorjad's domain, and Forsla dwelled in Flamehunt, southeast of the mountains. If disturbing a god wasn't enough to frighten youngsters, the legends also claimed that was where the Merluks, who guarded the child-gods, lived. The veil prevented the Merluks and other dangers of the forest from escaping into our lands.

"It isn't the stories that frighten him." Ezri grimaced. "He humors my interest because he's sworn to protect me, but he sides with my mother in thinking it all nonsense. He associates that bit of land with a bad experience we had there."

"What happened?" I asked when he paused.

Ezri glanced away, toward the fire. "We were attacked. On the first expedition my mother approved. The summer after my naming. She let me travel beyond the city walls in the trusted care of my tutor, and under the protection of Zan. We survived, obviously, but the experience left an impression."

"That must have been terrifying." I thought of Rys and the story he'd told of what happened to his family. Then that thought reminded me of Dern. Whatever was getting past the veil and threatening our clans, we needed to stop it. We needed to find the Inahi.

As though he'd read my thoughts, Ezri locked eyes with me. "I'll talk to the cook and make sure we have some travel cakes for tomorrow."

I nodded. Then, overcome by exhaustion, I stretched and yawned.

"Go on. Get some sleep." Ezri folded the map and handed it to Mia to hold while he helped me up. "We'll talk more in the morning."

"But you're not done with your dinner," I protested, even as I teetered on my feet.

"It's all right, Stormcat." Ezri lifted my hand and pressed his lips to my knuckles. "Zan will have us all up with the sun tomorrow. Best to get some rest while you can."

He nudged me toward Mia, who handed me the map, then led the way to our tent. Inside, all the cots but our two were occupied. Only one other guard was still up, mending a tear in her cloak.

I quickly changed into leggings and a fresh tunic for sleeping and folded my travel clothes before tucking them inside my trunk and closing the lid. The map I unfolded and spread out on the lid to take one last look before sliding everything under my cot. I had just laid down and pulled the blanket over me when someone blew out the last of the lanterns.

I thought it would take a long time to fall asleep in a tent full of strangers, but it seemed like I'd only just closed my eyes when I woke to daylight. I'd been dreaming of creatures lurking in trees, peering down at me through the dense canopy, and someone was calling my name.

I blinked my eyes open to find that someone was Mia, who was already dressed and standing at the foot of my cot. "Ezri-ruh said to let you sleep as long as possible, but they're nearly ready to pack our tent. So it's time to get up."

She turned and left, slipping out through the open tent flap into the soft sunrise glow beyond. When I sat up and glanced around, I realized that everyone else was also already up and out. Muffled shouts and the thump and bang of guards breaking camp passed through the canvas walls and made me wonder how I could have slept through that much noise.

I threw the blanket off and bent to pull my trunk out so I

could dress. In my hurry, I almost missed the tiny violet flowers scattered across the top of the map.

Pausing in time, I carefully lifted the parchment, holding my breath and moving slowly so as not to disturb the flower buds. I set the map on top of my cot and looked around the floor to see if there were more that I missed. There were none, so I returned to the map and noted the location of each little six-petal flower before collecting them into my hand.

The first flower I removed rested above my clan's winter compound. The next was near where Ezri had said we were camped for the night. The third sat in the triangle of land between the river crossings. Another lay north of the city, near the bay where the Stone River emptied into the sea. And the final flower lay above the city itself.

The tiny flowers reminded me of the ones I'd found next to my offering for the Inahi. These weren't moonbursts, but they were stemless, like the others. And they appeared to be marking our path of travel. I wondered if their placement on the map was significant, and if this could be another sign from the Inahi. If it was, that would mean they would have had to cross the threshold of our tent to leave this message for me. Something I'd been taught was impossible.

Mia called to me from where she waited at the tent entrance. Reluctantly, I tucked the five flowers into a pocket inside my trunk and retrieved my travel suit. After dressing, I returned my sleeping clothes to the trunk. The map I folded and slipped into a pocket in my travel cloak. Then I hurried to follow Mia out into the dawn, excited to find Ezri and tell him about the flowers.

"Will Zan be mad that I slept through the morning drills?" I asked.

"He called off drills." Mia led us through the bustle of

guards breaking camp, toward the cook, who was already packing gear into a waiting wagon. "Ezri-ruh and Zan met with Mage-ruh last night and decided it would be best to get an early start so we can make it as far as possible before nightfall."

I picked up the bowl of boiled grains the cook had left for me. Before taking my first spoonful, I asked, "Where are they now?"

Mia scanned the campsite. "Around. Somewhere."

I shoveled down my breakfast, keeping one eye on the cook's packing progress, and the other searching for Ezri's sun-streaked hair and bright tunic among the sea of black-clad guards. By the time I finished eating, there was still no sign of Ezri, but the tents and gear were nearly packed.

I quickly washed my bowl and spoon before returning them to the cook to load into the wagon. Then Mia led me to the horses. Even with all the rushing about, I couldn't stop thinking about the flowers. We were close. I could feel it. And today we were going to ask the Inahi for a meeting. I practically bounced along beside Mia, barely able to contain my excitement.

Ezri rode up just as I was about to mount Arge. "Good morning, Stormcat."

Mia gave me a boost into the saddle, and then led her horse to where Zan had stopped to talk with a small group of guards.

As soon as she was gone, I nudged Arge closer to Ezri's horse. "I have something I need to tell you."

He set his horse walking in the opposite direction of Zan and gestured for me to follow. "Did you sleep well?"

I guided Arge into a walk, flanking Ezri. "I did, but—"

He spoke over me to greet a pair of guards loading a cart

of tent poles as we rode past. Once they were behind us, and the next group was not quite within earshot, he gestured toward the wagons lining up ahead of us and spoke just loud enough for me to hear. "Let's get out in front before the wagons start rolling. Then we can talk."

We'd just passed the lead wagon in the caravan when another rider trotted up beside us.

"My Ruhl," she said, slowing her horse to a walk on the opposite side of Ezri.

"Mage-ruh. Good morning," Ezri replied.

"I'm still waiting for an answer." Her weathered face carried worried creases around her forehead and eyes. Her long, silver-streaked dark hair was tied back in a braid, as it had been when I caught a glimpse of her last night.

"I haven't forgotten. First, allow me to introduce you to Ayla-nah." He turned his head to grin at me and winked. Then he gestured to the woman who rode on his other side. "Ayla, this is the mage who taught me everything I know about the gods and our legends."

Mage-ruh sighed deeply and swore. "I see what you're doing, and I don't appreciate it."

Ezri laughed. "Come now, Mage-ruh. It would be rude of me to abandon my betrothed, and I told you I was going to inform her of what we discussed, anyway."

Ezri's mage shook her head. "If you must do this, you troublesome brat, you could at least remove yourself from the middle."

I gaped at her response. Surprised that she dared to talk that way to someone she supposedly served. But Ezri only laughed. Then he reined in his horse, dropping back long enough to let us pull ahead before guiding his mount around to the outside so that I was the one riding in the middle.

"Better?" he asked.

"It will have to do," Mage-ruh replied, before turning her attention to me. "My apologies, Nahla. This is not how I'd hoped we'd meet."

"You had hoped to meet me, Mage-ruh?" Her statement surprised me even more than the unusual dynamic between her and Ezri.

"Of course! I was delighted when I heard my niece had joined us and was returning with us to the city." The corner of her mouth turned up in a slight smile as she glanced at me.

"Niece?" I searched my memory for a long-lost aunt I had forgotten. My mother had been an only child, and I knew my father to have only brothers. My uncle Harn, who had died before I was born, and my uncle Feln.

"I suppose it was too much to hope you had been told of me." She sighed. "I'll never understand the way my brother's mind works, choosing to send you to the city wholly unprepared for what you would surely encounter there."

"Your brother?" I squinted at her, suddenly seeing the resemblance to my father in the shape of her nose and the set of her jaw.

"Yes. Your father banished me from the clan years ago, well before you were born. Then he forbade any clan member to mention me. But it doesn't matter what Teron-nah says. He can't change the fact that I'm still his little sister, Sera. Which makes me your aunt."

I sat speechless, staring at her. Sera. Sera-nah was what I'd overheard Goff say to Father. Ezri's Mage-ruh was my aunt. An aunt my father had disowned. An aunt who lived in the city. An aunt who was mage to the Ruhl. I didn't know what to say or where to start. I had so many questions.

"They knew. They knew you were in the city, and didn't

tell me? Did Mother know, too?" I wondered if the information would have made leaving any easier. My heart ached as my thoughts drifted back along the dirt road toward home.

"I'm sure that your father forbade it. He can be stubborn sometimes." Sera gazed at me with pity in her eyes.

"What happened? Why did he banish you?" I asked.

"I'm afraid that's a story for another time. I will humor your betrothed only so far. At the moment, there are more urgent things to discuss. Decisions to be made that he is avoiding." Her eyes narrowed as she looked past me. "Ezri-ruh?"

Ezri grinned. "Oh, did you want me to tell the story?"

"No, I do not, you miserable god-touched brat." Sera caught herself after she snapped at him and groaned. "My story is not yours to tell, and you know exactly what I'm waiting for an answer about. So stop baiting me. Out with it. What's it to be?"

I stared at Ezri, once again shocked at how Mage-ruh—my aunt—spoke to him. Perhaps this sort of disrespect was what caused my father to banish her. But again, Ezri laughed at her response. He didn't seem to mind at all. I was getting the sense that he might even enjoy it.

"Hmm." Ezri leaned forward so he could look around me. "What about the bits that are my story as well? Can I tell her those?"

"You can tell her whatever you want of your history once you've addressed my concerns. You do care about the safety of those sworn to protect you, do you not?" Sera raised her eyebrows and set her lips in a firm line.

That wiped the smile from Ezri's face and caused him to sit up straight in his saddle. "Of course I do."

"Then give the command." She stared at him, waiting.

Ezri's eyes met mine for a moment. Long enough that he

must have caught the look of confusion on my face. "First, tell Ayla what you told me and Zan, and let's see what she has to say about it."

"We don't have time for this, but I see your point," Sera grumbled before turning to me. "The veil is thinning. You know that much. Mage-nah told me you've been petitioning the Inahi."

I nodded, remembering my conversation with Ezri. The pieces began clicking together in my head. My aunt had been the one meeting with Mage-nah when I went looking for him. She had been his apprentice. The one who had gone to study at the Magery. No wonder Ezri had been so amused when I'd said I wanted to have words with the mage who'd taught him.

Sera continued her explanation, pulling me from my thoughts. "The way Ezri-ruh's grandmother used to explain it, the Inahi made it so our borders would appear to outsiders as an impassable stretch of sea, or impossibly tall mountains, or a deadly forest. Should they venture forth to explore the inhospitable terrain, they would be misdirected and only find their way back to where they started. This also worked to deter any creatures of legend who still dwelled in the deep forest from leaving it."

"The Merluks," I said. "Sworn to protect the gods."

"Yes." Sera paused. "Only now they're escaping. Slipping out past the veil. Gods know why. Yet, I've seen signs of them all along the outskirts of the Wandering Wood. I warned Ezri-ruh and Zan of this last night and recommended they make haste past Heartgrove and ride straight through to the safety of the city walls without stopping."

I thought of the map in my pocket and how far we'd traveled compared to how much further we had to go. "Is that possible?"

"No," Ezri said.

"Zan thinks it is. If we don't stop," Sera responded.

"A small group on horseback could make it, easily. But this?" Ezri gestured to the wagons rattling along behind us. He shook his head. "Impossible. Unreasonable."

"Then you and Ayla-nah should ride ahead with Zan. Mia can command the guards, and I'll stay with the caravan to guide them." Sera gripped her reins tight in her fists, her voice pleading.

"I won't leave them." Ezri sat tall and stared ahead, jaw clenched.

"Be reasonable." Sera leaned forward. "Think about Ayla. If we're attacked—"

Ezri cut her off. "Ayla? What do you think?"

I fiddled with the ring on my finger as I glanced back and forth between them. Stuck in the middle. Asked to make an impossible choice. I didn't want to leave the others any more than Ezri did, but I'd heard Rys's story of the attack on his family. One sparring session with Mia and the Shal clan guards was not enough to prepare me for a Merluk attack.

We could ride to safety. Or we could put an end to the danger once and for all. There really was only one way to stop this.

"We can't ride straight through," I said, turning to Ezri. "We need to make at least one stop."

Ezri nodded. "I haven't forgotten."

"Why?" Sera asked. "What stop?"

I turned my head to look at her. "You said it yourself. The Inahi left me a message. We need to contact them again to ask for a meeting. We can't do that inside the city walls."

Sera sighed. "Heartgrove. You want to visit the temple."

"There's a temple?" I gaped at her.

"What are they teaching in the Nahl crèche these days?" She scowled. "Don't tell me that my brother is following the lead of the Shal and eradicating the mage lore."

"Ayla knows her mage lore," Ezri said, before I could respond. "It's only that you've been too long in the Magery. Almost no one outside that place knows about the temple anymore."

Sera scoffed. "The Nahl did, back when I was your age. But you're right. Ever since your mother took over as Shal, the Nahl clan won't venture past the Little River crossing." She paused, rubbing her palm across the back of her neck as she stared at the road ahead. "The temple is too far in, though. I don't think it's safe to go that deep into Heartgrove."

"We can stay at the edge of the forest," I said.

She nodded. "All right. If this is your decision, and we're going to stop to camp, I'll need to tell the scouts what to look for."

"You could go with them," I suggested.

"That would be easier, I suppose." She looked at Ezri.

He raised his eyebrows. "Since when do you take orders from me?"

"You are impossible. Worse than your aunt was—may her soul rest among the stars." She shook her head. "I'll ride out with the scouts. But if we can't find a good place to camp, I'm sending you two ahead with Zan. I have no interest in facing the wrath of your mother if anything happens to you. Especially given her feelings about—"

"I don't take orders from you, either," Ezri said, cutting her off. "And I'm not going ahead. So you better find a suitable spot."

"Impossible." Sera grunted. She whistled three short notes, then urged her horse forward.

As she rode away, three guards galloped past us, following the cloud of dust kicked up by her horse's hooves.

"Does everyone know she's my aunt?" I asked once we were alone again.

Ezri shook his head. "Not everyone. Zan does, but the rest of the guards don't. My mother does. They don't get along, though. And that's stating it kindly. My mother doesn't want me associating with any of the mages, least of all Sera. Luckily, Sera doesn't have much reason to attend Council, and she never comes to Shal House or Ruhl House."

"But she's your mage."

Ezri laughed. "The whole Mage-ruh thing is a bit of a joke. I call her that, but Sera has no official title. Mage-sha wants Sera to be her successor, but my mother refuses to approve her for the position. So, Mage-sha continues on in the role, such as it is. Sometimes I think the Magery named me Ruhl instead of Vorn-jah just so that I would have the power to overrule my mother."

Before he could say anything more, Mia rode up. She slowed her horse to a walk beside mine.

"My Ruhl, Zan saw Mage-ruh depart and wants to speak with you," she said.

"Well then, why didn't he ride up here himself?" Ezri scowled.

Mia blinked. "I... I think he would prefer it if you drop back and ride closer to the middle of the caravan. Both of you."

Ezri sighed. "I'll drop back. You stay here and ride with Ayla-nah."

"Yes, my Ruhl." Mia dipped her head.

Ezri brushed his fingers across the back of my hand. "If I'm not back right away, don't worry. I'll find you when we stop after the river crossing."

#

Wᴇ reached the banks of the Little River at mid-day. As the wagons continued across the bridge, those on horseback stopped alongside the river and dismounted to give the horses a rest and let them drink and graze.

I led Arge as close to the edge of the forest as I dared before sliding out of the saddle to let her nibble on the grass while I searched for Ezri. I spotted him talking with Zan and Tavo on the far side of the road. Then I lost sight of him as another wagon rolled between us, blocking my view. When it passed, Tavo was still there and staring directly at me, but Ezri and Zan were gone.

I jumped when someone tapped me on the shoulder.

"Looking for me?" Ezri smiled and a lock of his thick, wavy hair fell across his forehead.

I placed my hands on my hips and returned his smile, cocking my head to one side. "Actually, I was. How did you manage to—"

He reached for my hand and cut me off before I could finish asking my question. "Come on. Before Zan catches us."

Ezri headed toward the point where the river entered the forest, and I hurried to keep up, pulling Arge along after me, just as Ezri was leading me. The rushing and burbling of water around boulders and branches blocked out the clatter of wagon wheels and the chatter of guards. It grew louder the closer we got to the river, filling my ears with its intimidating roar.

Ezri stopped next to a wide, flat rock. The lower edge dipped into the clear water as it tumbled past, but the upper part was dry, and positioned just below a tall tree.

"What do you think?" he asked. "Is this close enough?"

I glanced around. "How long do we have?"

"How long do we need?" He flopped down on the flat rock, stretching out his arm to dip his fingers into the water. Leaning on one elbow, he turned his head to grin at me. "If it were up to me, I'd stay here with you all day."

I busied myself tying Arge's reins to a branch and snuck a glance behind me to see if we had an audience. There was no sign of Tavo or any of the guards or their captain, but I was fairly certain Ezri was flirting with me. He was still smiling, watching me and waiting for a response. And we were alone for the first time since he'd cornered me in an alcove before my sister's wedding and told me he was going to have to kiss me.

I brushed my hands off on my leggings, hoping to relieve them of the dampness gathering on my palms. "I usually wait and watch after I place the offering."

"That would be nice." Ezri removed a wrapped bundle from a pocket inside his cloak. He unfolded the wrapping to reveal two traveling cakes and some dried fruit. "Unfortunately, I don't think we're going to have time for that. It took all my charm to convince Zan to let me stray this far from the rest of the group."

One look at the food had my mouth watering. My stomach grumbled. I hoped the river was loud enough that Ezri hadn't heard. "I'm surprised he didn't insist on coming with you."

Ezri looked up and lifted one corner of his mouth, grinning as he held out one of the cakes to me. "Here. I think we have enough that you can eat one."

"Thanks." My cheeks warmed with embarrassment, but I took the dense cake from him and broke off a small section before handing it back. "Let's use the rest of this one for our offering, and you can have the other."

Ezri shook his head. "It's my first offering, so I want to offer a whole one. You enjoy that one. It will be a long ride to dinner."

"But what about you?"

"Don't worry about me. I'll go pout around the cook's wagon until they give me more." He shrugged one shoulder, then gave me a sample of his best smoldering look before sitting up and breaking into a full grin. "Now what do we do?"

I shook my head. "Remind me to find you a copy of Lorjad's Laws for Travelers."

He waved a hand. "Take it up with old Mage-ruh tonight. It will be excellent dinner entertainment."

I bent down and picked up a sturdy twig lying near the toe of my boot. Then I crouched down next to Ezri. "I expect I know the answer, but I'll ask anyway. Do you know any runes?"

Ezri took the twig from my hand, bent over the surface of the flat rock, and drew two curves before leaning back so I could admire his work.

I smiled and shook my head at the heart he'd drawn. "That. Is not a rune."

He cocked his head to one side. Tapping the end of the twig against his chin, he squinted at the mark. "Are you sure?"

"Yes." I sat down on the upper edge of the rock so that his drawing was between us. Then I plucked the twig from his hand. "We're asking for a meeting, right?"

Ezri nodded.

"All right." I glanced around, looking for a smaller rock positioned just so. It took a moment before I spotted a round, flat stone that looked as though it had been smoothed by years in the river, but had somehow landed on the bank, out of reach of the water. I pointed to it. "Put the cake there."

Ezri scrambled to the far side of the boulder and set the cake on the rock. "Like this?"

I knelt next to him, gripping the twig in my hand like a pen. "I've been using Estrel's Hands, since that's the rune for divine gifts and assistance. But I think we should try one of Jusala's runes if we're asking for a meeting."

"It's always Jusala." Ezri sighed, sitting up and crossing his legs in front of him. "I suppose this is her forest, though."

I nudged his shoulder with mine. "It has nothing to do with that. It's because she's the goddess of diplomacy and balanced judgment."

"Yes, exactly. The goddess I'm meant to model myself after as Ruhl, as Sera and Mage-sha have lectured repeatedly." He frowned. "But I see your point. Estrel is renewal and miracles. Lorjad is journeys and fresh starts. Solnat is abundance, hearth, family. Forsla is strength and courage. Jusala it is."

I tapped the end of the twig against the edge of the stone. "But which rune?"

Ezri set his elbows on his knees and his chin in his hands. "Well, I showed you the only one I know."

"Yes. You did." I grinned. "Mage-ruh will be so proud."

He laughed. "All right. What are our choices?"

I scowled, wishing I'd thought to bring the little book of runes Mage-nah had given me. The book that must have been Sera's. I wondered if that had been his way of trying to tell me about her, but I pushed the thought aside to consider later and focused on picturing the runes in Jusala's suit.

"You know, Jusala's Heart is a rune. It just doesn't look like that one." I pointed to Ezri's drawing, behind me on the rock.

"See!" He brightened. "What's that one stand for?"

"What you might expect. Friendship. Love. Partnership." My cheeks warmed.

Ezri raised his eyebrows. "Will you show me how to draw it?"

I glanced back toward the road. We were still alone. "Later. Right now, we should focus on the offering."

"Right. The offering." Ezri pressed his lips together. "That's probably not the right rune for asking for a meeting."

"No. Nor is her Crown or her Claw." My eyes drifted to the water rushing past as I tried to remember the remaining two runes. "Jusala's Scales... or maybe... her Sight?"

"What do they mean?" Ezri asked.

"Jusala's Scales represent balance and harmony, which is what we're trying to restore. Jusala's Sight represents a crossroads, or a decision." I sketched the two runes on the rock between us as I explained.

"Hmm." Ezri studied my etchings. "A crossroads is a meeting place. I think we should go with that one. The other seems like it may be asking for more. Like the one you said you usually use. Estrel's something or other?"

I shook my head. "Estrel's Hands." I sketched that rune alongside the others. "I think you're right. Do you want to draw it?"

He stared at the twig I held out to him, then glanced down at the runes I'd sketched. "Would it be better if I did it?"

I shrugged. "You are the Ruhl."

"All right." Ezri scowled, but took the twig from me. He studied the rune for Jusala's Sight. Then he leaned forward and crawled toward the offering.

"Hold what you're asking for in your mind while you draw the rune," I said.

Ezri's body blocked my view. Since I couldn't see what he was doing, I listened for the scratch of wood on stone. It took longer than I expected before the first scrape reached my ears. When he was done, I scooted back to give him some room so he could sit beside me, facing the river.

"Do you think it will work?" he asked.

"I suppose we'll have to wait and see." I glanced over at the offering.

A pair of whistled notes, followed by another identical pair, cut through the sound of the river.

Ezri groaned. "Zan."

"Looking for us?"

"He knows where we are." Ezri paused as the pair of whistled notes repeated. "He wants to get moving."

I stood and brushed off my leggings before offering Ezri my hand to help him up. "Come on. If we can't stay, the Inahi will have to come to us."

Ezri took my hand, and I balanced against his weight until we were standing face to face. But he didn't move away. Instead, he tilted his head to one side as he studied my face.

"What is it?" I asked, lifting a hand to make sure I'd brushed any remaining crumbs lingering on my lips.

He took a step closer and tilted my chin up with his free hand. "It's just... I'm glad I found you."

My heart raced as his lips reached for mine. When they brushed against my skin, my eyes fluttered closed. His warm mouth parted slightly, and I leaned into his touch.

I hadn't wanted this, and at the same time, kissing Ezri felt as natural as breathing. I'd only known him for a few days, but his lips set my skin tingling. Everything else disappeared, and I wanted to stay right there for hours.

Zan's insistent whistle, louder this time, startled us apart. We both turned toward the sound.

Ezri's hand wrapped around mine. "We better get back."

"Let me just untie Arge," I said, already moving away.

He released his grip on my hand, only to capture it again when he fell into step beside me. "I'm sorry we couldn't stay longer."

I snuck a glance back over my shoulder at the travel cake to confirm it hadn't disappeared when we weren't looking. "I'm surprised Zan gave us as long as he did."

Ezri laughed. Then he started coughing. He covered his mouth with his free hand, but when the coughing didn't stop, he stopped walking and released me so he could search his pockets.

"Are you all right?" I placed a hand lightly on his back, but he shrugged me off.

He retrieved a tiny vial from somewhere in his cloak, pulled out the stopper, and took a sip. Then he slipped the vial back into his pocket and bent over, placing his hands on his knees to catch his breath.

"Sorry," he whispered. "It's nothing."

"Nothing?" I'd seen that vial before. Zan had given it to him in the gardens the night we'd met.

"Nothing," he confirmed, standing up. "Just a nasty cough. That elixir Mage-sha made me fixes me every time." He smiled.

"Are you sure?" I asked.

"All better." He wrapped his hand around mine. "But thanks for worrying about me."

We walked back to join the others and found Zan waiting for us with Ezri's horse. He exchanged a look with Ezri but said nothing. I wondered if he really had left us alone, or if he'd been keeping watch from a distance. Ezri helped me into my saddle, then pressed his lips against the back of my hand before turning away to mount his own horse.

For the rest of the afternoon, we rode together in the middle of the caravan with Zan flanking Ezri's far side. Ezri maintained a steady stream of conversation, which made me forget about the vial and his strange behavior, but every time I looked at him, my lips tingled from the memory of our kiss.

12

AT camp that night, even after another grueling training session, worse somehow because it was led by
Zan instead of Mia, I couldn't fall asleep. I couldn't
stop thinking about the Inahi and when or if they'd respond.
And every time I thought about our offering, my mind would
drift to that kiss. My feelings were a knot of confusion.

As I lay awake on my cot, listening to the sounds of the
other women breathing, I tried to untangle the knot in my
chest. Twisting and turning, restless and unable to quiet my
mind or soothe my heart, I finally gave up.

I slipped my legs off the cot and slid my feet into my boots.
Then I reached for the trunk and lifted my cloak off the top,
fastening it around my neck over my sleeping tunic and leggings. I tied my belt around the waist of my tunic so that I
had a place to stash my hunting dagger, which I retrieved
from beneath my pillow as I turned to leave the tent. Stepping carefully around cots, I pulled my cloak tight around my
shoulders, pausing once at the tent flap to make sure I hadn't

woken anyone before slipping outside.

Once out under the stars, I took a deep breath and shivered. I knew I would be cold without my warm riding clothes, so I set off at a brisk pace, walking through the camp to the outer edge, where the guards patrolled, keeping watch for any creatures that might escape the forest. Sera had warned everyone to stay well away from the woods, and I had no plans to go wandering off on my own.

Keeping the camp to my right, and noting where I'd started, I told myself I'd make one loop around the perimeter to shake off my restlessness. Then I would return to my cot and sleep.

At first, I wasn't concerned that I hadn't crossed paths with any guards. I didn't worry until I estimated that I'd made it halfway around the camp and still hadn't seen anyone. Even then, I convinced myself that there would be guards up ahead, probably walking the loop in the same direction as me, but faster.

It wasn't until I'd reached the stretch closest to the Heartgrove when I finally spotted two figures talking in the moonlight. I stopped short at the sight because they were standing at the edge of the forest, nowhere near where I would expect the guards to be patrolling, especially after Sera's warning.

I stepped back into the shadows of a nearby tent, where I had a good view of the pair. Fairly certain I hadn't been spotted, and unable to hear the conversation because they were so far away, I strained to get a glimpse of either of the faces.

They were silhouetted by the moonlight. One figure, clearly taller, bent forward to get a closer look at something the shorter figure held up between them. He had a broad chest and slim waist, but wore his long hair free-flowing. It fluttered against his back in the wind. He looked familiar, but he was too far away for me to be sure.

The angular head of the shorter figure appeared wider at the top than at the bottom in profile, more beast than human, even though it sat atop a body that could have belonged to any of the more thickly muscled guards. The creature moved to unwrap the bundle it presented to the man, and I caught the curve of long, sharp claws punctuating the end of each finger. A bolt of instinctive fear flashed through my body.

I adjusted my stance into a ready position, preparing to run, but froze as a hand clamped down on my shoulder. I jumped, recoiling from the touch, and released a high squeak of surprise before twisting away and crouching to free myself and prepare a defensive maneuver.

"Easy, Ayla-nah, it's just me." Mia released her grip on my shoulder and held both her hands up, palms facing me. "I heard a noise and woke to find your cot empty. I followed your footprints to make sure you were safe. Is everything all right?"

Adrenaline ran through my veins, and I forced myself to breathe deeper and slower. I looked over my shoulder to where the two figures had been standing, but they had vanished. "I just needed some air," I said. "I couldn't sleep."

"You shouldn't be out here, alone, in the middle of the night," Mia said.

Before I could respond, the sound of heavy footsteps approaching made me jump again. Both Mia and I reached for our daggers, even as I realized it was probably just a patrolling guard. Finally.

As the person came into view, a shaft of moonlight fell on their face.

"Tavo." I sighed, relieved to see another familiar face before tensing again as I finally realized he had been the familiar figure I'd just seen conversing with that creature in the moonlight.

"Oh." Mia glanced back and forth between my face and Tavo's. Her mouth pulled into a thin line, and she took a step back.

I instantly regretted greeting the Jahlo without adding the clan honorific to his name as I realized what this looked like. I cringed.

"Mia. Wait." Tavo rushed forward, surprising me. He reached out to touch her arm. "It's not what you think."

Mia shrugged his hand away. She focused on me as though Tavo did not exist. "Nahla, I must insist that you return with me. It isn't safe to be out alone."

I swallowed and nodded.

When Mia started back toward the tent, expecting that I would follow, I spun to face Tavo, holding out a hand to stop him. "What were you doing?" I hissed the question at him, trying to keep my voice low.

"Not. Now," he snarled back, twisting away so he could chase after Mia.

I followed after them, thoughts swirling. Dern had claimed Tavo said he'd look out for me, but I had a hard time believing that whatever he was doing with that creature was meant to be helpful. And what was that creature, anyway? I'd never seen or read about anything that looked like that.

Tavo's pleading whisper floated back to me, faint on the wind. I glared at the back of his head, wanting answers, but unsure how to speak to him without Mia. They disappeared for a moment around a turn, and I lost track of him. When I stopped next to Mia outside our tent, he was gone.

I opened my mouth to explain and ask where Tavo went so I could go after him, but Mia held up a hand to stop me.

"Whatever you two were doing out there, it doesn't matter," she said. "Tomorrow we'll be back in the city. But until we are safely inside its walls, don't go wandering off again. Zan will have my head if any harm comes to you."

"There's nothing going on between me and Tavo-jah. I didn't know he was out there. I just wanted to get some air." I wrapped my arms around myself to keep warm. "I couldn't sleep. I'm sorry."

"Just don't do it again." She moved closer to the tent, reaching up to unfasten the flap.

"You and Tavo-jah?" I'd thought there was something going on between Dern and Tavo, but I could have been wrong. I felt bad enough about what she must think of me, but I would feel so much worse if I'd ruined her relationship because of a misunderstanding.

"No." Mia fumbled with the loop fastening, struggling to stretch it around the hook.

"He seemed upset," I added.

Mia grumbled. Giving up on the tent flap, she turned to face me. "I have no interest in him, if that's what you're asking. He's been trying for years. Ever since he came to the city to represent the Jahl clan on the Council. If you two were..." She sighed and shook her head. "Then that only makes it worse."

Relief bubbled up inside me, past the knot of worry in my chest. "Mia, really. No. I thought there might be something between him and my brother Dern because of how he reacted after Dern was attacked, but me? Never. I was just as surprised as you were to find him out there."

Mia frowned, and again I considered telling her about what I'd seen, but hesitated. The Jahl clan were our allies. My father and my brothers would say I should trust Tavo.

But what I'd heard in the stables made me think he might be a threat to the Ruhl, and I needed Ezri if I hoped to convince the gods to restore the veil.

I didn't know who to trust. I wanted to prove to my father and brothers that I could handle this so they would stop treating me like a child, but there was so much I didn't understand about the power dynamics surrounding the Ruhl. I was determined not to mess this up. At the very least, I couldn't tell Mia what I'd seen before I told Ezri.

"I need to talk to the Ruhl," I said, taking a step back. "I'm not going to be able to sleep until I do. Can you take me to his tent?"

Mia squinted at me. "Can't it wait until morning?"

"I don't think so," I said.

Just then, a scream pierced through the night air. Howling followed the scream. Then more screaming cut through the howls.

Mia rushed to my side as guards began stumbling out of tents, pulling on tunics and strapping on weapons belts as they ran. She glanced between me and the steady stream of her fellow guards. Her hands wrapped around the handles of the knives sheathed at her waist.

"Just take me to the Ruhl," I said, suddenly worried that whatever had been out there had brought friends, and we were already too late. "Please."

She gave me a long look and shook her head. Her eyes scanned the camp, searching for any nearby danger. "I don't think that's a good idea."

A flash of silver caught my eye as the howling increased in volume. I turned, searching for the movement, but Mia was faster. She stepped between me and the woman approaching on horseback before either of us recognized the figure as

Mage-ruh.

"Mia," Sera's voice called out as she approached. "Go join the others. I'll stay with the Nahla."

Mia adjusted her stance and only lowered her knives to waist level, keeping them at the ready. "Did Zan send you?"

Sera's horse stopped in front of us, and she sat high in the saddle, her long grey hair glowing in the moonlight. "No, I believe he's with the Ruhl."

Mia shifted and then stilled. "What are you doing on horseback at this hour?"

I turned to search for the source of another scream that came from behind us and sounded more animal than human. That primal scream was silenced, but another rose to take its place.

"Merluks," Sera whispered, staring into the darkness toward the screaming and howling.

"Answer my question," Mia said, lifting her knives slightly and steadying her breathing.

Sera was going to end up with a knife in her chest if she didn't respond, but Mia had a point. It was suspicious that she'd arrived at our tent so quickly and on horseback. I had only just met this relative of mine, and I was inclined to trust her. But long-lost aunt or not, after what I'd seen at the edge of the forest, I wasn't sure I could trust my instincts.

"Sera," I said, attempting to bring her attention back to the most immediate threat.

Sera locked eyes with Mia. "If you won't trust me, then get her to Ezri-ruh and help Zan guard them." Then she pressed her heels into the sides of her horse and took off into the night, heading straight for the howling that had moved toward the far edge of the camp, not far from where we'd been earlier.

Mia sheathed one knife and grabbed my arm with her now free hand. "Let's go."

"I thought you were going to kill her," I whispered, allowing her to pull me along.

"I would have. My duty is to protect you, and I won't leave you unless Zan or the Ruhl himself dismiss me." She tugged at my arm, keeping us close to the edges of tents for cover, but pulling me toward the center of the camp, away from the sounds of the fighting.

After a series of turns, she stopped us alongside a tent like the one we'd been sleeping in. I wondered how she could tell them apart. They all looked the same to me.

Mia whistled a few notes. The response came from the tent directly across from us. The same few notes, only slightly altered. She tugged at my arm and pushed me toward the tent, watching around us as we crossed the open stretch for any sign of movement.

A body appeared out of the darkness and took position near the door flap as we approached.

"Zan," Mia whispered.

"Get inside," he hissed, lifting the canvas flap.

We slipped under his arm and into the tent. As my eyes adjusted to the darkness, I realized Ezri wasn't alone inside the tent. As he paced the small space, Tavo sat hunched over his knees on the edge of the only cot. Mia's grip on my arm tightened when she spotted him there.

"Mia, with me, outside," Zan whispered. He stood in the doorway, holding the tent flap open.

Mia hesitated.

Ezri stopped pacing long enough to reassure her. "We'll be fine. Go."

"Keep quiet and listen for the signal," Zan said to Ezri.

He waited for Ezri's nod of agreement before gesturing to Mia.

"With me," Zan repeated. This time his words sounded more like a reassurance and less like a command.

Mia shot a glance back at us as she followed him from the tent. She whispered something to him on her way out, and he swore under his breath. Then the tent flap slapped shut behind them, and they were gone.

Once they were outside, Ezri crossed the tent to me and reached to caress my cheek before slipping his hand around my shoulder and pulling me close to him.

I leaned against his chest. "Sera thinks it's Merluks."

"I'm sorry," he whispered. He pressed his cheek against the top of my head. "It's my fault."

"Why?" Tavo asked, reminding me we weren't alone. "What haven't you told us, my Ruhl?" He lingered on that last word, that title, his tone flirting with disrespect.

I turned my head toward him and caught the glint of metal in the darkness as he shifted his knife lazily between his hands. "I think the better question is what haven't *you* told *us*," I said, keeping my voice low.

Whatever that creature was, I was almost certain it wasn't a Merluk. I'd always been told Merluks were great hairy beasts with yellow vertical-slit eyes who prowled on four legs. Long white claws extended from each of their mighty paws. They were nocturnal and depended on their excellent night vision and hearing for hunting because their sense of smell wasn't great.

In the stories I'd read, Merluks didn't walk around like humans, and they didn't have horns on their heads. Based on what I'd seen at the edge of the forest, either what I'd been taught was wrong, or it wasn't Merluks attacking our camp at all.

"What makes you think I know anything about this?" Tavo glared at me. "What have you seen?"

I shivered at the subtle threat.

Ezri stared at us. "What's all this about?"

"Nothing." Tavo shifted again, letting his breath out in a huff. "It's late, and the attack has us all on edge. Perhaps we should just—"

A crash outside the tent cut off whatever it was he was going to suggest. We all turned toward the sound and found ourselves staring at the inside of a tent wall. A low growl rumbled beyond the canvas, followed by a grunt and a soft thud accompanied by a wounded howl.

Creatures farther away howled in response. A sword swished through the air and there was another thud. This time, the lifeless body slid against the canvas, leaving a dark mark in its wake.

My racing heart slammed against my ribs. I stepped away from Ezri and reached for the knife in my belt. Tavo was already on his feet, knife ready.

Then Zan's voice cut through the canvas. "I said, quiet in there. You want to draw them all to you?"

Ezri crossed the tent and returned holding a sword. The three of us stood with our backs toward each other, facing the tent walls, waiting. The sounds of fighting grew faint until I could barely hear them over our breathing. Then something bellowed, releasing a long, low cry that sounded like it came from the edge of camp. Screeches followed, along with the thudding and scampering of bodies in retreat.

"What was that?" Tavo asked.

"Something called them off," Ezri whispered.

Zan pushed back the tent flap. "They're gone."

"What happened?" Ezri asked.

"I don't know." Zan shook his head. "They were closing in, circling us. And then..."

"That sound," Ezri said.

Zan nodded. We moved toward the tent flap, but he held up a hand. "You may want to wait until we get this cleaned up."

"Nonsense." Ezri pushed past Zan and stepped out into the night.

Tavo followed him, and I slipped out last. Down each path leading away from the tent lay at least one grey lump.

Ezri sucked in his breath as he took in the carnage. "Did we lose any?"

Zan nodded.

Ezri's shoulders slumped. "Prepare the bodies. We'll burn them at sunrise."

I walked around the tent to where we'd heard the growl and stood looking down at a thin beast about the size of a child, covered head to foot in thick, shaggy grey hair. I watched as Mia retrieved a knife thrown with deadly accuracy into the beast's back. She rolled the body over and stared at the round, hornless head with large, rubbery ears pointing straight up on either side of its furred face.

The fur hid all features except two unmoving, vertical-slit yellow eyes positioned above a mouth with row after row of glistening, pointy teeth. I shivered. Whatever I'd seen in the forest wasn't a Merluk. It had to have been some other creature that had also crossed the veil.

Mia knelt to wipe her knife in the grass and looked up at me. "I think you can put that away now." She nodded at my hand, which still held my weapon.

I slid it back into its sheath as she stood to face me. "I want to help."

"You should get some sleep," she replied. Blood dripped down her neck from a cut on her jaw.

I tore off a strip of fabric from the hem of my sleeping tunic and offered it to her.

She pressed the fabric against the gash and gestured to the beast. "Get the arms. I'll get the feet."

As the first rays of sunlight illuminated the horizon, we built pyres for the fallen guards, putting our faith in the stories that said Merluks wouldn't attack in daylight. I still jumped at every unfamiliar sound as I helped to build the large bonfire around the Merluk corpses, using the broken boards from the damaged wagons as kindling. Eventually, we returned to the tent to wash and change and pack our things. By the time the sun crested the horizon, the camp had been dismantled and packed away, and the survivors had gathered around the pyres.

Ezri moved among the crowd, and they fell silent. "These few fought with the strength and courage of Forsla. They died defending us. We honor them and their sacrifice. Inahi guide their souls."

The gathering repeated the blessing, and Mage-ruh stepped forward holding a torch. She cast a handful of coal dust over each of the bodies, then bent to light the branches beneath. As the pyres burned and the gathering stood watching the flames consume the fallen, she walked to the bonfire and set it aflame.

Slowly, the guards dispersed, finding their horses or taking their places in the wagons. I crossed the field to retrieve Arge for the last day of our journey. As I walked, I let my eyes wander across the ground that had so recently been covered in tents, and then in hairy Merluk bodies.

When I found Arge and reached for her reins, I noticed a pattern of purple flowers hidden in the grass near where she had been grazing. I bent over them and realized that they weren't attached to stems. They appeared to have been placed there.

I bent to confirm these were the same delicate six-petal flowers in the same violet hue as I'd found lying on the map the previous morning. Again, there were five of them. This time they were aligned in a sort of zig-zag pattern, with the second placed higher than the first, the third level with the first, the fourth lower, and the fifth level with the first and third.

I searched the heads around me for Ezri but couldn't find him. So, I memorized the way they'd been laid out, collected each of the tiny flowers, and tucked them into the pocket in my cloak. Then I reached for Arge's reins and hoisted myself into the saddle.

I'd just settled myself when Ezri rode up beside me. "Ready, Stormcat?"

I nodded and urged Arge into a walk. Ezri fell in beside me. Mia and Zan joined us, and we took our place in what was left of the caravan of wagons, horses, and people returning to the city.

For once, Ezri didn't look like he wanted to talk. He rode silently, lost in his own thoughts. There wasn't anything I could say that would make him blame himself less. Even the flowers I'd found would have been seen as a failure because, at best, they meant the Inahi had visited us, but too late.

For the first time, I wondered if the gods really had abandoned us. Whatever the flowers meant, the Inahi weren't helping. Something wasn't right, and if we didn't fix it soon, the clans would be wiped from this god-touched land.

13

BY mid-morning, the thick stone walls of Shal City stretched to the sky in front of me. The city was hidden behind them, except for the peaked roof of a large stone structure that rose like a fist with one finger raised, pointing at the sky. Either the building was enormously tall, or they had built it on a bluff overlooking what must be the sea beyond.

I'd yet to see the expanse of blue water I'd heard so much about from my uncle, but the scent of the air changed when we crossed the Lower Stone and entered the stretch of valley that lay on this side of the city walls. Unlike the plains, this valley was rocky and dry with patchy tufts of grass and a scattering of short, gnarled trees.

The wind blew steadily across the land, sucking the moisture from my skin, and whipping up dust from the road. Aside from the fascinating sweet and salty scent of the breeze, I didn't understand why Ruhala's youngest son would have wanted to settle here. Everything was so harsh. Bright sun.

Whipping winds. Parched landscape. But once we were within sight of the city walls, Ezri's mood improved. Or, at least, he sat up straighter in his saddle and paid closer attention to the activity around him.

The closer we got, the easier it was to pick out the guards dressed in black tunics that dotted the top of walls. I had no idea the Shal clan had so many of them. Just the group that had accompanied Ezri combined with the batch on patrol at the wall rivaled the total number of Nahl clan guards. No wonder our elders had been so eager to gain an alliance.

Unfortunately, now that we knew we weren't dealing with raiders after all, I was even more convinced that the Shal clan would be no help. Based on what Ezri had told me, they openly shunned the gods, and I'd seen what the Merluks had done to their guards. They were no better equipped for fighting off Merluks than ours were. Still, the Magery would be our best hope of finding an answer, and it lay inside those walls. So I also sat eager in my saddle as every hoofbeat brought us closer.

As we approached the ribbon of water that surrounded the walls, the pair of guards positioned above the gate blew a steady note through long twin pipes set on either side of the archway. The pipes extended down from above the top of the wall, coming to rest on a stone ledge set into the base of the arch. From there the pipes curled up into a wider bell shape, aimed out at the road. The deep bellow resonating from their upturned ends reminded me of the wind howling across the plains, and a pang of homesickness pierced my excitement.

The effect was fleeting, ruined by the thunderous clatter of horse hooves moving off the soft dirt road and onto the planks of the bridge deck ahead. When it came time for me to guide Arge across the threshold, sunlight flashed off both the water and the smooth stone walls, making everything almost too bright to look at directly. I squinted and blinked as I struggled to maintain my composure in the saddle.

Once we cleared the gate set into the thick stone wall, and the sparkling reflections were behind us, I caught my first glimpse of the houses lined up in rows inside. The stone structure with the tower that I'd seen from outside the walls rose behind them, framed by nothing but the bright blue, cloudless sky. I sucked in my breath at this first view of what I guessed to be Ezri's home.

He must have heard me because he laughed and said, "Impressive, isn't it? If you think that's good, just wait until you're up there, looking out over the sea."

My heart raced at the reminder that, after leaving home and traveling so far with these strangers, I would finally get a glimpse of the sea and waves made of water rather than wheat.

People appeared along the road, emerging from stone houses, leaning out of windows below straw thatch roofs, waving, whispering, standing on tiptoes to get a better look at us as we passed. I tried to remember to smile. I fingered the signet ring my father had given me and reminded myself that, even though it wasn't the real reason I was here, I was representing the Nahl clan.

I sat up straighter, lifting my chest to better display the silver bar that held my cloak closed at my neck, and I let my long, dark braid swing freely at my back, proud of the outward symbols that marked me as a Nahla in this new land of sun-streaked hair and sun-bleached stone.

We followed a wide cobblestone street through the village, with the tower looming ever closer above us. Finally, we passed the last of the houses and villagers and started up a switchback path, which narrowed so only two could ride comfortably abreast. The line of guards ahead of us lengthened as they paired off for the climb. Ezri remained by my side while Mia and the Shal guard captain fell in behind us. As we reached the first bend and turned the corner, I noted the wagons were no longer following us, and Sera had slipped away as well.

When the path straightened, I looked up at the stone structure rising above us, trying to count the floors from the visible windows. "Is this where you grew up?" I asked.

"No one actually lives in the tower." He pointed at the topmost floor. "We station guards up there where they can see out in all directions and alert the city of any approaching danger, either by land or by sea." He returned his hand to the reins and continued to explain. "Below that are the Council chambers. And below them is the reception hall."

We rounded the next bend, and I realized what I had mistaken for one large stone structure was actually a tower surrounded by several smaller buildings.

Ezri pointed again, this time at one of the smaller buildings. "That's the Ruhl House, home of the last Ruhlini and her children. My father inherited responsibility for managing it until the next generation's Ruhl came of age, after my aunt Belyn died. Since the Magery declared me Ruhl, now it's mine."

He surveyed the courtyard as it came into view at the top of the next switchback. Then he pointed to an almost identical structure on the opposite side of the tower. "That's the Shal House. My mother lives there with my uncle Jeln and his son, Jace. That's where I grew up. Mostly."

"Mostly?" I asked.

"It's complicated." Ezri turned to look at me. "The Shal clan has always come first for my mother, while my father felt great guilt over the loss of his older sister. They separated when I was young. Curon, my father, moved out of my mother's Shal House and into the Ruhl House. I've had rooms in both houses for as long as I can remember."

"Oh." I regretted pushing on what was obviously an old wound when the fresh one of the previous evening was still raw. It seemed unnecessarily insensitive. Especially since, if I'd paid better attention to Goff's lectures about clan lineage, I might not have stumbled so easily into such a delicate topic.

Ezri continued, as though he was speaking of someone else, not his own childhood. "My father claimed me as Eldest of the Ruhl line and insisted I be raised at Ruhl House. My mother fussed, but she was much happier tending to clan business than managing an energetic and curious child." He shrugged and turned to point out the other buildings. "Over there are the kitchens and there are the guards' quarters. The Magery is out past the stables and training ground, near the north gate."

"Is that where the wagons went?" I asked, following his lead in changing the subject. "I noticed they are no longer following us."

Ezri nodded. "There is another, less direct route up the other side of the hill. They'll come up near the stables. It's actually faster to go that way, but when the former Shalo, now Ruhl, takes a company of guards off to secure a betrothal, the clan expects a bit of a parade on our return."

My cheeks warmed when he smiled at me. I turned away from the intensity of his eyes, sparkling in the sunshine, to realize we had arrived in the courtyard. The path widened again, and Zan rode up alongside. Mia joined him, and they both dismounted as Tavo, who had been riding ahead with the guards, walked over to meet us.

"My Ruhl," Tavo called in greeting, sneaking a glance at Mia and ignoring me.

Ezri acknowledged Tavo before dismounting and handing his reins to one of the young apprentice guards, who'd run up to assist us. Then he turned to offer me a hand down from my saddle. But I'd already dismounted. As my feet touched the ground, I found myself looking up at him.

A smile broke across his face, and he held my gaze as he said, "Mia, could you show Ayla-nah to her rooms in the Ruhl House so she can freshen up before dinner?"

"Yes, my Ruhl," Mia replied.

Ezri turned to Tavo as the horses were led away. "Tavo-jah, you don't mind relocating to the Shal House this visit, do you?"

Tavo's eyes widened and his nostrils flared as he opened his mouth to respond.

"Good," Ezri said before Tavo could speak. "I'm glad that won't be a problem."

Ezri turned back toward me, capturing both my hands in his. His eyes flicked to my lips, but he hesitated. The corner of his mouth lifted in a sly grin, and he kissed my cheek instead before setting off with Zan toward the tower and leaving me, Tavo, and Mia staring at each other in the courtyard.

"Nahla?" Mia prompted, extending her arm towards the Ruhl House. "This way."

Tavo closed his mouth and pressed his lips into a thin line. His eyes narrowed as he looked back and forth between Mia and me. He was probably wondering if I'd told her what I'd seen.

"See you at dinner, Tavo-jah," I said, and started after Mia.

He caught my arm and held me back. "Watch yourself,

Ayla. Remember where your loyalties lie. I didn't think you, of all people, would be fooled by a charming smile."

"Let go." I wrenched my arm from his grip. "They already believe we're secret lovers, and you're only making it worse."

He took a step back and flipped his long hair over his shoulder. "Just keep your head down, stay out of my way, and do what your father sent you here to do."

I pretended to ignore him as I turned my back on him and walked toward where Mia had stopped to wait for me, hoping my face revealed none of the turmoil boiling inside. Stay away from what? I couldn't risk being caught alone with him, but I needed to find out what he was planning.

#

They had already delivered both of my trunks to the rooms Mia led me to in the Ruhl House. After introducing me to Nye, the woman from the household staff who had been assigned to help me unpack and prepare for dinner, she left.

Nye ushered me through the sitting room and the bedroom to a luxurious bath, where she instructed me to strip down. She scurried away with my soiled traveling clothes as I slid into the warm water and sighed, letting all the tension ooze out of me into the stone tub.

After a thorough scrub, I wrapped myself in the warm robe Nye left for me. Then I wandered back into the bedroom and flipped open the lid on the smaller of my two trunks. I spread out the map Ezri had given me and set it on top of the dresser. Then I retrieved the flowers I'd saved and set them in their places on the map, matching them to where I'd found them as best as I could remember.

I returned to my trunk to find the little notebook of runes that I now believed had belonged to my aunt. Setting aside the smaller boxes of trinkets and supplies that had been placed on top, including the Nahl clan headpiece my mother had given to me, I dug down to the items that lined the bottom. The little notebook was there, along with the book Goff had given me as a going-away present.

Thinking the trunk was empty, I began to close the lid, only to spot a lump of something bunched up in one of the bottom corners. When I lifted it out, I instantly recognized the charm I'd found clutched in Dern's hand after he'd been attacked. So much had happened between then and now that I'd nearly forgotten about it.

The click of the door in the sitting room, followed by Nye's voice announcing her return, pulled me from my thoughts. I returned the charm to the bottom of my small trunk, along with the rune notebook, and closed the lid.

I gathered the wilted flower petals from where I'd set them on the map and pressed them between the pages of the book Goff had given me. Then I turned to search for the larger of my two trunks, the one that held my clothes so I could dress for dinner.

I found it at the end of the enormous bed, under another large trunk that I didn't recognize. I propped open the lid of the unfamiliar trunk. Inside were new garments in an array of colors. Nye entered the bedroom just as I lifted an item off the top of the stack and shook it out.

"What are these?" I asked, examining the dress I held.

"Those are the clothes the Nahlini ordered for you. Shall I hang them while you comb out your hair?" she asked.

I handed her the dress, then sat on the bed to watch as I combed my hair and braided it.

Nye took each item from the trunk and hung them carefully, sighing to herself and running her hands over the delicate fabric. After the dresses came the tunics and leggings, all fashioned in a similar style to my travel costume. Flattering while still functional.

"Which would you prefer to wear for dinner this evening, Nahla?" Nye gestured toward the now-hanging dresses.

The first dress that caught my eye was a pale golden hue that featured wide, bell-shaped sleeves and a long, straight skirt, shaped to allow me full range of motion while still skimming my lean curves. The bodice crossed in a low "V" that wrapped artfully into the flowing fabric of the skirt. Simple. Functional. I touched the fabric. Silky smooth. Now I understood why that woman had been sighing to herself as she hung the dresses.

I scanned the other dresses, admiring the Shal clan dressmaker's work, before returning to the first one. I lifted the dress off the hanger and held it before me, then turned to lay it out on the bed. "This one. This one will do nicely."

Before the fabric could touch the quilt, Nye lifted it from my hands. She gestured for me to remove my robe, then gathered the fabric so she could slip it down over my head. The silky fabric cascaded down across my skin as I slid my arms into the bell-shaped sleeves. After adjusting the bodice and smoothing the skirt, Nye directed me to the mirror and found a chair for me to sit on so she could finish arranging my hair.

Mia arrived just as Nye finished twisting and pinning up my braid. I collected my secret hairpin knives from the top of the dresser where I'd left them and slid them into place. My hand hovered over the Nahl clan signet ring I'd been given. I hesitated before deciding not to wear it and tucking it back into my small trunk.

Mia waited for me at the door to my rooms. She was also wearing a dress, only hers was the same inky black of her guard uniform and embroidered with the Shal rose crest on her chest, above her heart. But I spotted no sign of her twin daggers. Perhaps it was a sign we were finally out of danger, here behind Shal City's stone walls.

"No weapons?" I asked, wondering if perhaps I should have also left the hairpin knives behind.

Mia grinned, the skin of her cheek stretching tight across her old scar. She shifted her leg just enough to reveal the long slits that ran up the sides of her skirt and the black leggings she wore underneath. A sheathed knife adorned each of her boots.

"Follow me," she said, sliding her leg back beneath her skirt. "They'll be waiting."

A wave of fear flooded over me as I realized that the fancy clothes only served as an illusion of safety. Though, unlike on the road, I hadn't the first clue what danger threatened, or how to prepare myself for a dinner that required guards with hidden knives.

Mia led the way down the long hallways of the Ruhl House, and Zan met us outside. Rather than crossing the courtyard to the Shal House, he escorted us to the tower.

"We're eating here?" I asked, wondering if I should have worn my ring after all. Ezri had said the tower was where the Council met.

"We hold all formal dinners here, Nahla," Zan explained. "Tonight's dinner is significant because the Ruhl and the Council members have returned." He turned his head to look at me and frowned slightly. "And then there is also the matter of your status here."

"My status?" I asked, confused.

"Ezri-ruh and your father agreed you would return to the city as Ezri's betrothed. But your father seems to have taken this opportunity to have named you as the Nahl clan's representative in the Council." He dropped his gaze to my hand and a look of surprise crossed his face. He stopped walking, and I had to take a step backward to avoid running into him.

"So, which is it, Nahla?" Zan took a step closer to me, forcing me to turn my head up to maintain eye contact with him. "Are you here to marry the Ruhl? Or to spy for your father?"

The memory of my encounter with Tavo flashed into my mind. I glanced toward Mia, but Zan had positioned himself so I could no longer see her.

I blinked and swallowed before looking up to meet his eyes. "I am here because I agreed to marry the Ruhl. What does it matter if I also represent the Nahl clan on the Council, at least until we are married?"

Zan maintained eye contact with me, not moving or relaxing a muscle, only slightly working his jaw with his lips closed tight. Then he said, "They won't let you do both."

My eyes narrowed. "My father did not consult me in his decision."

"Zan," Mia said.

A flicker of calm passed over Zan's face in response to Mia's voice. "If you're not here to spy for your father, then what were you doing meeting with Tavo-jah before the Merluk attack?"

Ezri walked up and placed a hand on Zan's shoulder. "Is this what's keeping you?" He gestured towards me. "Interrogating my betrothed? If you want to protect me, you'd do better to be on time. You're making Filna-sha angry with your delays, and I'm suffering the consequences."

He tucked my hand into the crook of his arm to lead me away, then lifted his free hand to cover mine, where it rested lightly on the soft blue fabric of his tunic. He turned his head to catch my eye as we walked. "You look stunning this evening."

I breathed a sigh of relief as I looked up at Ezri and remembered that at least he was on my side. "Thank you," I said.

His eyes traveled over my hair and skimmed down my neck before following the line of my bodice to where it plunged toward my skirt. A rush of heat flushed my chest, and I looked away. Without my realizing, we'd stepped inside the tower. I glanced around as my eyes adjusted to the change in light and found that we'd entered what appeared to be the reception hall.

The circular room featured vaulted ceilings and thick white stone columns that marked a slightly smaller circumference about two-thirds from the center of the room. A few sections between columns were closed off from the center room to provide private rooms, separate from the larger space. On the far side of the room, opposite the entrance we'd walked through, an arch had been built into the exterior wall and set with twin oak and iron doors. The doors were pushed open and a cool breeze wafted through, ruffling my hair and pressing the silky fabric of my skirt and sleeves against my skin.

I clenched Ezri's arm and stood on my tiptoes to see what lay beyond the doors. "Is that...?" I asked, still not tearing my eyes from the archway and what I imagined lay beyond.

I could feel Ezri's eyes on me. "The sea?" he asked. "You want to go have a look?"

"Is there time?"

"Well, lucky for you, tonight we will dine on the balcony." I looked up at him with wide eyes and he smiled. "Ready?"

I nodded. As we proceeded across the reception hall, I imagined what it might be like to celebrate Midwinter here, with the hall decorated in black and green to honor Forsla, who ruled the blessing of maturity, and Jusala, who blessed the named. Then I remembered what Ezri had said about his mother banishing their clan mage. Even if they did still celebrate naming and maturity, it wasn't likely the ceremonies would look anything like they did on the plains.

Now that I'd seen where Ezri had grown up, I wasn't surprised that he hadn't been able to find the Inahi. I would need to convince him to leave the city and the Council's politics behind if he wanted to convince the gods to restore the veil.

14

E'D almost reached the archway when the curvy figure of a woman appeared, silhouetted in the opening. "Ezri? Enough already. You're keeping everyone waiting."

"We're on our way, Mother," Ezri replied.

The Shal shifted in the doorway. She made a brief sound of either acknowledgment or dismissal, then placed one hand on her hip and lifted a goblet to her lips.

I stiffened, and my grip on Ezri's arm tightened. In my excitement about setting my eyes on the sea, I'd forgotten for a moment that we would be joining others of the household for dinner.

He caressed the back of my hand in a soothing motion. "Relax. It will be fine."

I looked up at him, and he smiled and winked at me. I released the breath I had been holding in and took another. When I looked back at the archway, the Shal turned away and walked back out onto the balcony, out of view.

"You needn't fear her," Ezri whispered to me. "She won't bite."

I knew a bit about mothers and sons from watching my mother fuss over my older brothers, and I remembered what Ezri had said about the Shal's feelings about gods and folklore. I suspected Ezri was just trying to make me feel better, which I appreciated. But I still braced myself for our introduction.

We stepped out of the tower and onto the balcony, where a salty breeze caught the stray hairs that framed my face and swept them across my forehead. In front of us, beyond the thick stone railing of the balcony, lay the mixed blues of water and sky. I turned my face into the wind and breathed in, resisting the undignified urge to run to the railing. Instead, I pulled my gaze away from the blue horizon and scanned the other people mingling around the long wooden table set for dinner.

"Ah! See, Filna-sha? Here he is. Our Ezri-ruh, returned." A man dressed in a pale pink tunic walked toward us. An embroidered rose pattern stitched in a rich shade of plum wrapped around the collar and continued down the front placard, ending just above his round belly. "And this must be the Nahla."

He stopped in front of us and reached for my free hand, bringing it to his lips to place a dry kiss on the back of it. I smiled and bobbed my head.

"Cala-nah, is it?" he asked. My smile disappeared for a moment in shock, but I forced it back into place and was forming a reply when Ezri spoke.

"Ayla-nah, Uncle."

The man's eyes narrowed slightly. He inclined his head and repeated, "Ayla-nah," stressing my given name. Then he looked from me to Ezri. "You chose the younger girl?"

A woman in a long, jewel-green dress, tied at the back with a grey ribbon that wrapped under her full bust, sashayed forward and snaked her arm around the man's, pressing herself to his side. She pouted as she appraised me through narrowed eyes and long lashes.

Ezri ignored his uncle's comment and turned to me. "Ayla-nah, may I present my uncle, Jeln-sha and his partner, Vie."

"Vie-sha," Jeln corrected.

"Apologies, Uncle." Ezri cocked his head to one side. "Did I miss your wedding while I was away? Congratulations are in order, then."

I glanced at Ezri out of the corner of my eye, searching for a hint that might help me decipher the note of sarcasm I detected in his voice.

The glare Vie fixed on Ezri confirmed my suspicions. Rather than confront him, she snatched her hand away from her partner's arm and pivoted to stalk away.

Jeln reddened and sputtered as he stared after her, torn between following Vie or responding to his nephew.

"Ah, well. There's still time." Ezri tsked at his uncle, then dipped his head and guided me away.

"What was that about?" I whispered to him.

"He was being rude to you." Ezri steered me toward the other guests standing near the railing of the balcony, and I caught the eye of a young man as we walked past. He had been watching us with a lopsided grin. The mischief in his eyes reminded me of Kilm.

"Who's that?" I asked, nodding toward the young man and returning his smile.

"Jace-sha. Jeln's son," he said. "The new Shal clan heir."

"Really?" I wondered why he seemed to enjoy watching

Ezri insult his father. Tavo's warning whispered to me. After only my first introduction, I was already feeling like he and Goff had been right. I told myself it was only a dinner. I could manage without making my clan look foolish.

"Mother," Ezri called out as we neared a woman whose form matched the one I'd just seen outlined in the archway. Her thick, wavy hair was cropped close to her head, and she was shorter than she'd appeared in silhouette. As we approached, she turned away from the two women speaking with her near her near the balcony's railing.

"Mother, may I introduce you to Ayla-nah?" Ezri turned to me and said, "Ayla-nah, my mother, Filna-sha, the Shal."

I held my hands up, slightly in front of me with my palms open and facing the Shal in the traditional clan greeting I'd been taught. I bowed my head slightly, breaking eye contact, and waited for her to clasp my hands. Nervous that I had done something wrong and embarrassed myself, I lifted my head. As I did, her hands finally touched mine. She folded her fingers around my palms, and I folded mine around her small, plump hands in response.

"She honors the traditions," Filna-sha said, as she released my hands and reached to retrieve her goblet from the railing. "Interesting selection, Ezri."

The other two women shifted and fidgeted, waiting for their introduction, but Ezri ignored them and frowned at his mother. "Does it matter so little to you, Mother?"

"In this, you are your father's son, truly. You know what I think, and now is hardly the time to revisit the subject." She took a sip from her glass and looked up at him, placing her free hand on her rounded hip.

"If you feel the need to bring this..." She jabbed her chin in my direction. "Dirt-loving, nomadic traditionalist here to further your plans, then so be it. But don't expect me to take an interest. And don't keep our guests waiting for dinner."

Filna-sha nodded at her companions and brushed past me on her way to the dining table. The two women drifted around us to follow her.

I flinched away from her as she passed, stung by her hateful words, but unsurprised by yet another chilly reception. I turned my head away from the guests and looked out over the sparkling water, unwilling to let Ezri's clan ruin my first glimpse of the overwhelming expanse of water that crashed against the cliffs below.

Ezri reached for my hand and wrapped his warm fingers around mine. "She didn't mean that," he said, moving closer to my side.

I swallowed and blinked, then glanced at him with watery eyes and forced a smile. "Sounded pretty convincing to me."

His smile widened. I couldn't tell if this was a performance for the dinner guests, or if he was amused by my response.

"She just doesn't understand." He hooked a finger under my chin and tilted my face up to his. "Don't worry. Once we find them, she'll see."

"If she doesn't think you should try to find the Inahi, what does she want you to do? Does she know about the veil?" My vision had cleared and the sting from the Shal's insults was beginning to feel more like anger.

Ezri's eyes quickly skimmed the crowd, then returned to lock with mine. "We'll discuss it in the Council meeting tomorrow," he said, keeping his voice low.

I looked past him, out to the sea. "We should be riding out to the forest tomorrow," I whispered.

"Soon, Stormcat." Ezri tugged me closer and wrapped his arm around my waist. Then he guided me back toward the dining table where the others were gathering and taking their seats.

As we walked, I glimpsed Tavo standing alone, off to the side of the group. He shook his head and stalked away when he caught me looking at him. He would surely report back to Vorn about my encounter with the Shal, and then my father and Goff would hear of it as well. It was another reminder that I had no idea how my reception affected their plans because they didn't think it was worth informing me of them.

"After the Council meeting?" I asked. My eyes drifted to the table, where almost everyone was already seated.

As I watched, Tavo slid into the chair just to the right of the empty seat at the head of the table. He met my gaze, raised an eyebrow, then leaned toward the woman seated next to him and said something that made her laugh.

Since Ezri's mother already occupied the seat at the opposite end of the table, flanked by the women who'd witnessed her insulting me, I guessed that empty chair was for Ezri. Unfortunately, the seat directly to the left of it was also already occupied. There was only one other unoccupied chair, midway down the side looking out at the sea.

I tensed, and Ezri paused.

"Are you all right?" he asked. "I could ask—"

"I'll be fine." I cut him off before he could suggest making a fuss and rearranging the seating. Asking people to move so I could remain within reach of Ezri's protection would make me look weak. I could survive one dinner alone.

After Ezri helped me slide my chair into the table, he bent to place a kiss on my cheek, then walked to the head of the table to claim his place. Zan helped him slide into his chair, and then took a step backward, his eyes constantly surveying.

With almost twenty people at the table, my position near the center kept me well away from the need to make casual conversation with the Shal, but it also prevented me from speaking with Ezri. I turned to my right and almost jumped when I recognized the young man sitting next to me.

"Greetings, Ayla-nah," he said, his lips twisting into the grin I'd seen earlier. "I don't believe we've had a chance to be introduced."

"You're Jace-sha," I said, remembering. "Jeln-sha's son."

His smile widened. "Yes. Though I hope you don't hold that against me."

Unsure how to respond, I took a moment to glance around the table. "It is nice to be seated next to a friendly face. Though, I'll admit, I wasn't expecting a formal dinner so soon after our arrival. Do you often dine in such large parties?"

"I believe you will come to see, Nahla, that here in the city, where two deeply entwined households live across the courtyard from each other, daily orbiting this massive tower, the gravitational pull of even a simple family dinner attracts anyone with enough density to believe they might influence those two powerful forces."

"It appears you have devoted some thought to this topic," I replied.

"When one has spent most of their life as an insignificant outer moon, one has some time to think. And, of course, to be buffeted about by forces beyond one's control." Jace lifted his goblet from the table and raised it toward me.

I lifted my goblet to return the gesture as I asked, "And, you, I presume, are this outer moon being buffeted about?"

"We might in fact have that in common, Nahla." He tapped the edge of his goblet against mine and raised his eyebrows as he grinned at me.

I looked from him to his father, who sat at the end near the Shal, and was leaning toward her. The look on his face was intense and his hands gestured emphatically, but he spoke in a tone low enough that his voice didn't carry to our ears.

Jace's eyes followed my gaze. "He'll probably be annoyingly pleased that Ezri-ruh sat you next to me and interpret that as a positive sign. But you never know with our Ruhl." He sighed, and his smile drifted into a sullen pout. "Could be he's just realized that all the other insignificant moons at this table would use what little gravity they have to absorb you and leverage you to their advantage."

The older woman seated on my other side leaned around me to speak to Jace. "Enough. They're not that bad, and you know it. No sense in frightening the girl."

Jace flicked an eyebrow at the woman and pursed his lips. "Yes. Because they've been so kind to you, haven't they, Mage-sha?"

The elderly mage sucked in a long breath and appeared to grow taller in her chair. Her voice, when she spoke, boomed low and directional, aimed precisely at her target. "Young pup, you know nothing of what I've been through with this family. Where you see moons, I see Estrel's stars." She paused. "Remember who you are. Both of you," she added, before returning to her meal.

Her words sent a tingling down my spine and stirred a guilty feeling in my gut. She was right. And the last thing I wanted was to make a poor impression on the Shal clan's mage, even if the Shal had limited the woman's duties and banished her to the Magery. Perhaps especially then.

Jace and I both sat up straighter. We ate in small, proper, measured bites, listening to the burble of conversation around us. It didn't take long for our silence to prompt others sitting nearby to begin asking me questions.

They wanted to know more about my clan and my home-land. Their ideas about life on the plains were a far cry from reality. One woman wanted to know if we ate nothing but raw meat. Her partner marveled at my comment about how we had trained birds to carry messages across long distances. I did my best to hide my frustration at their lack of knowl-edge about life outside the city walls.

I smiled and nodded at their comments and tried not to laugh at Jace's sarcastic asides and explanations about who was who, which kept me entertained through the many courses of fish and fruit, hard breads and soft cheeses, unlike anything I'd ever tasted before.

"Jace," I whispered, toward the end of the dinner, looking at the mound of white dripping with red sauce on my plate. "What is this?"

"This?" Jace asked. "Have you never had fruit ice before?"

"Fruit ice," I wondered aloud.

"You eat it with your spoon," he said, pointing to the as yet unused utensil next to my plate. I lifted my spoon and reached with it to pierce through the thick sauce and lift some of the white substance.

"Wait," Mage-sha said as she noticed what I was about to do.

I paused, spoon in mid-air, and looked up at her. I hadn't realized she'd been listening to our conversation.

"Have a sip of that first," she said, pushing a small glass toward me. "Swirl it around your mouth and swallow. Then take a spoonful of the fruit ice." She smiled with the excite-ment of a small child as she instructed me.

Still holding the spoon in one hand, I lifted the delicate etched glass to my lips and inhaled the musky, dried fruit smell as I sipped. The liquid tingled as I swirled it in my mouth and burned my throat as I swallowed. Slipping the spoonful of white and red into my mouth, I sighed as the cool fruity flavors seeped into my tongue.

"I still remember my first taste of fruit ice," Mage-sha said, watching me as I swallowed that first bite.

"You don't have fruit ice on the plains?" asked Jace.

"No," I said, as I lifted my glass to my lips so I could repeat the experience.

"Fruit ice is a delicacy of the Shal," she explained. "No ice on the plains, and no fruit in the mountains."

I nodded as I lifted the glass to my lips for the third time.

"Careful." Jace pressed his fingers against my wrist, stopping me. "That is some powerful liquor in that cup."

My tongue had already felt heavy and thick, but I'd thought it might have been the cold fruit ice. At home on the plains we had several fermented beverages made of the grains from the fields, but I was only ever allowed to drink the watery kinds, never the clear, still liquids my father shared with visitors after dinner.

I took his advice and left the cup on the table as I finished the fruit ice, scraping the plate clean with my spoon. When I finished and looked up, I realized that Jace and I were the only two left sitting at the table. Mage-sha was gone. Ezri's mother had moved to the far end of the balcony with a few others, including Ezri. And the rest of the guests were making their way toward the tower.

As I watched from my seat, Mia stepped behind my chair and set a hand on my shoulder. "Nahla, the Ruhl asked me to tell you he will be busy for some time. He wanted you to know that the Council will meet after breakfast tomorrow."

A wave of something like relief at having survived the evening washed over me, clashing with the disappointment I felt at having been abandoned by Ezri.

Jace shifted in his chair to face me. "Ayla-nah, it was a pleasure dining with you this evening. I hope we will see each other again soon."

"I'd like that." I stood and lifted my hands with palms facing him.

He stood facing me and grasped my hands, bowing his head low. When he straightened, he lifted the etched glass from where I'd left it on the table and handed it to me. "If you find that you have trouble sleeping, just finish this."

"Ready, Nahla?" Mia asked, once Jace left.

"Are you going to walk me back to my rooms?" I asked.

"Yes, Nahla."

I frowned at Ezri's back, where he stood at the far end of the balcony. "And have you been instructed to make sure I stay there?"

Zan, who was standing near Ezri, turned his head to look straight at us.

"Yes, Nahla," Mia replied.

"I see." I took a sip from the glass and swallowed. "Well, let's go then."

Mia walked toward the archway. Just before I turned to follow her, Ezri glanced back at me. It was too far and growing too dark to tell, but I thought I caught a look of apology, or perhaps longing, cross his face before he returned his attention to the group he'd been speaking with.

I followed Mia in silence, back through the tower to the courtyard, as I replayed the night's events in my mind. The Shal's insults stung, but Zan's accusations hurt more than Filna-sha's name calling. I wanted to know if Mia also had concerns. If she trusted me, or if Ezri was the only one who did.

"Mia, do you think I'm a spy?" I asked.

She remained quiet for several strides before finally saying, "I don't know, Nahla."

"I'm not." I sighed and covered my face with my free hand, then dropped it to my side, fingers balled into a fist. "Is it because of Tavo-jah? I told you I had no idea he was out there last night."

Mia didn't respond and remained silent until we were almost at the door to my rooms. Then she stopped and faced me. "There are many who would like to harm the Ruhl. Relations between the clans have been deteriorating for years now. You must understand. His safety comes first for Zan. For me."

She watched my face for a reaction, but I waited for her to continue. "Ezri-ruh says he trusts you and we must keep you safe while you're here. We were ordered to keep you safe, as though you are an extension of him."

"I see," I replied.

At least Ezri trusted me. That was something. But I still wondered if he truly cared for me, or if it was just an act. Tavo was right about that much. Ezri was charming, and I barely knew him. Yet, I'd given up my home and my love and my family to be here. All to find the Inahi. To save the clans from the dangers beyond the crumbling veil.

I wanted to explain that to Mia. I wanted to tell her that if Ezri hadn't begged for my help, I wouldn't even be here. But doing so would break my promise to Ezri.

Instead, I met her eyes once more and said one last time, "I may be the dirt-loving, nomadic traditionalist that the Shal believes me to be, but I'm not a spy, Mia."

I stepped past her, into the main room of the suite they had settled me into, and closed the door to the hall behind me. With a sigh, I slid the hairpin knives out of my braids and returned them to my small trunk in the bedroom. After returning the signet ring Father gave me to its place on my finger, I paced back into the main room and stood at the doors that led to a small balcony overlooking the courtyard.

Perhaps it didn't matter if none of the others trusted me. I didn't need them to find the Inahi. I only needed Ezri. Once the gods agreed to repair the veil, I could go home and put all this behind me. But there would be a Council meeting in the morning. I would need to get through that first.

Nye knocked, pulling me from my thoughts, and entered my suite to help me undress and prepare for bed. I traded my silk gown for a newly woven soft tunic and leggings. Then I let her brush out my hair and re-braid it in one long column. When she finished, I sent her off and resumed my pacing, fingering my ring as the Shal's insults repeated in my mind.

Filna-sha was right. I was a traditionalist, and so were my people. I'd always been proud of that, but I could see now that the Shal clan might have almost as much disdain for those of us who honored the gods as we did for those who ignored them. At least I would be prepared for her insults when I faced her again at the Council meeting in the morning.

It only bothered me a little that I didn't know what the Council was meeting to discuss. Despite what Zan thought, I wasn't here to play at politics on behalf of my clan. I was here to help Ezri find the Inahi. That was all. But, alone in my room and farther from the forest than even the Jahl clan's caverns, high in the mountains, there wasn't much I could do besides pace and worry.

Unfortunately, my knowledge of our legends and gods would not help me in the Council. I was good at gathering information and making sense of it, but not at trading witty remarks—something that seemed to come naturally to Ezri. He'd stepped in with both his uncle and his mother, buying me time to compose myself. With the right knowledge, I might recover faster and do better than paste on a polite smile. Alternatively, I could ignore their jabs and focus my attention on finding the Inahi and going home.

Returning to the bedroom, I ran my hand over the cover of the book Goff had given me. The title read *Clan History: Lineages, Politics, and Magery.* Though I was certain there was information within that would help me improve my diplomatic skills, it was the flowers pressed between its pages that I was most interested in.

I laid the map out on the bed, placing one set of flowers on top of the map and the other set directly on the blanket to recreate the way they'd been arranged when I'd found them. Ezri still didn't know about the flowers I'd found after the Merluk attack. I needed to tell him. But maybe I could figure out what they were saying first.

I unlocked my small trunk to retrieve the notebook Magenah had given me. Placing the flowers had given me an idea. I'd been scratching runes on the rock near my offering. If the Inahi were trying to communicate a message with the flowers they'd been leaving for me, perhaps they were replying in runes. It was worth checking.

When I lifted the notebook out of the trunk, the charm I'd found in Dern's hand came with it. I started to put it back, then I noticed the symbol carved into the rectangular stone hanging from the leather cord. It looked a bit like a rune, but not one that I was familiar with, and not one that matched the shape of the flowers. Still, as long as I had the notebook out to study the runes, I could search for the symbol on the charm as well. Perhaps it would give me some clue as to what it was for and why Dern was carrying it.

Once everything was in place, I settled back against the pillows with the notebook. I'd waited days to study the contents of this slim journal. And that was before I knew my aunt had created it. An aunt I hadn't known existed and who lived in the Magery, where I hoped to study after I found the Inahi. No wonder Ezri had so easily agreed to my demands.

But before I could secure my future, I needed to understand why the Inahi had not only ignored our request for a meeting, but allowed a band of Merluks to attack our camp instead. I flipped open the cover and began.

15

AT first, I thought the voice that broke through my dreams came from the creature stalking toward me, clicking together the long, sharp claws that extended from each of its fingers. Then the voice said, "Nahla, you will be late if you don't get up now," and the creature disappeared, replaced by the darkness of my closed eyelids and the realization that it was morning, and Nye was here to help me dress for my first Council meeting.

I turned my face toward the warm sunlight and inhaled the sea breeze that blew through the open window. When I finally opened my eyes and sat up, I spotted Nye waiting in the doorway to my bedroom. It was a good thing she'd come to wake me. I'd stayed up much too late, and I might have slept straight through the Council meeting. But she didn't leave once she saw I was awake. She set a small basket of bread on the top of the dresser, then just stood there, waiting.

"Have you been assigned to help me dress every day?" I asked.

"Yes, Nahla," she replied.

"I appreciate your help." I chose my words carefully so I wouldn't offend her. "But tell me, does everyone in Ruhl House and Shal House have someone to help them dress?"

"No, Nahla. Only the Ruhl and the Shal. But you are to be married to the Ruhl, and Ezri-ruh instructed the house staff to treat you as we treat him."

"I see." I swung my legs over the side of the bed and stretched. I'd have to talk with Ezri about it. But in the meantime, it didn't seem wise to send her away. "Well, I suspect you know more than I do about appropriate attire for Council meetings. What do you suggest?"

While Nye considered the options in my new wardrobe, I scooped up the books from my bedside table and deposited them on the dresser next to my small trunk.

"I've selected a few items from your wardrobe for you to choose from, Nahla," she said.

When I turned to look, I found she'd hung a few embroidered tunics on the wardrobe door. The one that immediately caught my eye was golden, a similar shade as the dress I'd worn to dinner. It reminded me of the grass on the plains at this time of year. The cuffs of both sleeves and the V-shaped bodice were embroidered with a warm orange thread, laced with strands of silver. The combined effect looked like sun rays bursting out over the horizon at dawn. Brown leggings and a wide brown and green belt, woven through with silver threads, completed the outfit.

The colors seemed fitting. Yellow was Solnat's color, representing abundance and family. Green belonged to Jusala and stood for justice and diplomacy, while orange was the color of the Nahl clan, and the stitching reminded me of the sun rays embroidered on the black tunics of our guards. The combined hues would send a powerful message.

I ran my fingers over the silver threads in the belt and confirmed they were the same as those in my travel belt, meant to provide a lightweight armor. My clan had spared no expense to ensure my safety. And yet, the Ruhl House and the tower were both well-guarded. Aside from my less than warm welcome, I couldn't imagine what danger they expected me to find in a fortress that sat high on a bluff in a city surrounded by thick stone walls.

With Nye's help, I dressed quickly. After slipping my soft leather boots over the leggings, I slid the Nahl clan signet ring onto my finger. Then Nye helped me arrange my hair in a series of braids that formed a crown on my head. Mia arrived as she finished tucking the last strands into place.

"Nahla," Mia said, bowing to me.

"Good morning, Mia." I stood and turned to face her, remembering our last conversation. I searched her face for some sign that she'd had a change of heart and decided to believe me, but she kept her face unreadable. "I was wondering... I'd like to continue my training and practice the forms you and Zan started teaching me during our travels. Do you think we could train together later?"

"I train at dawn with the other guards, Nahla," Mia responded.

"I see," I said, letting my disappointment show on my face. "I guess I'll need to make other arrangements."

Mia pursed her lips and sighed. "I'll talk with Zan. He wanted you to train. He shouldn't mind me spending a few hours working with you. I'm assigned to watch you, anyway."

Her offer didn't contain any of the enthusiasm that I'd been hoping for, but it was better than nothing, and maybe it would give me a chance to win her over, eventually. "Great!"

I caught my excitement and tried for a more controlled response. "I mean…"

"Come, Ayla-nah." Mia allowed a small smile to flash across her lips before she turned away to open the door for me. "You don't want to be late to your first Council meeting."

"Thank you, Mia." I grabbed one of the swirled buns out of the basket of bread Nye had brought for me before slipping out past her into the hallway.

I bit into the slightly sweet bread, savoring it as I chewed, and led the way, retracing our path from the previous evening, down the long hall and across the courtyard to the tower. Inside the grand hall, Mia pointed me toward a staircase that climbed to the Council chambers above. She stood aside at the top of the stairs as I entered through the stone archway into a circular room where the others were already gathered. She remained there, outside the door, when Zan closed it behind me.

I scanned the room and realized that I'd been the last Council member to arrive. Filna-sha stood near the opposite end of the circular room, looking out one of the window slits that sliced into the thick stone walls of the tower. Ezri leaned over the back of a nearby chair, talking with Tavo. A woman who I recognized as one of the pair who had been talking with Filna-sha on the balcony sat opposite Ezri and shuffled through a stack of papers.

At the sound of the door closing, Ezri looked up from his conversation and walked over to intercept me. Tavo reclined in his chair and turned to watch. Ezri placed a quick kiss on each of my cheeks and slipped an arm around my waist to lead me to the table.

"Can we begin now?" Filna asked without turning.

"Yes, Mother," Ezri replied. "Come join us at the table." He held a chair out for me, and I slipped into it.

"I'm perfectly comfortable over here, thank you," she replied, tapping her fingers against the stone on the window ledge, still gazing out across the city, at what, I could only imagine.

"Suit yourself." Ezri relaxed into the chair he'd been leaning against when I entered. He looked over at the woman with the papers. "I call this meeting to order. Pin, will you please announce our first and only order of business for today?"

Pin gathered the pages of parchment and straightened them. She shot a glance at me over the top of the parchment, but her eyes quickly darted away when they met mine. "My Ruhl, there are two items on the list that was submitted to me. I believe the first order of business is your intended."

A flash of surprise crossed Ezri's face. He reached for my hand across the table before he spoke. "I see. The Nahl has agreed to my marriage to his daughter, Ayla-nah. The ceremony will take place after the Midwinter festival."

"After Midwinter?" Filna asked, finally turning from the window and stalking to the table to stand near her son. "What nonsense is this? If you're going to marry her, let's just get it over with. Why must we wait?"

Ezri clenched his jaw as he looked up to meet his mother's gaze. She'd positioned herself between Ezri and Tavo, and since the Jahlo could no longer see Ezri, he stared at me instead.

Tavo raised an eyebrow and lifted the corner of his mouth as though we were sharing a joke. Since I wasn't sure exactly what he found so amusing, I ignored him and returned my attention to Ezri, waiting for his response.

"That was my agreement with the Nahl. We would wait

until after Midwinter, when Ayla-nah comes of age," he said.

Filna made a hissing sound as she took a step closer to her son and gripped his shoulder. "And yet Teron-nah sends this child to sit on the Council and represent her clan. If she is old enough to do that, she is old enough to marry," she said, her voice sharp.

Ezri's eyes narrowed, and the Shal softened her voice to a purr. "Ezri—my Ruhl—these terms are not acceptable."

"Unfortunately, these are not your terms to accept or decline. This is between me and the Nahl, and I agreed."

"Then you, my son, are a fool." She released his shoulder and paced back to the window.

Ezri scowled at her back. "Your objection is noted. Now, do you have anything else to add? Or can we move on to the real reason we agreed to meet today?"

Filna spun around and leaned against the windowsill. She raised her eyebrows, studied her nails, and said, without looking up, "Either she is a member of this Council, representing the Nahl clan's interests, or she is your betrothed. As far as I am concerned, she cannot be both. I suggest you end this arrangement or marry her immediately. Enough of these games." She let her eyes lift briefly to meet Ezri's before looking back down at her hand.

Tavo shifted in his seat and caught my eye. He stared at me intently, as though encouraging me to speak, but I had no idea what to say. There seemed to be no point in arguing with her. If she didn't approve of me sitting on the Council, she'd need to wait for Father to send someone else before they could discuss whatever it was Ezri had called this meeting for. That was fine with me because I didn't want this role, and the more time I spent sitting in a stuffy tower discussing politics, the less time I had to find the Inahi.

Tavo coughed as though clearing his throat, breaking the awkward silence. "My Ruhl, the Shal has a valid point."

My mouth dropped open. That was not what I'd expected him to say after his warning me to remember my loyalties. I'd been told the Nahl and Jahl clans always aligned themselves together against the Shal clan.

Tavo leaned forward and smiled at me. "You two are so obviously in love, I don't see any good reason to wait. Surely the Nahl could be convinced to agree, don't you think so, Ayla-nah?"

If he was aligned with my father, I didn't understand why he would push for me to marry Ezri right away. Either I really didn't understand what my father was doing, which was entirely possible, or Tavo was up to something else. Given his increasingly odd behavior, there had to be another reason that he wanted the Council to proceed without me, or my clan's involvement.

As I opened my mouth to respond, I glimpsed a stone pendant hanging from a leather cord around his neck. The flat rectangular stone was barely visible, poking out through the V in the neckline of his tunic. It looked nearly identical to the one I'd found clutched in Dern's hand after he'd been attacked. Except I couldn't tell if Tavo's charm, if that was what it was, had any markings etched onto the surface.

I sucked in a breath at the sight before mastering my composure enough to counter his response. "If Ezri-ruh wasn't able to convince my father, I can't imagine that he would change his mind about me being too young just because I asked. Especially when Midwinter is less than two moons away."

"Too young. Please," Filna scoffed. "That's ridiculous. Delna-ruh married the Jahl when she was just fifteen. Your father knows this better than anyone." She narrowed her eyes at me. "Games."

"All right." Ezri leaned back and shoved his hand into his already tousled hair. "If neither of you agree to allowing Ayla-nah to represent the Nahl clan, then Ayla-nah, I suppose I must request that you write to the Nahl and ask him to send a replacement. Or give up the Nahl clan's right to a seat on the Council of Clans."

"Or dissolve the betrothal," Filna-sha added. The corners of her mouth twitched upward as her eyes met mine across the room.

I ignored her. "Of course, my Ruhl. If you'll excuse me, I'll take care of that right away."

Ezri's hand slapped down on top of mine as I pushed my chair back from the table and prepared to stand. "No. Stay. Please."

"My Ruhl?" I hesitated.

Ezri locked eyes with me. He took a breath, then exhaled. "Until the Nahl responds, Ayla-nah will remain as the Nahl clan representative. Now, perhaps we can discuss the other, more pressing item on the agenda? Pin?" Ezri prompted.

"Of course, my Ruhl." Pin shifted her papers. "The next and last topic on the list is the report filed by the captain of the Shal guard regarding the attack that occurred during your recent travels."

"Yes." Ezri slid his hand from mine and pressed his palms flat on the table. "Merluks attacked our camp. They killed five of our guards before retreating."

"Correct." Tavo folded his arms across his chest. "And you're the Ruhl. The solution is obvious, is it not? I assume you have spoken with the Inahi and asked Estrel to repair the veil?"

"Don't be ridiculous," Filna said. "We don't need gods to solve this problem. We'll just double the size of the guard and increase patrols at the city walls."

"But what of those on the plains and in the mountains?" Ezri asked. "If the veil falls, the Nahl and Jahl clans will be vulnerable to attack. They don't have stone walls to protect them."

"Then they should build some and begin acting like civilized creatures," Filna said. "Why must we support them?"

Tavo turned to Filna. "I agree that the Shal clan has no duty to defend us. And, to be clear, we have no desire of your protection." He looked at Ezri. "But, my Ruhl, we do expect that you will do whatever is in your power to restore the veil. If the Inahi can help, then you must go to them." He smiled. "You are, after all, the eldest of your line, are you not?"

"Perhaps the Jahl clan does not wish for help, but you only speak for your clan. The Nahl did request a dispatch of guards." Ezri's voice crackled with anger. "And I intend to see that he gets the reinforcements he needs."

"Wouldn't your time be better spent speaking with the gods, my Ruhl?" Tavo asked, his tone almost taunting.

"I will also consult the Inahi and ask for their help." He paused and coughed. "This meeting is over." He leaned back in his chair and slipped his hand into a pocket in his tunic.

Zan opened the door in response to Ezri's proclamation. Filna-sha exhaled in a loud huff, shot a glance at her son, and stalked to the door. She pushed past Zan and retreated down the stairs. Pin followed quickly in her wake, followed by Tavo.

Ezri and I remained seated at the table. Once the others were gone, Ezri leaned back and closed his eyes.

"Ezri." I leaned toward him and reached for his hand.

"Welcome to Council, Stormcat," he said, then opened his eyes and grinned. "Let's leave this stuffy tower and go find something more enjoyable to do, shall we?"

"Wait." I glanced at Zan and then at the open door where Mia still stood with her eyes on the stairs. "We need to talk, and it may be easier to do it here, now that we're alone."

Ezri looked at Zan for a moment until it appeared they'd reached some sort of silent agreement. Then he turned back to face me.

"I have a better idea. It's not the forest, but there's some-place I want to show you." He leaned toward me across the table and lifted my hand to his lips. His silky hair brushed the back of my hand as his lips touched my skin.

The combined effect sent a shiver down my spine. I hadn't forgotten that the last time we were alone together, he'd kissed me.

"Is it the Shal clan library?" I asked. "Because I think we should go there next."

"Let's get outside for a bit first. Mia and Zan can join us." He leaned toward me and added in a whisper, loud enough for Zan to hear, "I'm sure they wouldn't let us out of their sight anyway."

A mix of relief and disappointment twisted in my gut. While that probably meant there wouldn't be any kissing, it didn't sound like he was in much of a hurry to follow up on his declaration to the Council.

"What did you have in mind, my Ruhl?" Zan asked.

"I think we should show Ayla-nah the cave." Ezri tucked my hand around his arm and led me past Zan and Mia and down the steps. "I'm glad you chose sensible clothes for our meeting today," he said as we stepped into the sunlight. "I don't think we would have had time for you to change. As it is, we don't have much time."

Zan hurried after us, with Mia trailing close behind him. "Are you sure about this, my Ruhl? The tides..."

Ezri waved a hand and cut him off. "Zan, you worry too much. Let's stop in the kitchens so you can convince Mamma Fae to part with a basket of food. We don't have time to wait for lunch." He looked again at the angle of the sun in the sky and then began walking toward one of the stone buildings that surrounded the tower.

The kitchens were much like the kitchens in our compound at home. Bakers and cooks bustled about, tending to their creations. Ezri led us through the chaos and walked up to a large woman with her hair tucked up under a close-fitted cap. She was stirring a deep pot over the smoldering fire in an enormous stone hearth. She didn't look up as we approached, but when we were within an arm's reach she spoke. "Ezri-ruh, what are you doing in my kitchen? Do I need to remind you of your effect on my staff? Or will a burnt dinner be a better lesson for you?"

Someone close behind me snorted. I turned my head to be sure I'd heard correctly and found Zan stifling a laugh. The woman looked up at the sound.

"And you!" she said. "You let him in here? You should know better!"

"Sorry, Ma," he said. "You know how he is."

"Oh, Mia, my love, what happened to you out on the road? Come here and let me see that scratch." She set down her ladle and beckoned to Mia.

"It's nothing, Ma," Mia said, even as she stepped closer so that the cook could examine the deep gash on her neck. Only the tip of it was visible, just above the collar of her tunic, but somehow this woman had spotted the injury from half a room away.

The cook muttered to herself as she examined the wound. "That mage gave you something for it, yes?"

"Yes, Ma, she saw to it right away."

"Good. Good." She turned back to Ezri and added, "Well, out with it. What do you want?"

"Mamma Fae, this is Ayla-nah, my betrothed. I was hoping to take her on a picnic. Mia and Zan will join us, of course, to keep us out of trouble." He grinned at Fae. I was beginning to realize this was his signature maneuver for getting whatever he wanted. "Could you send us off with one of your delightful baskets?"

"Keep you out of trouble." Fae huffed as she reached up to a high shelf to retrieve a basket. "As though that were possible." She shook her head as she snatched up a loaf of bread and a few pieces of fruit. "Too handsome for your own good." She hurried away, disappearing inside an adjacent room, then returning with several items wrapped in cloth. "Your father let you get away with anything. Only child." She tucked another cloth over the top of the basket before shoving it into Ezri's outstretched arms. "Spoiled. That's what you are."

"I couldn't agree more," Ezri said, laughing.

"You'll be back for dinner," she added, more command than question.

"I wouldn't miss it," Ezri said. He gave her a slight bow and reached for my hand. "Now, I should clear out of your kitchens and let you work." He pulled me along behind him as he made for the nearest door.

On the way, I noted the kitchen staff whispering to each other and the young women trying to hide their blushing stares. Behind us, Zan and Mia had been pulled into a motherly embrace. They escaped with promises to return soon.

Once we were outside again, I turned to Zan. "So you do have a sense of humor."

Ezri threw his head back and laughed. "Only around his mother."

Zan scowled.

"That was your mother?" I stared at Zan, searching for a resemblance. "I thought that was just a nickname."

"In a way, it is," Ezri explained. "Mamma Fae adopts all the strays. She took Zan in when he was just a baby, and when Zan and I found Mia, she took Mia in, too."

"Mamma Fae is the kindest, most generous person I know," Mia said.

"Wise, too," Ezri said. "And she makes the best bread. My stomach is rumbling just thinking about it." He handed the basket to Zan. "Here, take it, or I'll eat it all before we even get to the cave. And come on, already. We have to hurry."

Ezri led us to the top of the cliffs looking out over the sea. We walked along the edge until we reached a staircase cut into the stone. Then we began the long descent to the beach. The sea stretched out to the horizon where stormy blue-grey patches covered in ripples met the clear blue of the sky. Birds swooped overhead and waves lapped against the shore. My legs ached by the time we'd reached the sand and began our trek along the beach to a place where the cliff seemed to rise up almost directly out of the water.

"My Ruhl, are you sure about this?" Zan asked. "The tides have already started to come in."

"We have enough time, if we hurry." Ezri pressed up against the cliff and continued on the thin strip of shore.

We rounded a bend, and the tower disappeared from sight behind us. My boots were covered in sand and getting damp by the time Ezri turned his head to call out over the noise of the surf. "Almost there!" Ahead, I could make out a break in the rock. The waves were swallowing the remaining sliver of beach, and I pressed closer to the cliff face.

I'd been so focused on the sand and surf that I hadn't realized we'd reached the cave entrance until a crescent of beach opened up, burrowing back into a crack in the cliff face. I took advantage of the additional dry land and moved farther away from the foaming waves. The sea had been beautiful from above, but this close, the swirling, rushing water sent shivers of fear down my spine. It seemed like one false step, and I would get swept away.

When I looked up from the waves, I spotted Ezri framed by a gap in the rock.

"Come on." He beckoned me to follow before disappearing into the darkness.

I hesitated and glanced back toward the waves. The fizzing edge of the water lapping against the cliff face had already erased our footsteps. I realized I'd have to go inside if I expected to stay dry. Mia and Zan followed Ezri, leaving me alone on the beach. I took a deep breath and walked forward, into the cool darkness.

Ezri lit a series of lanterns secured to the ledges inside the cave. Once my eyes had adjusted to the dim light, I realized the walls were covered with drawings. Most of them were rough outlines of creatures. Some I recognized. Others I'd only seen illustrated in our clan's book of legends. But they weren't all drawings. An arrangement of runes had been chiseled into the center of one wall.

When I walked closer, I realized they were the symbols of the five gods that had been carved in a ring, with Estrel's mark at the top. The rune that represented the Inahi was at the center, with lines running out to each of the god marks to create a sort of wheel. I'd never seen those runes arranged that way before. And they were surrounded by other carved symbols that I didn't recognize.

Except one. There was one I'd seen before. My eyes were immediately drawn to it, and I froze in place.

16

I WALKED over to the cave wall so I could run my fingers over the carvings. I traced the ring of god runes before reaching up to touch the symbol that had caught my attention. The same one that was carved on the charm I'd found clutched in Dern's hand. "I've seen this before."

"Koto," Mia said, with a hint of an accent.

"Koto," I repeated, attempting to imitate her accent. "What does it mean? This symbol isn't one of our runes, is it?"

"It's an Agrisse symbol for a creature that's common throughout Agrion. They say they're merchants. We think they come from the kingdom of Valthonia." Her fingers brushed across the scar on her face before tucking a stray strand of hair behind her ear.

My eyes moved to the other two symbols that surrounded the ring of god runes. They had been carved at equidistant points around the ring. Their positioning reminded me of the way the flowers had been placed around my offering on the day of the Gathering festival.

"Are these also Agrisse symbols?" I asked.

Mia nodded. "That one is the symbol for human. The other means mage."

"Mages in Agrion still have magic, though," Ezri said, coming up behind me. "Mia thinks that's why there's a different symbol for them."

"Does that mean that the Koto aren't human?" I asked, turning to Mia.

She grimaced. "They have bodies like humans. Their heads are shaped more like an impex, but with a shorter snout and thicker horns that—"

"That curl forward like this," I said, cutting her off as I realized she was describing the creature I'd seen silhouetted in the moonlight. The one that had stalked me in my dream.

"You've seen one?" she asked.

"I... I think I may have. Near the forest. The night we were attacked." I had wanted to tell Ezri about what I'd seen first, so he could decide what he wanted to do about it and who he wanted to tell, but after the Council meeting, I felt like we were running out of time. If Mia knew something about these creatures, and they might be a threat to the clans, she might be able to help.

"Why didn't you say something?" Zan asked, stepping closer until he loomed behind Ezri.

Ezri waved him back. "Give her a chance to explain before you jump at her."

"Before I caught up with you?" Mia asked. Her body had gone tense. She stood with fists clenched at her sides. Only her thumb moved, rubbing against the green stone ring wrapped around the lower part of her first finger.

"You said she was meeting with Tavo-jah," Zan snapped at Mia.

Ezri reached toward me. He set his hand on my shoulder, and I could feel his eyes on me, but I kept my attention focused on Mia and Zan.

"I told you she'd gone out walking, alone in the middle of the night, and that we ran into Tavo-jah," Mia said. "You drew your own conclusions."

"So did you," I said, reminding her he hadn't been the only one to make assumptions.

"I believed you," Mia replied.

"You could have said so." I crossed my arms.

"If we could just back up a bit," Ezri said, interrupting us. His hand slipped from my shoulder down my arm until his fingers wrapped around my elbow. "How about we start at the beginning? Hmm? And maybe discuss this while enjoying some food? I don't know about you, but I'm starving."

He led me over to a ledge wide enough for the four of us to sit relatively comfortably. Zan followed with the basket, but Mia stood staring at the images on the wall. Ezri helped Zan spread a cloth out over the rock while he chewed on a hunk of bread he'd snatched from the basket.

"Mia?" he called around his mouthful of partly chewed bread. "Join us?"

Zan and I positioned ourselves on opposite sides of Ezri, who had arranged himself cross-legged in the center-back of the ledge. He pulled the basket toward him and started emptying the contents, one by one, onto the cloth spread out between us.

Mia shook her head. "You're sure that's what you saw?"

Before I could respond, Ezri spoke. "I said, let's start at the beginning." He pointed at the empty spot across from him on the ledge. "Now, come sit down." He held out a round orange-red fruit as an offering.

"Yes, my Ruhl," she said, eyes narrowed. She perched on the edge of the ledge, half-facing us, and took the sunset-colored fruit from Ezri. She took a bite and stared at the carvings as she chewed.

"Now," Ezri said. "Ayla, why don't you tell us what happened that night?"

I took a bite of cheese and chewed while I considered where to begin. "I couldn't sleep. So I decided to go for a walk. Sometimes that helps me settle my thoughts."

"All right," Ezri said, nodding. "That sounds reasonable. Doesn't it, Zan?"

Zan made a noise, but I could tell he thought I was making this up.

Ezri rolled his eyes at Zan and turned back toward me. "Then what?"

"I walked around the perimeter of the camp. I assumed there would be guards patrolling there, so it would be safe. But there were no guards. Only two figures standing off near the trees. The silhouette of one of them had a large head and horns, like the creature Mia described. The Koto." I looked at Mia, but she just continued to chew and stare at the drawings.

"And the other?" Zan asked.

"Human." I hesitated, unsure if I should mention my suspicions about Tavo. I decided it would be better if I let them draw their own conclusions. "I... didn't get a good look. It was dark. I don't know. Then Mia found me, and when I looked again, they were gone."

Mia turned her head slightly and caught my eye. She'd stopped chewing, and I watched her swallow. "Tavo-jah."

I met her eyes. "Maybe. I don't know."

"It has to be. If he wasn't there to meet you, why else would he have just appeared out of nowhere?" she asked.

When she put it that way, I wasn't sure how to reply. Tavo was definitely up to something. I just didn't know what, and I didn't know how to find out. He wasn't going to tell me. I'd already tried asking.

Zan scowled. "So you want us to believe that you weren't meeting Tavo-jah that night? You just couldn't sleep, took a walk, and came across a creature that shouldn't be able to set foot on our lands because of the veil." He shook his head and looked at Ezri. "And you believe this?"

Ezri leaned back against the wall and crossed his arms. "I do. It fits with everything else we've been seeing. We hadn't seen any Merluks until that night, either."

"He has a point, Zan." Mia turned to face the rest of us, curling her legs beneath her on the ledge.

Zan leaned forward, his eyes locked on mine. "We know the Nahl and Jahl are plotting something. It's much more likely that the Nahla was out there to meet with the Jahlo about whatever it is their fathers are up to."

"Then how did she know what these creatures look like?" Ezri sighed. "Zan, I know you're only trying to protect me—"

"They want you dead." Zan cut him off. "You've read the reports from our agents. You heard Tavo taunting you in that Council meeting. And yet you insist on trusting her." He slid off the ledge and started pacing.

I stared at Ezri. Was it possible that our clans were plotting against him and not the Shal? But why?

"I trust her because we made a deal." Ezri spoke with a quiet calm that pebbled the flesh on my forearms with warning.

"Yes, I know." Zan scoffed. "You're in love, and it's rendered you incapable of behaving sensibly."

"Zan. Stop. Listen." Even spoken softly, each word was a command.

Zan's body went rigid with tension. He stopped pacing and faced Ezri, but remained silent. The automatic response of a trained guard to their commander.

Ezri grimaced. "Whatever the Nahl and Jahl are up to, Ayla isn't involved. She's here because we made a deal. She agreed to this betrothal so that she can help me find the Inahi. That's all."

I stared at him, surprised that he trusted Zan and Mia with our secret. Then again, the ties of loyalty between them had been forged in childhood bonds. They were nearly siblings, in a sense. And I knew how I felt about keeping secrets from my siblings. From Rys. A pang of guilt constricted my chest.

"Find the Inahi?" Zan raised his eyebrows. "The leaders of two clans are trying to assassinate you, your uncle would be more than happy to assist them to ensure that Jace-sha is the one to inherit the Shal clan leadership from your mother, and you seriously intend to go chasing gods? You do realize Tavo is just taunting you? He's looking for any excuse that might make the Magery reconsider their decision. He doesn't care about some nonsense written in a legend."

"It's not nonsense," I said. "The Inahi have been sending us messages. We can find them. And then, once the gods repair the veil, everything can go back to normal again."

"You think finding the Inahi is going to be what keeps Ez-ri-ruh from getting killed?"

"Zan..." Mia's tone as her voice trailed off left the lingering sensation of an unspoken warning.

Zan put his hands up, palms facing us. "All right. Let's put the bit about the Inahi aside for a moment and focus on the rest. Assuming we trust the Nahla—"

"Ayla," Ezri interrupted. "Call her by her name. Say Ayla-nah, if you must, but at least stop speaking about her like she's not sitting right here."

I bit my lip to keep the bubble of surprised relief from escaping my mouth as some embarrassing squeak or worse, laughter.

Zan glared at me. "Fine. Assuming we believe that Aylanah was just out for an innocent stroll, as she claims, and stumbled onto a meeting between a Koto and the Council's representative from the Jahl clan, what does that mean? What do these Koto have to do with anything?"

"Maybe it has something to do with the Merluk attack," I said, remembering. "Merluks can't strategize like humans."

Ezri leaned toward me. "You said you'd seen that symbol before. Where? In the folklore?"

"No." I shook my head. "On a charm."

Mia's hand paused on its journey to deliver a bite of bread with cheese and meat to her mouth. "What charm?"

I exhaled. "The day you arrived at our compound, my brother was attacked. Some guards found him and brought him to our clan mage. He was unconscious and very badly wounded. And he had a charm clutched in his hand."

"Who told you this?" Zan asked.

"No one. I was there when they brought him in." I rubbed my palms against my leggings, remembering. "I found the charm and stuck it in my pocket. With the festival and...everything...I forgot about it until I arrived and unpacked."

"Where is it now?" Mia asked.

"In my rooms. In the Ruhl House."

"We need to destroy it. Immediately." Mia hopped down from the ledge.

Zan gestured to the mouth of the cave. "We're not going anywhere until the tide starts going back out. What's the urgency?"

"If it's what I think it is, then it's a charm that means the wearer is under the protection of the Koto." Mia squinted at the cave entrance. "But it also means the Koto can see through that person's eyes. They claim they have to in order for the magic to work."

"Through my eyes?" I tensed. "Now?"

Mia shook her head. "No. Only if you were wearing the charm."

Ezri's hand wrapped around mine, causing my fingers to release the grip they'd had on my knee. But his comfort and her words only soothed me for a moment. Until the image of Tavo, leaning across the table as he spoke to me in the Council meeting, surfaced in my mind.

"You think the Koto are spying on us?" Zan asked. "But why?"

Mia shrugged. "I don't know. I only remember the charms because my parents warned me about them when I was a child. They didn't explain any more than that. My father said if I ever saw someone wearing one, I should tell him or my mother right away."

"That charm." I forced the words out of my frozen mouth. "It's not the only one. Or at least... I don't think it is."

"You've seen another?" Ezri asked, caressing the back of my hand with his thumb.

I nodded. "On Tavo-jah. He was wearing it at the Council meeting this morning. It was tucked inside his shirt, and the symbol wasn't facing outward, but the necklace looked identical to the one I found clutched in Dern's hand."

"This has to be more than a coincidence." Mia looked at Zan. "We need to keep a closer watch on him."

"Don't you think that's exactly where I'm headed once we get out of this dripping cave?" Zan stalked over to the ledge and ripped a hunk of bread off the end of a loaf in a manner that made me glad we had to wait for the waves to recede before we could return.

Mia scowled as she watched Zan chew. "You should let me handle Tavo-jah."

"No," he said. "I'll be the one to interrogate him."

"The direct approach will not get you anywhere," Mia said. "It will only alert him to the fact we're on to him."

"She has a point," Ezri said. "And Tavo-jah's been trying to get Mia's attention since he got here. If she shows an interest…"

"I said no." Zan returned to pacing in front of the drawings on the cave wall.

"Zan." Mia leaned against the ledge. "You have to admit, this could work."

Zan stopped in front of Mia. He shoved a hand into his hair and gripped the roots tightly. His nostrils flared as he inhaled. "I'm not letting you throw yourself at that Jahlo when I can accomplish the same thing with a few hours of interrogation."

"I can't let you do that, Zan. It will destroy any remaining shred of relations with the Jahl clan, and the Nahl will follow like they always do." Ezri glanced at me. "No offense."

I grimaced, wishing I could contradict him, but in my limited experience, he wasn't wrong.

"There has to be another way," Zan said.

"Look, I don't like it any more than you do, but Mia can handle herself." Ezri slid off the ledge and took a step toward Zan. He arched an eyebrow. "She was trained by the best, right?"

"Your flattery is not helping," Zan muttered.

Mia walked over and placed her hands on Zan's shoulders.

"It will be fine. All I have to do is convince him I've changed my mind."

I sighed as I considered this plan against what I knew of the Jahlo. "Even if you do, I still don't think he'll confide in you, Mia."

"Finally. Someone is making some sense." Zan jerked his arms up at his sides.

"But Ezri's right," I added quickly. "You can't interrogate him, either."

"So, what exactly are you suggesting?" Zan asked.

"He might confide in me. If he thought..." I glanced around at the three faces staring at me. "If he thought I was trying to help."

"Well, that's a convenient suggestion," Zan said, rolling his eyes.

"Zan," Ezri growled.

"What? It's true and you know it." Zan shrugged.

"You can trust me. I could go to him and ask for his help. Tell him I don't know what I'm doing in the Council. He'd jump at the opportunity to guide me." I looked down at my hands and fingered the signet ring Father had given me. "I wouldn't even really be lying."

Ezri stepped over to me and put his arm around my shoulder. "You're wrong, you know. You did great this morning."

"Liar," I said, half-smiling.

"It might work," Mia said.

"Let's say you get him to help you." Zan stalked toward me. "How does that help us?"

I squirmed under his scrutiny, but held his gaze. "Well, for starters, whatever he tells me to do will be something that helps him with whatever he's planning. So we might get a better idea about what that is. And, assuming he knows I saw him out there that night, if he thinks I'm on his side, it might keep him from doing anything rash."

"I still don't like it." Zan crossed his arms over his chest. "But I can't think of anything better."

"You'll have to be careful," Ezri said. "He can't know that you're actually working with us."

"I know." I glanced over at the carving on the wall.

Ezri sighed. "So that covers the immediate threat, but now we think we have at least two types of creatures breaching the veil, and still no sign of the Inahi."

"Actually," I said. "We may have received a response, and I have an idea about what it means. That's what I wanted to tell you about, after the Council meeting."

"Response?" Zan aimed his glare at Ezri. "What's all this about?"

Ezri explained how we'd left an offering for the Inahi, and I told them about the flowers I'd found on the map and again the morning after the attack.

"Both times there were five flowers." I scooped up some small pebbles that were scattered over the top of the ledge. "At first, I thought the ones on the map were marking locations. But last night, I noticed that, if you disregarded the map, both times the flowers appeared in the same pattern. Like this."

The others gathered around as I arranged five of the pebbles on the ledge in front of me.

"You think the Inahi are leaving you flowers?" Zan scoffed.

"Wait." Ezri leaned closer until his shoulder brushed against mine. "Is it a rune?"

I grinned at him. "That's what I thought, too. I searched through this notebook that Mage-nah gave me before we left. I think it belonged to Sera, but I haven't asked her about it yet."

"Did you find anything?" Mia asked.

I nodded. "The closest rune this pattern matches is Estrel's Mouth."

"That's the one you said you'd been using to mark your offerings, isn't it?" Ezri asked, gripping my forearm as his eyes widened with excitement.

I smiled, thrilled that he'd been paying such close attention, but shook my head. "Close, but no. I've been using Estrel's Hands. Estrel's Mouth looks like this."

I picked up another small rock and scraped a curving line between the pebbles I'd placed. First looping down, then rising and arching up to make a sideways S shape. "On a rune card, it's bracketed by Estrel's symbol."

I pointed at the carving on the wall, then scratched a vertical line on either side of the rune to demonstrate.

Ezri stood and walked over to the carving.

Mia asked, "What does it mean?"

I stared at Ezri's back as I answered. "According to the notebook, it's a symbol that's associated with the Ruhlini. I think that's why I didn't recognize it. I've never seen it outside of a rune deck. In that context, it's interpreted somewhat differently. But I think, based on my aunt's notes, that when it's not bracketed with Estrel's symbol, it's meant to represent the one who can speak with the gods."

Ezri's fingers reached out to touch the symbol for the Inahi at the center of the ring. "Why are they leaving these messages for you, and not for me?"

"Maybe they don't know how else to get your attention." I set down the rock and wiped my hands on my leggings before sliding off the ledge so I could walk over to Ezri. "You live in a city surrounded by stone. The Inahi can't reach you here."

Ezri turned to face me. "Then I need to go to them."

"Oh, no." Zan hurried over and set a hand on Ezri's shoulder. "Do not get that look on your face. You are not going anywhere except back to the Ruhl House, where I can keep you safe."

Ezri shook his head. "Don't you see? With the veil thinning and the clans fighting for power, there is nowhere that I'm safe. I need to do this. It's what I was born to do. At least according to the Magery."

Mia called to us from closer to the mouth of the cave. "The tide has retreated enough for us to return. We should go."

Zan dropped his hand from Ezri's shoulder, but kept his eyes locked with Ezri's. "If you must do this, then I'm going with you. But let's at least wait until after Ayla-nah talks with Tavo-jah."

I wrapped my hand around Ezri's, pulling his attention from Zan. "He has a point. You know how much I want to find the Inahi, but we need to know what Tavo-jah is up to and deal with these charms first. Especially if they're as dangerous as Mia thinks they are. You're no good to anyone if you get killed."

Ezri cupped my cheek in his palm. "That's exactly why we should go to the forest and find the Inahi first. Before he can get to me."

"Give me tonight. Let me try. If it doesn't work, we'll go tomorrow."

"Not without me," Zan said.

"Or me," Mia added.

Ezri glanced at each of them, then turned his attention back to me. "I'll take you to the Magery when we get back so we can brief Sera and see if there's anything else in the mage lore that might be helpful."

My heart soared at the idea of finally getting to see the Magery. "Good."

"All right. Let's get out of here." Ezri took a step closer to me. When Zan turned away, he bent his head close to mine, and in a low voice added, "No more secrets. No more wandering off. If you need a midnight walk, you take Mia with you. Got it?"

"Yes." I nodded.

"I'm serious," he said, giving my hands a brief squeeze. "Promise me."

I sighed. "Fine. I promise."

With one last glance at the carving on the wall, I followed Ezri to the mouth of the cave, where Zan and Mia waited with the remains of our picnic stuffed back into its basket. Then Zan led the way out of the cave, and Mia lingered behind us.

I looked back over my shoulder. "Mia? You coming?"

"Hmm?" she asked, lost in thought.

"Mia, let's go," Zan called from up ahead.

Mia's head snapped toward Zan's voice and her hand dropped to her side. She blinked once, then hurried to catch up.

17

WE traversed the sliver of wet sand revealed by the retreating tide until we reached the bottom of the stairs cut into the cliff side. When we finally reached the top, panting and sweating, with our hearts thumping in our chests, we ran into a group of guards heading to the barracks. Zan and Mia paused to talk with them, but Ezri tugged my hand and led me away, around the back of the Shal House.

"Where are you taking me?" I whispered. "I thought we were going to the Magery."

"We will," Ezri explained. "But, as long as we're here, we might as well check the Shal's library to see if there's anything useful there."

He led me down the hallways. Colorful hanging tapestries caught my eye, and I turned my head to stare at them as we passed. A few times, I tried to stop to get a better look, but Ezri kept us moving. He tugged at my hand and hurried me along as I followed him around a few more corners.

"Why are you in such a rush?" I asked.

"Because," he said, just before skidding to a stop on the plank floor. He caught me and pulled me toward him, then lifted the edge of a tapestry and pulled us behind and through a hidden door. At the top of a short flight of stone stairs, he pushed open another door, and we burst out into the sunshine and sea breeze. "I wanted a moment alone with you before Zan catches up to us."

I turned my face into the wind, letting the breeze blow my hair behind me, and looked out over the sparkling blue waters at the horizon. "It's beautiful," I whispered.

Ezri stepped behind me and slipped his arms around my waist. "So are you."

I tensed at his unexpected words. "Ezri, I—"

He spun me around until we were face to face, and the rest of my explanation about how I'd already given my heart to someone else, how I thought that after we'd found the Inahi and I'd earned my place in the Magery, things might be different, lodged in my throat.

My eyes locked with his, and he bent his head closer. His warm arms pulled me against him. "I really want to kiss you again."

I blinked at him. "But you told Zan and Mia—"

"I told them we made a deal. That doesn't mean I don't have feelings for you." He tucked a strand of hair that the wind had freed from my braids behind my ear. "When I'm with you, I can't stop looking at you. Reaching for you. And when we're apart, I can't stop thinking about you. About that kiss. You feel it too, don't you?"

I swallowed my objections and nodded, because it was true, and I'd promised him no secrets. "It's why I couldn't sleep that night."

He grinned. "Maybe we should try it again?"

I knew I should resist his charm and tell him about Rys, but I needed to know if the sensations of that first kiss had just been nerves. My hands lifted to wrap around his biceps. "Just a test."

My eyes fluttered shut as he pressed his lips to mine, warm and soft. That same spark traveled through me, lighting up my core. Even though I wanted to feel nothing, I couldn't ignore the way my skin tingled everywhere we touched.

He pulled away until only our foreheads were touching. "Anything?"

I opened my eyes to catch the teasing grin on his full lips.

"Perhaps a bit more, then." He leaned in and kissed a spot just below my earlobe. His warm mouth traveled along the sensitive skin on my neck, and I sighed.

As much as I didn't want to admit it, there was a spark of something between us. I'd been so sure that I wanted to return to Rys once this was over, and yet, after only a few days, these feelings for Ezri had made me question everything. Maybe, if I stayed to study at the Magery after we found the Inahi, there would be time to figure it out. It would be all right as long as we weren't forced to marry right away.

A cough in the doorway made me jump, but Ezri just grumbled and pulled me closer. "Go away, Zan," he said, his breath warm against my skin.

"Of course, my Ruhl," Zan replied. "Since it's clear that love has definitely not clouded your judgment, I'll just leave you two here and go find Tavo-jah."

Ezri grumbled again. He reluctantly pulled away from me to face Zan. "If I thought for a minute that you would actually let me out of your sight, I might even let you."

"Though I'm tempted to leave you alone and take this opportunity to give that Jahlo a taste of what he deserves, I know you'd only run off to the forest as soon as I'm gone," Zan replied. "Besides, you should be thanking me for finding you before the Shal did."

"She's home?" Ezri tensed.

Zan nodded once. "Those guards were the ones who accompanied her into the city. They said she cut the visit short after arguing with the proprietor because someone had taken her usual table."

"Interesting." Ezri frowned. Then he turned his gaze to the sky. "The closing bells will ring soon. If we hurry, we can get to the Magery just as the classes are ending. With Lorjad's Luck, we can catch both Sera and Mage-sha before they leave."

Zan agreed, then started back down the stairs. As soon as he was gone, Ezri caught my hand in his. He leaned close and pressed a quick kiss to my cheek, then whispered, "To be continued."

A shiver of anticipation ran down my spine. Then we were moving, hurrying down, shutting the doors behind us, and slipping out from behind the tapestry into the hallway below, where Zan was waiting for us. Ezri squeezed my hand as he stifled a cough. Zan shot him a pointed look that I couldn't read, but Ezri just shook his head and gestured for Zan to lead the way.

We started back the way we'd come, but at a slower pace. Just as we reached the first turn, a voice called from behind us.

"Ezri, dear. Is that you?"

I didn't need to turn to know who it would be. Only Ezri's mother would dare to call him by his given name, with no mention of his title. I tensed. My previous encounters with her didn't leave me eager to talk with her again.

Ezri paused and turned. "Yes, Mother?"

She took her time closing the distance between us, her small, curvy form wrapped in a silky material that floated above a series of layered sheer skirts. When she stopped in front of us, her gaze drifted to where Ezri's hand held mine. Other than that brief glance and her huff of annoyance, she spoke only to Ezri and didn't bother acknowledging me or Zan.

"Where are you off to at this hour?" she asked. "You'll be late for dinner again."

"There are still several hours until dinner, Mother," Ezri replied. "We were just on our way to pay a visit to the Magery to arrange the wedding. It won't take long."

"I see. That's splendid news." The sour pout of her lips contradicted her words. "I suppose having a mage perform the ceremony is unavoidable. But I must insist on it being Ren and not her troublesome apprentice, even if the woman is the Nahla's relation." She looked down her nose at me and affected a dramatic shiver before shaking it off and clasping her hands together in front of her chest with a smile. "It's a good thing I caught you. I'll just go along with you to make sure it's all arranged properly."

"I don't think that's necessary, Mother." Ezri gave my hand a reassuring squeeze. "I'm sure you have better things to do."

"Nonsense! What could be more important than the marriage of my son?" She pushed past, choosing to squeeze between us and forcing Ezri to release my hand.

When I stepped aside, a movement down a side corridor caught my eye.

"Ayla-nah? Is that you?" called a voice. The figure stepped into the light, and I recognized Ezri's cousin, Jace. "Ah, hello, Auntie Filna-sha. And Ezri-ruh, I almost never see you in

Shal House these days. But lucky me, your sweet Nahla is just the person I've been searching for."

"I'm afraid she's already spoken for," Ezri said, smiling at his cousin.

"And you know that's not at all what I mean." Jace winked.

"Jace, my boy, whatever it is that you could possibly need with the Nahla, it will have to wait. We're on our way to the Magery." Filna turned to walk away.

"Ah, Auntie, I do apologize, but I think that will have to wait. Pin has important papers that need the Nahla's seal so they may be sent off without delay. She said it was something to do with Council business?" Jace shrugged and lifted an eyebrow at Ezri.

"That is unfortunate," Ezri said, exchanging a glance with Jace and a brief nod. "But Pin's right. Ayla-nah needs to send that message to her father." Ezri turned to me and took both my hands in his. "I'll see if Mage-sha is free to join us for dinner tonight. Perhaps we can arrange the wedding details over a nice family meal."

"Of course, my Ruhl," I said, getting the sense that it was best to follow his lead.

Ezri kissed the back of my hand and mouthed the word "later" to me while he faced away from his mother.

"Excellent." Jace offered me his arm. "Let's be off then. Shall we, Nahla?"

"Zan, would you send a message to the Magery for me?" Ezri said as Jace and I disappeared down the hall. "I should get back to the Ruhl House and finish reviewing the reports that stacked up while we were gone. Mother, I'll see you at dinner."

Jace leaned toward me and whispered, "He'll owe me for that save."

"You mean there are no papers?" I whispered back.

"Such a smart girl." Jace patted my hand where it rested in the crook of his arm. "I knew my charming cousin brought you here for a reason."

"What just happened back there? And where are you really taking me?" I glanced back once more before we turned down a hallway I didn't recognize.

"Oh, it doesn't matter, really." He shrugged. "We could go anywhere you like. Though, if you really do have a message to send to your father, I can assist with that."

"How did you know about what happened at the Council meeting? Did you plan that?" I asked.

"Oh, you are a sweet thing." He chuckled. "Remember what I said at dinner? Insignificant moons are often ignored in the company of the flashier heavenly bodies. But stealth makes it easier to observe the orbits of others."

"You were spying."

"Precisely." He grinned.

"But why did you interrupt?"

"Did you want the Shal to accompany you lovebirds on your visit to the Magery?"

The answer was no, but I wasn't sure I wanted to be honest with someone who spied in passageways. Ezri's mother clearly disliked me. But she was the Shal, and Jace's aunt. So I held my tongue and responded with a question. "Why did she even want to come with us in the first place? I thought she hated the mages."

Jace threw his head back and cackled. "You may be smarter than Filna-sha thinks you are, but you still have much to learn."

"Secrets," I muttered. "Everyone with their secrets."

"Welcome to the city, Nahla." Jace stopped at an intersection in the hallway. "Shall I return you to your rooms to write your letter? Or would you prefer a tour of the Shal House, first?"

His question gave me an idea. "I don't suppose you can take me to wherever it is that the Shal clan keeps their folklore?"

"Of course, Nahla, if that's what you'd like, I'll take you to the Shal House library."

"Excellent. And then, maybe you can educate me about the Shal's feelings regarding mages in general, and why she dislikes my aunt in particular?"

"Ah... an excellent choice for story time." Jace tapped a finger against his chin, then led me down a short hall and through an archway into a room lined with dusty books on shelves. A large wooden table served as the centerpiece of the room.

"Shall I also get what you need to write to your father?" he asked.

I nodded and turned to the shelves. While I waited for him to return, I ran my hands along the spines, reading titles, looking for any volumes that might have stories about the Inahi, amazed at the quantity of books gathered in one place. I'd just started to calculate how long it would have taken the apprentices in the Magery to create this many volumes when a thick book of folklore caught my attention. I slipped the volume off the shelf and brought it over to the table where Jace had already laid out paper, quill, ink, and sealing wax.

Jace glanced at the dust-encrusted cover as I set the book on the table. "I thought you'd already picked a story for me to tell?" He raised an eyebrow at me, and the corner of his mouth lifted into an impish grin.

"This is for later," I said. "Do you think they'll mind if I borrow it?"

"They?" He frowned. "I live here, too, you know."

"Well, it is the Shal House," I said. "I just thought…"

"Yes, yes." Jace waved his hand in the air. "I suppose all this belongs to the Shal. But, unless my dear nosy aunt manages to live forever, or my most excellent cousin revokes his title as Ruhl, I suppose they will have no choice but to allow me to inherit at some point."

"Would he do that?" I asked.

"Allow me to inherit?" His lips quirked into another lop-sided grin.

"No," I sighed. "Revoke his title." I reached across the table and pulled a sheet of paper toward me.

Jace slid the quill and ink to me. "I doubt it. He is quite serious about his duty and responsibility to the clans. And his appointment as Ruhl is for life."

Something in Jace's statement made my skin prickle. I shook off the feeling as I reached for the quill. "She didn't want him to be named Ruhl. Is that why she hates the mages?"

"Oh, it goes back much further than that, I'm afraid. Shall we begin story time?" He paused, waiting for me to nod before continuing. "I suppose it all started when Edan-ruh was dying… Belyn-ruh stood to inherit the title of Ruhlini from her mother. Then Edan-ruh died and Belyn-ruh followed shortly after, along with the baby she was carrying. And everyone blamed the whole mess on your aunt."

I scowled. "My aunt? Why? What did Sera do?"

"Did anyone tell you how your aunt ended up in the city in the first place?"

"She came to study at the Magery."

"Yes, and shortly after she arrived, she became friends with

Belyn-ruh. The two were very close. According to those who were there, Belyn-ruh told Sera-nah all her secrets. Which meant your aunt has been in the thick of things for quite a long time."

"But..."

Jace held up his hand. "Shh, and let me tell the story. As Belyn-ruh's best friend and confidante, your aunt found herself in the middle of quite the family scandal. You see, my father thought he was going to marry Belyn-ruh. But dear, sweet, innocent Belyn-ruh fell in love with your uncle, Harn-nah, instead.

"When her father found out that Belyn-ruh was pregnant with your uncle's child, and your aunt had been helping them hide that fact from everyone, he quickly changed his betrothal negotiations with the former Shal. Instead of matching Belyn-ruh and my father, he offered his son, Curon-ruh, as a match for my aunt, Filna-sha, instead."

"Belyn-ruh and my uncle?" As far as I'd been told, my uncle had died an untimely death. He had been only a little older than me, and he'd never had a chance to declare for anyone, let alone father any children. "Are you sure?"

"Ask my cousin if you don't believe me. He knows. Unfortunately, as you may have guessed, the story doesn't have a happy ending. The young lovers were on the cusp of their happily ever after, planning to reveal their secret affair after Filna-sha and Curon-ruh's wedding. But, as Lorjad's Luck would have it, my father caught them sneaking out of the wedding feast together. He's never been one to let things go easily, and he still had it in his head that he was going to marry the next Ruhlini." Jace shook his head. "So he confronted Harn-nah. They fought. Harn-nah fell off a balcony and died."

I gaped at him. "Your father killed my uncle?"

"To hear my father tell the story, the fall was just an un-fortunate accident." Jace cringed, then squinted at me. "You appear genuinely surprised. Did your father never tell you how your uncle died?"

"It seems there are quite a few things my father never told me. I only knew that Harn-nah died very young. No one ever said more than that." Perhaps this was what my father had meant when he said Ezri's family has caused enough trouble for us already. "They blame my aunt for all of that?"

"For the whole tragic affair." Jace leaned back in his chair and sighed.

"But... why? Just because she helped her best friend keep a secret?" I lifted the quill and twisted it in the air as I considered this new aspect of our family's history.

"Sera introduced the lovers. She helped them hide their affair. And then she failed to save them from their fate." He ticked the offenses off on his fingers. "This is, perhaps, one of the only things the Shal and your father agree on."

I looked away from the quill to meet Jace's eyes across the table. "What do you mean?"

"Your uncle died and your clan lost their opportunity to marry into the illustrious family of the late Ruhlini—until now, of course. Your father probably didn't care that Sera introduced the lovers. That bit, I'm sure, he thought was a stroke of genius that would have allowed the Nahl clan to se-cure the upper hand in the Council. But Sera ruined that op-portunity. And here you are to fix her mistakes." Jace smiled his sly smile at me and watched my face as I absorbed what he'd just told me. "Such a stroke of genius, I think, to marry both his daughters off. One to the Jahlo, and the other to the Ruhl."

"You think he planned this?" I knew my father had. That's

what Mage-nah had written in his notes on my father's reading. But I hadn't realized his maneuvering was so obvious to everyone else.

"It's simply politics, Nahla. Though, what I can't understand is why he didn't marry you both off right away. Why wait?" He tilted his head and studied me with narrowed eyes.

I ran my finger along the edge of the feather on the quill, avoiding his gaze. "Father thought I was too young."

"Yes. That is what the gossips have been saying. But my charismatic cousin can be quite convincing." Jace paused. "He always gets what he wants."

"What are you saying?" I snuck a glance at him.

He gave me a knowing look. "Our parents may be driven by their ambition, their judgment clouded by the outcome of what should have been a love story with a happy ending. But I trust my cousin, Nahla. I will do what's best for the Ruhl because I believe that is what's best for the clans. Perhaps it's time for you to consider who you serve?"

His words echoed what Tavo had said to me when we first arrived. I'd been the one to beg my parents to delay the wedding. Perhaps my father had wanted me to marry right away. Perhaps he knew that Ezri would do as he wished as soon as we'd returned to the city. I knew so little about my father's plans. It did seem as though he was as political as Jace thought.

I dipped the tip of the quill into the ink bottle. "If you'll just give me a moment to write a few lines and then help me deliver this to Pin, I would appreciate it."

"Of course, Nahla. Take your time."

18

I RETURNED to my rooms after leaving my letter with Pin. Writing to my father had left me feeling sad and a little homesick. I dreaded preparing for another dinner with the Shal, but at least I had time to study the book of folklore I'd borrowed before I had to face her and her insults again.

I was considering how Cala might deal with the Shal's behavior when muffled voices echoed down the corridor from the direction of my rooms. In the dim light, I could just make out the two figures standing outside my door.

Tavo had Mia backed against the wall. He leaned over her with one hand pressed against the wall behind her. His other hand was reaching toward her face.

"Mia?" I called, hoping that a simple warning that they were no longer alone might cause Tavo to back off.

He pivoted to face me, but kept his hand on the wall next to Mia's head. He rested his other hand on his hip as his lips curled up in a grin. I wanted to smack the smug look off his face, but I didn't need Goff's diplomacy lessons to know that wouldn't help me get any information out of the Jahlo.

"Hello, Nahla," he drawled.

Mia took advantage of my arrival to side-step away from Tavo. She straightened her tunic before meeting my eyes.

"Is everything all right?" I asked, directing my question at Mia.

"Yes, Nahla," she said. "Zan sent me to find you. I stopped here on my way to the Shal House to see if you'd returned and found Tavo-jah waiting for you."

"I see." I turned to Tavo. A quick glance at his collar confirmed that he'd removed the necklace he'd been wearing during the Council meeting. "Sorry to keep you waiting. I was composing a letter to Father."

"Right. I'd almost forgotten about that." He pushed off the wall and stretched lazily. "Don't worry about me. I was perfectly entertained here, catching up with Mia."

"As it turns out, I wanted to talk with you as well." I gestured toward the door to my rooms. "Why don't you come in for a bit?"

Tavo glanced between me and Mia. "Are you sure we should be speaking alone in your rooms? What will Ezri-ruh think?"

"Ezri-ruh trusts me. It shouldn't be a problem. Unless there's some reason he shouldn't trust you?" I raised my eyebrows.

Tavo scowled. "Of course not."

"All right then." I opened the door and gestured for him to go ahead of me. "If it makes you feel better, I'll leave the door open while we talk. Mia, would you mind waiting out here for a bit?"

Mia flashed me a look of warning behind Tavo's back. "I'll

wait, Nahla."

After giving her a reassuring nod, I followed Tavo into my sitting room. "I suppose you're coming to talk with me about the Council meeting this morning?" I asked, setting the book of folklore down before taking a seat at the far side of the room, near the windows and the door to the balcony.

"I thought I warned you to stay out of my way." Tavo kept his voice low as he perched on the edge of the chair closest to me.

"Perhaps it would help if you told me what way that is so that I can improve my chances of staying out of it." I folded my hands in my lap to hide my nerves.

"Just do what you're here to do." He waved a hand in the air between us. "Marry the Ruhl and keep out of the Council, and we should be fine."

"My father gave me that seat on the Council, and he was the one who requested the delay in my marriage." I glared at him. "What I don't understand is why you appear to be asking me to go against his wishes. Why are you siding with the Shal?"

"Was it really his idea? The delay?" Tavo leaned toward me with a sly grin.

"What are you implying?" I raised my eyebrows in what I hoped was a look of innocence.

"I can't imagine your father refusing you anything. If it was his idea, and you truly are in love, do you expect me to believe that you didn't ask him to reconsider?"

"Why would I? It's tradition for there to be a delay between declaration and marriage. Cala's rushed wedding was an exception. One that was, thankfully, still blessed by the gods. Even her reading—"

"Cala-jah got a reading before her wedding?" he asked, interrupting.

"Yes." I paused, recalling what she'd told me. "I believe she went to Mage-nah for a reading the morning of the Gathering."

"That morning?" Tavo stood. "You mean, before Vorn even arrived?"

I frowned, quickly thinking through my knowledge of clan customs, hoping I hadn't said something wrong. I wasn't certain that I knew all the Jahl clan variations on our traditions, but I was fairly certain there wasn't any reason for them to have an issue with what Cala did. "People go to the clan mage for readings all the time. Cala was anxious about her future, and I think it helped calm her a little to hear Mage-nah say she was to be married and that she would be happily settled with many children. Though she admitted that she initially feared the cards were referring to Ezri-ruh because there was something Mage-nah said about a death that would bring her husband to power, and Ezri-ruh's father recently died, so..."

Tavo's eyes narrowed. "Mage-nah saw all that in the cards? Even before Vorn's declaration?"

"It's not that dramatic of a prophecy." I shrugged, still not understanding why he was so interested in this and hoping I could steer the subject back toward Ezri and the Council. "Everyone was expecting Cala to receive a declaration at the Gathering. They might have thought it would be Ezri-ruh and not Vorn-jah, but what does that matter?"

Tavo paced to the window. He stared outside for a moment, then turned and said, "It's getting late. If you'll excuse me, I must go and write a letter to the Jahl before dinner."

He couldn't leave. Not before I got some useful piece of information out of him.

I stood and reached for his arm. "If you're worried about

your father, I'm sure he's fine. If Mage-nah had seen any concern for his health, I'm sure Cala would have mentioned it. He likely only meant that Cala and Vorn-jah would become Jahl and Jahlini one day, as is our custom. You shouldn't worry."

Tavo pulled away from me. He brushed a hand across the section of tunic I'd touched, as though my fingers had somehow left dirt marks that needed to be scrubbed clean. "If you want to be helpful, make sure the Ruhl keeps his end of the agreement he made with your father and dispatches those guards to the plains."

"But—" I scrambled to think of something to keep him talking, but he cut me off before I could.

"And tell the Ruhl that I won't be joining his family for dinner this evening." Before I could say anything else, Tavo turned and stalked out the door.

I'd taken a few steps after him when Mia hurried inside.

She shut the door behind her. "What happened?"

"Well," I sighed. "That didn't exactly go as planned."

A knock interrupted me before I could explain further. Mia held up a finger, then opened the door to see who was there. After a brief exchange, she closed the door and turned to face me.

"Ezri-ruh's here to escort you to dinner. And Mage-sha is with him. Should I let them in?"

I glanced down at the simple tunic and leggings I'd worn to the Council meeting and our visit to the cave. Grains of sand still stuck to my boots. "Tell him I need a minute."

I removed my boots and took them out onto the balcony to brush them clean. Then I selected a sweeping violet dress with a bodice trimmed in gold embroidery from the wardrobe. After adjusting the layers of fabric in the skirt, I shook out my hair and swept it up, pinning it in place with my hairpin knives. Then I slipped my soft leather boots back onto my feet.

"Ready," I said, standing in front of Mia for inspection.

"Excellent choice, Nahla," she said. "Zan is here as well. He'll accompany you and Ezri-ruh to dinner while I return to the guardhouse to change."

"Wait." I held up my hand, then hurried back to my dresser to retrieve the charm she'd said we needed to destroy. "Here."

Mia took a step back. "Do you have anything you can wrap it in? I shouldn't touch it."

I squinted at her, then glanced down at the charm I held in my open palm. "Why not?"

She looked over her shoulder at the door before meeting my eyes. "The reason I know about the charms is because my family was being hunted by the Koto. It's why we tried to escape across the sea. To get away from them."

"Oh." My gaze drifted to the scar on her face. I glanced away, focusing instead on searching my trunk for a scarf or a handkerchief I could use to wrap around the charm. "Do Zan and Ezri know this?"

"They know my family was trying to escape Agrion. They know I made it and my parents didn't. But I never told them about the Koto. I thought I would be safe from them here." Mia's hand curled around the hilt of her knife.

I wrapped the charm in the first scarf I found, then turned to hand her the bundle. "Ezri and I will find the Inahi. You'll be safe here again. I promise."

"You can't promise that, Nahla." She gripped the bundle tight with both hands.

I grimaced, remembering that there was more than one of these charms within the city walls. "Tavo wasn't wearing it tonight, when he came here."

Mia shook her head. "No. I noticed that as well."

"Let's not keep Ezri and Mage-sha waiting." I gestured toward the door. "We can decide what to do about that after dinner. At least we'll know we have dealt with this one."

Mia walked me to the door and opened it, stepping aside so that when the door opened, the only thing Ezri saw was me.

"Stormcat." His eyes locked with mine. "You look stunning."

He guided the older woman who accompanied him toward a comfortable chair as Mia slipped out behind them and shut the door. I recognized her as Mage-sha, the woman who had scolded Jace and me at dinner the previous evening. She had pale, wispy short hair and a pink, wrinkled complexion, and she carried a thick book tucked under one arm. A beaded pouch dangled from her other hand.

"Ayla-nah, I'd like you to meet Mage-sha," Ezri said.

I offered my hands in the traditional greeting and bowed my head.

She placed her things on the table so she could wrap her cool, dry hands around mine. "May the Inahi bring you blessings, child."

"And many blessings to you, Mage-sha," I replied, lifting my head and returning my hands to my sides.

Her eyes were large and bright under thin, almost translucent eyebrows. They stood out as the most distinctive feature on her face and made me shiver with their intensity when she met my gaze.

"I asked Mage-sha to come a bit early, so she might give us a reading before dinner," Ezri said. "Since our plans to go to the Magery were interrupted."

"A reading? Why?" I asked, wondering why both he and Tavo were suddenly so fixated on rune card readings.

"Mage-ruh suggested that it might be helpful, considering what we have planned for tomorrow." Ezri winked at me.

"Sera also asked me to bring you this." Mage-sha gestured to the book she'd placed on the table next to its nearly identical twin.

"I see you got to the library after all," Ezri said, picking up both books and moving them to the side so Mage-sha would have room to shuffle her rune deck. "Have you checked it yet?"

"There hasn't been time," I replied as Mage-sha settled herself in a chair and pulled her rune deck from the beaded pouch she carried. "Tavo-jah was waiting for me when I returned. He just left before you arrived. I'm surprised you didn't see him."

"How convenient." Ezri raised his eyebrows. "We must have missed him."

"Odd. A little too convenient, maybe?" I sighed. "Unfortunately, he left before I got him to tell me anything useful."

"Too bad." Ezri gestured for me to sit opposite Mage-sha. Then he pulled another chair closer so he could sit next to me.

Mage-sha offered him the deck, and Ezri cut it. Then she dealt out three cards, setting them in a triangular formation. We all leaned over the table as she studied them with her piercing grey eyes. Her fingers hovered over the two cards closest to her, but I couldn't take my eyes off the card at the top of the arrangement.

There it was again. Estrel's Mouth.

Mage-sha muttered over the cards while rocking slightly in her chair. "Mmm. The danger is closer now."

Ezri shifted in his chair. "Yes, but what about the Inahi?"

"Give me a moment, my boy." She lifted the fourth card off the top of the deck and placed it in the center. Then she hummed as her fingers flitted between the cards, poking them, caressing them, but always coming back to linger over the two cards closest to her.

One was from Solnat's suit. It took me a moment to identify it as Solnat's Eye. That wasn't a rune I'd seen many times before. If I hadn't been studying Sera's rune notebook so closely, I might not have recognized it. The other rune was Forsla's Horn. The fourth card, at the center, was Lorjad's Stick.

"Yes," Mage-sha said, leaning back in her chair and turning her sharp gaze on Ezri. "You shouldn't delay. Leave tomorrow at dawn. I wouldn't wait much longer, my boy."

Ezri ran his hand through his hair and frowned. "It's still there, isn't it?"

Mage-sha nodded.

"What is?" I asked, trying to recall the meanings of the two runes Mage-sha had been so focused on. Lorjad's Stick represented a journey or a new beginning, and Estrel's Mouth was the symbol Sera had associated with the Ruhlini. But I couldn't remember what the other two stood for, and I'd never been properly trained in reading runes. That was something they taught at the Magery.

Mage-sha kept her eyes locked on Ezri, and I realized she was waiting for him to answer.

I turned toward him. "Ezri?"

"My death," he said.

I recoiled, finally remembering the rune that stood for endings. "Solnat's Eye. But what does that have to do with the Inahi?"

Ezri hesitated. "It's been like this since before my father

died. At first, I thought maybe his death had been the one Mage-sha kept seeing in the cards. But it remained, even after he was gone. And then we found out there were other reasons to believe it's me."

I recalled his argument with Zan in the cave. "You think my father and the Jahl are trying to assassinate you? But why would they when you're the one who can speak with the gods? It's right there." I pointed to Estrel's Mouth.

"You know the runes, Nahla?" Mage-sha turned her gaze to me.

"Some. I've been training as an apprentice mage. I'd planned to attend the Magery before..." I waved a hand, gesturing to indicate Ezri and the room and the general situation I'd found myself in.

"Sera said that Mage-nah speaks highly of you." Mage-sha nodded, and signaled for me to join her on her side of the table.

Once I stood at her side, she explained her reading of the runes. "Solnat's Eye represents death and endings. Forsla's Horn represents betrayal. Those who would act against you. Both are the runes of reversal in their suits. The symbols that represent the opposing force of that god.

"What's especially interesting is that Estrel's Mouth, which, as you said, has been a symbol linked to the Ruhlini and the power to speak with the gods, also falls in the reversal position within Estrel's suit, while Estrel's Bowl, the rune that stands for what most would consider a reversal of Estrel's gifts, appears in the fifth and final position of that suit."

Ezri shifted in his chair. "Mage-sha..."

Mage-sha motioned for him to be quiet. "I know. Now is not the time for lessons. It's the time for dinner. Give me a moment longer."

"Go on, then." He reached for one of the folklore books.

"Is that important? That they're all reversal cards?" I asked, trying to remember what Estrel's Bowl meant. "Why would Estrel's Mouth be considered a reversal?"

Mage-sha smiled up at me. "You ask questions like a mage, my dear. You would be a valuable addition to our ranks."

Heat warmed my cheeks. "Thank you, Mage-sha."

She gestured to the cards. "All reversals, except for the one at the center that ties them together. A journey. While Sol-nat's Eye haunts Ezri's readings, the others are new twists on previous themes. You are also a new twist. Which means perhaps this journey will result in a new beginning, reversing the reversals. You see?"

My mind bent, trying to follow her interpretation.

She patted my hand. "It's all right, dear. It takes years of practice to become acquainted with the language of the runes. It will come in time. For now, just take my advice. Leave at dawn."

"For the forest?" I asked.

Ezri bolted upright with the folklore book open in his hands. "There's more here!"

"More?" I hurried around to look over his shoulder at the page.

"Something's been spilled all over the bottom here, covering up the rest of the text, but I don't remember you telling me this part. It's new, isn't it?" He pointed at the section of text above a large black blob that covered most of the text on the lower half of the page.

"It looks like someone spilled ink." I pressed my fingers to the dry page. "Which book is this? The one from the Shal library?"

"No. The one from the Magery." He gestured to the one

he'd left open on the table. "That one seems to also be missing a page, but this one appears to have been tampered with in a different way."

I read, starting at the top of the page. "'...they agreed and told their mother to accept the offer from the Inahi. In a matter of days, even the simplest spells were no longer possible.' That's where the story in our folklore book ends."

"So this part is new to you?" Ezri asked, pointing at the next paragraph, the last one visible above the spill.

"Yes." I continued reading. "'As the years passed, children grew to adults who couldn't even remember the colors of magic. But the tradition of the mages continued. Ruhala created a Magery where each of the clans sent promising students to apprentice and learn the arts of healing and the traditions of their faith. Each clan maintained a mage, who had learned to heal using potions instead of spells and performed the ceremonies associated with the five blessings. Even without magic, the tradition of rune reading continued. Then, when Ruhala reached the end of her days, she journeyed to the Gods' Seat one last time.'"

"The Gods' Seat?" Ezri asked, looking at Mage-sha. "Do you know what that means?"

"Perhaps." Mage-sha stood and held her arms out for the book. "In her final days, Edan—may her soul light the darkness—woke in the night, determined to leave her bed. Her skin was hot, and she was babbling about something that sounded like nonsense. I thought her fever had taken a turn for the worse, so I gave her medicine to calm her and help her rest."

"Did she say where it was?" Ezri asked.

Mage-sha frowned as she considered his question. "I don't believe she did. Sera sat with her the following night because they needed me to perform the marriage blessing at Filna-sha and Curon-ruh's wedding. We should ask her if Edan talked about it again."

Zan walked in as Mage-sha was talking. He waited for her to finish, then said, "My Ruhl, we should be going."

Ezri nodded. He took the book back from Mage-sha. His eyes skimmed over the page one last time before he closed the tome and set it on the table with the other book. "Whatever it is, and whatever happened there in the story, seems to be important enough that someone wanted to destroy the knowledge. Probably the same someone who wants me dead so that they can control who inherits my grandmother's power next."

"A death that would bring him to power." The words tumbled from my lips as I remembered what I'd said to Tavo about Cala's reading.

"What's that?" Ezri asked. "Something else from the legends?"

"No." My hands flew to my face, and I gasped as I realized what I'd missed. "Oh, no. I'm sorry. I'm so sorry."

"What? What is it?" Ezri took a step closer to me.

"We were talking about my sister's reading with Mage-nah." I gestured to where Tavo had been sitting. "And after I said that, he got much too quiet. I should have known. I'm sorry. I should have—"

Ezri wrapped his arms around me. "Slow down. Start over at the beginning. Who were you telling about your sister's reading?"

I leaned back so I could see his face. "Cala's reading before the Gathering. She said that Mage-nah told her there would be a death that would bring Vorn-jah to power. I mentioned this to Tavo-jah when he was here earlier. He seemed very interested, asked me some questions, and then got very quiet. At first, I thought he was mad, then I assumed he was just worried about his father's health. Before I could reassure him, he asked me to tell you he wouldn't be at dinner and hurried out."

"Where did he say he was going?" Zan asked, stepping closer.

I glanced over at him. "He said he wanted to send a message to the Jahl."

19

ZAN looked at Ezri, and I turned my head in time to catch Ezri's raised eyebrows. I could only guess at whatever question and response had silently passed between them. I hoped that it hadn't been another seed of doubt taking root in the fertile soil of Zan's reluctance to trust me.

Ezri met my gaze. "So, you thought Mage-nah meant the Jahl, but now you think he might have meant me, right? Because of what Mage-sha said in the reading just now?"

"Yes." I tensed. I felt like such a fool.

"It's all right. You didn't know." He slid his arm around my shoulders as he directed his next questions to the captain. "Zan? The aviary?"

Zan shook his head. "I don't think it's a good idea for me to leave you unguarded right now."

"Then accompany us to dinner and send Mia to check when she joins us?" Ezri suggested.

Zan nodded, then retreated out into the hallway to wait

for us.

"Mage-sha, are you ready?" Ezri asked.

She'd packed her rune cards back into her beaded pouch, but her eyes were still on the two books of folklore. "If you bring that back to the Magery, I might be able to dissolve some of the stain from the page. It will depend on what ink they used to print the story and what sort was spilled on it, but trying won't make it any worse."

Ezri nodded, then offered Mage-sha his arm. "We'll pick it up after dinner, and then I'll walk you back to the Magery. If Sera's around, I'll ask her about the Gods' Seat, while you work your magic."

Mage-sha swatted at Ezri's arm with her pouch. "It's not magic, my boy. You read the legend. 'Even the simplest of spells were no longer possible.'"

Ezri chuckled as Mage-sha made her way to the door ahead of us, and I took the offered place on his arm.

"After dinner, can I go with you?" I asked once we were alone.

"Tonight?" he asked, raising his eyebrows.

My cheeks warmed, and I tried to explain as he led me out into the hallway. "You made me promise not to go out walking alone, but what if I'm out walking with you? Would that be all right? I'd like to speak with my aunt."

Ezri ducked his head closer to mine when I paused to shut the door to my rooms. "I think, given Mage-sha's reading, it's best I don't let you out of my sight."

"That's going to make it hard for you to sleep," I whispered back.

Ezri's slow grin made me realize the double meaning of my response. "I expect it will."

"Will you two hurry up?" Zan turned to glance back when

he realized we hadn't followed him and Mage-sha down the hall. "The sooner I see you safely to dinner, the faster I'll be able to return with some answers."

"On our way," Ezri called to Zan. Then, after wrapping his hand around mine, in a lower voice he added, "The sooner we get through dinner, the sooner we can get out of here."

My body buzzed with excitement at the promise of visiting the Magery and then heading out into the Heartgrove to find the Gods' Seat. We were closer than ever to finding the Inahi. I could feel it. The anticipation eclipsed my dread of dining with the Shal again, which was a good thing because the walk to the private dining room in the Ruhl House proved to be a short one.

"We need to keep up appearances with my mother so she doesn't figure out what we're planning and try to stop us. As the Shal, Zan and the guards report to her, not me. She extends her protection to me because I'm her son, but she won't hesitate to use them to stop me if she thinks I'm getting in the way of her plans to do away with the position of Ruhl so she can once again make me her heir," Ezri explained as we walked down one stretch of hallway to a T-shaped intersection with another hall that appeared to parallel the back wall of the Ruhl House.

Zan and Mage-sha turned left, and we followed, continuing about halfway to the intersection with the hall that accessed the rooms on the far side of the house. Mia was waiting for us and opened the door to the dining room as we arrived. Mage-sha, Ezri, and I entered to find the Shal, her brother, his consort, and Jace already inside.

"You appear to be making a habit of these delays, Ezri," Filna-sha said. Her eyes shifted to me. "I don't like it."

"Well, we're here, now. Shall we sit?" Ezri asked, gesturing toward the table at the center of the room. "I've promised to walk Mage-sha back to the Magery after dinner, and I don't want to keep her out too late."

"Thank you, dear." Mage-sha patted Ezri's hand. "I appreciate your kindness to an old woman."

"Mage-sha," Jace said, coming forward and offering his hands in greeting. "How lovely that you could join us this evening."

"What about Tavo-jah? Is he not joining us?" Filna-sha asked.

"Not tonight," Ezri said.

The Shal shrugged one shoulder. "No matter. At least Mage-sha has come so we can make arrangements for your marriage."

Ezri pressed a hand to the small of my back and led me to one end of the table. After helping me into the chair to his right, he took his seat at the head of the table. Filna-sha took the seat at the opposite end. Jace helped Mage-sha into the seat next to me as his father and Vie took the seats on either side of the Shal. Then Jace circled around behind Ezri so he could sit opposite me, leaving the space between him and his father empty because of the absent Jahlo.

As everyone settled into their places, a server slipped through a door I hadn't noticed in the wall at the far side of the room. She circled the table, filling our goblets with a dark red wine. When she finished, she retreated from the room, and a different server entered, carrying two large platters heaped with bread, cheese, and nuts. He placed one at the center of each end of the table.

Jace leaned forward to serve himself from the platter. I watched him for a moment, then offered to help Mage-sha reach what she desired. While everyone busied themselves with the food, Ezri reached for his goblet.

"I'd like to make a toast before we begin," he said.

A hush fell over the group as everyone set down their plates and reached for their own goblets.

"To my betrothed, may this be the first of many family dinners we share together." Ezri smiled as he raised his goblet to me.

A brief pang pierced my heart at the mention of family and the reminder that these people were nothing like my brothers and sister, or the parents I'd left behind. I raised my goblet to meet his and tried to match his smile. The joy that radiated from him warmed me even more than the small sip of wine I took to honor his gesture.

As I set my goblet back on the table, a movement on the far side of the room caught my eye. It was there and gone in a blink. Then Ezri's goblet tumbled from his hand. He gripped the table, staggered, then plunged to the floor.

I jumped to my feet and crouched down next to him, where he'd fallen. "He's choking. Mage-sha!"

She was already moving when I glanced back at her. Jace hurried to her side to help her kneel, then helped me roll Ezri, who had gone still, onto his back.

"I don't think he's breathing," I whispered.

"Guards!" Filna-sha yelled. "Where are the guards? You there. Go find the guards and get them in here!"

I glanced up in time to see the server who had brought in the platters of food. He met my eyes briefly and froze. The swinging movement of the pendant tucked under the collar of his tunic caught my eye. He jerked his body toward the door when he realized what I was looking at.

"No!" I sprang to my feet. "Stop him!"

Mia already had the door open. She blocked it with her

body when he tried to push past her. Then, in one quick movement, she grasped his wrist and twisted his arm behind his back, just as Zan appeared in the doorway behind her.

"What happened?" he asked, his eyes moving from me to Ezri's body, motionless on the floor, before taking in the positions of everyone else in the room.

Filna-sha, who had come around the table to see what was going on with her son, ignored his question. "Did he have an attack? Where is his medicine?"

Medicine. I remembered the vial of liquid that Zan had given Ezri the night we met and the potion he drank when he'd had that coughing fit, the one he'd said Mage-sha made for him.

"He usually keeps it in his pocket." I bent to search for the vial where I'd seen him tuck it away before, but Filna-sha's hand clamped down on my shoulder.

She held me back. "Not you. Someone else. Jace. Check his pockets. Assist Mage-sha."

I tried to pull away from her. "Let me help."

She tightened her grip the more I squirmed. "No. You're not going anywhere near my son. Not until we figure out what happened here. Do you think you're fooling anyone, trying to accuse Ruhl House staff of harming my son?"

I glared at her, then turned to Mia and Zan. "His neck. I think he's wearing one of those amulets."

Zan frowned but turned to the server. He tugged on the cord and extracted the stone pendant from where it hung under the man's tunic. After studying it for a moment, he held it up for Mia to see. "Is this it?"

Mia flinched away from the charm. "Yes."

Zan jerked his head toward the door. "Take him away and restrain him. Dispatch a unit to sweep Ruhl House for more and send a second unit to Shal House to retrieve the Jahlo. Send a third here to secure this room, then meet me in the Ruhl's chambers when you're done."

"Yes, sir." Mia shoved the server ahead of her through the door.

"What are you doing?" Filna-sha asked, twisting me away from Ezri and shoving me toward Zan and Mia. "Take her as well. Whatever's going on here, she's responsible for it, I'm sure. First Belyn and now my son. When will it end? I told him to stay away from those people!"

Zan looked at me and scowled.

I silently begged him to trust me and not send me away. I only hoped that Zan could see I was innocent, even though I knew, since he was the captain of the Shal's guard, he would be honor-bound to do as she commanded.

"Do it. Now," the Shal commanded when Zan didn't respond right away.

His gaze flicked to Ezri. "I can do nothing until more guards arrive. In the meantime, I think we should focus our attention on your son and perhaps get him to a more comfortable location. Mage-sha, do you agree?"

"There is nothing more I can do for him here. I need my satchel, but I left it at the Magery," she said.

"I'll go," a soft voice said.

I turned to see who'd spoken just as Vie stepped forward.

Zan squinted at her, most likely evaluating her motivation for volunteering and weighing it against the need to get the supplies Mage-sha needed to help Ezri. "Jace-sha, go with her. Jeln-sha, help me lift the Ruhl and carry him to his room. Ayla-nah, you come with me so I can keep an eye on you. Help Mage-sha."

Jace followed Vie out of the dining room at Zan's command, and I used the distraction to twist out of Filna's grip.

Mage-sha looked up at me. "He's breathing," she said. "Barely. And his pulse is faint. I don't think it's his lungs. I think it's something... else."

"It's obvious he's been poisoned," Filna said. "And mark my words, the Nahla is behind it."

Zan and Jeln took positions on either side of Ezri as I helped Mage-sha stand. We took a few steps back to give them room. Then they hoisted his limp body between them, taking care with his head as they maneuvered his arms around their shoulders.

"My Shal," Zan said once he had Ezri settled. "I think it best that someone stay here to make sure that no one disturbs this room before my guards have a chance to investigate, and I don't think you'd like me to leave Ayla-nah here alone. So, unless you think you can help me carry your son, I will need you to remain here until the reinforcements I sent for arrive and then direct them to begin the investigation."

Filna glared at me. "I will keep the Nahla here with me and instruct *my* guards when they arrive."

Mage-sha straightened beside me. "If you want me to save your son, the Nahla must come with me. She has been trained as a mage apprentice, and I will need assistance."

Filna hesitated. Worry flickered across her face, softening her features for a moment before her scowl returned. "I don't want that Nahl clan traitor anywhere near my son."

"Then your son will die," Mage-sha said, folding her arms across her chest.

"Enough." Zan's commanding voice clamped all our mouths shut. "No one is dying on my watch. I will take responsibility for Ayla-nah and see that she is confined for questioning once we have secured another assistant for Mage-sha."

Filna's eyes narrowed. "Send for one immediately, and don't take your eyes off her, even for a moment, Captain."

"Of course, my Shal," Zan responded.

"I also need Ezri-ruh's goblet," Mage-sha said. "I'll need to test it once my satchel arrives."

I started forward to fetch it, but Filna stopped me. "No. I'll get it."

She backed toward the table, keeping her eyes fixed on me until the last moment before bending to search the floor near Ezri's chair. Ducking down, she retrieved the goblet from where it had fallen and rolled under the table. She straightened, brushed a lock of hair back from her forehead, and handed the goblet to Mage-sha.

A pained look crossed Filna's face as her eyes shifted to her son. "Take Ezri to his chambers and see that he survives. I will stay until the guards arrive. Then I will join you there."

Zan dipped his head. "My Shal."

Zan and Jeln, supporting Ezri between them, led the way down the hall to Ezri's rooms. Mage-sha and I followed. Her grip on my arm tightened every few steps.

"Will he be all right?" I whispered.

"I'll do what I can, but we will need to identify the poison quickly," she said.

Strong heart, strong body, strong mind, keep him in health until your Star calls him to shine. I murmured the Star Litany, even though I doubted Estrel could hear me, surrounded by stone and with no offering.

Mage-sha must have heard my quiet prayer, though, because she made the sign for Estrel's blessing. Releasing her grip on my arm, she placed the thumb of her free hand against her breastbone, holding her hand perpendicular to her chest and turned her gaze briefly skyward.

"Let's see what else Mage-nah has taught you," she said when we reached Ezri's rooms.

While Zan and Jeln worked to make Ezri comfortable on his bed, I glanced around, familiarizing myself with the layout and noting the similarities between the rooms I'd been assigned and Ezri's suite. The main difference appeared to be the small office adjacent to his sitting room. His bedroom was a bit larger than the one I'd been given, but otherwise, they were very much the same.

"Captain?" Mia's voice called from the doorway. She held a leather case that was almost the same size as my small traveling trunk.

Zan stepped away from the bed. He thanked and dismissed Jeln, then waited for the Shal's brother to leave before signaling Mia to come inside and shut the door behind her. "What do you know?"

"Tavo-jah is missing and so is Mage-ruh. According to Jace-sha, the Magery seemed to be in disarray when they arrived. Luckily, one of the students was able to help them locate this." She set the case down near Ezri's bed.

"The Magery is always a bit chaotic, but Sera's absence is worrying. She wouldn't have left without you." Mage-sha shook her head as she made her way past the others and opened her case. "Ayla-nah, take this and pour it into that goblet. Swish it around at least ten times. Make sure you cover as much of the interior surface and rim as possible, then pour the contents back into the jar. We'll have to wait a bit for the reaction, but it should give us a hint of what we're up against."

I took the jar Mage-sha handed me and carried it over to the goblet, waiting to see what Zan would say before adding my thoughts to the discussion. He was already so suspicious of my family, it probably wouldn't help to mention that, given the state of the Magery, we should probably assume my aunt had been compelled against her will to accompany Tavo, wherever he'd gone.

Zan might have come to the same conclusion, only he was more likely to guess that she'd been an accomplice. After all, I was helping Mage-sha test Ezri's goblet for poison. Something mages were fully capable of producing.

"Did anyone see him leave?" Zan asked. "Is his horse gone? He could have gone to the stables after leaving the aviary. He had enough time after leaving Ayla-nah's rooms to get halfway back to the Lower Stone Crossing before I checked on the messages he sent."

"So he did send a message, then?" I asked, unable to contain my curiosity.

"Two," Zan confirmed with a scowl. "One to the Jahl and one to your father."

I snapped my mouth shut and turned away to focus on swirling Mage-sha's potion around the inside of the goblet without spilling.

Mia spoke up, answering Zan's questions. "His horse was gone, but if he packed a bag, he didn't take everything. His trunks are still in his rooms at the Shal House. I assigned a pair of guards to search his things and sent another cluster to the Magery and a pair to the stables to keep watch."

I'd known Tavo longer than anyone else here in the city. I hadn't wanted to believe he would hurt anyone, but his actions made him look very guilty. With Ezri lying motionless on the bed, I almost wished we had let Zan interrogate Tavo when we'd had the chance.

Zan ran a hand through his hair. "Send a party after him. Search everyone leaving or entering the city. And send our two fastest riders directly to the mountain caverns to stand watch. I want a report back immediately if he returns."

"Yes, sir." Mia turned to leave, but before she could reach the door, the Shal burst into the room.

"How is he?" she asked. "The guard at the door informed me that Tavo-jah and that meddlesome mage from the Nahl clan have fled. Is that true?"

Zan grimaced. "Mage-sha can speak to Ezri's state, but as for the rest, it's true. Both Tavo-jah and Sera are gone, though we have not yet determined that they are together."

Filna scoffed. "Of course they are. The cowards tried to assassinate my son and then fled before they could be caught. But Ezri won't die, will he, Mage-sha?"

"I would not be so quick to accuse Sera if I were you." Mage-sha wiped her pale brow with a piece of cloth before stepping forward. "I've confirmed that the Ruhl has indeed been poisoned and given him a general antidote, but I won't be sure it's the right one until he either wakes up, or we correctly identify the poison."

Filna shoved past Mia to get inside the bedroom. After a long look at her son, her eyes connected with mine. "Have you sent for a proper assistant from the Magery?"

"I was just about to, my Shal," Zan responded.

"The Nahla is done here. Get someone else to help. I want her out." Filna pointed a finger at the door. "Based on the convenient disappearance of Tavo-jah and Sera-nah, I'm accusing the Jahl and the Nahl of treason. The Nahla is lucky I'm not sending her to the detention cells. Instead, I want her escorted to her room immediately. She's to stay there until this mess is resolved."

Zan frowned but held his tongue. He nodded to Mia, and Mia placed a hand on my shoulder. "Come, Nahla."

"No. Not her," Filna commanded. She called for the guard standing watch outside the door. "You. Escort the Nahla to her rooms. And make sure she stays there."

Mia let her hand drop from my shoulder.

I handed the jar, refilled with the potion that I'd swirled around inside the goblet, to Mage-sha. Then I took one last look at Ezri. His wavy hair spread out on his pillow, framing his face. Through the tears welling up in my eyes, he almost appeared to be sleeping, if not for the choked grimace his lips had frozen in.

Before Filna could make another fuss, I backed out of the bedroom, as she moved to Ezri's bedside. I moved through the sitting room, toward the hall, intending to make it easy on the poor guard waiting there, assigned to watch me.

Zan stood with his arms crossed in the doorway to Ezri's bedroom, keeping his eyes on me as he'd told the Shal he would. Even though I'd known Zan wouldn't be able to resist obeying the Shal's commands forever, I'd hoped she'd see I wasn't to blame. But arguing with her would get me nowhere. I had no choice but to obey and retreat.

I'd only taken a few steps when the sight of a figure pushing past the guard in the doorway made me stop in my tracks. My mouth dropped open and my heart lurched. "Rys? What are you doing here?"

"Captain," Rys said. He walked past me into the sitting room and turned to face Zan. "I got here as soon as I could. I have a report."

"Captain?" I stared at them. "Zan, what is this? What's going on? Rys, what are you doing here?"

"Dex," Zan addressed the guard, still standing in the doorway. "You have your orders. Take the Nahla to her rooms."

"But..." I glanced back and forth between Rys and Zan,

searching for an explanation.

"I'll send someone to let you know when the Ruhl wakes up," Zan said to me before focusing his attention on Rys.

Dex clamped a hand around my arm to drag me from the room, but I twisted out of his grip and stormed past him. As I marched down the hallway toward my rooms, I tried to come up with some other explanation, but there was only one. Rys was one of Zan's spies.

I held myself together long enough to get inside my room and shut the door behind me, leaving the guard who had followed me outside. Then I fell to the floor and sobbed.

20

I AWOKE to someone knocking softly on my door. Exhausted, I must have cried myself to sleep on the floor where I'd landed. I stood slowly and cracked the door open. Mia's serious face greeted me. I searched her expression for any hint of good news.

"How is he?" I asked, opening the door wider, only to realize that she was alone. The guard who had been assigned to watch me was gone.

Mia didn't answer. She just slipped past me, into the room, and shut the door behind her. "Grab your things. Whatever you think you'll need. And hurry. We don't have much time."

"Is it Ezri?" My heart clenched.

She shook her head. "According to Mage-sha, he could wake up at any moment. That's why we need to hurry. It's almost dawn."

"Dawn?" I glanced at the windows, registering the faint light that had begun to color the sky outside. "We're not still planning on going to find the God's Seat, are we?"

She frowned. "That's still up for debate. Mage-sha is arguing for it based on whatever it was she saw in the Ruhl's rune card reading. She thinks it's the only way to keep the Ruhl safe."

"So, this is a rescue?" I hesitated only a moment before hurrying into the bedroom to change into my traveling clothes. The map Ezri had found for me and my aunt's little notebook of runes went into the pocket inside my cloak.

"Are you ready?" Mia asked when I returned to the sitting room.

I glanced over at the books of folklore still lying on the table. They would be too big to take with us, but I wanted to bring them with me if we were going to stop at the Magery on our way to the forest, as we'd planned. I picked them up and carried them with me to the door.

"Books?" She raised her eyebrows.

"They may prove useful. And even if they don't, I need to give one of them back to Mage-sha." I hugged the two tomes against my chest.

Mia looked skeptical, but she didn't argue. "We need to move quickly and quietly. If we cross paths with any guards, let me do the talking. Ready?"

I nodded, my pulse racing. "Ready."

She opened the door wide enough to peek outside. Once she'd determined the hallway was still clear, she motioned for me to follow and shut the door behind us.

"With any luck, no one will be sent to check on you until breakfast, and by then you'll be far from here," she whispered.

Mia set a brisk pace, retracing the path Zan had led us down to our ill-fated dinner. She sped up as we passed the dining room, keeping her body between me and the open door. Inside, I glimpsed guards moving about the room. I tensed, every muscle in my body ready to run.

Once we made it past without notice, I breathed a sigh of relief, only to realize we were approaching the turn that would lead us to the hallway outside Ezri's rooms. I sucked in a new breath and held it as Mia extended her arm to block me, signaling for me to wait while she looked around the corner.

After she made sure there wasn't anyone lingering in the hallway who might catch her sneaking me into Ezri's rooms, she motioned for me to follow. We hurried down the last stretch, then slipped inside the unguarded door to Ezri's rooms, only to be greeted by Rys.

"What's he doing here?" I asked.

"He's one of Zan's spies," Mia said, confirming my suspicion. "He's been helping us."

A hot stab of rage flared in my chest. I dropped the books on the table and lunged toward Rys. "You were spying on me? For how long?"

"It's not like that." A frantic, pained look flashed across his face, but he quickly hid it behind an emotionless mask. "I can explain."

"Then do it." I pushed his shoulders, trying to get another reaction, but he only took a step backward. "Tell me why I should believe a word that you say. After everything…"

Mia set a hand on my shoulder, reminding me we weren't alone. When I glanced over, I found Zan standing in the doorway leading to Ezri's bedroom with his arms crossed.

"I've been reporting to Zan for as long as I've been a guard," Rys said, squaring his shoulders and standing up straighter. "I'm loyal to the Ruhl and will do what needs to be done to protect him, even if that means spying on my clan."

"Your clan?" The words tasted sour in my mouth. "How

can you even call us that? How can you even face me with no apology after you've been lying to me all these years?"

My fingers balled into fists at my sides. In that moment, I wanted to erase all that time I spent kissing him and loving him and pinning all my hopes on him. I felt like a fool, and I couldn't bring myself to ask the questions that burned bright in my mind.

Had it all been a lie? Had he really felt nothing for me? And possibly worst of all, were they all in on his charade?

As if he read the thoughts in my head, Rys shook his head slightly. His eyes burned into mine, trying to convey some message to me, but my rage clouded my vision until I had no hope of understanding whatever it was he was trying to say.

"Ayla? Is that you?" a faint voice called from somewhere behind Zan.

My anger washed away on a wave of relief. "Ezri?"

Zan stepped aside so that I could push past him. Ezri lifted his head from the pillow, but Mage-sha kept one hand on his chest, preventing him from trying to sit up. With the other, she took his wrist and felt for his pulse.

"He's awake now," Mage-sha said, with only a hint of scolding in her tone.

"What happened?" Ezri asked, setting his head back and blinking up at us as we gathered around his bed.

"You were poisoned, my boy. It will take you time to heal." Mage-sha released her grip on Ezri's wrist. "And that's only after we find the antidote."

"Who?" Ezri croaked out the word.

Mage-sha held a glass of water to his lips as Zan explained about Tavo and Sera.

"Did you find anything in Tavo-jah's rooms?" I asked.

"Not much," Mia said. "The guards collected his things and

brought them here for Zan to look through. They're in the Ruhl's office."

"Perhaps, now that Ezri-ruh is awake, I could have a look through Tavo-jah's belongings to see if I can find anything that might help us identify the poison?" Mage-sha suggested.

Zan nodded. "That would be helpful. If you don't mind?"

"I would rather enjoy the task, truthfully. These old eyes have seen many things. It would be my pleasure if they could assist with restoring the health of Edan's grandson." Mage-sha started toward the bedroom door.

Mia followed her far enough to instruct Rys on Mage-sha's task. We waited while she asked Rys to assist Mage-sha. I tried to hide the emotions warring within me. Half of me wanted to put a stop to everything until I could confront Rys. The other half insisted it would be better to stay focused on Ezri and ignore the hurt that still throbbed in my chest.

I'd come here to find the Inahi and help Ezri protect the clans. That was what mages did. My heartache didn't matter in the face of the dangers threatening our border. Threatening Ezri's life. And Mage-sha's reading had been for me and Ezri, together. So maybe the messages I'd been receiving had been leading me here all along, so that I could return Edan's grandson to the Gods' Seat, wherever it was. There would be time to deal with Rys later.

Mia shut the door to Ezri's bedroom. "Now what?"

Zan paced to the window. "It's nearly dawn."

"Ezri can't leave. You heard Mage-sha. The poison is still at work inside him. He needs to rest." I moved closer to Ezri, taking the place of Mage-sha at his bedside and reaching out to hold his hand.

His fingers curled around mine. "I can go. I need to go. If she doesn't find an antidote—"

Zan cut him off before he could finish his morbid thought. "If I have to hunt down that Jahlo myself, we'll find the antidote. You're not going to die."

I considered our options. As much as I didn't want to admit it, Ezri had a point. We didn't know where Tavo had gone. He may have returned to the Jahl caverns, but he could have crossed the border, or taken a ship to Agrion or Valthonia. It would take time to hunt him down. Time we might not have. Not if Ezri really had inherited the ability to speak with the Inahi. I hadn't had much luck deciphering their messages.

"The messages." I fumbled for the map I'd tucked into my pocket. "Maybe they aren't runes, after all. Maybe they're marking a path."

"What do you mean?"

I unrolled the map and spread it beside Ezri's legs on the bed. Then I glanced around the room, searching for some small objects I could use as markers. My eyes landed on Mage-sha's bag. If she kept supplies in there, she'd probably have starflower seeds. One of the first jobs assigned to a novice was harvesting starflower seeds because we used them in so many potions.

I hesitated for a moment, glancing toward the door and wondering if I should ask permission first. But there wasn't time. Mage-sha would understand. I rummaged around in her case until I found what I was looking for, then I returned to the map to address the questioning looks on the others' faces.

"Here's where the flowers were lying when I found them on the map." I placed the seeds down in order, working from the leftmost one that had been closest to our clan's compound, to the rightmost one that had been just outside the city walls. Near the Heartgrove.

"They don't follow the road," Zan said.

"But they align with the places we stopped along the way," Mia added.

"Except this one." I pointed to the last seed.

Ezri propped himself up on one elbow so he could get a better look at the map. "It's near the Heartgrove."

"What if they're leading us to the Gods' Seat?" I met Ezri's gaze.

The spark of mischief in his eyes returned. "Let's go find out."

Zan waved his hands. "Hold on. Wait. You're not going without a guard, and your mother will have me locked up if I let you leave here with the person she's accusing of plotting to murder you."

"If you stay here, you can cover for us, keep her out of my rooms, just until we return. And Mia can come with us," Ezri suggested.

"Can you even walk?" I asked.

"Only one way to find out." Ezri pushed himself up and swung his legs over the side of the bed.

I moved the map out of his way, gathering the seeds into my hand just as the door opened and Mage-sha returned, carrying a small wooden box in her hands.

"Just what do you think you're doing?" she asked, staring at Ezri. "I thought I told you to rest. Lie down this instant."

Ezri took a moment to catch his breath before fixing his most charming grin on her. "I'm sorry, Mage-sha, but I can't do that. I need to go find the Inahi."

Mia stepped closer to Mage-sha. Her eyes were focused on the box Mage-sha was holding. "Where did you find that?"

"This?" Mage-sha held up the wooden cube, and I realized the surfaces were carved with a pattern of bars that looked almost like a maze from where I was standing. "It was buried under a heap of what I assume were Tavo-jah's clothes. I've never seen anything like it, and it was the only object that was at all curious among his things. Do any of you know what it might be?"

"No. But the pattern." Mia held up her hand, displaying the large stone ring that covered most of the lower half of her first finger. "It's similar, yes?"

Zan closed the distance between himself and Mia, positioning himself between her and the box Mage-sha held so that he could get a better look at both. "Very. Do you think it's Agrisse?"

"What would Tavo-jah be doing with a wooden box from Agrion?" Ezri shifted toward the end of the bed. "Does it open?"

I followed his progress, ready to help him if he tried to stand.

"There's no opening that I've been able to find," Mage-sha replied.

"It may not be from Agrion," Mia said. "I can't be sure where my ring came from, originally. My grandmother gave it to my parents when I was a baby. I think it's a protection spell of some sort. It hung from a cord above my cradle until I was old enough to wear it on a cord around my neck. I'd only just been able to fit it onto my thumb when we fled Agrion."

"What was your grandmother trying to protect you from?" Zan asked.

"Koto," I said, remembering what she'd told me.

Zan stared at Mia, who confirmed my guess with a nod. He looked like he wanted to say something more, but Ezri spoke first.

"Can I see it?" Ezri asked.

Mage-sha slipped past Zan and Mia, still locked in some silent conversation, and handed the box to Ezri. That seemed to break whatever spell they'd been under, because they joined us, and we all watched while Ezri turned the cube over in his hands, studying it from every angle.

"I don't see any sign of a lid or a hinge, either." He held each face up, studying the varying patterns. They each featured a unique arrangement of nested lines and angles. All except one side. That one had concentric circles carved into the polished wood.

Ezri pressed his thumb against the middle circle, and we all sucked in a breath at the sound of a faint click. He grinned up at us. Then he let his fingers play along each ring in turn, but nothing more happened until he reached the outermost ring.

That one slipped a bit when he touched it. He twisted it until it clicked into place. Then his fingers danced back toward the middle, trying each ring until he found another that moved. Another twist and click, then another. Like tabs fitting into slots.

When he finally took the pressure off the final ring, it slid out from the surface. Ezri turned the cube so that the side angled down as he lowered his palm. The ring continued to slide out, revealing itself to be a cylinder that had fit snugly inside the box.

Ezri held out the cube, and I took it from him. Then he unscrewed the cylinder. "Empty."

"Let me see." Mage-sha gestured for him to hand it over. She angled it into the light and humphed with satisfaction. "Almost, but not quite."

Zan, Mia, and I leaned closer. Inside was the residue of a fine powder. It wasn't much, but if it was the poison that had been used on Ezri, it might be enough for Mage-sha to brew an antidote.

"Gotcha." Zan's face broke into an expression that might have been joy on anyone else, but looked particularly dangerous on him.

"I'll need to return to the Magery to see what can be done." Mage-sha frowned at Ezri. "I don't suppose you'll agree to wait for me before running off, will you?"

Ezri grinned up at her. "Weren't you the one who said we should go right away?"

"That was before. Now—"

Ezri cut her off. "Now it's even more urgent. What if you can't make an antidote? What then? Besides, Ayla thinks she knows where we need to go."

I quickly explained my interpretations of the Inahi's messages to Mage-sha.

She nodded. "There's a trail that leads up into the Heart-grove, very close to the north gate. The novices use it to forage the plants we need from the forest for potions. But the path is uphill, and Ezri-ruh..."

"Can he ride?" Mia asked. "If he can sit in a saddle, I'll return with horses after I walk Mage-sha back to the Magery."

"I'm sitting now, aren't I?" Ezri replied.

"We'll still need to get you from here up onto your horse, and the longer we wait, the more people will begin moving about," Zan said. "If we're going to make this work, we need to hurry."

"We'll leave right away," Mia replied, gathering up Mage-sha's case. "Mage-sha?"

"Be careful." Mage-sha set her palm on Ezri's head. "May Lorjad's Luck be with you."

Zan reached out to touch Mia's arm. "Stop at the barracks and get a fresh pair of guards to keep watch on Mage-sha while she works."

We watched as they left, then Zan turned to me. "You, too. Out. I'm not about to send Ezri-ruh off into the forest dressed like that. He needs to change into traveling clothes."

"Of course. I'll just…" I hesitated, remembering that Rys was probably still out there, standing guard. "Wait in the sitting room."

Sure enough, Rys had just closed the door on Mia and Mage-sha as Ezri's bedroom door clicked closed behind me. He turned toward the sound, and our eyes locked.

"Ayla." The gentle tone I remembered had returned to his voice.

"Don't," I whispered, moving closer to meet him near the entryway and reduce the chance that Ezri and Zan might overhear us. "There is nothing you can say that can change how much you've hurt me."

"I know. I know I've hurt you." He kept his voice low as he closed the remaining distance between us. "But it's not how you think. They didn't know about us. I didn't realize that my reports would end up making him interested in you. It wasn't supposed to be this way."

My body tensed with the effort of holding back my emotions. "You're right. It wasn't supposed to be like this. You had a chance to stop this. You could have spoken up. But you made your choice. You chose your loyalty to him over your love for me. If you ever really loved me. If any of that was real. Not that it matters, because now I'm betrothed to Ezri."

"Ayla, please. Don't say that." He reached for my arm, but I shook him off. "Of course my feelings for you were real. Are real. I still love you. How could you doubt that?"

"Because the whole time I was falling in love with you, you were spying for them." I gestured behind me, toward Ezri's bedroom. "How am I supposed to believe anything you say?"

Rys caught my waving hands and pressed me back until I was caught between him and the wall. He pinned me with his gaze before dipping his head down. After a heartbeat of hesitation, his lips met mine with all the hunger I remembered, and I melted into him. As much as I wanted to forget, to deny what we had, his kiss brought everything rushing back.

I pulled away. "I can't. We can't."

"I'll tell him." His fingers brushed against my cheek. "I promise. Just say you'll give me another chance."

I shook my head. "Not now. We're so close. There isn't time to explain."

He brushed the tip of his nose against mine. "I won't go back. Not without you."

The metallic click of Ezri's bedroom door opening had us springing apart. I had only a moment to catch my breath before Ezri limped into the sitting room with Zan's assistance.

"Ready, Stormcat?" The hope and excitement in his eyes sent a spear of pain through my gut.

I shoved down all of my feelings, locking them away to deal with later. "Let's go."

21

ZRI and I rode through the gate as the sun crested the horizon. Zan agreed to have Mia accompany us as our guard while he stayed behind and attempted to hide our absence from the Shal. The only argument came when Mia volunteered to go after Tavo. But the words were barely off her lips before Zan shut that down. He said he wouldn't risk her that way, especially now that he knew the Koto had been hunting her family.

So Ezri, Mia, and I set off together, following the road out of the city until it began to curve away from the forest. At that point, I left Mia with Ezri and rode across the parched, rocky ground, toward the edge of the forest to find the trail Mage-sha had told us about. It took a few passes back and forth along the base of the hillside before I found what I was looking for.

What Mage-sha had called a trail looked like little more than a gap between the low bushes that looked to have been beaten down over the years by generations of browsing impex. But I couldn't find any other way up, so I signaled to the others to follow.

After Arge crested the first ridge, the narrow path opened up to a wider trail that wound its way beneath the trees. We continued the slow climb up the tiered hillside until it flattened out. At that point, the trail was just wide enough for us to ride side by side.

Ezri brought his horse up to ride next to me, and Mia fell in behind us. I monitored Ezri's labored breathing as I inhaled the scent of fresh pine mixed into the crisp sea breeze. Around us, the birds came to life with the morning light, chattering and chirping as they went about their business. I allowed myself a moment to bask in the relief at being out of the city and back in a place where I felt more at home.

"I'm sorry you had to find out about Rys that way," Ezri said, breaking my sense of peace. "I didn't realize you knew him that well."

My insides twisted with guilt as I prepared to tell Ezri the truth.

"I hope you can forgive him. It's really my fault that Zan chose him in the first place," Ezri said before I could find my words.

"Your fault?" I asked, confused.

"Rys wouldn't have told you—Sera made him swear to keep it secret—but our paths crossed when we were both much younger." Ezri paused to catch his breath. "Remember the story I told you? About how we got attacked near the river crossing on my first trip out of the city?"

I nodded, my mind already doing the math and putting the pieces together, even before Ezri confirmed my suspicion.

"There was another family camped near the crossing that night. A Nahl clan family. Sera thought it would be safer if we all stayed together. She caught up on news from your clan while Zan and I sparred with their son. Rys."

"That was the night his family was attacked," I said.

Ezri nodded. "Sera and his father woke at the first sound of something approaching. They went out to check on their herd of onks while his mother stayed back with us. When the shrieking started, Zan tried to leave. She held him back and made us promise to stay inside the tent. Then she went out to help defend us." Ezri winced.

"Are you all right?" I reached for his arm to keep him steady in the saddle.

He remained bent over, breathing fast and shallow, and didn't answer right away. I opened my mouth to call back to Mia for help when he shook his head and straightened. "I'm fine."

We rode in silence as his breathing evened out. Then he tried to continue his story. "When it was over, Sera did what she could to help his mother, but his father—"

I interrupted him. "I know what happened with his family. The entire clan knows that much. What I don't know is why they never mentioned that they weren't alone."

"Sera thought it would be better for Rys and his mother if they didn't mention she was with them. Rys argued with her. He thought he could convince the Nahl to change his mind because of her service to the clan in protecting them and saving his mother. But she made him promise to keep it a secret. He insisted on repaying her in some way. So she told him to return the favor to another in need someday, and he declared he would promise himself to the Nahl clan guard as soon as he returned. Then he swore an oath of loyalty to me."

"To you? But why?"

Ezri swayed in his saddle. "I think Zan made an impression

on him. He is older than us. He was already serving in the Shal clan guard, and Rys knew he'd sworn an oath to protect me. That's why he was traveling with us."

I sighed. Everything Ezri said matched with what I knew of Rys and made perfect sense. I still hated that he'd lied to me and kept all this a secret, but knowing why softened the hurt. Glancing ahead, as I gathered my courage to explain exactly how well Rys and I knew each other, I realized the trail was about to split. One path led out toward the sea cliffs, and the other led deeper into the forest.

Before I could ask Ezri which way he thought we should go, a rustle in the bushes drew my attention. I kept Arge moving at a steady walk as I peered into the brush alongside the trail to see if there was a creature lurking there. I spotted nothing. Ezri hadn't even looked, so I wondered if I was imagining things.

When we reached the place where the trail split, I drew Arge to a halt. "What do you think?"

Ezri took a moment to consider the options before starting down the path that led deeper into the forest. We hadn't gone very far when another rustle in the brush, first on my right, then on my left, put me on alert for danger. I glanced back at Mia, but she didn't appear concerned. Ezri also kept riding as though he had heard nothing.

My muscles tensed as I searched alongside the trail, listening for something besides the birds, the wind, and the hooves of our horses in the dirt. The next time I heard the sound, I signaled for Arge to stop, and held up a hand to alert Ezri to do the same. My other hand went instinctively to my belt for the knife Mia had given me.

Ezri's horse stopped next to mine. Before he could speak, I raised my finger to my lips. Together, we listened. Then he must have heard it, too. His eyes narrowed, and he looked into the bushes on the side of the trail. I turned back to signal Mia, only to discover she was no longer there.

I slid out of the saddle, heart pounding, and took Arge's reins in one hand. With my other, I gripped the knife. Then I stood, barely breathing, and stared into the bushes, waiting for another sound or some sign of life, or for Mia to appear behind us. I considered suggesting that we turn around and glanced over to catch Ezri's eye.

He kept his gaze fixed on the path in front of us, then nudged his horse forward as though in a daze. I didn't bother getting back into the saddle. Instead, I led Arge along the path beside Ezri, further into the forest. My skin prickled as every sense in my body shifted to high alert.

Both horses stopped after we rounded the next bend and discovered three stormcats facing us, standing side by side and blocking our path. Each one had a tiny creature straddling their neck, just behind their tufted ears. I almost thought I was imagining the whole thing because the harder I tried to focus on the creatures, the more they seemed to grow fuzzy and indistinct. But, if I focused on some other point, like the tip of a stormcat's nose, and only looked at the creatures indirectly, they became more distinct. They were almost human in feature, but clearly miniature in size. They sat, silent and serious, astride their mounts.

Inahi, I thought, my heart beating faster, scared, but also excited. *We found them.*

The stormcat in the middle stepped forward, and a voice said, *Yes. We've been waiting for you.*

I didn't see the lips move on any of the Inahi, but I was sure I hadn't spoken out loud, and Ezri had not been the one to respond. I glanced at him to see if he had also heard the voice, but he was still staring at the stormcats.

"We mean no harm," Ezri said, lifting both hands so his palms faced the three Inahi.

If you had, you wouldn't have made it this far, came the reply. Again, the response echoed in my head, but I couldn't detect a voice or speaker.

I turned to Ezri. This time, he looked at me, eyes wide with surprise.

"What did you do with our companion?" I asked.

She is safe but must remain here, said the voice. *She may not proceed to the Gods' Seat.*

Ezri and I exchanged a look. Excitement that we'd finally succeeded won out over concern about Mia, who we trusted could take care of herself, and we followed the Inahi further into the forest. As the trails became skinnier, Ezri and I could no longer walk side by side. One of the Inahi led the way. Arge and I followed behind, with another Inahi slipping in between me and Ezri. The third Inahi rode at the end of the line, and I hoped it was monitoring Ezri because I could no longer see him.

The older, taller trees in this part of the forest blocked much of the early morning light from reaching the ground. Their thick branches made it harder to see the trail, but somehow the Inahi remained strangely illuminated. Their shapes were much brighter and more distinct without the sun shining on them.

We traveled for some time in silence. My mind churned, wondering where they were taking us and what we'd say when we arrived. The rustle of the leaves above us and the crunch of twigs beneath hooves, paws, and feet kept my already excited senses on edge. I couldn't make out what was up ahead, but I could feel the presence of more of these creatures nearby. Then, after several more steps, I noticed what looked like stars blinking between the limbs of the trees above, but they also appeared closer to the ground, especially near the base of an enormous tree trunk ahead.

It took a moment before I realized they weren't stars, but more Inahi moving about between the trees and along the forest floor. As my eyes adjusted, I could tell they were traveling up, around, and between the trees on pathways and suspended bridges.

Behind me, Ezri sucked in his breath at the sight of the Inahi moving about. Then we both exhaled in awe at the wide tree trunk just ahead of us. The thick trunk extended up nearly as high as the Council tower before splitting into five enormous branches that arched out and up in low, wide curves. It looked like the hand of a giant, raised up from the earth and reaching for the stars.

Welcome to the Gods' Seat. You are safe here, but do not attempt to leave until we release you.

Ezri grunted as he slid from the saddle, and I hurried over to help him stand.

Leave your horses and follow me. I wasn't sure which of the Inahi had been speaking. Their lips didn't move, if they had lips. It was hard to tell because the details of their shape became indistinct when you looked at them directly. For all I knew, they were all speaking at the same time. Or perhaps they took turns. Or maybe only one of them could communicate with us. There was nothing in the folklore about the details of communicating with the Inahi.

When the Inahi who had been leading us turned away and began walking off the path, I followed it toward the base of the wide tree. It laid one hand on the trunk, then walked in a circle around it, trailing its hand along the bark. Once the

Inahi completed its circle, it stopped and turned back in the other direction. Then it stepped forward and seemed to disappear inside the tree.

I craned my neck, trying to see where it had gone. Ezri shuffled closer to me. When we didn't move toward the tree trunk, the other two Inahi who had been escorting us nudged us forward. I hadn't even realized they were still behind us.

As I took a tentative step forward, the Inahi that had disappeared into the tree reappeared and motioned for us to approach. Ezri matched my small, cautious steps. I kept close to him in case he faltered, and wondered if he was also near bursting with awe and excitement, knowing that we were finally here. We'd done it. We'd found them. I reached over to give Ezri's arm a squeeze.

As we approached the tree trunk, the Inahi disappeared again. I watched carefully and pointed out the opening in the trunk in case Ezri had missed it. The gap was just wide enough for us to slip through sideways.

Ezri let go of my arm and slipped inside first. Once inside, I could see his profile, bathed in the interior glow. I slid in beside him and looked around. The inside of the trunk was illuminated by glowing orbs scattered around the ground near the walls. The tree was mostly hollow, with stairs cut into the inside of the trunk. Several feet above our heads, the stairs ascended through a small opening in the ceiling.

The ceiling and the walls were not smooth. They looked like they still bore the marks of a very large chisel that had been used to hollow out the inside of the tree. The ceiling only covered a little more than half of the space above our heads. In the section where there wasn't ceiling, the inside walls of the trunk extended all the way up to what might have been a dome, far above, that let some of the morning light inside.

What struck me most was that everything seemed to be fit on a scale meant to be comfortable for both human and Inahi. Near the center of the space there was a glowing fire, small but warm, enclosed in a circle of rocks almost as tall as the Inahi. There was a small opening on one side where the fuel could be inserted. The smoke rose out of a chimney that cleverly routed it out of the trunk. There were also pallet beds cut into one side of the trunk, and I could smell food, even though I couldn't see where the mouthwatering aroma originated. I wondered if they hosted other human visitors, or if only the Ruhlini had been welcome here.

I could sense and almost see several Inahi moving about in the space. The Inahi who had led us inside motioned to some lumps near the fire, and I realized they wanted us to sit there and relax.

Rest, said the voice in my head. *You have had a long journey. We will bring you food.*

Ezri began to ask a question, but an Inahi held up its staff. *We will talk after you eat. Sit. Rest.*

We moved closer to the fire, where we both collapsed into the lumpy pillow-like chairs. Then the Inahi presented us with steaming food in clay bowls. I had no idea what it was, but it smelled delicious, and I found I was starving. Ezri, maybe being extra cautious because of the poison his body was still fighting, sniffed the food in his bowl and poked at it. While I ate quickly, he took a small bite, chewed slowly, considered the flavor, and then repeated the process. I had nearly finished my portion before he had even taken five bites.

While we ate, the Inahi moved around us, feeding the fire, bringing more food, carrying things from here to there. None of them seemed bothered by our presence.

Warm, with a full belly, feeling relief at having finally found what we were looking for, I let my eyes blink closed. Allowing myself to relax, as the Inahi had instructed. I must have dozed off because an image of my father surfaced in my mind. He was standing near the well in the gardens outside the lodge, reading a message.

The details were so clear that I could hardly believe it was a dream, and yet it didn't feel like a memory, either. Just as I realized this, Father finished reading the note, folded it, and handed it to Tavo, who was standing nearby.

"Tell him I agree to his proposal," Father said.

My eyes snapped open. I sat still, staring into the flames, trying to hold the picture of the scene in my mind, but it was gone. The reality of the vision disturbed me, and I sat up, wondering what I should tell Ezri.

When I looked over at him, I noticed he hadn't finished eating. His attention was still on the Inahi. I followed his gaze around the room, noting there were now about ten of them, as best as I could tell, engaged in various tasks. Some were near the fire, feeding fuel into the flames and checking pots that hung from rings above the heat. Others were hunched over a bench covered with beakers and vials at the opposite side of the space. Surrounding the bench were books on shelves. In a way, the Gods' Seat reminded me of Mage-nah's tent.

One of them approached us. *You may go up now, if you're ready. Or rest longer, if you prefer.*

Ezri met my gaze and raised his eyebrows, as if asking me for permission.

"Are you ready?" I asked, giving his arm a nudge.

He set down his bowl and shifted forward, but struggled when he tried to stand. I helped him up, then let him lead the way to the stairs.

We took our time climbing. Ezri's grip on the rail carved into the wall made it clear that he was still suffering. I worried about the toll the poison, combined with this journey, was taking on his body, and hoped the Inahi might offer him something to help until we could get back to the Magery and the antidote that Mage-sha was brewing.

The stairs led to a wide platform with a ladder that we had to climb to emerge through a hole that brought us up onto a strip of plank that bordered the dome I'd glimpsed from below. Around us, the five enormous branches stretched out and up. Above us was only sky.

If the five branches were fingers, the landing we stood on was part of the palm that stretched between them. The rest of the palm was about half dome and half balcony. Littered around the balcony were more of the lumpy pillow seats we'd been sitting on near the fire. A few Inahi walked around the outer edges of the platform, and one sat near the center, not on a pillow, but on a mat of some sort.

Approach, the voice in my head commanded. I motioned for Ezri to go first, but he just stared at me, frozen, like he didn't have the first idea what to do. So I took the lead.

I took his hand and began walking toward the Inahi at the center of the platform. As we got closer, I noticed the other Inahi had stopped what they were doing to watch us.

Sit, the voice said as we passed the cluster of lumpy chairs closest to where it sat.

I chose a seat and gestured for Ezri to sit down next to me.

Welcome to the Gods' Seat. I am the Inahi Prime. I am pleased you have found your way to us. We have much to discuss.

I raised my open palms and bowed my head, hoping the traditional clan greeting would translate here. Then I spoke out loud, unsure how else to communicate with this Inahi elder. "Thank you for guiding us. We are honored that you have accepted our request to meet with you."

It has been too long, my child. The Prime's words filled my mind. *But we had to be certain. And we do not enter the dwellings of the humans. So, we left you signs that we were watching you. Signs that we hoped would lead you here.*

"Yes. Thank you." I motioned to Ezri. "They helped me bring Edan-ruh's grandson to you. Our Ruhl."

Yes. Your Ruhl. But he is not our Labharon, and technically, there is another with greater claim to the title of Ruhl.

"What do you mean?" Ezri asked, leaning forward.

My body tensed, hoping the Inahi wasn't going to tell us that, after everything, Vorn really should have inherited the title.

The eldest of Edan's line is the beloved child of Belyn and Harn.

"That's impossible," Ezri said. "That baby died."

That baby did not die. That baby was hidden to protect it from those who would prefer that the title of Ruhl be inherited by another. The true Ruhl's mark will be revealed when the time is right.

"But then why are we here, if Ezri is not the true Ruhl?"

We do not care who holds your title of Ruhl. We seek only our Labharon.

"What do you mean? What's a Labharon?" I asked.

My child, the Labharon is not a title you can inherit. The Inahi choose the Labharon, as it is written in the legend of Ruhala.

"The legend with the ending that someone tried to destroy." I glanced at Ezri.

Yes. Long ago, when the clans formed the Council, they gave our Labharon the title of Ruhl. They chose the name to honor the first Labharon, Ruhala. After many generations, all but the oldest of your mages had forgotten there was a difference. That is why you are here, Ayla of Nahl clan.

"Me?"

Yes, you, my child. We have chosen you as the next Labharon.

I pressed my back into the curved support of my chair, leaning away from the Prime. "But why?"

We have been watching you. You honor us and keep the old ways in your heart. You are the rightful Labharon. The heir of the gods. The only one who can communicate with us.

"If that's true, then why can I hear you and speak with you as well?" Ezri asked.

Because our Labharon wishes it to be so. We may speak to other humans, but only in the presence of our Labharon. We grant our Labharon a portion of our powers, so she can speak with us from anywhere.

"Are visions included in these powers?" I asked, thinking of the strange not-quite-dream I'd had while sitting in front of the fire.

Yes. Glimpses of what's happening in other places, with others you care about. You will be capable of that and more. But it will take time. We will train you to use these new gifts.

"Inahi Prime, I appreciate this great honor you bestow upon me. I will work to be worthy of it." I bowed my head and fixed my gaze on my hands, clasped tightly in my lap.

You are worthy, my child. That's why we've chosen you.

Warring emotions swirled inside of me. My deepest dream had been to meet the Inahi, and now I had not only met them, but they had chosen me as their Labharon. I couldn't believe it. But part of me also worried about Ezri's feelings. Would he be disappointed or relieved that the safety of the clans now rested on my shoulders? Either way, it fell on me to pose the question we'd come all this way to ask.

"Then, as Labharon, I beg you, Inahi Prime, please ask the gods to repair the veil."

Alas, the veil will fall, my child.

"Does that mean that you won't take our message to the gods? Or that the gods won't help us?" Ezri asked.

Your people made their choice. They let an ancient evil into your lands. Because of this, the veil will fall. It has, in truth, been thinning now for a generation, but Jusala's Scales insisted that balance be restored. So Estrel chose to give you back your magic. It will return to your people over time, if you cultivate it. All the babies born into your clans since the rift have had their magic potential restored. Unfortunately, not all of these children will keep their magic. If they are not trained before they come of age, they will lose their powers.

"But who will train them?" I asked. "No one in the clans, not even our mages, remember a time with magic, let alone how to wield it as a true mage."

You will train them, Labharon, once you have completed your training.

"How long do we have until the veil disappears completely?" Ezri asked.

Perhaps one year. Perhaps sooner if the evil continues to spread throughout your lands from its source. Certainly, this will be your last winter under our protection.

"What can we do? How can we keep this evil from spreading?" I asked.

You must stop it at its source. Let your powers guide you.

"But where is this source you speak of?" Ezri added.

My stomach sank with the heavy feeling of dread. "I think I know where we need to go."

22

THE Inahi Prime dismissed us, and another Inahi appeared to lead us back down and out to our horses. From there, a pair of Inahi on stormcats led us back to the trail. Through it all, I kept a firm sense of where I was, and knew I could find the Gods' Seat again.

The Prime had said I would need training, and that I would need to train the others who had regained their potential for wielding magic, but they had ushered us out with no mention of when I should return. With Midwinter approaching, another batch of potentials, myself included, would reach maturity. According to the Prime, we'd lose our magic if we weren't trained. And, when the veil fell, we would need our magic to keep our clans safe.

I tried to catch Ezri's attention so we could discuss what we'd learned, but he kept avoiding my attempts. He remained quiet for the rest of our time with the Inahi and gave me no hint as to how he was feeling. I didn't know if he was in pain or preoccupied with reflections based on our conversation with the Inahi Prime. The farther we got from the Gods' Seat, the more worried I became.

When we finally emerged onto the trail, Mia was there waiting for us. I turned to thank the Inahi who had led us back, but they were already gone.

"Sorry to keep you waiting," Ezri said to Mia.

Mia cocked her head to one side. "Waiting? What do you mean?"

I pointed to the sky. "We've been to the God's Seat and back. It's nearly midday."

"That can't be." She tilted her head back to look up past the treetops. "You never left."

"We left." Ezri winced. "And now we need to get back."

"Are you all right?" I asked, reaching over to touch his arm.

He turned to face me, and I noted the strained look on his face. "We need to find Mage-ruh. I think we know now why Tavo-jah took her when he left."

"Mage-ruh? Really? What about..." I hesitated, unsure what to say in front of Mia. "...the rest?"

Ezri shook his head. "We'll deal with that later. Whatever this evil is, it can wait. We have to find the baby. The—" He caught himself and shut his mouth before starting again. "She was there. She knows. I'm sure of it."

Mia walked her horse closer to Ezri. "You look pale. If you've found what you were looking for, we should get you back to the Magery."

"No. You're not listening." Ezri grimaced and clutched his side as he forced the rest of his words through his clenched teeth. "We need to go after them. Right. Now."

"Ezri, please." I nudged Arge closer in case Ezri slipped in his saddle. "You're not going anywhere like this. Let's get you back. You don't know. Zan may have already found them."

A ghost of the vision I'd had flickered in my mind. The nagging sensation that something wasn't right wouldn't leave me. Even though it was clear we needed to get Ezri back to the Magery, I somehow knew that I was needed elsewhere. I had to get back to our clan's winter compound, and fast. But my reminder that Zan was already looking for Tavo was enough to get Ezri moving back down the trail.

I waited until we were back at the road before telling Mia to go ahead without me.

"You're not going after her alone, are you?" Ezri asked.

"No." I stared at the road, remembering how long it had taken us to travel to the city and the Merluks that had attacked us along the way. "Do you remember what I said to the Inahi? I think I know what we have to do, and it means that I have to go."

"Go where?" Mia asked.

"Home."

"Your home is here now," Ezri said.

I sighed. "Not yet."

"You can't ride all the way back to your clan by yourself," Mia said. "You have no supplies, and you'll get lost with no one to guide you."

"I can follow the road."

Mia shook her head. "Roads are for wagons. There are faster ways. Help me get Ezri back, and I'll go with you. We'll be there before nightfall that way."

Ezri straightened, then winced. "If you're going, I'm going, too."

"No." Mia and I spoke at the same time.

"I can do this." I reached out and squeezed his hand. "Please. Let Mage-sha help you. I need you to live."

Ezri scoffed. "You don't need me. You're... No one needs me. Not anymore."

"That is not true, and you know it." I brought Arge up alongside Ezri's horse, then turned to cup his face in my hands. I waited until his eyes locked on mine. "Think. Please, Ezri. No one has to know. You must return. You must live. Lorjad's Stick, remember? New beginnings? Please?"

He swallowed. For a moment, I was sure he would resist me. Then he gave in and nodded. "New beginnings."

I guided his horse alongside mine as Mia rode ahead. She returned with Zan, who had just arrived at the gate to get a report from the guards. As he took over responsibility for getting Ezri back to the Magery, he gave me a nod. I hoped that meant Mia had filled him in on our plan.

I sat up straight and forced a tone of command into my voice. "I want to see him healed by the time I return."

The corner of Zan's mouth twitched. "I'll keep him safe, Nahla."

I leaned over and kissed Ezri on the cheek. "I'll be back soon."

"Be careful," he said.

"I will."

As Mia and I watched Zan and Ezri's horses plod along on their way back toward the north gate, I wiped the tears that I'd been holding back. He was right about the need to find Belyn and Harn's child. If the clans knew Ezri wasn't the rightful Ruhl, he would lose his place on the Council. The clan leaders would likely begin to fight outright for control, abandoning their more subtle political maneuvering. There would be no way to keep them united because the treaty that gave the Ruhl family control of the Council was entirely based on a title handed down within that family.

But that search could wait a bit longer. At least until after I dealt with whatever this evil was and learned to use the powers granted to me by the Inahi. In the meantime, if we kept what we'd learned about the Labharon a secret, no one would have to know that the Ruhl and the Labharon were not the same thing. Then Ezri could remain on the Council to lead the clans through the dangerous times that were inevitably ahead of us, once the veil fell. We could make it appear as though it was him who could speak with the Inahi, as long as I remained at his side. But that would mean giving up Rys.

But first, Ezri needed to survive. And I needed to put a stop to whatever this evil was that had made us lose the protection of the gods. That meant confronting my father and figuring out what he knew. There had to be a reason for the vision I'd received.

Filled with determination, I turned to Mia. "Lead the way."

She set her horse to a walk, and before long we were galloping away from the city, across the rivers and plains, only stopping as much as necessary. As she'd promised, the walls surrounding the Nahl clan compound came into view as the sun dipped to touch the horizon. By sunset, we were riding through the gate.

I didn't bother stopping at the stables. Instead, I led us directly to the lodge. Mia took Arge from me and promised to see that she was well cared for while I rushed through the great room, into the courtyard, searching for my father.

"Ayla? Is that you?" Goff said, spotting me. "What are you doing here?"

"Where's Father?" I rushed toward my brother, not bothering to explain myself. "I must speak with him right away."

Goff squinted at me. "He's in his study. But why? Ayla, wait—"

He called after me, but I was already moving, and the door shut behind me, cutting off whatever he was going to say next. It opened a moment later, but I was halfway down the hall before Goff caught up to me.

"What's going on?" He jogged up beside me, then slowed to match my pace.

I ignored him and walked past the guard stationed at the door. "Father?"

I spotted him sitting at his table, bent over some papers. He looked up as I entered with Goff.

"Ayla, what are you doing here?" he asked.

"I need to talk to you," I said, fixing my gaze on him.

He stopped and looked up at me. "Didn't you receive my message? I told you to tell the Ruhl that I'm sending your uncle. He was planning to join you in the city after Midwinter. I didn't realize there was any urgency."

"Father, tell me what you know about this plot to overthrow the Ruhl."

"What plot?" He sat back in his chair and folded his hands, resting them on his belly. "Has something happened?"

"Yes. But I want to hear what you know about it."

"I've received no news from the city, if that's what you mean," he replied.

"You know that's not what I mean."

"Ayla, what's all this about?" Goff asked.

"Tell me," I said, ignoring Goff and keeping my eyes locked with Father's. "Tell me the truth. Are you involved in this?"

"Involved in what?" Goff asked.

"That's enough, Goff." Father stood. He stepped around the table to stand before me. "I have nothing to tell you."

"So you deny any involvement?"

"In what?" Goff asked.

"Tell him, Father."

"There's nothing to tell." He shrugged and moved back behind his table. He bent his head and shuffled the papers on his desk.

"What's going on, Ayla? Why are you here and what's gotten you so riled up?" Goff edged toward me.

I recalled the vision I'd had earlier, searching for any useful details that might help me. "If there's nothing to tell, then what are those papers there on your desk?"

Father's eyes flicked up, meeting mine without lifting his head.

"That's just a proposal the Jahl sent for Father to review," Goff replied. "Tavo-jah was here earlier to deliver it."

"Tavo-jah was here?" I asked.

"Yes, but he's gone now," Goff said.

"And did you ask what he was doing here and why he wasn't in the city?" I asked.

"What is this all about, Ayla?" Goff asked.

"Father, this is your last chance. I need to hear you say it," I said, turning away from Goff's question.

"There's nothing to say. It is as Goff explained. This is just another proposal the Jahl clan plans to present in the Council. I don't know what you think is going on. Perhaps you should tell us." He folded his arms.

"Ezri-ruh was poisoned, and the Shal is accusing you and the Jahl because of the suspicious way Tavo-jah and my aunt are suddenly nowhere to be found." I observed Father's face for any sign of surprise and found none.

"You really believe that Father would conspire with the Jahl to poison the Ruhl? To what end?" Goff scoffed. "Really, Ayla. I'd hoped you were smarter than that."

I ignored Goff. He could continue to be blindly loyal if he

chose. I wanted the truth. Pinning my father under my stare, I pressed my palms against his desk and leaned forward. "And now Goff says that Tavo-jah was just here. To deliver papers. Where is he now?"

"This is the first I'm hearing of this poisoning." His face gave nothing away.

"So the Jahl did not approach you about a plan to overthrow the Ruhl and replace him with Vorn-jah?"

"What the Jahl does is not of my concern." Father shrugged.

"I see." I nodded, then took a half step back. "Well, Father, I've learned something that may interest you. We've found the Inahi. They've confirmed that the veil is falling. And if Ezri-ruh is our only hope to convince the gods to protect us, what do you think will happen if he dies and Vorn-jah takes his place?"

"If Vorn-jah inherits the title of Ruhl, he will be the one to convince the Inahi to restore the veil," my father said.

"It doesn't work that way, Father. You, better than anyone, should know this. Look what happened when Belyn-ruh died. Did Sera not warn you?" I cocked my head to one side, watching him.

Father clenched his fist and slammed it down on the table. "Do not mention that name in my presence. I don't care what lies you were told in the city."

"They aren't lies, Father. It's all there in the legends." Another small lie, but he wouldn't know. Neither of them had studied the legends. Not the way I had, and they both knew that. "If the eldest dies, then we must wait for the next generation to reach maturity."

"Vorn-jah is the eldest," Father said, automatically.

"Then you are involved in this, aren't you?"

"Nahla, you'd be wise to stay out of this." The warning

tone in Father's voice didn't intimidate me anymore. Not after what I'd learned.

"How can I, Father? Ezri-ruh is my betrothed. You agreed to this arrangement yourself. I think I have every right to know what's going on. To know what my own father has been plotting. This must stop now, or the gods will desert us, and our lands will be overrun."

"Father, what's going on?" Goff asked.

"They killed your uncle!" He swept his hand across the table, sending the papers flying. "Then they let the baby die. They think they're better than us. Every year we send our harvest to them. The Jahl sends metals and gems. And what have they done for us? Nothing! They look down their noses at us from their walled city. They've forgotten the old ways. The traditions. And that spoiled Shalo has been corrupted by his mother. Nothing will change with him leading the Council."

"You don't know Ezri-ruh, Father." I kept my voice soft, but firm.

He scoffed. "And I suppose you do?"

"Ezri-ruh wants what's best for the clans. He'd listen to your concerns if you gave him a chance. Instead, you removed Uncle Feln from the Council. You left everything to the Jahl and his scheming sons. Is the Nahl clan meant to trade one ruler for another? What of our power?"

"The Jahl respects us."

"Really? The Jahl hasn't even told you everything about his plans. Has he? Or do you admit to knowing about this plot to poison the Ruhl?"

"Enough!" He gripped the edge of his desk hard enough to turn his knuckles white. "What did you come here for? What do you want?"

An image flashed through my mind. *Koto. In the Jahl clan's caverns.* I blinked as my mind sorted through what I'd learned and searched for a path forward.

"We are going to the caverns." I locked eyes with my father. "And you will not sign those papers."

Goff stepped toward me. "There's no need for Father to go. I'll go with you. Father needs to stay and run the clan."

"No," I said, not breaking eye contact with my father. "Father goes. You stay."

I still wasn't certain how much Father knew, but I'd decided putting him in the same room as the Jahl would make that apparent. Plus, if there were things the Jahl had been keeping from Father, I wanted him to see first-hand that he couldn't trust him to do what was right for the clans. Especially if this new vision was true.

My father nodded.

"Good. That's settled." I crossed the room and bent to pick up the papers he'd scattered on the floor. "I'll hold on to these. Get your things and meet me in the stables."

I pivoted and kept walking until I was outside the lodge. It had taken all of my courage to stand up to Father, but I'd survived, and we were going. Heading toward the stables to find Mia, I took a deep breath and tried to calm my hammering heart.

#

We camped in the foothills that night. Our horses were spent after the hard ride from the city, but Mia agreed it was best to keep moving. So we borrowed fresh ones for the journey, even as Father stood by, trying to convince me to wait until morning to leave. I was more worried about what would happen to Mia if the Koto really were waiting for us in the caverns than I was with sleeping for a few hours at the base of the mountains so we could start up the trail at first light.

As we secured the horses and made a fire, the wind howled down on us from the mountains that loomed above. Their sharp teeth hid Estrel's stars. The bite of the cold blowing down from the peaks warned of winter storms on the horizon. I shivered and pulled my cloak tighter around my shoulders as I helped Mia unload bedrolls and Father nursed the faint embers of our fire. He had said little since we left the compound.

The Inahi had said we needed to stop the evil at its source. I wanted to test my ability to contact them to ask if I was on the right path, but I wasn't sure how. I wasn't going to leave the safety and warmth of the fire to wait beside an offering, and they'd already excluded Mia from our first meeting. It seemed like they wouldn't come to me while I was with her and my father, especially if he was involved in this mess with the Jahl.

Feeling silly, I tried calling to them in my mind. I sat down on my bedroll, closed my eyes, and thought the word, *Hello.*

I was about to try again when an image of an Inahi riding a stormcat, waiting near an outcropping of rock, flashed in my mind. I opened my eyes and glanced around until I caught the flicker of firelight on stone. *We are here.*

My eyes searched for a shimmer in the darkness.

This is as far as we will follow you, Labharon, the voice said. *It is dangerous for us in the mountains.*

Because of the Koto? I thought. *Or the Jahl?*

He thinks he controls their power, but he is wrong.

Are we too late? I wondered.

Perhaps. Perhaps not. You are right to go and see yourself.

What about my father? I asked.

He will have to make his own decisions, as you will have to make yours. Be careful, Labharon.

I looked over at my father, curled up in his blankets with his back to the fire. I couldn't tell if he was asleep, and I didn't want to say anything in front of him until I knew for certain what side he was on.

Mia seemed to understand. She met my gaze and nodded. "Get some sleep. I'll keep watch." She jerked her chin toward my father.

"Wake me if you need to sleep," I said. Then I curled up in my blankets and lay staring up at the stars until my eyelids grew heavy and I slept.

23

WE rode single file up the switchbacks carved into the side of the mountain. From time to time, one of the horses would kick some loose rock over the edge and I'd watch it crash down the steep mountainside. The temperature dropped the higher we rode, and the bracing wind bit at our faces at every turn.

My eyes stung and watered from the cold, dry air, and I almost missed the entrance to the caverns. I blinked and realized Mia's horse had stopped. So I pulled mine up short behind her.

"We're here," she said. "But I've seen no sign of the guards Zan sent to watch for Tavo's return."

"Maybe they're inside." I looked around. "Where should we leave the horses?"

"It flattens out around that bend," Father said, pointing to where the trail disappeared around a turn up ahead. "We can leave them there, for now. But we'll need to move them before nightfall."

Mia nodded and led the way around to the shelf of rock that overlooked the valley below. We tied up the horses and returned to the cavern entrance on foot.

As we came within sight of the entrance, a figure emerged. I wasn't the only one who recognized the long dark hair and the fur-lined vest. Mia sprang forward and leapt at Tavo, knocking him back toward the cavern entrance. They stumbled, and Tavo struggled to get free.

"Stop!" I yelled. A wrong step would send one or both of them tumbling over the edge. Mia twisted Tavo's wrist behind his back and Tavo winced.

"Nice try," Mia hissed. "But you're not getting away again."

"I'm not trying to escape," Tavo said. "If you missed me so much, you should have said something." Tavo smiled and adjusted his body to take some pressure off his wrist.

Mia scowled and wrenched Tavo's wrist a notch higher. "What did you do with my guards?"

"The mountains are no place for city-bred guards. We gave them a choice. Return home or get thrown in the brig with the Ruhl's spies."

"What's this all about spies?" Father asked.

Before Tavo could say anything more, I stepped forward. "Let's go," I said. "Everyone, inside."

Mia forced Tavo to turn and marched him back down into the caverns. Father fell into step behind them, calling out instructions where the tunnels branched in different directions. I followed last, marveling at the glowing lanterns set onto ledges in the smooth stone walls.

After several turns, the tunnel opened up into an enormous cavern wrapped with ledges and balconies cut into the stone. At the center of the main floor were tables surrounded by people. In the sea of dark hair, I spotted my sister's auburn curls. She was talking with a man who looked like an older version of Vorn on the far side of the room and turned her face up to us when the room fell silent at our entrance.

Her mouth fell open, and she reached for a young girl nearby. She motioned for her to move closer to the man I guessed to be the Jahl. Then Cala turned and ran up the steps to meet us on the balcony.

"What are you doing here? Has something happened? Is it Mother?"

Father hugged Cala. "No, no, dear. Your mother is fine. So are your brothers."

"Oh! Good!" Cala turned to me. "But why are you here and not in the city?"

"I missed you, too," I said and smiled. She rolled her eyes and held out her arms to me. I stepped forward and hugged her close. "Not here," I whispered to her. "Is there somewhere more private we can talk?"

She pulled back and studied my face. "Alone?"

"Vorn-jah and the Jahl as well," I said.

She nodded. "Follow me." She turned to retrace her path down the stairs, but paused and half-turned to look over her shoulder at Mia. "You may want to let go of his arm for now, if you don't want to start a fight."

Mia frowned but loosened her grip on Tavo's wrist. "Fine, but if you make any moves, I won't hesitate to bury my dagger in your heart."

"I'd love to see you try." Tavo rubbed his freed wrist and flashed Mia a smile.

Cala's brow wrinkled with worry, but she didn't say another word. Instead, she turned and started down the steps again, leading us to the main floor. We followed her across the room. Heads turned to watch us as we passed. Katz was the only one I recognized. I caught him whispering to a young boy who looked identical to the girl Cala had left with the Jahl.

Vorn intercepted us before we'd crossed to the far side of the room. "What's this?" he asked Cala, placing a hand on her shoulder. He bowed his head briefly to Father, then shot a glare at Tavo.

"They want to speak with you, and the Jahl. In private," Cala explained.

Vorn nodded and hurried across the room to where the Jahl stood waiting. He whispered something into his father's ear, then dismissed the girl. She went running over to her brothers while Vorn walked ahead, with his father, out of the main cavern and into a tunnel. Once they'd started moving, Cala led our group out behind them.

We followed Vorn into a smaller cavern, outfitted with chairs and a round table. His father sat, but the rest of us remained standing around the table. Veins of exposed gemstones striped the stone walls surrounding us, hinting at the riches of the Jahl clan.

"Sit," Vorn said.

Mia remained standing, blocking the path to the doorway. But the rest of us took seats in chairs around the table.

"Now," Vorn said. "What is this about?"

I felt a prickling sensation on my skin, and the hairs on my neck rose. "There was an attack on the Ruhl."

Vorn nodded. "Yes, we've heard. Is he all right?"

"He is recovering," I said. The sensation that we were not alone in the room overwhelmed me.

The Jahl scowled at me. "Surely you didn't travel all the way here and risk getting caught in the coming storms just to tell us this?"

"She thinks you have something to do with this, Ve-hlm-jah." Father turned in his chair to face the Jahl. "What do you have to say?"

"I say you have no proof." He lifted his chin, then relaxed back in his chair. I'd heard that he was slightly younger than Father, but the Jahl's lined face and frail posture made him appear much older.

"We have proof," Mia said.

"Then, by all means, let's see it," Vorn commanded, spreading his hands with his palms raised.

My skin prickled again, and I glimpsed movement in the shadows at the far end of the room, but when I looked, there was nothing there. I turned my attention back to Vorn. "To craft an antidote, Mage-sha needed to know the poison. We have the poison, and I know where it came from."

Tavo shifted in his chair.

Vorn shot him a look. "So you say."

"I do." I turned to Tavo. "We found it when we searched Tavo-jah's belongings."

"Just because you found something in my rooms doesn't mean it's mine." Tavo swung his arm over the back of his chair. "I've had several... visitors in my rooms during my stay in the city. Any of them might have left something behind. It's been known to happen."

"Yes, well, I have other reasons to believe this item is yours." My eyes caught another movement in the shadows, but this time I didn't turn to look. I reached out to feel for the presence like I had with the Inahi. There was definitely something there.

A sound near the door distracted me. A woman, older than Cala, but with a youthful, unlined face and up-swept hair, slipped into the room carrying a tray. "Refreshments for our guests?"

"Thank you, Mother," Vorn said.

Delna, I thought. She cocked her head and turned to meet my gaze. Her eyes widened and her mouth opened slightly. I blinked, and she turned her focus to setting the tray on the table. For a moment I wondered if she had heard my thought, but that would have been impossible.

"Would you join us?" I asked.

Delna looked to her husband, who grumbled something unintelligible. Vorn nodded at her, and she took a seat at the table. Cala helped serve the tea and passed around a plate of biscuits.

When everyone had been served, Vorn turned to face me. "I believe you were about to tell us how you came to believe the poison belongs to my brother."

"Do you realize how close we came to losing Ezri-ruh and what that means for the clans?"

Vorn shrugged. "Tell me. Tell me why you're so concerned about losing your betrothed. Have you fallen for him so quickly? Tavo tells me he can be quite charming. Have you forgotten your loyalties already?"

"My loyalties?" I pushed my chair back and stood. My fingers gripped the edge of the table, nails biting into the wood. "I've been with Ezri-ruh to speak with the Inahi. They say the veil will fall. And if the clans don't stand united, how will we face the kingdoms beyond the veil? Or the creatures threatening our borders? If our alliance crumbles, the safety of my family, my clan, everyone I love, will be threatened. Is that what you want?"

To test my theory about something lurking in the shadows, I turned on my heel and paced away from the table, closer to the presence I felt.

"What do you know of what's beyond the veil, Nahla? What if those creatures you speak of were offering to help us, to trade with us?" Vehlm asked. "Perhaps we could all be as rich as those pampered stone lovers who care nothing for our traditions and hoard all our wealth for themselves."

I spun around to face the others, purposely turning my back on the shadows. "Tell me, then. What do you know of these creatures beyond the veil?"

A hand gripped my throat, and the points of long nails pressed into my skin. Mia drew her daggers and shifted to find a better position for an attack. Cala gasped and Delna cowered. But somehow, I knew it wouldn't hurt me. Yet.

"What is the meaning of this, Vehlm-jah? What is this, this thing?" my father asked, standing from the table and pointing at the creature who held me. I knew without turning that it would be a Koto, like the one I'd seen in the forest.

Vehlm sat, smiling, and folded his hands in his lap. "Our new allies, Teron-nah. Aren't they marvelous?"

"Vorn, tell it to let go of my sister." Cala gripped Vorn's arm and squeezed. Mia slid closer, searching for an opening to take out the creature who held me in its grip.

Vehlm shook his head. "Tavo, disarm the Nahla's guard and bind her hands. I've had enough of these city-dwellers and their accusations." Vehlm sat back in his chair and waited while Tavo rose and made his way across the room to stand in front of Mia.

"It's probably best if you don't struggle," Tavo said, flashing Mia a satisfied grin.

Mia grunted and lunged at Tavo, but Tavo was faster. He stepped out of the way easily and plucked the dagger from Mia's hand. My mouth dropped open, and I gagged, forgetting for a moment the Koto's grip around my neck.

Mia didn't give up easily. She lunged again for Tavo, this time prepared for Tavo's speed, and nicked his forearm. Tavo twisted and danced from the tip of Mia's dagger, then swung around and snagged her in a headlock. With a twist of her wrist, he disarmed her and brought the dagger point to her chest.

"No!" I screamed. The Koto gave me a shake, and I struggled against its grip. Sharp nails bit into my skin.

"Aw. Don't play hard to get," Tavo said, face close to Mia's ear. He gave Mia a squeeze and toyed with the dagger point pressed against the cloth of her tunic.

Mia wrapped both hands around Tavo's on the hilt of the blade and wrestled for control. Tavo tightened the headlock. Then, with one smooth twist of his wrist, he sent Mia's dagger skidding into a corner of the room. He grabbed one of Mia's wrists and twisted her arm behind her back.

"Doesn't feel very good, does it?" Tavo asked. He gave Mia's arm a yank. Then he released his arm from around her neck and twisted her other wrist behind her. Capturing both of her hands in one of his, he pulled a lace free from his vest so he could bind Mia's wrists.

"Now that you have the guard restrained," Father said, turning back to Vehlm, "let Ayla go."

"First, we talk," Vehlm said.

Cala squeezed Vorn's arm again and begged him to free me, but he shrugged her off. Delna caught my eye, and I heard her voice in my head. *Patience.* My eyes went wide, and my heart beat faster. How could she do that?

"This wasn't part of our arrangement," Father said.

"I thought you weren't interested in the dirty work. Only in the spoils. Hmm? Have you changed your mind? Bit too late for that now, I think." Vehlm's bony fingers slid along the arms of his chair.

"Your plan failed," Father replied.

"It matters not if the boy lives or dies, Teron-nah. Your daughter is right about one thing. The veil will fall. But our new allies will help us take what is rightfully ours back from those heretic stone-lovers."

"*Our* allies? Are you making deals on behalf of my clan now, as well as your own?"

"Come now, Teron-nah. I'm not going back on our arrangement."

"Free my daughter and leave her out of this."

"You were the one who brought her into this, and now she knows too much to return to the city."

"Let her go, and I'll call off her betrothal. I'll keep her in our compound, at least until we settle this."

"No. We'll keep her here in the caverns until we settle this. She can have a cell next to Sera's. We'll take good care of them both."

"Sera? Sera's here?" I pulled against the Koto's grip, but it held me firm.

"Yes. Another little present from Tavo. He's done so well. Always bringing us information, and now he's brought us the Mage-ruh." Vehlm grinned.

"What is the meaning of this, Vehlm-jah?" Father asked.

"It's simple. We've suffered under the thumb of the Shal for too long. You've said it yourself. We agreed they needed to be taught a lesson. You withdrew from the Council, and we're destroying what's left of it. We'll leave them isolated, in their city, without our resources and with no hope of help from the Inahi. Meanwhile, our new allies will open up trade routes with the neighboring realms. They'll pave the way for us. And we will hold the power, not Filna-sha and her clan.

They will be nothing without us."

"But why eliminate the Ruhl? What part does he play in this?"

"You heard your daughter. The Inahi can't help us. The Koto will be our guides and protectors. Come, let us sign the papers and finalize our treaty. It's just as I've said before. We have joined our clans in marriage and they will lead the future generations."

"But Cala gave up her clan affiliation when she married your son."

Vehlm waved his hand as if to brush away Father's comment. "Those are just vows in a ceremony, Teron-nah. She's still your daughter. Come. You read the treaty. It's all there, as I say, is it not?"

"Father, no!" I said, but the Koto squeezed, and I choked on my words. I needed to get loose of this Koto and get Mia back her dagger. Pressing my hands to my head as though I was overcome with emotion, I secretly palmed my hairpin knives. Then I closed my eyes and imagined the Koto's hand around my neck. With only my mind as my guide, I stabbed down hard into the Koto's flesh, hoping its scaly red hide was softer than it looked.

The Koto cried out in pain and released its hold. I dashed to Mia's dagger and bent to retrieve it. By the time it was in my hand, Tavo had moved to stop me, leaving Mia free.

"Give it here," Tavo said, holding out his hand for the knife.

I lunged at him. He dodged the point and gave me an opening to slip out of the corner. I ran for Mia, but Tavo caught my arm before I fully slipped past him. I lifted my foot and slammed it down on the toe of his boot, then lifted that knee to his groin. I didn't quite hit my mark, but I got close enough to cause him to double over in pain. By this time, everyone was standing and shouting.

Mia backed toward me while monitoring the others. I sliced the cord that held her wrists and placed the dagger in her hand. When I looked up, the Koto had disappeared and Cala was sobbing, clutching at Vorn. But the room fell silent with the thud of Mia's knife as it buried itself in Vehlm's chest.

Delna collapsed and Vorn reached for his mother to catch her before she hit the floor. Tavo howled and rushed at Mia, but Father intercepted Tavo and held him back.

I froze. My eyes met Cala's across the room as I realized that Mia's actions had likely just freed our land of the evil the Inahi had warned us about, but also might have torn apart my family.

24

THE Jahl clan guards escorted Mia and me to a dimly lit cavern and slammed a barred metal door shut behind us, locking us inside. Their footsteps echoed as they retreated down the tunneled corridor, leaving us to contemplate our fate.

"I'm sorry, Nahla," Mia said. "Once I realized it was him the Koto were using as an anchor, I had to stop him."

I turned away from the bars to face her. "An anchor?"

"He let them in. Without him, the Koto won't be able to cross the veil."

"Unless he's not the only one," I said.

A groan from the back corner of the chamber alerted us we were not alone. My body tensed. I was still on edge after being held captive by that Koto.

"Who's there?" Mia asked. She positioned herself between me and the sound, but the only answer was another moan. She crept forward, into the darkness, and I followed close behind.

The figure, sprawled on the floor against the back edge of the chamber, attempted to press up to a sitting position but failed and collapsed with another groan onto the bare stone. However, the movement allowed me a glimpse of braided hair and a profile.

"Sera?" I pushed past Mia so I could crouch next to the figure.

I watched her take a breath before she turned her face toward me. "Ayla," she said. "Is it you?" Her eyes fluttered closed.

"Are you all right?" I reached for her and tried to help her sit up, but she cried out in pain, so I stopped. Mia helped me arrange her more comfortably, with her head cradled in my lap. I brushed loose strands of hair back from her dirty brow and waited for her response.

Her lips pressed together, and she nodded once. "I will be now."

As my eyes adjusted to the light, I noticed the dried blood staining her clothes and her exposed skin. "What happened? Who did this to you?"

She took a breath and winced, squeezing her eyes shut as her face contorted in pain.

"It's all right," I said. "Just rest. We'll get you out of here." I motioned to Mia, and she examined Sera's body, cataloging her visible injuries while I cradled her head and caressed her hair.

Sera moaned when Mia moved her limbs or shifted her tunic to get a better idea where the dried blood had come from. When she finished, she stepped toward the barred door and signaled me to follow.

"Sera," I whispered. When she didn't respond, I shifted slightly to remove my cape. Then I bundled it up and adjusted her head so it lay pillowed on that instead of in my lap. I stood carefully so I wouldn't disturb her and walked over to join Mia.

"She needs a mage," Mia said, keeping her voice low. "There's not much I can do."

"Is it bad?"

She shrugged. "It might be."

The slap of feet against stone in the corridor alerted us that someone was returning. I turned my head and found Cala breathless, just outside the bars, panting as though she'd run the entire way. My heart leapt at the sight of her.

"Cala." I rushed toward her and slid my arms between the bars, reaching for her hands.

"Ayla." She sighed, clasping hands with me. "I'm trying, but he won't listen to reason."

"Tell me," I said. "What has Vorn-jah said?"

"He wants to hold you two until the Ruhl will agree to the Jahl clan's demands."

"What demands?" I asked.

"Never mind that," Mia said. She gripped the bars. "You're the Jahlini now. You have the power to release your sister. She doesn't need to pay for what I did."

Cala took a step back. "I... I..." She wrapped her arms around her waist. "I can't," she said.

"Fine." I reached for her through the bars. "It's all right, but we need the clan mage. Sera's badly wounded and needs help. Can you bring someone to help her?"

"Who's Sera?" she asked.

"It's a long story, but for now, the only part that's important is she's our aunt."

"What? We don't have an aunt."

"I assure you, you do," Mia said, crossing her arms. "She's

in here bleeding, possibly dying."

"Please, Cala," I begged. "Bring Mage-jah or send a message to Mage-nah."

"I'll tell Father," she said.

"So you're planning to let her die, then?" Mia shook her head and turned to face me. "Your father hates her."

"It's true," I said. "He banished her from our clan. I'll tell you all of it, but please, bring a mage. Even if you can't convince Vorn-jah to let us out. Please?"

"Your guard killed the Jahl." Cala stared at Mia.

I wouldn't apologize for Mia's actions. "The Jahl let enemies into our lands." I hoped, once she got over her shock, Cala would understand what that really meant for us.

"I didn't know. Vorn didn't know. I swear it." She took a step closer.

"You're sure?" I hated that I had to ask and hated that I had to doubt my own sister would tell me the truth.

"I didn't know." She grasped my hands.

"Please, Cala. The clans are in danger. We need to get back to warn Ezri-ruh." I didn't mention that I also wanted to see if he was all right, if he'd survived the poison.

She nodded. "I'll get the mage and Father and see what I can do about Vorn."

"Thank you." I squeezed her hands before releasing them. She stretched her arms through the bars to rest them on my shoulders. I gripped her shoulders in response and we pressed our foreheads together, the closest we could manage to a hug with bars between us.

When she closed her eyes, tears glistened, trapped between her lashes.

"It'll be all right," I said.

"Mage-nah was right," she said.

I opened my mouth to speak, but she released my shoulders and fled down the corridor, back into the center of the caverns. I listened to her go, thinking about how it had been me telling Tavo about Cala's reading that had started all of this.

Perhaps Vorn-jah hadn't known of his father's plans, or perhaps he did, but Tavo must have known. My mind shifted through the possibilities. If he'd been responsible for the poisoning and played a part in letting the Koto into our lands, he would also have to be punished.

I paced as I waited for the Jahl clan mage to arrive. Mia watched me from where she sat, monitoring Sera's breathing. She tried to catch my eye, but I needed to think. So I kept moving. Pacing. Thinking. Trying to find a way out of this situation.

Cala had mentioned the Jahl clan had demands. I thought back through everything I'd learned since the Gathering, searching for a hint of what they might want.

Father and Mage-jah arrived before I could wear a groove with the tread of my boots, back and forth across the cavern floor. The young guard accompanying them rattled his keys as he searched for the right one.

"Stay back," he warned, inserting the piece of metal into the lock on the door. "I'm letting the mage in, but if either of you tries something…" He sliced a finger across his neck.

Mia shifted up onto her feet, itching to pounce on the guard. She could probably take him down, but if she did, we'd still have to find our way back out through the corridors and caverns without being stopped. I grabbed her arm, squeezing it hard to let her know she shouldn't try anything. Not yet.

The guard twisted the key, and the door clicked open. Mage-jah slipped inside, carrying a bundle I hoped contained medicines.

"Help him," I whispered to Mia as the young man hurried to attend to his patient. I tilted my head toward my father. "I'll talk to Father."

"What's all that whispering about?" the guard asked. He shut the door but didn't lock it. "I warned you. Don't try anything."

I gave Mia a nudge toward the back of the chamber before stepping closer to the bars. "May I speak with my father, please?"

The guard glanced between me and Father, unsure how to respond. "All right. But I'm not moving. I'm standing right here to make sure you don't try something."

I took a tentative step forward. Then another to close the distance between me and the bars that separated me from my father.

"You didn't know?" I asked.

He shook his head. "I'm sorry. It appears you were right."

"I believe you." I pressed my lips together, wetting them. "The clans are in danger. I have to get back to the city."

"I understand."

"We don't have much time. I can't tell you any more right now. You have to trust me. I'm trying to help our clan."

He nodded. "What can I do?"

"Take Sera with you. Mage-nah can help her."

His face hardened. "She's no longer welcome in our clan."

"She's family. She's your sister. You've already lost one sibling. If you leave her here, they will kill her." I watched for any hint of his emotions, but as Nahl of our clan, he hid them well. I waited for his response.

"All right," he said. "If Mage-jah can't help her, I'll take her home."

"Thank you."

He reached between the bars and clasped my hands in his. "Save the clans, Ayla."

"I'll do my best."

Mage-jah stood and shuffled toward the guard.

"That's it?" Mia yelled after him.

The mage glanced back over his shoulder, then shuffled faster. "Let me out. I've done what I can."

"You've barely done anything." Mia stood and stalked toward Mage-jah. "At least leave whatever's in that bundle."

The guard opened the door a crack and pulled Mage-jah out by his robe, but not before Mia snatched the bundle of herbs from his hands. The guard pretended not to notice and slammed the door shut, twisting the key in the lock. "Visiting time's over. Let's go."

"I'll talk with Vorn-jah and return for Sera," Father said. He pushed ahead of the guard and Mage-jah, disappearing into the corridor.

I watched them go. The longer we stayed locked up in here, the more I lost hope of returning to Ezri. We needed a plan. I turned to discuss it with Mia just as a movement caught my eye. A figure emerged from the shadows. *Delna.*

Hello. Her soft voice filled my head like the words of the Inahi. I stood, staring, wondering how this tiny woman knew how to communicate this way. She crept closer. I matched her, step for step, until we met with the bars between us.

Delna handed me a book, slipping the spine between the bars so I could take it from her. I examined it, first caressing the cover with the palm of my hand. The leather was soft and worn. What looked at first glance to be brown leather had once been blue. The gold catch holding it closed shone brightly against the dull, faded cover.

"That was my mother's," Delna said. This time she spoke aloud, but it was the same voice I'd heard in my mind.

"Edan-ruh's diaries," I whispered, still staring down at the cover.

"Yes," she said. "They haven't been much use to me, but I think they might be of some use to you." In my mind, I heard her add the word *Labharon*.

I looked up and met her eyes. "How?"

"I think you'll find much of what you need to know is in there. I hope you don't mind that I picked the lock and read it. I've spent many long years isolated up here in these caverns." Tears gathered in the corners of her eyes. "I wasn't much older than my twins are now when he brought me here."

"I understand." I remembered my reaction to my betrothal and could only imagine how much worse it could have been to be only fifteen, have your mother die, and then be forced to leave your family and marry a man you hardly knew.

She pressed her hand against the lock on the door. I thought she'd meant to steady herself, but a brief white flash sparked against the metal. The mechanism clicked, and the door swung open.

"How did you...?"

"It's all in there," she said. "But I had to teach myself. I lost my chance. Don't lose yours." She swung the door open wider. "Come on."

I glanced back at Mia. She was already moving toward the door.

"What about Sera?" I asked.

"I'll make sure Teron-nah takes her," Delna said, staring into the darkness. "Don't worry. She saved my life once. I owe her."

Hurry, she said again, only to me.

I slipped out of the barred chamber, and she shut the door behind me, not bothering to lock it. Then she turned and said, "Follow me."

We crept behind her, pausing when she paused, sticking close to her shadow. I hugged Edan's diary to my chest, eager to read it once we were far from the caverns.

We encountered no one as we crept closer and closer to the tunnel that would return us back to the surface of the mountain, and I wondered if Delna was using her magic to keep us hidden. I whispered a prayer to Estrel that, by some miracle, our horses would still be there, waiting, when we emerged.

25

ITH all the commotion surrounding the Jahl's death, no one had bothered to retrieve our horses and take them to whatever cavern held the Jahl clan's stables. Because of Delna, we were gone before anyone realized. And after riding back down the mountain, moving as quickly as we dared, we rode hard for our clan's compound so Mia and I could retrieve our horses and return the ones we'd borrowed for the journey to the mountains.

We had hoped to sneak in and out without encountering any of my brothers, but Dern was waiting in the stables when we arrived.

"I'm coming with you," he said, leading Orem, who was already saddled.

"Does Goff know this?" I asked as I dismounted, handing the reins of the horse I'd borrowed to a waiting stable hand and hurrying past Dern to get to Arge's stall.

"Aren't you the one who was attacked?" Mia asked. Looking down on him from the saddle, she blocked his path to the door with her horse. "You can't come with if you can't keep up. It's not safe."

"I can keep up," Dern insisted as I unlatched the stall door to lead Arge out.

Mia swung herself down from the saddle, then lunged at my brother, causing Dern to flinch away. "That's what I thought," she said, her voice smug. "You stay."

"Why do you want to go to the city all of a sudden?" I asked, fastening Arge's lead to a hitch so I could get her ready to ride.

Dern scowled at Mia's back as she followed a stable hand to the opposite end of the building. "You wouldn't believe me if I told you."

"Try me." I retrieved Arge's tack and got to work preparing her for our journey.

"I think Rys was right about the Merluks," he said, keeping his voice low, even though we appeared to be alone. "Now that I'm well enough to travel, I need to warn the Ruhl. There's no one else who might believe me... Except maybe you."

"Did you see them?" I asked, adjusting the straps on Arge's saddle. "Is that what attacked you?"

Dern nodded.

"You had a charm in your hand when the guards found you." I paused to watch his reaction. "Where did you get it?"

"Did you take it?" He stepped closer to me. "Tavo asked me about it when I woke after the attack, but I couldn't find it. I told him I must have dropped it. He seemed to think Ezri-ruh or that guard captain of his might have taken it from me, when I was unconscious."

I raised my eyebrows. "Did Tavo give you that charm?"

He grimaced. "He said it would keep me safe, but when I rode out to meet him, those creatures came after me. They burst out of the forest and chased me down before I could reach the Ruhl's party. Then, when they caught me..." He choked on his words and gulped them down before continuing. "They ripped the charm right off my neck. I grabbed it before they could take it from me, but that's the last thing I remember."

I moved closer to him. "Did Tavo tell you anything else?"

"About that charm?" He shook his head. "No."

"What about his plan to poison the Ruhl?" I squinted at him.

Dern gaped. "What? He would never."

"Are you sure about that?" I asked, cocking my head to one side.

Dern opened his mouth, then shut it. After a breath he said, "If you'd asked me at the Scattering, I would have said yes without hesitation. But now? I don't know. He followed your party back to the city, even though he'd said he was going to spend the season with me. He stayed until he was sure I would be all right, but his reasons for leaving were..."

Dern's voice trailed off as the corners of his mouth twisted into a scowl. "Why? What happened?"

"It's a very long story, and I don't have time to tell you. I could use your help, but you'll have to stay here." I paused long enough for him to object, but his curiosity must have conquered his desire to warn the Ruhl about the Merluks.

When he didn't immediately refuse, I continued. "I need you to promise me you'll send me a message if Tavo shows up at the compound. And keep an eye on Goff and Father for me. If they try to make any treaties with the Jahl, I want to know." I turned away to finish securing the buckles on Arge's tack, not bothering to explain that Vorn was now the Jahl and our sister the Jahlini. Dern would find out soon enough.

"Promise me?"

Dern scowled. "You want me to spy on Goff and Father? What's going on, Ayla?"

Arge was ready, and I was out of time. I took hold of the reins and walked closer to Dern so I could set my hand on his shoulder and look him in the eye.

"Please? I believe you. About the Merluks. I've seen them, too. They attacked our camp on the way to the city. But Merluks aren't the worst of what's coming. The Ruhl and I are trying to keep the clans safe. So if Goff and Father make any moves to align with the Jahl, or threats against the Ruhl and the Shal, I need to know."

Dern nodded. "All right. I'll trust you, for now, and let you know if I hear anything. But when you get back to the city, send me a message and tell me the whole story?"

"I'll do what I can." I gave him a quick hug, then led Arge past him to where Mia was already waiting for me at the door.

Once we were clear of the compound, we let the horses run, cutting back across the plains toward the city. There was plenty of time to reflect as we rode on the many things I hadn't noticed. I should have paid more attention. I should have seen Rys for what he was and learned the lessons Goff tried to teach me. Fixating on my obsession with finding the Inahi caused me to ignore everything else. And perhaps that's why they'd chosen me to be their Labharon.

But if I hoped to save the clans, the only thing left to do was the one thing I'd been avoiding from the start. My duty. And the plans that took form in my mind as Arge galloped toward the Shal City walls all hinged on whether Ezri lived.

By silent agreement, we avoided the main gate, opting for a more direct route to the Magery. We arrived at the north gate just after sunset, pausing only to see our horses to the stables before doubling back to the guards stationed outside the Magery doors.

"Dex. Tem." Mia greeted the guards as we approached. "Is the Ruhl inside?"

Dex nodded to Mia. Then his eyes fixed on me, and he lunged forward.

Mia stepped between us, blocking him. "The Nahla is with me. Is Zan here?"

"Let me pass. That Nahla was accused of poisoning the Ruhl." Dex attempted to shove Mia aside. "I've been ordered to take her to the holding cells once she's been found."

"Who ordered you? Zan?" Mia asked, gripping his arm and forcing him back toward the Magery doors.

"No. The Shal." Dex twisted his arm, but Mia refused to let him go.

"I'm going to ask you one more time, and this time, I expect an answer." Mia angled her head into Dex's line of sight. "Where. Is. Zan?"

"Inside. Guarding the Ruhl," the other guard answered.

"Thank you, Tem." Mia gestured for me to go ahead through the doors.

I hesitated, my eyes on Tem. She hadn't moved to restrain me, but her body had tensed when Dex lunged at me, and she didn't look like she was going to let me pass.

When I didn't budge, Mia turned to Tem. "Zan is expecting us. Go up and let him know we're waiting."

Tem nodded once, then disappeared through the doors. She reappeared a moment later, this time to hold the door open and wave us inside. Mia waited until I'd gone past before releasing Dex and following me up the stairs inside the entrance.

The stairs let us out in a hallway. I looked to my left, only for Zan to call to me from the right. Sure enough, I turned to find him walking toward us from a room near the end of the hall.

"How is he?" I asked.

"Better." He gestured for me to go past him, toward the open door with the light spilling out into the hallway. "Go see for yourself."

I hurried ahead and burst into what turned out to be a small infirmary where Ezri stood, waiting next to a small table that held two half-full bowls of still-steaming soup.

He closed the distance between us, pulling me into his arms. "You're back. I was worried."

"You were worried?" I laughed with relief. "I was the one who was worried."

He stepped back, holding me at arm's length. "Did you find the source?"

I nodded. "I think so. Was Mage-sha able to create an antidote?"

His eyes skimmed past me. "What did you do with Mia and Zan?"

"Ezri?" I moved my head until he met my gaze. "The poison?"

He dropped his hands from my shoulders and paced to the door. After a brief glance down the hall, he shut it. "We need to talk."

"What happened?" I stared at him. He looked fine. There was color in his cheeks. He was moving around without effort, and he wasn't breathing in shallow gasps the way he had been when we left the Inahi. "Zan said you were better."

Ezri took my hands and led me to the table. Once we were both sitting, he said, "Mage-sha brewed an antidote. It seems to have stopped the poison from doing any more damage. I am better. But I'm not fully healed."

"But you will be."

He shrugged. "Perhaps. But it doesn't matter now, does it? You're the Labharon. You are the one who should be given the title of Ruhl. Or, Ruhlini, I suppose."

"Shh." I leaned toward him, lowering my voice to a whisper. "You haven't told anyone, have you?"

He shook his head. "No. Of course not. I was waiting for you to return before I said anything."

"Good." I sighed, sitting back in my chair.

"Why does it matter?" he asked. "Did something happen?"

I snorted. "So much. But, listen. I don't think we should tell anyone what we learned from the Inahi. At least... not yet."

"What? Why not?" He raised his eyebrows.

I covered his hand with mine. "I've had a lot of time to think about this."

"As have I."

"I think it will be better if you continue as Ruhl, and we let everyone believe you are the Labharon. So long as we are together, no one will question anything. And this way, I can train with the Inahi while you continue to lead the Council."

"This will mean we have to marry," he said.

"I know." I folded my hands in my lap.

"You're giving up on becoming your clan's mage?"

"I am," I said, staring down at my hands. I was giving up on more than just that, but it was the right thing to do. I had a chance to help more than just my clan. It was time I accepted that and moved on from childhood dreams.

He remained silent for a moment. Then he said, "Rys told me."

I closed my eyes. When I opened them and looked up, Ezri

was leaning forward. "He's why you said you couldn't marry me, isn't he?"

I swallowed, then nodded.

Ezri stood. He paced a few steps away, then turned. "Why are you doing this? You don't owe me anything. We found the Inahi. Our deal is done. I can end the betrothal. If we tell everyone the truth, you'll take your place as Ruhlini. I'll go back to being my mother's heir, and you'll be free to become a mage, return to your clan, and marry Rys."

Everything he said was true. And it was everything I'd ever wanted, all laid out before me. My childhood dreams within my grasp. But there was something more important than what I wanted.

I stood to face him. "I could. But the most important thing now is keeping the clans safe. You said it then, and it's even more true now. The alliance between the clans is too fragile. Even the return of magic won't help us if we cannot keep the clans united."

"And you think lying to them is going to help?"

I shook my head. "Of course not. But the next few moon cycles are critical. If we wait until after Midwinter, after I've trained the first batch of potentials, after we're married, it will make it easier for us to convince my father and Vorn-jah to remain aligned with the Shal. If you end our betrothal, and we tell them I'm the Labharon, that will almost certainly sever the alliance. Once you hear what happened in the caverns, I'm sure that you'll agree. You and I are the only thing holding it all together."

I explained to him everything I'd learned from my father and the Jahl. Then I told him about the Koto and how Mia had killed Vehlm-jah. I showed him his grandmother's diaries, given to me by his aunt, who could somehow wield magic.

"Vorn-jah is Jahl," Ezri said, sinking into his chair with a sigh. "And Mia…"

"Zan will find a way to help her. And together we will protect her because she acted to protect the clans."

Ezri ran a hand through his hair. "I know. I would have done the same. But…"

His voice trailed off. For a few breaths, he stared off into the dark corners of the room as though they held an answer. Then his eyes returned to mine. "Are you sure this is what you want?"

Zan knocked and opened the door before I could respond. "Mia's gone. She told me what happened, and then she fled before I could stop her."

"Where did she go?" I rushed past him to look down the hall.

Zan paced across the room. "She refused to tell me where she was going. She insisted it would be better if I didn't know. But there are Merluks out there. And at least one clan that probably wants her dead. We need to find her."

I caught Zan's arm and forced him to stop. "We'll find her."

"How? Do you know where she went? Did she say something to you?" He scowled at me, eyes narrowing.

I glanced over at Ezri and raised my eyebrows, hoping he would know what I wanted him to say.

He shifted in his chair, hesitating only a moment before catching on and speaking up. "The Inahi will help us."

"What's this?" Zan looked back and forth between us. "What's going on?"

I sighed. It was no use trying to keep secrets from Zan. I gestured to Ezri. "Fine. Tell him. But only him. And maybe Mia, once we find her."

Ezri filled Zan in on what we'd learned from the Inahi. He

finished by asking, "What do you think of Ayla's plan?"

Zan studied me with a look on his face I didn't recognize. It appeared almost like respect. And not the sort reserved for the people he served as captain of the Shal's guard, but the one I caught him giving those, like Mia and Ezri, whom he held in high regard. I was sure it wouldn't last, but it was a satisfying change.

"I think she has a point," he said. "Vorn-jah is married to her sister. And you are his cousin. If his mother is also on the Nahla's side, as she must be since she helped Ayla-nah and Mia escape, then you stand a much better chance of holding the alliance. I agree. None of us should speak another word of this to anyone."

Ezri stared at me. Then he turned to Zan. "Can you give us a moment? Alone?"

Zan nodded. "I'll be outside."

"I don't like it," Ezri said as the door clicked shut behind Zan.

"Do you have a better idea?" I asked.

Ezri scowled. I waited until he shook his head.

"No." He sighed. "But I can't do this to Rys. Not after... He pledged his loyalty to me. He gave you up for me. When he told me, I... And I thought... These past few days, I thought there might be something." He reached toward me, then stopped and shook his head. "But I don't want to marry someone whose heart is elsewhere. I won't."

I took a step forward, closing the distance between us before he could turn away. "You're wrong, you know. My heart isn't elsewhere. It's torn. It has been since that first kiss. Or maybe even before that. Maybe since that first dance at the Gathering."

He lifted his eyes from where my hand rested on his forearm until they locked with mine. "Does he know that?"

"I'll tell him. Tomorrow."

"Tell him what?"

My jaw clenched. I swallowed the lump in my throat. "That it's too late. That I can't go with him. That my heart has found a new home."

"Has it? Are you sure?" His fingers brushed against my cheek as he searched my eyes for answers.

I hesitated, remembering the last time I was alone with Rys. That kiss. I needed to erase it from my memory if I hoped to make Ezri believe my words.

My gaze dropped to Ezri's lips, and I leaned closer until I could feel the warmth of his breath on my face. Curling my fingers into his hair, I pressed my mouth to his and let my eyes flutter closed. The slide of his lips against mine as he wrapped his arms around my waist and pressed me against him sent that spark coursing through me again. Everywhere my skin tingled with awareness while our surroundings dropped away until we were just the points where our bodies touched, and I couldn't get close enough.

It wasn't the same hunger, the same fire, that consumed me when I kissed Rys. This was different, and equally undeniable.

"All right." Ezri paused to catch his breath, the tip of his nose teasing mine. "I believe you."

"I don't know." I grinned at him. "We may need to try it again."

26

WHEN Mage-sha came to check on Ezri, we broke apart, cheeks flushed. She smirked knowingly, and after making me wait in the hall while she checked on her patient, she agreed to let me stay in the Magery that night. After a short and silent debate that involved a series of meaningful looks exchanged between Ezri, Zan, and me, we agreed to tell Mage-sha the truth about what we learned from the Inahi.

When we finished answering her questions, she said, "We'll say you've decided to train as a novice, since you cannot sit on the Council. All novices start with a period of secluded study. No contact with their family or anyone outside the Magery until that phase of their study is complete."

"But won't the other novices know when Ayla isn't here?" Ezri asked.

Mage-sha tapped her finger against her chin. "Ayla-nah has already been through some training with Mage-nah. I'll use that to explain why she isn't training with the others. And we may use Sera's absence to our advantage here as well."

Zan nodded. "We can say Mage-ruh is tutoring her the way she tutored Ezri and me."

"Yes. Exactly." Mage-sha patted Zan's shoulder. "I'll send a message to Delna-jah to inform her of our plans and ask her to keep us updated on Sera's progress."

Mention of Delna reminded me of the Ruhlini's diary. I retrieved the leather book from the pocket in my cloak and showed it to Mage-sha. But after two nights of light sleep at the base of the mountains, I couldn't keep my eyes open for long. Eventually, I curled up on one of the cots while they flipped through the pages and discussed the contents. I missed all of it because I fell asleep as soon as my head hit the pillow.

In the morning, I walked with Ezri and Zan back to the Ruhl House. Then, after returning to my rooms to bathe and change clothes, I set out for the guard barracks to find Rys. I planned to leave for the forest as soon as possible, and I couldn't leave without talking with him. Zan had briefed the guards and the Shal on what had happened in the mountains.

The news that the Jahl had admitted his guilt and been killed cleared my name enough to keep me out of the holding cells, but Zan had assigned Tem to accompany me, just in case I ran into trouble. Her presence only reminded me of Mia's absence, and I itched to get back to the forest so I could ask the Inahi for their help in locating the woman I'd begun to think of as my friend.

One of the guards in the common area of the barracks directed me to Rys. Tem stayed behind to talk with the others while I followed her friend's directions down two halls to the bunk room on the right.

I paused in the doorway to gather my courage, but Rys

must have heard me, or sensed my presence, because he turned away from the small bag he'd been packing to face me.

His eyes lit up, and he smiled when he spotted me. Then he scanned my body, finding my empty hands, and the brightness on his face clouded over. "You're not leaving."

I took one step into the room. "I can't."

Rys moved toward me, closing the distance between us, but stopping an arm's length away. "But I told him. He said he would break the betrothal."

"He tried. But I wouldn't let him." I crossed my arms.

"Why not?" Rys frowned.

"Because you were right. I need to do my duty. I have a chance to help unite the clans in the face of what's coming. If I go home now, I'll have to live with knowing I could have done more, but I ran away from my responsibilities."

"Do you love him?" he asked, taking a half step closer.

"I..." I hesitated. The truth was, I didn't know. I definitely had feelings for Ezri. And yet even though Rys had hurt me, he'd been my first love, the boy I'd thought I'd marry. Facing him, I knew I still wasn't completely over him. "I need to see this through."

"Ayla—"

I recognized the look on his face and held up a hand to stop him from saying something that might break my resolve. "I'm going to study at the Magery. Starting tomorrow. I'll be secluded as a novice until just before Midwinter."

Rys stared at me, eyes narrowing. "So you're not getting married?"

I shook my head. "Not until Midwinter."

He moved closer to me, lifting his hands to cradle my face. "Ayla, what's really going on?"

I blinked and tried not to get lost in his deep brown eyes.

The words wanted to spill from my lips, but I pressed them closed. Swallowed them down.

"You said, 'in the face of what's coming.' What's coming, Ayla? What has you this scared?" he asked.

"The veil is falling. Because of what the Jahl did." I decided I could tell him that much.

"And you think you can help?" His fingers brushed a strand of hair off my forehead, tucking it behind my ear.

"I'm going to be a mage, and I'm going to marry Ezri." I pulled away from him. "I need to go."

My heart ached and tears stung my eyes as I fled from the barracks, past the stables, to the courtyard that surrounded the tower rising between the Shal House and the Ruhl House. I stood there for a moment, trying to catch my breath and clear my head.

By the time I was done training with the Inahi, Rys would be erased from my heart. He'd made his choices, and now I'd made mine. It was time to move on.

Only, there was one last task I needed to complete before I could return to Ezri and prepare for my departure. Gathering what was left of my composure, I marched past the tower to the Shal House. Inside, I asked the first person I saw where I might find Jace. They directed me to the library.

I thanked them, then made my way down the halls, silently begging Lorjad that I wouldn't cross paths with the Shal. When I found my destination, the door was closed. I knocked, waiting until Jace called for me to enter before stepping inside.

He looked up from the book he'd been reading and dipped his head in greeting. "Nahla."

"Shalo," I responded. "I need you to send a message to all the clans."

"Why me?" Jace squinted at me.

"I need someone who knows how to throw a party." I flashed a weak imitation of Ezri's charming smile at him.

"And you think that person is me." Jace raised his eyebrows.

"Call it a hunch." I shrugged. "Am I wrong?"

"Go on…" He waved a hand in the air, inviting me to come closer.

I shut the door behind me and moved to stand across the table from him. "Invite everyone who will come of age this year. Tell them that, in celebration of his coming wedding, the Ruhl will host a Midwinter festival. The festivities will begin a week before Midwinter."

"That's late in the season for travel." Jace closed his book and studied me.

"That's why I need you to convince them it will be worth it to make the journey. I'm counting on you to make sure that everyone attends."

"Does the Ruhl know what you're planning in his name?" he asked.

"He does, but the Shal has not yet been informed of our plans."

"I suppose you want me to plan this festival for you as well?" His eyes narrowed.

I nodded. "And help us convince the Shal to allow Magesha to perform the maturity ceremony."

Jace rolled his eyes. "Anything else?"

"No."

"I'll take care of it." He dismissed me with a wave.

I backed out of the library, shutting the door behind me. Then I hurried out of the Shal House and across the courtyard to the Ruhl House.

Zan spotted me as I approached Ezri's rooms. I signaled him to remain quiet so that I could slip past and surprise Ezri. But Ezri looked up from Edan's diaries as soon as I stepped into his room.

"You're back early," he said. "How did it go?"

I perched on the arm of his chair. "Jace agreed to arrange the festival. I'm leaving at dawn to train with the Inahi."

He tapped Edan's diaries against my thigh. "That wasn't what I was asking about."

"As well as could be expected." I didn't want to talk about Rys. "I'm leaving for the forest at dawn, now that everything's settled. There isn't any time to waste."

"I know." Ezri's fingers found my chin and nudged it until I turned my face toward him and met his eyes. "Are you all right?"

I nodded, unable to speak from the lump of worry in my throat.

He stretched up until his lips brushed against my ear. "I'll be here when you return."

27

I SLEPT in my travel tunic and leggings, curled up beside Ezri in his bed, and woke at first light. After brushing my lips against Ezri's cheek and whispering a plea to Estrel to keep him safe, I slipped silently from his room, only to find that Zan had already retrieved my luggage from my rooms.

Two saddle bags filled with my gear were waiting for me in Ezri's sitting room. With one last look over my shoulder, I carried the bags out into the hall and made my way to the stables. Once I'd settled onto Arge's back, I pulled the hood of my cloak over my head and rode down past the Magery, to the gate that would take me back to the forest and the Inahi that awaited me there.

When I reached the start of the trail the novice mages used, I found three Inahi riding stormcats waiting for me.

It's time.

"I'm ready," I said. "But I need to return before Midwinter."

Yes. It's more important now than ever that you train the

others.

"Why? I thought we put a stop to the evil you spoke of when Mia killed the Jahl."

The gods are missing.

Sign up for my newsletter to be the first to know when new
books release and get some Mage Lore bonus scenes!
http://www.emenozzi.com/newsletter.html.

ACKNOWLEDGEMENTS

This book has been in the works for a very long time. Thank you to everyone who has read excerpts and previous versions, from my very first UC Berkeley Extension critique group to my other Bay Area writing group, and all the way through to my present-day Struggle Bus Crew.

Special thanks to Elizabeth Buege, who picked this story out of a sea of other manuscripts in the 2016 Pitch to Publication contest, and to the RWA judges who gave the original version of the first chapter first prize in the Athena contest.

Thank you to the 2017 Madcap Creating Worlds Workshop participants and instructors for their feedback and plotting help.

Massive thank you to Kaitlin, who wouldn't let me shelve this story and encouraged me to revise it one more time. And extra thanks to Anne, who gave me the feedback I needed to take that last revision and work out the rough bits.

Thank you to my excellent cover designer, Elizabeth Mackey, and to my stellar copy editor, Shannon Page.

I definitely would not have been able to do this without my mom cheering me on and my husband patiently listening to my angst and encouraging me to keep going. Big hugs and thanks to both of you!

And finally, to you, dear reader, thank you for exploring this world with me. I hope you enjoyed it and are excited to read more.

ABOUT THE AUTHOR

Elizabeth Menozzi is an award-winning writer of science fiction and fantasy with romance. A former Midwestern girl, she currently resides on Orcas Island with her husband. In her spare time she is a trail runner, planner geek, and devourer of books.

You can find out more on her website at http://www.emenozzi.com/.

Also by E. Menozzi

Eve of the Fae
Dawn of the Fae
Will of the Fae
Hunter of the Fae
Ash of the Fae
Tales of the Fae

www.ingramcontent.com/pod-product-compliance
Lightning Source LLC
Chambersburg PA
CBHW021218310726
48971CB00006B/1601